JOSEPH COVINO JR

FRANKENSTEIN RESURRECTED

AN EPIC PRESS BOOK

Published by *EPIC PRESS*
PO Box 30108
Walnut Creek, CA 94598

First *Epic Press* Edition published 2005

In loving memory of my beloved father, Joseph Sr.

ACKNOWLEDGMENT

My sincerest heartfelt thanks is rendered to *STEVE HOLMES*, Director of Design & Animation Training for Total Training Inc., for lending his kind and admirable aid to the debut of both *Epic Press* and this its first title. This British gentleman is as generous and gracious as he is a master instructor extraordinaire! Without his informative and invaluable assistance this project would've remained but a doubtful prospect. And for that my gratitude can be nothing but infinitely great.

C O N T E N T S

Prologue: Pursuit to Hell..................................7
One: Spirits of the Dead...............................23
Two: Land of Mist and Snow.....................41
Three: A Lost Friend Found........................59
Four: Dark Night of the Soul.....................77
Five: Dawn of Death...................................95
Six: Birth of Doom....................................113
Seven: Inhuman Sacrifices........................129
Eight: Creator Confronts Creation..........145
Nine: Retreat to the Refuge.....................163
Ten: Beauty Fled the Beast.......................181
Eleven: Insanity Incarnate........................197
Twelve: A Being's Birthright.....................215
Thirteen: Insensate Sensations.................233
Fourteen: Emotive Emotions....................249
Fifteen: A Monster's Enmity.....................265
Sixteen: A Monster's Soul.........................281
Seventeen: A Maker's Misery.....................299
Eighteen: A Monster's Mate Lost..............317
Nineteen: A Family Reunited.....................331
Twenty: A Family Ravaged........................347
Epilogue: The Creator Restored................365
Footnote: Frankenstein—A Profoundly Christian Parable..383

PROLOGUE:
PURSUIT TO HELL

"I had formed in my own heart a resolution to pursue my destroyer to death; and this purpose quieted my agony, and for an interval reconciled me to life."—Victor Frankenstein

JOSEPH COVINO JR

Out of the thickly oozing wall of murky mist and fog burst my hardwood sledge—pulled swiftly across the endless expanse of Arctic ice, frost and snow by my strenuously striving, striding team of sledge dogs. Their laborious panting and hardworking exertion meshed lustily with the swish of the ice-runners as their toughened feet dug deep into the shivery surface, driving me and my sledge over the frozen waste at a furiously spanking pace.

Onward my sledge bowled along, skidding smoothly over the glassy ice at deliberate, breakneck speed. Their tails curled smartly over their strongly muscled backs, my ever true and trusty dogs protruded their broad, sturdy chests and plunged us headlong—deeper and farther into the vast, frigid wilderness—working their wiry, tireless legs against all time and eternity. And at my relentless urging they took me in grim tow. Neither the freezing cold nor the heavy load would daunt their indomitable spirit or slow their synchronous and springing run—nor would even the visibly brewing storm looming ahead on the lurid, icy horizon. Savagely I snapped my leather tug-lines, lashing my tightly harnessed huskies into a flying and reckless fury.

A wrenching tightness squeezed my chest. And my own labored breath fumed right ahead of me, freezing instantly into frost rime which thickly incrusted my whole face from my hardened lips to my frost-fringed eyeballs. Stormy gusts beat up and down my racked and enfeebled body, ripping at my skins and plastering matted hair across my deeply furrowed brow. Biting cold—cutting, creeping, consuming cold—slit its way through the tightest and minutest openings. And along with the cold, swelling slowly to a violent intensity, blew the wind—raging, riotous wind shrieking across the ice, churning up air and snow and whipping them toward the darkening, threatening skyline. And although my sledge skimmed swimmingly over the frosty surface I suffered severe, face-disfiguring frostbite and desperately but stubbornly fought off a withering attack of crippling snow-blindness.

My present plight and predicament were such that they drained and devoured all deliberate thought or resolve. Rage and revenge alone drove me on, invigorating me with strength and fortitude, infuriating me and inflaming my blood, yet keeping me calm and coolheaded whenever death and destruction would threaten to overtake and hurl me into oblivion. My perennial roaming would end only with death, for which I had prostrated my faltering limbs and prayed many times. But rage and revenge kept me very vital and alive. After all I dared not die and let my archenemy—the archfiend—live! For many months then it had been my toilsome task to fruitlessly hunt and chase after him, for somehow he always managed to elude me and evade death—how I hardly ever knew. And although he would ever escape me I would ever follow on his trail.

For anyone just starting out in life, for whom misery was new and despair unknown, how could they ever know what insufferable pain I had suffered? I was irrevocably damned by some hellish demon, yet I pressed on, carrying along with me my own private and perpetual hell. But some ministering spirit kept company with me and showed me the way; and when I faltered most would unexpectedly brace me and deliver me from imminent disaster. And so I kept up my pursuit and bent my course ever northward; the heavily falling snows thickened and the cold deepened to a bitter degree almost too excruciating to bear.

Calling on God in Heaven to pull me through and push me forward, I pushed on with revitalized zeal and determination until the great northern sea stood out a long way off, forming the uttermost bounds of the sea line. Overlaid with ice it was set apart from land only by its abounding but boundless space and turbulence. Once there I bent to pray, and with all my heart, gave thanks to my ministering spirit for bearing me harmless to the place where—in the face of my archenemy's provocative mockery and ridicule—I looked forward to meet up and do battle with him.

Now I was gaining in my pursuit, although losing it before, and slowly but surely catching up with him—so much so that when I first saw the sea floating before my eyes he was only one day's ride ahead of me. With me treading so closely on his heels he bent his steps northward across the ice-covered sea to some nameless destination, leading to neither dry land nor even solid ground. Surely he must soon perish and be swiftly engulfed by the bottomless pit of imperishable frost, ice and snow. My heart sank at the thought and suffered in silent but passing pain that he escaped me once more; and that I must now set out on a self-destructive and impossible journey across the pathless and trackless masses of sea ice—submerged into deadly cold which I could hardly hope to ever survive. But at the thought that my archenemy—the archfiend—should yet outlive and survive me, my rage and revenge revived, and like a surging and powerful flood tide overwhelmed every other feeling or sensation.

Exactly how many days had passed since I left land and set out across the frozen sea I could barely tell; but I had felt the depth of misery, which nothing but the deathless lust for a just revenge, making my blood boil, could have enabled me to endure. Mammoth and misshapen mountains of ice many times blocked my path and progress; and many times the bellowing swell of the ground sea fell on my ears, threatening to swamp and sweep me away eternally. But once more the snow settled, froze over and hardened, saving my sledge from being swallowed up in the frigid, watery waste. By the ration of food I had eaten I would reckon that I had passed three weeks on my crossing; and the lingering remnants of hope returning to my flagging heart, reviving my depressed spirit, many times drew out tears of frustration and despair from my eyes. Hopelessness and heartache had truly almost devastated their prey, and I should have already sunk abysmally low beneath the weight of all this wretchedness.

My passage to this desolate place had been torturous and difficult—climbing up and down lofty ice-hummocks; wading up to my waist through drift snow; and scudding across slippery ice incrusted with frost, snow and grainy, crystallized salt which corroded and ate away at my sledge's ice-runners. Survival there ebbed and flowed rhythmically between intense tedium and turmoil. And except for the oncoming darkness which deepened the ghostly, grayish purple hues of the irregular outlines and formations making up the snow-swept landscape, every visible thing varied in only one dominant and monotonous color: snowy white.

More than I ever could or would be in this bleak and barren world, I was then completely and utterly alone with myself; for the Arctic waste is in essence a place of emptiness: no sight, no smell, no sound—nothing beyond the reach of my sheepskin gloves. Diffuse sunlight seeped through my head-embracing cap, coming from all points of the compass but with no points of reference, nor even any perception of depth. I was totally cut off from all outer reality to that point when all the senses reach to desperate but fruitless limits, when before long they slowly wear out from the effort, sensing in the end absolutely nothing.

Although freezing cold the snow falling in the shape of icicles and stars soon turns dry as dust, making the Arctic waste a pendulous, undulating and granular desert surface of frost, ice and snow which is sheared and stripped level by the screaming wind. From northern peoples I learned how to read and find my way unerringly across the wide open expanse of icy, sometimes hilly desert waste, having neither distinguishing landmark nor steering device to pilot by. To make out my direction I relied instead on rolling, furrowed ridges of snow formed by the stormy currents. Experience taught me at what angle to cut across those ridges so to get to any specific spot—the way to safely move along over an unending stretch of ice buried deep and unseen beneath the desert snow. At times the icy ground I passed over became very irregular and uneven, turning into a rough and rugged mixture of furrowed cracks, snow banks, deep pools and craggy hummocks which often ranged before me in hilly rows, or else split and broke off into jagged masses of floating, drifting ice. This hummocky nature of the ice made driving or dragging my heavy, hardwood sledge extremely laborious—so much so that I could plainly see the visible signs of overexertion springing up in the very pained expressions of my footsore and weary dogs. But even so these ever faithful and loyal servants would follow their master's obsessive ordeal into outright oblivion.

Freezing water instinctively terrified my dogs, and much against their will I often drove them through vast, glassy looking sheets of water up to their exposed undersides. But I had only one, single-minded course to steer—straight and undeviating over the ice: and once I forced my wretched dogs across the water they grudgingly set off at full speed, but hardly ever wet anything while hauling their heavy load. Sometimes, though, I would badly misjudge the watery surface, wrongly thinking the ice would bear the burden of our weight. And once we would venture to cross the ice would break up and cave in, plunging us up to our strained necks in frozen water—up out of which I would strenuously crawl, enraged and infuriated!

Then my flagging dogs were stumbling over the snow-packed ice from sheer exhaustion, breaking their stride and looking ready to drop. Driving my sledge up a sloping ice-hill I held tight to the handle-bow and stood with one foot on the ice-runner while pedaling in the snow with my other foot. Bending my knee to rest my weight on my supporting leg I pushed my sledge onward up the rising surface with long, sweeping strokes from my free foot. Smoothly I heaved and shoved the sledge along—pushing, letting the sledge slip, slide and catch up to the dogs and then pushing again.

As my sledge hobbled to the hilltop I stood with both feet

on the ice-runners and let my dogs pull me forward. Once
mounting the crest of the ice-hill my sledge lurched ahead
with sudden violence. Balancing my weight on both feet I
braced myself in back of my sledge and dug my heels into the
snow to slow down my dogs. Momentarily my sledge lagged,
buckling and creaking in budging over the top. And then it
was dragged abruptly down the steep slope of the hummock
slantwise—instead of bows first—so its heavily sidelong tilt
pitched all its weight onto the lower ice-runner, breaking it and
ripping off the heads of the upright pop-pets from the bearer,
which itself fractured and broke. A flurry of freshly fallen
snow just as abruptly whipped me off my sledge and sent me
flying headlong through the air. Desperately I hung on to my
careening sledge—I had to hang on to stop my dogs and keep
from losing them!—toppling it over! Roughly I tumbled and
plowed into the snow but still clenched my tug-lines, hanging
on tenaciously as my dogs dragged me and my overturned
sledge trippingly downhill!

"Whoa!" I yelled frantically through my gnashed teeth.

My dragged body scooped out a lengthy furrow of spewed
slush and snow until my dogs slowly stopped dead in their
tracks at the foot of the ice-hill. By wrenching fits and starts
my dogs erratically yanked me along—prone across the ice—
until one among their team, hobbling and collapsing under his
own weakened weight, crumpled up into a heavily panting heap
of hairy fur and steamy vapor. Finally I rolled to a dead stop.
Sluggishly I crawled over to the sprawled dog, sagging under
his own languishing fatigue. I folded him affectionately in my
arms, trying vainly to comfort him in his last fitful moments,
gently embracing his lolling head, warmly caressing his forlorn
brow. Shivering all over his whole racked and broken body
convulsed uncontrollably, his slackened tongue dangled weakly
from his gaping jaws, and his spiritless eyes glazed over as he
finally drooped and died—lying deathly silent and still.

"Buffer," I murmured over him, heaving a soul-sick sigh.

"Now the evil one has claimed yet one more innocent victim. Now I have one less ally to stand up with me against the demon. Farewell my brave fellow."

Laying down the dog's lifeless head softly onto the snow I stood up, wobbling weakly as I looked out in anguish over the vast icy plain spreading far and wide before me—limitless, shore-less and without the slightest sign of human passage or presence: with the express exception of one.

Sometimes my archenemy—the archfiend—fearing that if I lost all track of him, I might falter and die, left some marker to guide me. Whatever his thoughts were whom I hunted I could never know. At times, though, he left taunting messages carved in a flat scrap of timber or wooden plank stuck upright in the snow goading me to an enraged fury. Just then I found one such marker standing up in the snow, shaken slightly by the swirling wind. Limping, I stepped slowly up to it. With deliberate, circular motion I rubbed the palm of my glove over the wood and wiped it clean of frost and snow. Plainly inscribed in the wood were the lettered words:

My regime is far from fallen. You live and my reign is supreme, my power is absolute, my domain complete.

With the harshness and hopelessness of my struggle, the mad, maniacal glee of my enemy grew by slow and relentless degrees. His mocking words fortified my firmness and resolve. I made up my mind to triumph and gain total victory in my final cause: his utter destruction! Suddenly I caught sight of a dark figure astir on the frozen waste. I strained my eyes and made out the shape of a moving sledge. And then I recognized the familiar but gigantic and grossly misshapen form riding in its rear.

"Ah, ha!" I cried out excitedly as a blazing surge of hope returned to my heart.

Abruptly my eyes erupted with tears which I hurriedly wiped away so they would not dim my vision, making me lose sight of the demon. But the burning teardrops blurred my eyesight until, caving in to the depressed spirits oppressing me so heavily, I wailed out loud. Only I had no time to unduly linger: so I cut loose from my dogs their dead fellow, gently tugging at his tightly fitted harness, casting off the padded collar, back-strap and belly-band looped snugly around his neck, torso and forelegs. Pulling taut the loosened dragropes, or traces, I upraised my upset sledge, gathered my scattered provisions and resumed my pursuit.

What reached my ears, even through the clamorous noise of the gathering windstorm blowing up over the ice, was the demon's distinct and diabolical laughter, echoing all around the frozen wasteland. His sledge was yet in sight; nor would I again lose sight of it except during those brief, passing moments when some craggy ice-hill would put it out of sight by blocking it from view with its broken and jagged ice-rocks. Truly I had gained a great deal of ground; and when I had my archenemy—the archfiend—in sight at the point of being overtaken, within real reach of being put to death and destroyed, my heart pounded inside me, making my head throb.

Before long my sledge, rickety from its split but workable parts, glided into a wide open field of shapeless but rugged sea ice and slid to a noisy stop. At first sight the place appeared perfectly still and silent except for the softly swirling, slowly swelling wind, blowing boisterously to thump and tug at the icy sheets then shrouded by an icy mist. All over was shed a spotty play of iridescent colors silhouetting roughhewn blocks of black ice bulging in the background. As formless and frozen as my surroundings looked I knew they were convulsively changing their composition—I could hear them!—cracking, rumbling and dashing as massive slabs of sea ice shifted and jostled together to constantly rearrange and realign their chaotic and cluttered formations. With stormy strength, biting, blustering gusts incited and intensified the gathering gloom; and floating, drifting slabs were beginning to grate and grind noisily against each other.

Starkly alone in the middle of this disordered maze of ice rested the demon's sledge and dogs at a deathly standstill. But the demonic prey I was in pursuit of was nowhere to be seen. All around the bleak and barren waste I looked intently, straining my nervously darting eyes. Unthinkingly I was already half-cocking my big-bore flintlock blunderbuss; and pursing up my cold-chapped lips, blowing air through its vent. Covering its shallow, oval pan I tore open a paper cartridge and poured powder down its short but solid brass barrel, flared at its bell-shaped muzzle. On top of the powder I rammed wads of paper and buckshot, plunging forcefully, blowing powder through the vent and into the pan. To make sure powder poured into the pan I turned the gun on one side—pan downwards—sharply slapping its walnut stock.

"Where are you, vile devil?" I cried out furiously, glancing around, anxious and afraid. "Come out of hiding and show yourself!"

My archenemy—the archfiend—gave me no answer. Then a tempestuous wind was blowing up and wildly whipping snow across the icy surface, swiftly disrupting the waste's deathlike silence. Then I saw it!—the shaggy outline of something gigantic hunkered belly-down, head bowed low, curled up snug on the ice and gradually being buried beneath a thick blanket of insulating snow. Grasping my gun in one hand by its heavy, octagonal breech, my other hand—petrified by cold—feebly fingered the graven twirls of its brass side-plate and slowly traced the shape of its slightly curved trigger guard. Cautiously I stepped up to the bodily bundle and fully cocked my gun. By slow degrees my finger curled around the trigger. Slowly, stealthily—I moved toward the mammoth mound lying silent and still beneath the bed of thickening snow. Icy frost crunched forbiddingly underfoot. Spurred by blind and bitter compulsion alone I brazenly stepped up to it, careless of my own safety and protection.

"Come out, foul fiend!" I shouted, fuming and quivering with rage, rejoicing and relief. "I have finally caught up with you! You are discovered and destined to die at my hands! I have come to kill you! Devil!"

Rashly I lunged forward and lashed out, letting a foot fly at the faintly heaving heap, kicking it forcefully with all my might. At first the snow-shrouded figure barely budged when my booted foot hit hard the rigid body burrowed beneath the snow bank. But in the very same frantic breath I found I had blundered perilously—for out of the snow with an explosion of frost and ice burst not the demon I was in pursuit of but—in his place: a great white ice bear!

At one jump I sprang back from this monstrous, murderous menace! Violently shaking off frost and snow from his shaggy, clear-white fur coat the giant bear hung his head down, glaring ferociously with his big, black eyes fixed directly on me in a threatening gaze; and his short, stubby ears pressed back flat against his head which swung low from side to side. Noisily champing his jaws he chafed and growled a deep, throaty warning of imminent danger.

Panic-stricken and paralyzed I stood aghast, staring intently at the ice bear's strikingly doglike face as he crouched low on his short, stocky legs, staring down his long snout at me, snarling and baring his sharp and protruding canine teeth. Slowly I stepped backward in retreat, keeping the glinting brass muzzle of my blunderbuss leveled and aimed at the glowering bear. Abruptly the bear raised up his massive and mighty frame, rearing up on his hind legs and roaring loudly, rabidly, reaching up sky-high and waving in the air his huge paws, jutting with enormous claws. Forward he waddled a few steps and then, without warning, he charged! Dropping down flat on his four furry feet, his shimmering back, rump and flanks rippling with buoyant blubber as he launched out against me, he shuffled smoothly across the ice with an aggressive but graceful gait.

Terrified and stumbling I fired off a point-blank volley at the bear from my blunderbuss as he rushed full-tilt against me—raging, roaring and un-struck—oblivious to either the blast or the buckshot. Jolted violently by the gun's powerful kick I slipped, tripping on a lumpy piece of ice, and fell backward onto the ground. And all I saw bearing down on me, fast and furious, was a flying blur of fiery eyes and flaming fangs obscured by a cloak of blinding white fur. Rolling roughly over the incrusted ice and flailing in the frost I struggled frenziedly to get back to my feet and run. But before I could move to take flight the bear bounded and pounced on me; and with one swift and deft movement swiped me with a punishing, bone-crushing blow from his immense paw. Tenaciously he clenched my thick skins in his jaws and picked me up—bodily—shaking his head and jerking me in his teeth before flinging me forcefully to the unyielding earth!

Wide-eyed and open-mouthed, my heart pounding in my chest, I threw up my hands in horror—waiting, breathless, for the bear to plunge his impaling fangs into my creeping flesh. Only the piercing pain never came. Quite unexpectedly the bear growled and whirled around wildly, his upraised claws and bared teeth ready to rip and tear as he poked his snout up into the air, sniffing curiously at some mysterious scent. Suddenly and drastically the bear changed his expression and I looked aghast as I watched his fearsome, ferocious face overrun and paralyzed by some convulsive and consuming pain. Then he dropped down and collapsed heavily, writhing into a sprawled, leaden and lifeless heap. And punched through his heart poked out a long whaling-lance—tipped with a bloodied and barbed spike of iron!

Struck dumb with wonder I strained to regain my footing and stand in awe of the mighty ice bear lying deathly silent and still at my feet, unable to believe my shocked senses. And out of the screaming, swirling and blinding barrage of freezing sleet and snow slowly stood out in full view the ghastly creature

I was in pursuit of: the demon himself—towering, titanic and hideously grotesque!

"So!" I said knowingly if winded, nodding and moving backward, matching his slow and sluggish footsteps as he inched towards me. "The obscene thing I created has become my own guardian devil!"

"I expected you to be the thankless ingrate," he answered me in his familiar, restrained but resonant voice. "But you are very fortunate you made me of such superhuman strength and stature."

"Very fortunate indeed!" I agreed heartily, riveting my eyes with disgust on his misshapen, rime-incrusted face, his sheer, shriveled skin yellowing and pulsating with transparent musculature and blood vessels. "You have saved my life so that I might destroy yours!"

"You are as wrong and misguided as ever." He glared malevolently at me through his yellow, watery eyes. "I have spared you death for killing you is a pleasure which I reserve for myself."

Shuddering I reached slowly into my skins to shakily draw out a loaded flintlock blunderbuss pistol and aim it at the demon. Parting his straight black lips and showing his crooked but pearly white teeth he grinned a grisly, malicious grin which wrinkled his stretchable cheeks.

"A fool's toy for a fool's mind," he said contemptuously, shaking a head matted with long, lustrous black hair. Stoically he pointed at my gun with a gnarled and swollen finger. "You cannot hope to defeat anyone with that but yourself."

"Shall I put it to the test then?" I challenged him bitterly, raising up my gun's flared brass muzzle and pointing it directly toward his monstrous head. "And blast your wretched brain to hell?"

"Do what you will," the demon said with sedate defiance. "Whatever you do will come to nothing for you are doomed to destroy only yourself."

"Then," I said in measured tones, taking careful aim at the demon, "let my doom hit its mark."

Just then I was jarred and knocked abruptly to the frigid ground by a violent vibration of the ice trembling beneath me. All around vast slabs of solid sea ice were astir, plowing into abutting slabs and pulverizing their colliding edges. And where jumbled slabs clashed their shattered edges crumbled and fell to pieces, bumping and lumping together, shooting up straight into elongated ridges rising high up above the frozen sea surface. On all sides massive blocks of ice were heaved upward until they cracked up, broke apart and tumbled down into huge, scattered chunks of ice-rubble. Before long the expansive field of sea ice was a crowded and confused mass of shifting slabs smashing together; and blocking out a chaotically and tumultuously moving landscape of jagged ridges which rose and fell with the heaping, splitting and toppling of bulging blocks of ice.

In the thick of this stormy turmoil the demon leaped forward to attack me, his great outstretched hands ready to grasp and rip me to pieces. Again I fumbled to aim and fire my gun—but it flashed in the pan, misfiring! Stumbling to my feet I flung my gun at the demon—hard!—but it only bounced off his massively strong chest. Then I saw my big blunderbuss, dropped during the bear attack, lying miraculously at my feet. I dove for it, laid my hands on it and snapped it up. Frantically I released the catch on top of the gun's breech. A bayonet hinged and folded back along the barrel-top sprang out—its long, triangular blade glinting sharply. A muzzle catch fixed it in place!

Charging the monstrous demon flung himself at me, reaching, groping to come to grips with me. I thrust at him with the bayonet, plunging it deep into his breast. But he laid hold of it with his immense hands and yanked it out, calmly casting it away with me still holding on to it! Painfully I tumbled over the rough ice to a standstill, waiting fearfully for the demon to close with me mortally once more. His murderous attack never came.

At my very feet the sea ice split and fractured, threatening to engulf me, my dogs, sledge and all. Suddenly a quaking upheaval shattered the solid slab beneath me, laying bare the deep-running black water lurking silently below, but then churning and swelling into a turbulent ground sea. All over convulsive wind and waves ruptured the ice-field into cragged sheets with a thunderous and terrifying uproar. And in moments a surging sea gushed and rolled between me and my archenemy—the archfiend—casting us both adrift on splintered and severed sheets of ice, separated by an ever widening lane of water. Over the uproarious noise the demon himself roared at the top of his voice.

"Follow me!" he bellowed, waving brazenly at me. "I head for the endless ice of the farthest north where you will perish from the cold—to which you made me invulnerable. Come on, then, my enemy. We have yet to fight for our lives but you must bear many long and torturous hours until that time comes."

"Gloating devil!" I yelled back at him, straining my voice. "Again do I swear revenge! Again do I curse you to torture and death! Never will I give up my pursuit of you until one of us drops dead! And then: with what gladness will I join my beloved wife—and my dear relations long since dead and gone! Even now they prepare to reward me for my terrible ordeal!"

"Prepare yourself!" the demon shouted contrarily, grinning and goading me. "Your trials have only begun—for soon we will set out for a place where only your own miserable death will gratify my eternal hatred of you: *Frankenstein!*"

And all across the frozen waste the noisy clamor of ice and wind together reverberated to echo the demon's venomous outcry of my name: *FRANKENSTEIN!*

ONE:
SPIRITS OF THE DEAD

"Wandering spirits, if indeed ye wander, and do not rest in your narrow beds, allow me this faint happiness, or take me, as your companion, away from the joys of life."—Victor Frankenstein

Through the thick, murky fog and the dark, lurid column of churning clouds tumbling down around them from overhead the three towering masts of the mighty, four hundred-ton, square-rigged bomb ship cut a creeping but penetrating passage. From her bluff bow to her lute stern the fuming fog seeped and spread all throughout her frost-incrusted decks as her heavy, yellow ocher hull sliced slowly but smoothly through the icy, Arctic waters. Out of the oozing fog bulged two massive, howitzer-class mortars mounted on revolving platforms set on the centerline in the ship's waist fore and aft of her main mast. And high astern sagged the bomb ship's wind-whipped Union Jack flag—its drooping folds flapping feebly over her plank-inscribed name: *H.M.S. IMMORTAL.*

Strenuously seamen chopped away in force with axes at the heavy fall of snow heaped up about the bomb ship's bow and persistently beat with sticks the bomb ship's rigging, glittering with ice-encased cordage, striving to keep her ropes stripped free of frost. And much to the biting discomfort of the bomb ship's leadsman—in whose frostbitten hands the line slid and got solidly coated with ice while being alternately cast and towed from the frozen sea—the bomb ship's hand-lead was kept constantly running to take soundings for depth.

Amidships above the main deck the bomb ship's jittery lieutenant, dressed in flannel breeches and jacket, leaned out far over the port gunwale to carefully inspect the long and narrow streams of broken blocks of ice flowing loosely alongside, grating and grinding noisily against the bomb ship's hull. Then the lieutenant scrambled to climb up a ladder stretching from the quarter deck to the poop deck, rising gradually above rows of six-pounder and twenty-four-pounder carronade guns, poking out through the menacingly scarlet squares of their staggered gun ports. He stepped up and stopped for a moment at the top of the poop, briskly rubbing together his lamb's wool mittens. And step by step he finally moved slowly toward his ship's commander, standing stoically at the poop's forward-facing rail and looking down intently on the wooden, frost-plastered decks below. But even as the lieutenant drew deliberately near from behind, his commander kept on looking dead ahead with vigilant and watchful eyes, flitting anxiously beneath his Scotch cap and flannel face-cover.

"We've struck soundings?" the commander asked sedately, without turning to look at his expectant lieutenant.

"We've tried for soundings," the lieutenant answered with regret, "but we get no bottom with seven hundred-eighty fathoms of line."

"And the state of the ice?" the commander asked, impatient. "What's the prospect from the spike plank?"

"We're falling on a lot of brash ice," the lieutenant reported calmly, "which is getting thicker and more solid, but larger floe-pieces are lying in our way, so it mustn't be too far distant by my reckoning."

Beneath his heavy woolen frock and muffler the commander shifted restlessly.

"It's so unnaturally quiet there's scarcely a breath of air." He shrugged off some shivery sensation. "But there's a distinct current coming from the southward."

"Perhaps the proverbial calm before the storm."

"We certainly need no prophet to foretell the coming of bad weather." Gravely he lifted up his worried eyes to the darkening, threatening thunderheads settling fast over the slightly fluttering topgallant sails. Abruptly he pointed aloft as if to support his own sentiment. "Look!"

"The blink of the ice," his lieutenant announced absent-mindedly, raising his eyes with wonder to take full measure of the silvery sky, shining with a radiant intensity which brightly tinged even the lowering line of rain clouds with a lucent, yellowish glow.

"The glare of this ice-blink is so bright," the commander agreed with a knowing nod. "It induces me to imagine that our destination is no more than one mile distant from the ship as the crow flies."

"Aye, Captain, we're of the same mind," the lieutenant said, throwing up a hand of warning. "Listen!"

Just then the attention of all the bomb ship's seamen was arrested by a distant but thunderous and uproarious roar which boomed like breakers crashing on a seashore.

"It sounds like surf!" the lieutenant speculated excitedly. "It could be an island."

"Unlikely," the commander differed, shaking his head. "Give the order to be vigilant."

"Keep a good lookout from the masthead!" the lieutenant shouted at the top of his voice. "And keep the lead going!"

Gradually the fog started to lift and clear, dissipating by very slow degrees. "We've struck soundings in one hundred-one fathoms!" the leadsman announced loudly. "We've found muddy bottom!"

Already the commander was squinting through his raised telescope.

"What's the prospect from the masthead?" the lieutenant called out.

"Something on our starboard bow!" the lookout shouted from the crow's nest.

"We've got muddy bottom with seventy-nine fathoms!" the leadsman announced again.

"Stand for it and see what it is," the commander ordered calmly.

"Bring to!" the lieutenant bellowed, setting the bomb ship's entire watch into bustling, spirited motion. "All hands! Look alive!"

Then the entrancing prospect of something landed looming ahead, and standing out of the smoky fog, showed up visibly on the expectant faces and expressions of all on board—in spite of the heavy hailstones showering down in flying, icy pellets, battering the bomb ship's ice-encased planks and piling onto her sides more sheets of frost with every forward plunge of her bow.

"I dare say I can hear the gale coming without first feeling it," the commander said with bated breath, pricking up his ears and listening intently to the soft soughing of the wind breezing gently, whisperingly through the almost silent and still rigging aloft.

"Something's just visible from the spike plank!" shouted another lookout conning from the broad walk laid down across the bomb ship before the mizzen mast—raised to give a clear, commanding view over the bow.

"It must be the main northern ice!" the lieutenant exclaimed.

"There it is on our leeward side!" the lookout cried from the crow's nest.

As the last of the fog melted away and scattered to the winds, the swell of the roaring surf filled the air, dashing with hurtling surges against the outward edge of a vast, solid mass of ice, shooting up from the surface and stretching from end to end all along the distant horizon. Wind and waves bore down violently on this compact and continuous body of ice, lying level on the skyline and reaching unbroken in nearly a straight, east-and-west direction. Formed of massive pieces driven tightly together, rising and falling with the rolling rush of breakers heaving furiously against it, the ice collided convulsively with the great frozen sea.

"The polar ice pack!" the commander said lowly beneath his breath, standing aghast.

"One endless, impassable wall of ice!" his lieutenant chimed in, looking equally aghast. "Surely it must reach all the way to the Pole!"

"Now it must be only a mile or two under our leeward beam!" the commander marveled, bristling with exhilaration. Gravely he gestured to the pilot's wheel erected nearby in back of them. "And presently it will be the duty of us all to make that barrier of ice our main bone of contention."

And a stern proclamation engraved in brass letters, spattered with frost and snow, circled the wheel with those immortal words: *England expects that every man will do his duty.*

§

From my stock-pot filled with dog feed, a mixed mess of bread-dust, pea-soup, seal-skin and whale oil I plucked out a last piece of musk-beef to gently wiggle in front of the numb, frost-nipped nose of my last sledge dog but to no avail: his lifeless snout had long since stopped sniffing for any semblance of scent. So over the thick, jagged, crumbly edge of the solid ice-slab I lay sprawled on, heaving, I shoved the last trusty mate of my sledge team, solemnly watching him splash, sink and slowly disappear into a whirling eddy of the icy, murky depths.

No longer did I care about keeping my dead dogs to eat as a last resort—not even to sustain and prolong my own utterly worthless and wretched life. No longer could I bear even to look on their rigid, rime-incrusted bodies; their stiffened, lifeless limbs; their deathly glazed eyes. No longer could I bear even the slightest sight of death laid out before my own disheartened, despairing and dying eyes. No longer did I care whether I myself withered and die—as I knew I surely should; and would. At the very bitter end of my relentless and vengeful pursuit I finally felt ready to give up the chase—and my ghost. Almost.

Along with the gathering gloom the expansive ice field had frozen over into a tangled maze of solid and thick ice-slabs spreading as vast as a boundless, wide open plain. And all over the ice field was splintered and misshapen by sharp and spiky projections tossed and thrust upward by the convulsive waters rampaging below; as the craggy ice-slabs were slammed and smashed all the while by uproarious wind and waves.

Shifting and astir—set in restless motion by the freezing, stormy currents sweeping along above and below the ice—the field's countless icy slabs crunched thunderously together: grating, grinding, colliding; climbing and then crumbling, transforming the smooth, level surface of the field into a jumbled mesh of rugged rifts and ridges. Many times great slabs of ice split and broke apart, laying bare the black water lying silent and hidden beneath, but running deep and flowing swiftly through the middle of these fluid-filled fractures; spilling over onto the ever-changing ice field itself. In less than no time the ice reclaimed any open spot by freezing over the darksome opening and overlaying it with a lurid, limpid layer of freshly incrusted ice.

One among countless others being crowded and clustered together by the blustering storm, the floating ice-slab I rested on drifted aimlessly as wind and waves scattered the craggy pieces of the shattered ice field to the four winds. Like a sledge dog would do I curled up in my skins and furs on the ice-slab, which was white as snow and looked just as soft, but was as hard and unyielding as stone.

For a short time a cloudburst poured down in steams and quick-froze as it fell, thickening and weighing down the air, making it as blighted and withering as the grave—and just as cold. Most sharply felt was the air's cutting, strength-sapping, death-delivering cold. Later on, though, I would watch with wonder the lively play of bright, iridescent colors shed by the intrusive sun across the icy wonderland, peaked with the black silhouettes of craggy ice-blocks poking out and darkening the frigid background. At other times the frozen ice field grew utterly silent and still: it was then that the ministering spirits I constantly called on to help me would infuse me with new life and spur me onward. Cold, hunger, exhaustion and despair were the slightest trials I was fated to suffer. I was damned by some hell-born demon and I bore the lowering burden of my own infinite, infernal hell. Even so some ministering spirit of goodness went along with me, guiding me and showing me the way; and when I lost heart and hope would unexpectedly deliver me from even the most desperate and hopeless ordeal.

As it went along this way my existence—or subsistence—proved to be so thoroughly abhorrent and repellent to me, only through restful and refreshing sleep did I ever savor any enjoyment or relief from my evil lot. Many times when most desolate and oppressed, I lay down on my icy sheet, slipping slowly into deep sleep; and my shadowy, unearthly dreams calmed and subdued me even to sheer ecstasy and euphoria. Sweet, soothing sleep! My ministering spirits, standing careful watch over me, replenished me with these grateful moments, even hours, of undisturbed peace and serenity so I might prolong my stamina and see my mission through to its inescapable end. Stripped of such blissful sleep I should have already buckled and collapsed beneath my ordeals, rushing to irrevocable wrack and ruin.

Throughout the day I was encouraged and emboldened by the bright prospect of night, for asleep and at rest I saw my long-lost friends and relations, my dearly beloved wife, Elizabeth, and my much-missed homeland of Geneva: and once more I caught sight of my father's kindly and benign features, overheard the soft inflections of my Elizabeth's voice and set eyes on the hale and hearty youth of my best and most revered friend, Henry Clerval. And many times when worn out and spent from my arduous crossing, I reassured myself that I was dreaming until night should overtake and overspread me, and then in reality I would revel in keeping company and fellowship with my closest and dearest friends. What consuming feeling did I cherish for them! How firmly did I grasp their precious faces since at times they haunted even my most wakeful and watchful hours, and reassured myself that they yet walked the earth!

In these tenuous moments of ease the lust for revenge raging inside me suddenly died out, and I bent my steps toward the demon's downfall, but more as a duty imposed by God in Heaven—the inborn instinct of some nebulous force to which I was oblivious—than as the devout and passionate compulsion of my soul. So rather than break down and cry I prostrated myself on the ice, and with a hopeful heart gave thanks to my ministering spirits for escorting me safely to this spot where I took heart and trusted—even in the face of my archenemy's scoffing contempt—to catch up and come to grips with him. Following then a short sleep, throughout which these ministering spirits of the dead hung about, inciting me to strike back and wreak vengeance, I resumed my relentless, perilous pursuit.

And thinking back on how I came to be in this barren, cold and desolate waste, I *remembered:*

§

To me the walls of both dungeon and mansion alike would prove equally repulsive. My life was eternally defiled and corrupted. Lying all around me I saw nothing but a thick, murky blackness, pierced by no light but the eerie glow of two fiery eyes staring down at me. At times they were the gentle and suggestive eyes of my best friend, Henry Clerval, drooping in decay, his darksome eyeballs almost deathly sealed by the rotted, half-shut lids and the long black lashes fringing them. At other times they were the lurid, liquid, yellowy eyes of the demon as they first stared down at me in my bedchamber in Ingolstadt, where my whole terrible and terrifying ordeal began. An overwhelming lethargy was my sole sensation—in which a dungeon was as pleasing a lodging as even the most grandiose palace. My sluggishness was scarcely disrupted but by fits of bitterness and desperation. In those most disturbed moments I struggled many times to do away with the life I detested, for it demanded endless diligence and deliberation to stop myself from perpetrating some depraved and deadly act.

Burdened by the oppressive memory of my many mishaps and misfortunes, even sleep gave me no rest from my relentless distress and despair. My dreams laid bare countless things which preyed perpetually on my mind and struck eternal terror into my heart. And just then toward the break of day, I was seized by some convulsive nightmare: about my throat I sensed the demon's monstrous clutches from which I struggled fruitlessly to break free, crying out hysterically in breathless panic! But as I desperately strained my eyes to see my archenemy, my eyeballs bulging from their sockets, I abruptly awoke and finally realized that the foul fiend's neck-crushing fingers were never really squeezing my throat at all. And the two great unearthly eyes staring down at me were really two yawning openings in my solitary cell window, divided by crooked iron bars, agape and ablaze with bright sunlight.

Stretched out on a shabby bed I sat up, shakily erect, shivering from the cold sweat bursting out of my pores and soaking my skin. Before long the clank of metal keys and the clang of grating, iron bolts fell noisily on my ears; the cell's heavy, solid wooden door swung wide open and a stern-faced jailer stepped inside my squalid cell, ordering me to get up and go along with him. Stoically the jailer led me through the desolate dungeon's long, bleak corridors, echoing our solemn footfalls until finally he stopped, turned on his heel and left me alone, in silence and solitude, at the entry to the dungeon chapel.

My footsteps clattered over the wide, cracked blocks of stone as I slowly set foot on the chapel floor, finding my way into its innermost sanctum. Before me stretched the long middle aisle, cutting a wide passage through rows of spare wooden pews, and opening up into a spacious, column-supported chamber crowned by an arched dome. Right ahead at the far end of the chapel rested a long wooden table set between two facing rows of tall, ornately carved wooden benches flanking the walls on either side. Behind the table facing me quietly sat an elderly man, clothed with authority and looking as judicious as I expected he should. Behind the man towered a lofty cross made of heavy and wide timbers erected crosswise atop a high, solidly-built pedestal. And through a tall arched window behind the cross, gloriously radiant sunlight threw down dusty rays all around the man seated below, shooting out all over from behind the crossed beams. As I slowly stepped up to the man sitting at the table beaming sunlight dazzled my eyes, blurring his face with its vastly scattered streams.

"Please sit down," he directed me, gesturing to the frontward pew. "I thought this would be a more hospitable place for us to meet."

I sat down, anxious but silent.

"You summoned me, sir?" he asked, closing at length a Bible he was leafing through and lifting up his expectant eyes to me.

"You are a criminal judge?" I asked, hesitant.

"Yes I am. But what need have you of a magistrate? I gather that you are being set free this very day."

"Freedom is a worthless luxury to me," I said, grim-faced, "for I have come to my senses only to find that I have yet to take my revenge."

"Revenge?" he said, surprised. "Against whom?"

"I have a charge to make!" I exclaimed with emphasis. "I know the murderer of my family, and I demand that you exert the full weight of your authority to effect his capture! I sent for you thinking this would be the surest way of apprehending him."

"Rest assured, sir," he encouraged me, smiling slightly, "I will spare no pains to catch the killer—whoever he is."

"I thank you," I said, grateful and relieved. "Then listen to the evidence I have to give. It is a story so monstrous that I should be afraid that you would never believe it, were there not a certain precision to the truth which, however fantastic, compels belief. My story is too coherent to be taken for a nightmare,

34

and I have absolutely no reason to lie or fabricate."

"I have no reason to suspect that you would speak falsely."

"Allow me then to tell you my history and give you a concise account of my experiences, marking dates and events briefly but accurately."

"Why don't you relate the most vital particulars first?"

As I thought back on my past calamities in telling my horrific story, I started to appreciate once more their sole source—the base creature whom I brought into being; the wretched fiend whom I set loose on the earth for my own self-destruction. When his hellish image flashed across my memory I was convulsed with rage, overpowered by a burning passion, and craved and prayed fervently that I might have him within my reach to wreak a savage and unforgiving vengeance on his accursed head!

The magistrate listened to me attentively and amiably. At first he looked soundly skeptical, but his expression grew more engrossed and intrigued as I spoke; at times he shivered with alarm, looking deeply dazed and dumbfounded but visibly filled with great doubt.

"You tell quite a ghastly tale, sir," he said finally, sounding intensely shocked and stunned, "like something akin to stories of evil spirits and the supernatural."

"Nevertheless," I cried, angrily raising my voice, my hate and hostility blazing in my eyes, "this is the creature whom I charge and for whose arrest and punishment I implore you to bring all your power to bear, for he is unspeakably evil! It is your duty as a magistrate, and I trust that your sensitivity as a human being will not rebel against your doing your duty in this case!"

"I would freely give every possible aid and comfort to your cause," he explained conditionally, qualifying his assurances, "but the being you describe seems to possess powers which would defy even my most forceful efforts. Who can chase after a creature who can cross mountains of ice, and can live in caves and dens where no man would dare to enter? Besides, some months have passed since he committed his crimes, and no one can even speculate to what place he has retreated to."

"I have no doubt that he hovers very near over whatever space that I occupy." I fidgeted and shifted restlessly in my seat. "If he truly has stolen away to the Alps he may yet be tracked, hunted down and killed like the wild animal he is. But I anticipate your resistance: you do not believe my story, and you have no intention of following the fiend to inflict the punishment he deserves!"

"You are wrong, sir," he contradicted me with care. "I will do my utmost. And if it is in my power to capture the creature, then rest assured that he will most certainly pay the penalty commensurate with his crimes. But I'm afraid, from what you yourself have portrayed his capabilities to be, that this will prove quite impossible. And so, while every suitable step is taken, you should perhaps resign yourself to disappointment."

"This cannot and will not be!" I cried out, quivering with rage which made the magistrate flinch in fear. "Anything that I can say will be in vain, for my vengeance is clearly of no import to you. But while I suffer it to be an obsession, I admit that it is the one, consuming preoccupation of my soul. My anger is indescribable when I think that the killer, whom I have set loose on mankind, still stalks the earth! You deny me my just due: so I have only one recourse, and I dedicate myself, either in my life or death, to his total ruination!"

"Sir," he addressed me imperiously, looking down his doubting, disbelieving nose at me. "I understand that you have been unwell and unsettled in your mind. Perhaps your story is the result of some morbid delirium or hallucination."

"No, I am not mad!" I bellowed, striking a palm hard with my fist. "I assure you I have only the firmest grasp on the awful reality of my predicament!"

"Sir," he started once more in his richly appeasing tone of voice.

"Stop!" I cried, throwing up my hands. "You know nothing of which you speak!"

And heaving a persistent sigh his wrinkled lips parted to condescend yet again.

"Fool!" I hissed scornfully. "How witless you are in your arrogance of knowledge! How inept in your pretense of humanity!"

So once I was freed from the dungeon I broke out and bolted full-tilt from its gate, enraged and infuriated. I charged up a winding and steep footpath until I reached a crumbling flight of stone steps, climbing trippingly until I got to a battered and cracked foundation, weedy and overgrown with foliage and underbrush. Winded, I collapsed onto a huge cornerstone block, sprawling close to a bare and empty but covered urn set down at that breezy, remote spot overlooking the dungeon's shingled roof and conical towers, poking forbiddingly out of the distant treetops. That urn's unspoken symbolism, betokened by its un-carved surface, bespoke its ominous and grievous meaning. I muttered it solemnly to myself: *death!*

When I set out from Geneva my first set purpose was to find some trace by which I might track and hunt down my archenemy—the archfiend. But my course of action was doubtful and for a long time I roamed around the borders of the town, undecided about what trail to follow. As darkness loomed I found myself at the gate to the fenced cemetery where together my little brother, William, my wife, Elizabeth and my father rested. I passed through and drew near to the slab headstones marking their graves. Everything was as silent and still as the grave, except the leaves of the trees being gently rustled by the whispering wind. As black and cavernous as a bottomless pit was the night's darkness, and the somber setting would have felt grim and foreboding even to the most stoical onlooker.

Unconquerable is death—the common lot of our humanity—and into its inescapable clutches we must all eventually surrender our limited and transient lives. But between the living and dead stands its impenetrable, separating barrier. And all around the grassy, woodsy cemetery I looked solemnly at the many symbols of our perishable mortality standing out sharply among the dark and dismal burial landscape, making up a curiously peaceful place for all the shared spaces of the restful dead. Rising obliquely from among the cemetery's thicket of trees and shrubs was a sinuous outline of many angular, irregular and solidly carved forms, showing up as silhouetted shapes which cast their obscure and pointed shadows against even the blackest tapestries of night—castellated mausoleums faced with the curved arches and tall columns of ancient temples, conical rooftops, domed rotundas, lofty obelisks and tapering pyramids—many half-buried in the damp ground and all battered and in ruins. Together with the spirits of the dead hovered round and spread their own long shadow, which I felt fall on my desolate soul even though it lurked unheard and unseen. Hovering round as well were other outraged and offended spirits having no stone cold graves to be laid to rest in.

Before long the consuming distress and despair which the cemetery's surroundings had at first stirred inside me turned swiftly into bitterness and desperation. My most dearly beloved relations were dead and gone and yet I lived and walked the earth. So did their murderer—and to murder him I must prolong my already played out life. At length I flung my body to the grassy ground, prostrating myself and kissing the burial soil, and with trembling lips cried out aloud:

"By the hallowed ground on which I bow and pray, by the spirits drawing near, by the unending pain which I bear, I swear: and by you, the dead of night, and the spirits which rule over you—to follow the devil who inflicted this pain until either he or I shall die in a death struggle. For this end alone will I prolong my life: to take my precious revenge will I once more see the shining sun and walk the solid ground of earth—or else these should be lost to my sight forever. And I appeal to you, spirits of the dead; and to you, avenging spirits of justice—to help strengthen and sustain me in my pursuit. Let the accursed and hell-born demon suffer insufferable pain. Let him suffer the punishment which now tortures me."

I had started my prayer with such conviction and devotion I was nearly satisfied that the spirits of my murdered relations overheard and gave me their blessing. But as I ended my prayer the avenging spirits took possession of me and fury choked my power of speech. Through the silence of the night I was abruptly answered by a deep and diabolical fit of laughter. It fell on my ears long and harshly; the highlands echoed it and I felt like all hellfire closed in on me with scoffing scorn and contempt. At that moment, no doubt, I should have been seized by desperate rage and have taken my own wretched life, but that my oath was overheard and that I was sworn to revenge. Finally the laughter died out when a familiar and hated voice, near to my ear, accosted me in a faint but distinct whisper.

"I am overjoyed, vile criminal!" it rasped. "You have willed to go on living and I am well pleased!"

Recklessly I dashed to the place where the voice distinctly resonated from but the demon escaped my vengeful clutches once more. And abruptly the great face of the moon rose and glowed, shedding light lavishly on his hideous and grotesque form as he raced away, taking fast and furious flight.

I awoke with a cringing, flinching start of fear—in sheer dread of the skulking demon until once more I felt the pinching cold and remembered, and realized, that I was no longer sprawled on the sodden ground of the Genevan cemetery, but instead on a floating ice-slab set adrift in the icy waters of the farthest, frowning, frozen North.

TWO:
LAND OF MIST AND SNOW

"There is something at work in my soul, which I do not understand....there is a love for the marvelous, a belief in the marvelous, intertwined in all my projects, which hurries me out of the common pathways of men, even to the wild sea and unvisited regions I am about to explore."—Captain Robert Walton

JOSEPH COVINO JR

Then scudding before the wind the mighty bomb ship bowled along, bearing down rapidly on the vast wall of ice looming right ahead. Through his raised telescope the bomb ship's grim-faced commander watched the surging swells roll and beat violently against the ice.

"We're running before strong wind with a very heavy cross sea," he told his lieutenant solemnly. "Cut sail."

"Cut sail!" his lieutenant shouted lustily to the spirited seamen struggling aloft in the bomb ship's ice-incrusted, wind-whipped rigging.

All across the shifting sea line held intently in his sight the commander could see the whole wall of ice astir with a wildly wavering motion. Massive pieces of ice at the edge of the pack violently undulated up and down, and by turns—while the billows rolled roughly along—alternately plunged into the frozen sea and then heaved upwards again at either end of the pack. Other floes of ice at the pack's edge broke up and fell to pieces, scattering and overspreading the sea with thickening brash ice, cast dangerously adrift in the bomb ship's way.

"Point her bow toward the most formidable pieces to turn them aside," the commander ordered.

"Steer toward the floe-pieces!" his lieutenant shouted obediently, but warning beneath his breath. "We'll likely lose our bowsprit."

"Preferable to letting our broadside hit the ice," the commander countered calmly. "Should she roll and dip her gunwale under the floes, she'll either lay open her side or get overset all at once."

With the crowded, confused and convulsive mass of closely packed ice then spreading over the frozen sea in all directions the mighty bomb ship shook sporadically but violently from colliding with loose chunks of drifting ice-floes, battering her hull.

"I fear the ice is getting too heavy to be pushed aside

by our bow," the lieutenant said seriously, looking intensely careworn.

"We cannot afford to lose a single inch of ground by bearing up to avoid the ice," the commander answered with grim and decisive resolve. "We will not put about. Make preparations to join the encounter."

"Aye, sir." His lieutenant nodded resignedly and shouted the order. "Secure the ship for concussions!"

And immediately, spirited seamen on deck hustled smartly to hang about the bomb ship's bow long lengths of hemp cable—with square, iron plates attached—as bumpers. Just as actively they tied down the bomb ship's masts with more ropes, battened and nailed down hatches.

"Totally impenetrable," the commander said lowly, visibly disconcerted as he ran his dazed eye over the fast-approaching wall of ice through his raised telescope.

Dead ahead one endless line of raging breakers rolled and dashed against massive pieces of ice, rising and falling with the wind and waves, smashing together so riotously that the bomb ship's officers could hardly make their orders heard by their crew.

"Can't we punch an opening into the ice and force our way through?" the lieutenant asked.

"How would you propose we do that?" the commander asked him quizzically.

"We could drive into the ice and divide it—floe by floe—with a full spread of sail," he suggested, his voice enthusiastic but serious.

"Highly inadvisable." His commander summarily dismissed the notion with a disapproving frown. "We cannot hold this course without putting ourselves in great danger. The storm that's brewing is almost upon us. Bring to at the edge of the pack until this wind eases off."

"Bring to!" the lieutenant shouted at the top of his voice, imparting his commander's order to the bomb ship's crew.

Suddenly a violent gale sprang up and blew with unrelenting fury, churning the heavy sea with a billowy ground swell. Blustering squalls swept across the tumultuous sea surface with a hefty downpour of hail and snow, falling in solid, steamy sheets and soaring as high up as the bomb ship's masthead. And careening mightily in the turbulent sea, her masts and rigging reeling aloft in the gusty wind, the bomb ship nearly toppled over onto her beam-ends, tumbling wildly toward the seething waters boiling over her leeward gunwale and overrunning her overflowing decks. Abruptly and menacingly the jostling, tossing mass of ice sprang up and floated before their awestricken eyes, staring them in their frightened faces.

"Come about and heave to!" the lieutenant shouted his commander's next order, straining feverishly to raise his shrill voice above the gale's deafening din.

Where the solid wall of ice collided with the great frozen sea, convulsively churning and hurling its mountainous waves wildly against the great frozen barrier, it burst explosively onto the icy blocks, plunging them deeply beneath the rippling billows and then rushing over their craggy edges, wholly awash with swirling froth and foam once the sunken pieces heaved upwards and shot up again from the stormy sea surface. And as far as the eyesight could reach every single floe rocked and swayed in its icebound bed, bobbing up and down, grinding violently against each other until some shattered on impact, falling to pieces into the rampaging upheaval.

"If this storm casts us against the ice," the lieutenant bellowed shakily, "we'll be dashed to pieces!"

"Then we'll have to take desperate measures to save ourselves!" his commander bellowed back at him. "All we can do is drive the ship directly into the pack itself and take refuge within it! Stand to until we can find an opening to run her head through!"

"Helm!" the lieutenant yelled with grudging obedience. "Stand ready to steer straight into the ice!"

"It's no use!" the lieutenant cried hastily, glancing around, anxious and afraid. "There is no opening!"

"There has to be!" the commander shouted, equally insistent. "Now stay on the alert and keep a sharp lookout for it!"

Laboriously plying the boisterous waters the mighty bomb ship bounded all at once over the billows before the blustering gale. And instinctively every seaman aboard laid firm hold of anything immovably fixed and secure.

"Perhaps it's presumptuous to expect even to survive such an unequal contest," the commander muttered fatefully, lifting up his anxious eyes to the soaring masts swaying wildly aloft in the lowering clouds, waiting breathlessly for the coming clash. "But we're about to pit the strength of our lowly ship against that of the great, icy barrier!"

"Brace for concussion!" his lieutenant shouted lustily one last time.

Slicing her way smoothly through the lighter ice the bomb ship collided suddenly and violently with the frontward wall of the polar ice-pack. And at the same frightful instant all seamen aboard stumbled, many among them losing their footing and falling prostrate. Above, the bomb ship's masts bent abnormally from the powerful collision, while below beams and timbers creaked abrasively from a fearsome and overwhelmingly heavy pressure. From the shock of impact the bomb ship abruptly lurched and reeled, bounding back in a moment of appalling alarm. Rolling pendulously beneath the bomb ship's unbending hull, a forceful billow drove her almost her full length into the pack's outer edge. Trailing billows plowed ferociously into her stern and pitched her broadside to the wind, battering her on all sides with relentless blows until her leeward side tilted against the ice itself.

"We're foundering!" the lieutenant yelled, straining his throat.

"All we can do is hold on and abide the issue!" his

commander cried.

Buffeted repeatedly from one floe-piece to another all seamen aboard could barely stay on their feet, let alone come to the bomb ship's aid. So violent was the tumult that the bomb ship's bell then tolled clangorously.

"She can't hold together for very much longer!" the lieutenant shouted.

"Our only chance is to get her before the wind and penetrate the pack!" his commander agreed, nodding nervously. "We have to crowd on more sail and force our way farther into the ice where the pieces are less violently agitated!"

"Aye!" the lieutenant answered, calling out his commander's unspoken but understood order. "Set more sail!"

Tottering with the strain of sail already spread the masts were put at risk by the seamen struggling aloft on the spars to put more pressure on the bomb ship's forepart. Just then the bomb ship's bow split apart a lumpish sheet of ice, forcibly cutting a passage through the solid field.

"We're breaking through!" the lieutenant shouted elatedly.

"No doubt we'll be embayed in the ice," the commander said, breathing a sigh of jubilant relief, "but by the blessing of Divine Providence, at least we've weathered the storm. We can give thanks to the Almighty for delivering us from impending danger."

Although the impetuous wind still blew a storm at sea, hurling roaring breakers against the jagged edge of the pressure-packed ice, the sky rising above looked perfectly clear and cloudless; while threatening thunderheads clouded over the stormy sea, sweeping along heavily until they reached an upright border roughly even with the ice-pack's outermost edge. Right at that spot shot up a sheer boundary line, dividing two separate and distinct skies—with lurid rain clouds scudding swiftly right and left—thickening or scattering on impact with it. And although the storm's turbulence constantly cast clumps of clouds irreversibly toward its limit, that natural line of demarcation never invaded the clear and serene sky overhanging the ice-pack itself.

"The ship is so becalmed," the commander said lowly, raising his disbelieving eyes aloft, "the vane at the masthead is hardly agitated." Then he turned his telescope astern, where a hazy, misty cloud of spume and spray, shooting up from the breakers booming at the ice-pack's edge exploded and burst into sight. "But the open sea is running with a vengeance."

As abruptly as it arose the storm rapidly subsided. And just then the sudden blast of a gun pealed across the vast, frosty ice field, piercing startled ears and drawing all awestruck eyes on board to its direction.

"What in God's name was that?" the lieutenant exclaimed with fearful wonder.

"It sounded like the report of a musket," the commander guessed.

"Gunfire out here?" the lieutenant said skeptically. "Who could possibly be this far out?"

"Besides us and the polar bears?" the commander quipped. "What's the prospect from the crow's nest?"

"What's the view from the masthead?" the lieutenant called out to the bomb ship's pilot aloft.

"I've sighted something very strange half a mile distant," the lookout reported excitedly, sounding startled, "something too incredible for words!"

"Tell us what it is!" the lieutenant shouted impatiently. "What do you see?"

"This is hard to believe," the lookout stammered, "but it looks like a man—a gigantic man—driving a dog-sledge hard and making haste for the north!"

"Farther north?" the lieutenant cried. "Who could this be?"

"Whoever he is he's making his way very quickly," the lookout shouted disappointingly. "I'm losing sight of him in the thick of the ice."

"This is beyond belief!" the lieutenant cried, taken aback. "We're supposed to be hundreds of miles away from any land, yet the sight of this phantom would suggest that we're not really so far north as we thought!"

"Can we track him?" the commander suggested.

"Can we follow the stranger's trail?" the lieutenant called out to the lookout once more.

"Impossible," the pilot answered gravely, "for now we're in even greater difficulty! The ice is surrounding the ship and shutting us in!"

§

Just then the mighty bomb ship coasted slowly along the narrow, smooth lane of water winding tortuously through the labyrinthine maze of frozen ice-floes, floating and jostling noisily together in all directions. Reflected lucent in the water were the bright, bluish banks of ice, along with all their endlessly varied shapes and forms, standing out in bold relief against the glassy plane, mirror-like surface of the icy canals turning and twisting chaotically among the clustered floes.

"Trim sails!" the lieutenant shouted to his fellow sailors toiling aloft. "Helm! Hold your course!"

Then he hustled over to the gunwale to oversee the activity of some spirited seamen, scrambling out onto the ice and tugging strenuously in concert on light lines cast to them from aboard ship.

"Watch the bow on the short turns!" he called out to them. Worriedly surveying the stern he mounted the poop deck once more.

"What's the state of the ice?" his commander asked.

"The channel we've just passed through is closing in on us fast from astern with no open water in sight," he reported solemnly. "Soon we'll have no room to turn much less put about."

"Perhaps the closing is only temporary," the commander confidently surmised. "Make for the far end of this lead. Once we get there we'll push our way through to any open water beyond."

"Aye." The lieutenant nodded his agreement as he called out the command. "Steady as you go!"

Just then the commander, squinting through his telescope, had in sight a singularly massive—and moving—ice-floe directly in the bomb ship's path.

"There's a big piece of ice turning around right ahead of us," he calmly observed. "Make fast to it immediately."

"Ice-floe dead ahead!" his lieutenant announced loudly. "Fix ice-anchors and secure lines!"

More ropes hitched to the bomb ship were cast to the seamen hustling on the ice. Attached to the ropes were hefty iron hooks which the seamen drove forcibly into the ice-floe, which pulled and stretched the ropes tight as it shifted heavily in the icy water. Creaking noisily from the strain the ropes towed the bomb ship to the outside of the ice-floe as it slowly twisted round and round.

"Following this floe should protect the ship from the passing ice by keeping the projecting points ahead and astern of her," the commander said, satisfied. "Should the floe be deeper in the water than the ship it'll keep us from going aground."

Around a projecting lump of the gnarled ice-floe the bomb ship slowly turned, drifting into a small bay blocked out of the ice field but surrounded by small, loose chunks of ice gradually hedging around her hull.

"Heave on those ropes!" the lieutenant called out to spirited seamen putting their stout shoulders to the cranking wheel of a windlass. "Secure to the floe with chain and anchor!"

Abruptly the mighty bomb ship stopped dead in the frozen water, lurching to a violent standstill.

"The channel's closed up completely behind us," the lieutenant reported gravely.

"Is there still no open water in sight?" his commander asked.

"None to be seen in any quarter."

"So we have no room either to turn or retreat."

"All we have room for is to work out how to extricate ourselves."

"Then we're beset by the ice," the commander said stoically.

"Aye, quite firmly fixed," the lieutenant confirmed. "Now we're part of the polar pack, which is carrying us along with it."

"What do the pilots recommend?"

"They're afraid we'll get stuck fast—permanently," the lieutenant stressed. "Their counsel is to liberate the ship by means of a canal cut with saws."

"Set all ship's companies to work," the commander ordered unhesitatingly. "If we can cut a passage through the ice perhaps we can drag and warp through a small opening."

His lieutenant nodded knowingly and shouted aloud.

"All hands with instruments to the ice!"

And at short notice spirited seamen scrambled again out onto the ice and fell to work all around the bomb ship's icebound hull, actively wielding axes, capstan bars, handspikes and ice-saws.

"This ice is too thick to saw through!" the lieutenant finally reported fatefully. "The ship is immovable! I fear we're hopelessly trapped!"

"It would appear," his commander casually agreed, "that the prospect of ever liberating ourselves is becoming less and less promising as time wears on."

Strolling over to rest his hands on the gunwale the commander paused to look all around, calmly surveying the vast, pathless plain of ice, surrounding the bomb ship and spreading all over in all directions—far off and away from those upturned and up-heaved masses pressing in so heavily against her hull.

"It could be a field of endless alabaster!" he marveled, thoughtfully taking the full measure of the violently agitated plane surface, piled up with countless, craggy and angular ice-hummocks scattered far and near. Because of closely compressed floe-pieces squeezing so snugly together the ice in many places was then heaped higher than the bomb ship's main yard.

"It looks to me like a stonemason's yard," the lieutenant grunted bluntly.

Suddenly the whole bomb ship shook again, rocked by massive pieces of the crumbling ice-floe piling up beneath her keel and bow, grating and grinding noisily against her heavily pressed hull, heaving her high above the level plane surface. A jagged, sharp point of the ice-floe grazed the side of the bomb ship, scraping abrasively across her planking as it glanced off.

"The ice is wedging us in so tightly," the lieutenant exclaimed, "we're being raised out of the water!"

Thunderously cracking and breaking up the ice field slowly shattered and fell to pieces far and wide—in places swiftly shooting up in rising piles of gnarled, pyramid-shaped ice. Immense ice-hummocks toppled over and plunged explosively beneath the frozen sea.

"Nothing made of mere wood can possibly withstand this pressure!" the lieutenant exclaimed again in a panicky tone. "We'll be crushed!"

His commander shook his head dubiously.

"Or else we'll rise and let the ice press on beneath us until it runs into other ice as hard as itself," he said, trying to sound hopeful. "Fortunately the bowed shape of the ship is favorable to her rising. And the formations of the ice are so rough and irregular that some parts of it are bound to take the strain before pressing much against the ship."

"Then there's no time to be lost!" the lieutenant cried fearfully. "If we don't rise with the pressure then our sides must cave in! What shall we do?"

With her timbers creaking and her masts quivering the mighty bomb ship heaved abruptly upwards, wildly convulsing, and then dashed downwards again, loudly tolling her bells as she tilted steeply sideways. So distortedly did she crumple up and sag—beams broke off, planks split, timbers cracked and, inside cabins, panels burst from their frames and doors flew wide open. Hard by the bomb ship's hull heaping piles of ice shot up, overturned above her bulwark and tumbled down, crashing and splattering all over her decks.

"The ice is doubling up beneath us!" the lieutenant cried out anxiously. "We're heeling over!"

"Unship the rudder before the ice carries it off!" the commander ordered, turning urgently solemn. "Then we must consult as to what is to be done. Summon all officers to the state cabin."

§

All around the table in the bomb ship's state cabin the commander assembled all officers in attendance to hold their urgent consultation.

"All officers are present and accounted for, Captain," his lieutenant announced.

"We're still secure to the ice-floe?" the commander asked.

"Aye," his lieutenant answered, "but our ice-anchors are slipping."

"Our rudder is unshipped?"

"Aye—and secured across the stern."

"Very well." The commander glanced around, nodding to recognize the rest of his officers. "My lieutenant and I are of the unanimous opinion that our present position is anything but a desirable one. So we're here to consult together with a view to decide on our future proceedings, as well as to adopt a suitable course of action. Master pilots, report."

"The ship is sustaining a very severe and heavy nip," the first pilot reported in a serious tone. "That is, she's being nipped or forcibly pressed in on both sides between two floes of ice. Being so situated she's in great danger of having her sides crushed."

"This ship is supposed to be strengthened against the ice, is she not?" the commander said scrupulously. "She's sheathed with plank of seasoned oak three inches thick—to say nothing of strong bracing inside her hull!"

"Aye," the first pilot readily confirmed, "she's as strong as iron and wood can make her!"

"Then kindly explain the reason why this ship is firmly fixed in an icy cradle but still listing in the ice," the commander demanded impatiently.

"Aye," the first pilot answered again. "She's heeling over to port at about five degrees. Broken masses of ice have passed beneath her bottom, becoming blocked by her keel. We've dug a fire-hole close to her port beam and found that the ice doubled beneath her bottom to a depth of some twenty feet."

"Our other master pilot agrees with that assessment?" the commander asked, looking around resolutely for concurrence.

"Aye," the second pilot answered hesitantly. "We found the pressure from the ice is mostly on her port side. This pressed her starboard side against the ice-floe, forcing her to list to port."

"Recommendations, gentlemen?" The commander looked around again, doubtfully, for concurrence.

"We must immediately commence cutting a dock and secure the ship within it," the first pilot volunteered confidently, "and sink charges of powder to assist in loosening the ice once the cutting is complete."

"Very well," the commander acknowledged, nodding and turning solemnly to face his lieutenant. "Divide our men into work parties and place them where their services will prove most useful."

And again with his grim and decisive gaze the determined commander looked all around in fatal earnest at his expectant officers, anxiously awaiting his command with bated breath.

"Let's get to it!"

§

Instinctively all hands laid firm hold on ropes, sensing the mighty bomb ship's torturously slow rise out of the water, creeping inch by inch ahead of the forcefully mounting ice, crawling and heaving sluggishly but inescapably upwards. Momentarily she rested motionless, barely balanced on her keel, turning over even further onto her port side, trembling violently from end to end. Her topmasts bent like whalebone, fearfully overstretching the already taut weather shrouds, crisscrossing the bomb ship and supporting her masts slantwise. As the pressure of the constricting ice squeezed, closing in even more tightly on the bomb ship's hull, huge, craggy blocks of ice slowly scaled her sides, threatening to tumble down on board while being beaten back by stout seamen stationed on the gunwale, lunging with spiked ice-poles. On the frozen surface itself other stalwart seamen stood cutting through the ice using long, broad and sharp-edged ice-saws. Back and forth they laboriously thrust their saws—hung by bolts driven through the heads of three spars each, forming triangular frames with tackle set up on the ice—working to a rhythmic but noisy cadence. Bomb ship carpenters marked out by lines the diagonal spans of ice to be sawed. And energetic seamen jumped up and down to loosen and dislodge the two freshly sliced slabs.

"Only rarely could the might of men prove capable of resisting the power of so much pressure," the commander thought out loud.

"It's been said," his lieutenant agreed with a knowing nod, "that any attempt to resist only heightens the calamity since any ship which ventures into the polar pack is doomed to be crushed to pieces."

"Then let's lend a helping hand in the form of an admirable defender," the commander solemnly suggested. "Employ the powder."

"Aye," his lieutenant said, shouting out the order. "Sink charges!"

On the ice skilled seamen filled preserved meat canisters with two to four pounds of powder stuck with a fuse run through their corks. Coatings of luting or tallow made the tins watertight. After lighting their fuses they lowered the charges a few feet into holes bored into the ice, suspending them in their dangled positions by strands of yarn spun from boat hooks. Exploding charges broke up and split apart the frigid ice-floe in all directions for a long way off.

"Heave on those hawsers!" the lieutenant called out to the striving seamen bearing down on the thick ropes hooked up to the ice to rock the boat side to side, slightly righting and settling the bomb ship.

"The ice-anchors are still slipping!" a seaman cried.

Far off and away from the mighty bomb ship, lying low among the stark, snowy landscape of rugged and jagged ice-hummocks, lurked a gigantic and grotesque creature, watching stealthily the persistent plight of the persevering seamen with yellow, watery and inquisitive eyes, burning hotly with confused curiosity in their drab, deep-set and dun sockets. Reflected limpidly in their liquid mirrors was the flaring glimmer of the exploding powder charges, thrown and set ablaze against the distinct lines of the bomb ship's soaring masts and sails. Across the creature's disfigured face and features, his pulsating blood vessels and muscles showing through his shriveled and yellowish skin, flashed the blazing bursts of fiery light.

"The immediate effect of introducing the charges

appears to be proving satisfactory," the lieutenant announced excitedly.

"No!" his commander cried, riveting his eyes intently on the ice field and shaking his head. "The charges have set the ice in fresh motion! It's closing in on us again!"

And a grisly grin crossed the creature's straight, black lips as he beamed a malicious and malevolent smile, creasing his stretchable cheeks, jeering as if he gloated wickedly over the bomb ship's perilous predicament.

THREE:
A LOST FRIEND FOUND

"….I should find no friend on the wide ocean; yet I have found a man who, before his spirit had been broken by misery, I should have been happy to have possessed as the brother of my heart."—Captain Robert Walton

JOSEPH COVINO JR

Standing astern on the poop deck the commander and his lieutenant carefully surveyed the foursquare berthing dock blocked out of solid ice and the placid pool of icy water the mighty bomb ship rode silently at anchor in.

"Have you taken your daily allowance of spirits, Captain?" his lieutenant asked unexpectedly.

"Why no," the commander said, surprised. "I believe I'm overdue."

"Will you join me then for a drink?" his lieutenant offered. "Supplied by the bounty of Her Majesty's most bountiful government."

"Delighted to."

"One pint of permissible brandy, sir." The lieutenant held out a small flask and poured the liquor into two jiggers he set down atop the rail.

"I thank you." The commander took the filled glass his lieutenant handed him with a grateful nod.

"I'd like to make a toast to you, Captain." The lieutenant slightly raised his glass.

"I'm honored." The commander's eyebrows rose.

"To the camaraderie you've fostered among the men by your injunction to dispense with titles of respect."

"I must commend you for your conduct as well, Lieutenant." The commander gave a ceremonious bow.

"How's that sir?"

"For doing honor to human nature," the commander complimented him. "During our entire voyage—even under the most trying circumstances—you've always remained calm and resolute. I've never heard you issue your commands with an uncivil oath, nor call a sailor by any other than his real name."

"As they say, Captain," his lieutenant said, flushed with blushing pride, "you have to pay respect to command respect—even if you do happen to have authority over another."

"Let's drink to that, shall we?"

After they tossed off their glasses the lieutenant pulled a long face, sullenly looking out over the vast, frozen waste of irregular ice spreading endlessly in all directions.

"This must be the most terrible place on the face of the earth," he said, pensive and sad.

"Terrible," the commander conceded, "but at the same time beautiful."

"I see no beauty—only eternal misery for as long as we're stranded here."

"In its terror, perhaps, is where the true beauty of this place really lies."

"There is nothing here!" the lieutenant protested, raising his voice. "Nothing but a miserable ocean entombed in ice— utterly lifeless and hostile."

"Its repugnance, I imagine, is part of what makes it so undeniably seductive. There is much in even this frozen wasteland to entice the senses, especially when Nature flaunts her beauty so wantonly. Don't you find it mystifying that that part of the earth which we now traverse is so desolate and forbidding, so completely severed from civilization, should prove to be a place of such profound fascination? Or that the mere absence of life should actually deepen its beauty?"

"Quite the contrary, I find this to be a most disagreeable and inhospitable place—much too cold and indifferent to claim any birthright of beauty."

"God's infinite wisdom is evident in all His works," the commander said in earnest. "Even Creation's deformities can prove pleasing. The God who made all and loves all shows no partiality. He favors neither the terrible nor the beautiful, yet He loves both equally."

"I must beg to differ." The lieutenant turned adamant. "All that's evident to me is that God has failed to favor us! He's let us sink to the bottom of this abysmal ice cellar. And I doubt very much whether He cares if we ever climb out."

"Then you believe that God has grown indifferent to us—that He has hardened His heart to us?"

"As coldly and callously as the ice itself—yes—I do believe it. He has forsaken us and left us here to die miserably."

"No, mister, you are wrong." Reassuringly the commander clasped his lieutenant's shoulder and gestured to the shore-less expanse of ice-incrusted ocean spreading all around before them. "Where else on earth could the wisdom of our beneficent Creator be seen or felt more strongly? Being so secluded from the rest of a restless world has the virtuous effect of provoking a contemplation of God's divine works; for here is a place where we cannot help but appreciate the many ways in which God has favored us with His generous gifts."

"All I'm provoked to contemplate, sir, is how powerless we're compelled to feel in the face of powers we cannot hope to overcome."

"That such a place defies domination is what makes its beauty—and terror—so sublime. You must admit that it does have a certain aura of mystery about it—a mystique, so to speak. Does it not?"

"And we're the brave and conquering heroes who've come to tame the untamed land?" his lieutenant asked quizzically. "Men have died in droves trying to tame untamed lands. And if it's all the same to you, sir, I'd rather not join them."

"I have no intention of letting us join them," the commander assured him. "But we do have a mission to perform—the least of which is to cast away the veil of secrecy and superstition which has always hung over these remote regions."

"Then like a sailor after a storm we should try to forget about past misfortunes."

"The one thing which makes us alike as explorers," the commander philosophized, "is that we choose—no, we dare—to explore of our own free will—in spite of the risks we run. God merely leaves us to ourselves and our own devices—free and unhindered. But we can still rely on divine power to will the course and might of those elemental forces which no mortal power can overcome."

"Then Divine Intervention should see us through our ordeal."

"Of that I admit no doubt."

"Since we're pondering the justness of our God," the lieutenant mused, "do you ever wonder what in God's name ever brought us here in the first place?"

"Many times."

"What brought you here, Captain—personally, I mean?"

"I followed the usual siren song, I suppose—the lure of adventure; the thrill of sailing uncharted waters no one else had ever sailed before; the challenge of possibly discovering something which might benefit others."

"And what of our benefactors?" his lieutenant asked skeptically. "Do you really believe they sent us here expecting us to find anything of any use to anyone in this frozen waste?"

"Perhaps the more wishful thinking among them," the commander answered with an acquiescent tone. "The profiteers hope we'll find for them their lucrative trade route across this obstructive ice. The curiosity seekers hope we'll stumble onto some trivial secret which might satisfy their exaggerated fascination with polar magnetism. At least that's my somewhat official interpretation of the situation."

"Have you a somewhat less than official interpretation?"

"For that matter I do."

"Would you suffer it to tell me plainly then?"

"Quite plainly," the commander said, heaving a weary sigh, "the richest and most influential patron of the Royal Society, sponsoring our expedition, sent us here for no other reason than to prove some incredibly farfetched theory he's conjured up a vision of."

"Which is?" the lieutenant asked, his interest invited.

"That the frozen sea encircling the North Pole is actually

free of ice!" the commander explained. "That beyond this impassable barrier we should supposedly sail an ice-free sea!"

"I refuse to believe what my ears have just heard!"

"That," the commander confirmed with a knowing nod, "and the tempting prospect, entertained by the Admiralty, that we may yet engage the French should they have sent their own foolhardy expedition here. Why else should they have fitted us out with so much heavy mortar armament?"

"How then do you contend with this unsettling knowledge?" his lieutenant asked earnestly. "That we've been used to run such a fool's errand?"

"I take heart in the sentiment that our vision of the unknown is shaped—not only by what we hope or expect to find—but by how we set about finding it—and why. And what we make of what we do find."

"Getting here has been such an exercise in futility, I dare say that nothingness is all we'll ever find in this God-forsaken place."

"Then we can only pray that the path to nothingness may yet yield something worthwhile," his commander heartened him, "for even this ghastly chaos can unfold priceless riches."

"Like a clear passage back to the open sea?"

"As the old saying goes about what makes a great explorer," the commander continued, overlooking his lieutenant's persistent pessimism, "he has the irresistible urge to press on into the unknown, even when common sense says: turn back!"

"If you could choose what we might find, Captain," his lieutenant asked fatefully, "what should prove most worthy to you?"

"A good friend to explore and discover with," the commander confided. "Someone to share in either the joy of our success or the sorrow of our defeat. Someone perceptive enough to either appreciate or temper my ambitions."

"Surely I am your friend, Captain." His lieutenant looked

abruptly downcast.

"You're my trusted lieutenant."

"Pray, then, could you tell your trusted lieutenant whether you truly believe we will ever get out of this crushing trap of ice?"

"I'm the Captain," the commander answered him simply. "If only for the sake of our men I have to believe we'll get out."

"But what would you tell your good friend you believed?"

For only a moment the commander brooded, collecting his truest thoughts.

"That as long as we remain alive," he said, "we're free to believe."

Just then a sudden rush of all hands on deck turned their heads, directing their curious eyes to follow a swarm of seamen scrambling to one side of the bomb ship. All was instant bustle and confusion as an agitated crew called out excitedly to someone swimming in the sea—in reality a lone, mortal man, along with a disabled sledge, afloat on a large floe-piece, drifting slowly abeam.

"In the name of God, who are you? Climb aboard!" the master pilot shouted to the mysterious man floating on the ice as the commander and his lieutenant came up on deck. "Here's our captain! He won't let you die in the frozen sea! A stranger alongside, sir!"

Straining his eyes to make out the bomb ship commander the shattered stranger called out to him in weary English, but in a Genevese accent.

"Before I come aboard your ship," he cried unexpectedly, "will you tell me where you're bound for?"

"You stand there on the verge of extinction and ask me such a question!" the commander answered him back, astonished. "I should think you would consider my ship to be a godsend which is beyond price!"

"Indeed! More precious than life itself! But I must know

where you're bound for!"

"Very well," the commander capitulated. "We're on a voyage of exploration and discovery towards the northern pole."

"Then I consent to come aboard," the stranger said weakly as he broke down and collapsed heavily onto the scraggy floe-piece, resting fully satisfied.

"Good God!" the commander exclaimed as he ran his awestruck eyes over the gaunt and haggard stranger carried aboard ship. "His limbs are all but frozen! Take him to the steward's room. Summon the surgeon."

But as soon as some eager seamen carried the rawboned man into a cabin he collapsed again, fainting and falling prostrate.

"Bring him back on deck into the fresh air," the commander ordered in the same breath, taking the full measure of the man's wasted frame. "His body's emaciated. Rub him down with some brandy."

Obliging seamen cast off the man's cap and sheepskin gloves, loosened and laid open his reindeer skins, briskly rubbing the exposed skin poured over with brandy.

"Here," the commander urged the sickly stranger, cradling his head in one arm while gently raising a flask to his frost-bitten lips. "Drink this. It'll bring you back to life."

Feebly the man's leaden lips parted just enough to swallow some brandy from the flask's narrow neck. And slowly he began coming back to life.

"Move him next to the chimney," the commander ordered.

And shortly the afflicted stranger was seated close to the radiating heat of the galley stove chimney and bundled up in blankets. Once he was settled and quietly at rest there, his thin and shaky hands grasping for a soup bowl, the commander himself raised a spoonful of broth to his quivering lips, moving weakly to eat.

"I am Captain Robert Walton of Her Majesty's Ship, Immortal," the commander introduced himself, warmly squeezing the stranger's wrapped shoulder. "And I welcome you aboard our vessel. Can you tell me your name?"

Visibly enfeebled and fatigued the shriveled features of the man's whole face lighted up at perceiving the commander's courtesy and kindliness—his shiny eyes beaming with gratitude. But he stayed strangely silent and gave no answer back.

§

A pair of familiar sailors hustled aft, heading hurriedly for the surgeon's cabin, speaking in soft whispers.

"Have you heard the rumors?" one asked the other.

"What rumors?"

"That this expedition we're on has some secret purpose which has been deliberately disguised."

"A secret mission? Of what kind?"

"I don't know," the one said gravely. "But I've gathered that it's so secret it's being kept hidden from even the officers appointed to carry it out."

"Then it would seem something quite sinister hangs over our heads. How did you get wind of it?"

"I sit on God's privy council," the one said facetiously. "And speaking of sinister I gather our ship's surgeon harbors some secret purposes of his own."

"Gather from whom?" the other asked, perturbed.

"Never mind," the one insisted. "Just take heed and be forewarned!"

Then the two sailors stepped up to the surgeon's cabin, knocking lightly at his door. Presently it creaked open by slow degrees, showing the distinct silhouette of a broad-shouldered, robustly-built young man against the lurid backdrop of a darkened but greenish-colored, eerily glowing room.

As the surgeon stepped up to his threshold, edging open his cabin door, its shadow passed over his straight thatch of reddish hair and fell away from the fine features of his face—large, dark blue eyes set widely apart beneath the sloping ridge of his broad forehead; a goodly but straight nose with sharply flared nostrils; and a resolute mouth naturally complimented by a firm, blocked chin.

"Yes?" he asked, raising his bushy brows curiously.

"Doctor Van Helsing, sir," the one sailor announced urgently. "The captain summons you to come on deck immediately."

"What's happened?" asked the young surgeon, striking an imposing pose.

"We've plucked a man out of the sea who needs to be attended."

Suddenly the surgeon riveted his intensely alert eyes directly on the sailor addressing him.

"A man?" he exclaimed. "Lead me to him at once!"

Presently the wretched stranger to the mighty bomb ship sat casting his anxious eyes back and forth between Captain Walton and Doctor Van Helsing, gnashing his teeth and staring blankly into oblivion with a look of crestfallen frenzy.

"He's unable to speak," the captain reported forlornly. "I fear his ordeal has drained him of all reason."

"He's no doubt overwrought by the weight of whatever burden he's had to bear."

"Treat him well," the captain ordered. "Once he's recovered to some degree move him to my own cabin. I will attend to him myself as far as my duty will allow."

Doctor Van Helsing simply nodded his mute assent.

§

Captain Robert Walton stepped hastily inside his cabin, quickly shutting the door on the off-watch seamen huddled restlessly outside. Then he promptly drew the curtain over his cabin's portal and turned on his heel to graciously greet his bedridden guest.

"It's with great difficulty that I keep my men at bay," the captain said, smiling warmly at him, "for they desperately crave to ask you a thousand questions. But I promise I will not permit you to be distressed by their idle curiosity. Because of the severe afflictions you've suffered in both mind and body, your recovery obviously depends on your having complete rest. And have it you shall."

His prostrate guest smiled sweetly but silently back, his face shining with appreciation.

"Still," the captain said conditionally, "I cannot help but wonder why you have come so far over the ice on so unlikely a conveyance."

Instantly his guest's benign face assumed an attitude of the deepest and darkest gloom.

"To give chase to one who flees from me," he said spiritlessly.

"And does the man you chase travel by the same means?"

"I spoke of no man," he objected adamantly. "But yes— the very same."

"Then I suspect we have seen him," the captain said, heartening him, "for the day before we picked you up we saw some dogs pulling a sledge like yours across the ice—with what at least looked like a man—a gigantic man—riding on it."

"Which path did the demon pursue?" the invalided guest asked insistently, straining every nerve to sit up in his bed. "You must tell me!"

"Demon?" the captain asked incredulously, gently laying a consoling hand on his agitated guest's shaky shoulder.

"Yes!" he scowled, heaving a sigh of utter disgust as he fell back heavily onto his bed. "The demon! The archfiend! The Devil incarnate himself!"

Struck downright dumb the captain simply looked aghast.

"No doubt I've aroused your curiosity—as well as that of your noble crew," his guest conceded, struggling to regain his composure. "But you've been much too kind and considerate to press me with any interrogations."

"Of course," the captain assured him. "Indeed it would be most presumptuous—to say nothing of ungracious—to accost you with any inquisition of my own."

"And yet you have saved me from a most monstrous and dangerous predicament," his guest said gratefully with reclaimed calm. "You have most graciously brought me back to life."

"Do you think the disintegration of the ice destroyed the other sledge?" his guest asked anxiously after a crisp pause.

"That I cannot answer with any measure of accuracy," the captain lamented, "for the ice had not broken up until almost midnight. So the driver could have reached a place of refuge by then. But of this there is no way I could say for certain."

"Then I must go on deck to keep watch for the sledge which was sighted," his indisposed guest insisted, straining once more to sit up in his bed.

"No, my friend, out of the question!" the captain gently refused him, prevailing on him with another consoling stroke to his shoulder. "For the time being at least you must stay here in the cabin, for you are much too frail to endure the severity of this air. But I promise that someone will watch for you and notify you immediately should the sledge again appear."

And again his disappointed guest laid back down on his bed, heaving another heavy sigh and resigning himself with sullen surrender.

§

Captain Robert Walton came up slowly to his enigmatic guest, looking much recovered from his sickness and standing vigilantly on deck at the gunwale, keeping a constant watch for the strange sledge which fled and flew swiftly before his own.

"A vast and lonely realm of deathlike silence and solitude," he mused aloud before turning to face his attentive host, "and yet so overwhelming in its magnificence. What are you in search of in such a desolate place as this, captain?"

"Officially," Captain Walton said with a shrug, "we're searching for a polar route to the Pacific, as well as exploring the possibility of reaching the North Pole, preferably by way of a navigable, northeast passage."

"For what purpose?"

"Our orders are to make the best of our way, proceed to the northward and use our best endeavors to reach the North Pole," the captain explained. "But our primary purpose is to steer a course from the Atlantic to the Pacific Ocean, on a heading as due north as possible, and try to find a quicker and safer route to the South Seas than the long and tedious voyage around Cape Horn—and by so doing venture to unite the two great oceans."

"Do you believe such a northeast passage between the two great oceans actually exists?" his guest asked, looking large-eyed with wonder.

"As of now," the captain confided, "everything beyond these northernmost latitudes is a blank on the charts. But among certain learned circles in British high society it's thought that the ocean around the North Pole is completely free from ice, and will allow for a direct route across the Pole to the Pacific."

"Isn't the sea in these higher northern latitudes eternally covered with ice?"

"For all anyone knows," the captain answered with an affirming nod, "the most forbidding obstacle to a navigable polar passage is, indeed, the sheer profusion of ice which chokes these northern seas."

"What of the Pole itself? Isn't it surrounded by a solid

mass of ice?"

"Theoretically at least," the captain clarified, "that wall of ice encircling the Pole is but a narrow band, beyond which—if it could be breached—would be found a clear and open sea."

"A circumpolar sea free of ice," his guest mused, taken aback. "That's somewhat of a fanciful idea."

"Perhaps," the captain readily agreed. "But our main benefactor seems convinced that the polar sea is at least sometimes navigable. To secure support for this voyage he solicited the Council of the Royal Society in turn to petition the Board of Admiralty to finance the expedition, which depends solely upon the dubious merits of this most implausible theory of an open polar sea. So if we could find an ample break in the ice we could conceivably pass through and make our way to the Pole."

"Oftentimes," his watchful guest suggested sedately, "the capacity of rational and intelligent men to deceive themselves is most extraordinary."

"Truly," the captain easily concurred, "but acquiring knowledge is the basis of all our orders under which we were dispatched. I am charged with careful exploration and observation, and to waste no opportunity for gaining any new and important discovery. I am then compelled to explore for discovery's sake. And surely the North Pole is an object of curiosity in its own right."

"Should your adventurous foray into the ice prove disastrous wouldn't even the most hopeful benefactor be persuaded that a wooden ship cannot possibly penetrate towards the Pole?"

"Our Queen's most learned minister declared at the outset of our voyage that knowledge is power," the captain told his doubtful guest in earnest, surprised at his seeming pessimism, "so even the knowledge of our mission's impossibility would prove worthwhile. That aside the irrefutable answer to all doubts and uncertainty is simply to go and see! So I'm determined to prosecute our assignment and see it through until we reach our goal."

"I beg your pardon, captain," his guest apologized penitently. "Forgive me if I sound discouraging, but I fear for you and your courageous crew should you pursue to the bitter end some fallacy of an ice-free sea at the top of the world, only to suffer untold tragedy."

"Even for all that," the captain insisted, "surely our present expedition makes us pioneers—the likes of those who have gone before us. We're destined to follow where mariners past have already led and shown the way."

"Beware that knowledge can come at great cost," his guest warned, turning darkly downcast and ominous, "and at great sacrifice. A mighty hoard can be heaped onto man's store of worldly knowledge. But countless innocents can die amassing it, and even those who live can be irreparably scarred with the agony of their attainment. They can return to the places of their youth and be so broken in spirit that even the joy of living is lost forever."

"Isn't our desire to explore and discover a natural instinct vital to our humanity?" the captain asked earnestly. "Successful races, I dare say, explore first and decide later what worth may come of it. Indeed, sir, I fancy that our very survival as a race depends upon it."

"Knowledge which is warped and twisted becomes an abomination," his guest answered, deadly serious, "and a bane to bear. We can sometimes penetrate past the threshold of exploring ground and reach a point of no return, beyond which nothing more can or even should be known!"

I would gladly give up my wealth, my life, my every ambition to further my cause," the captain protested, shaking his head contrarily. "My life or death would be but a small sacrifice to make to gain the knowledge I seek—to in turn gain and pass on the mastery of the elements which plague mankind."

"Misguided man!" his guest objected, castigating him. "Have you caught my insanity? Have you been made drunk from madness? Listen to me. Let me tell you my story, and you will sober up and come quickly to your senses!"

"You seem to hate yourself for having been the slave of your own passion." Captain Walton riveted his eyes and thoughts on his mysterious guest, trying intently to understand his innermost nature.

"Quite perceptive," his guest complimented but corrected him, "but I have been long enslaved by obsession, not passion. And a passion which turns into an obsession is dangerous, to say nothing of self-destructive, especially when you go in search of things forbidden and unattainable."

"I've been long in search of a friend," the captain said, abruptly changing their discourse and warmly clasping his guest's shawl-covered shoulder. "I crave a more intimate attachment to a fellow intellect than has ever been my fate. A man can boast of little joy who has never relished this gift."

"I quite agree with you." His guest grinned a ghastly wry smile but clasped the captain's hand with his woolen mitten. "We are unfinished creations, only half formed if someone brighter, wiser and dearer than ourselves—as such a friend should be—does not lend himself to help complete our weak and imperfect characters. Once I had such a friend, the most admirable of human beings, and so I'm competent to judge concerning friendship. You have your whole life and future ahead of you, so you have every reason for hope, not despair. But me—I have lost everything, and can never start life over again."

Captain Walton winced in deep-felt pain, feeling his heart melt as he drew in a deep breath and watched his guest's face express a serenely reconciled and unresisting misery; only he stayed silent and, without a word, retired to the captain's cabin.

§

Shortly the bomb ship's young surgeon stepped suddenly inside, admitting himself after knocking lightly at the door. Lying down in bed again the captain's guest sat up with a start, looking apprehensive at the surgeon's abrupt intrusion into the cabin.

"Victor Frankenstein!" the surgeon announced just as abruptly. "I am Doctor Abraham Van Helsing! I've been looking for you for a very long time, and I've gone to great lengths to finally find you."

"Looking for me?" the startled guest asked, taken aback. "How can that possibly be? Are we perhaps acquainted with each other?"

"Indeed we are, sir," the surgeon adamantly assured him. "In fact, I signed aboard this vessel for the express purpose of taking ship in search of you."

"For what reckless reason would you voyage so far to the Arctic ice searching for me?"

"My master sent me to go in search of you," the surgeon explained inexplicably, "just as you came to his asylum in London sometime ago in search of him."

For just a moment Victor Frankenstein brooded deeply on this mystifying mystery, puzzling over his somewhat recent past and struggling inwardly to remember—What? Whom?—until someone blindingly familiar flashed unexpectedly across his memory and clearly betrayed himself.

"Your master is the most distinguished natural philosopher in England," Frankenstein muttered disbelievingly, his features lighting up with the startling revelation then haunting his head, "whose knowledge and discoveries were absolutely vital to the completion of my final and most vile undertaking."

"Yes," Abraham Van Helsing answered him solemnly. "To fashion a female being of the human species."

FOUR:
DARK NIGHT OF THE SOUL

"I was like the Arabian who had been buried with the dead and found passage to life, aided only by one glimmering and seemingly ineffectual light."—Victor Frankenstein

JOSEPH COVINO JR

Victor Frankenstein stared blankly, and stood in awe of his startling visitor.

"How did you ever come to overtake me in this frozen waste?" he asked him, soundly stupefied by the young doctor's presence.

"For many months now," Abraham Van Helsing explained calmly, "it's been my settled purpose to follow you just as it's been yours to follow your creature."

"That fiend!" Frankenstein enunciated, lifting up his voice. "My enemy!"

"Led by every slightest tracing of the foot," Van Helsing went on, unperturbed, "I followed you from Switzerland along the Rhone River until I came to the Mediterranean Sea. Then I took passage in the very same ship bound for the Black Sea just as you did. And even as you did I headed northward and followed your trail through the wilds of Tartary and Russia."

"How could you follow in my track so precisely?" Frankenstein asked him doubtingly.

"Quite simply," Van Helsing assured him with confidence, "by the very same means you followed your creature—by his trail of fear and terror. Your creature left behind quite a clear and easy trail to follow. Frightened peasants, terrified by his awful sight, often told me of his route. So following him was as good as following you."

"How could you know which path to take once you reached the northernmost seashore?"

"Once I got to a certain hamlet on the White Sea," Van Helsing answered at length and in further detail, "I asked the villagers about your creature and gathered very precise information. They told me a gigantic monster, heavily armed, routed a family from their cottage by virtue of his horrific appearance. He made off with their store of winter food and loaded it onto a sledge, and even harnessed a team of trained dogs to drag it with. And to the great relief of the villagers, he—like you—shaped his course across the frozen sea; after which it was no difficult feat to take ship aboard this vessel in Archangel and be bound for the Arctic ice as you were, although I was obliged to delay my departure to collect certain instruments with which you are well acquainted."

"The instruments of life," Frankenstein muttered, struck with awe and disbelief. "How did you ever propose to yourself to take ship aboard a vessel bound for the Arctic ice?"

"I'm a Hollander!" Van Helsing boasted proudly. "It's commonly known that Dutch seamen, employed in the Greenland fishery, sail regularly to Spitzbergen from Archangel and other ports bordering the White Sea in ships such as this."

"This is a naval warship!"

"Fitted out for Arctic exploration!" Van Helsing clarified. "I had also heard of the lesser proposition of reaching the North Pole from Spitzbergen during the winter by going over the ice in sledges drawn by dogs. So with a view to finding out just how far this plan was practical, I questioned and got answers from Russians living at Archangel, who had wintered in those remote islands."

"And you concluded that making the crossing by ship rather than by sledge would be most practical—to say nothing of tolerable," Frankenstein suggested in half-hearted jest.

"And swifter as well," Van Helsing added with a nod. "It was only by the most fortuitous good fortune that I came to sign on aboard this vessel with the good captain, who at the time—as fate would have it—happened to be at Archangel enlisting sailors for the voyage."

"Do you believe this expedition stands any chance at all of reaching the North Pole?"

"If my Dutch seafaring ancestors had set their hearts on realizing their ambitions as strongly as I did," Van Helsing answered whimsically, "those winds and currents which drove them northward would have tempted them with the tantalizing prospect of reaching a place which had always been considered unapproachable. I've never considered a voyage to the Pole to be impossible."

"Why have you pursued me to this place?" Frankenstein asked him bluntly, his entire aspect turning gravely serious.

"My master has revolutionized medical therapy by his discovery of the continual evolution of brain-matter—the theory of which I helped him to develop," Van Helsing explained with infuriating leisureliness. "Now I've made it my own specialty."

"Why have you come here to find me?" Frankenstein persisted with impatient indignation.

"How much do you believe it advisable to confide in the captain?" Van Helsing asked in answer.

"Confide what in the captain exactly?" Captain Robert Walton asked inquisitively as he abruptly appeared, unexpectedly darkening the cabin door!

§

Oppressed heavily by depressed spirits Victor Frankenstein stood, tightly wringing his hands and brooding blankly at the spot where he wandered back on deck—and where Captain Walton stood watching him with bated breath which smoldered in the icy air.

"Even to a man broken in spirit," the captain said knowingly, "every beautiful sight to be seen in this miraculous realm—the sea, the sky—must still seem powerful enough to raise his soul."

"As you may readily gather, captain, I have endured great and disastrous calamity." Frankenstein turned at the last to look him, grim-faced, in the eye.

"I gather that you feel very deeply," the captain said, "but even though you may have suffered great distress and disappointment, when you take refuge inside yourself you become like your own guardian angel, within whose protective sanctuary no misery or despair can penetrate."

"Once I had decided that the horrible nightmare of my ordeal should die with me. But you have persuaded me to change my decision."

"How so?"

"You search for knowledge and enlightenment just as I once did. And I fervently pray that the fulfillment of your desires should never become a monster to destroy you as mine has."

"How do you mean?"

"I don't know that telling my tragedies will be of any use to you," Frankenstein offered, "but when I consider that you are pursuing the very same path that I did, exposing yourself to the very same dangers which have reduced me to what I am, I trust that you may infer a fitting moral from my story— one which may guide you if you succeed in your venture, or comfort you if you fail."

"I am resolved not to fail," Captain Walton said in earnest, "in spite of the dangers."

"Then make ready to listen to things which would normally be considered inconceivable," Frankenstein cautioned him. "Were we among more temperate surroundings I should fear to face your disbelief, perhaps even your disdain. But many things will seem more believable in this strange and savage domain, which would provoke the scorn and ridicule of those ignorant of the overwhelming forces of Creation."

"I feel I'm no stranger to those forces," the captain empathized.

"Then I feel certain that the bare facts of my story should speak well for themselves, and bear out the truth of the incidents of which it's made."

"As much as I'm pleased by your offer of confidence," the captain said with care, "I couldn't bear that you should revive your misery by telling your ordeal. Still, I feel exceedingly anxious to hear your story, partly out of curiosity, but partly out of a real desire to better your lot if it's at all within my power to do so."

"I thank you for your understanding," Frankenstein said, "but it's no use. My fate is nearly sealed. I await only one thing, and then I shall rest in peace. I appreciate your intention, but you are wrong, my friend, if you will let me so call you. Nothing can change my lot. Hear my story, and you will see how indelibly the die is cast. I will start my story tomorrow when you should be more at ease."

"You have my deepest thanks."

Captain Walton laid an affectionate hand on Frankenstein's stooped shoulder, turned on his heel and retired, leaving him un-afflicted.

§

Ever since I can remember I've always possessed an insatiable thirst for knowledge. I've thrived on investigating the causes more than the mere configurations of things. For me the whole world was a profound secret to explore and expose—a great, baffling mystery to solve. A consuming curiosity, diligent research to discover and unfold the hidden secrets of nature, a joy much like ecstasy as they were revealed to me—these are among the first impressions I can recall.

At times my temperament was violent and my moods volatile, but by some bent in my disposition they were turned not toward petty pursuits, but a burning desire to learn some notably select and special things. What I really longed to know were the very secrets of heaven and hell—and all the world which lay in-between. Whether it was the surface exterior of things or the innermost and mysterious nature of man which engaged me, I still concentrated my research on the metaphysical—or in its supreme sense—the physical secrets of Creation. But ultimately my passion for the pursuit of knowledge ruled and overran my destiny. I felt it rise like a wellspring from vile and infernal sources, but surging as it arose until it turned into a flood tide which has—in its tumult—engulfed and drowned all my hopes and ambitions. Misfortune and misery combined to corrupt my mind, and turned my hopeful prospects for great possibility into hopelessly desperate and self-absorbed preoccupations.

I've been infused with this devout desire to penetrate Nature's secrets for a long time. So with the greatest devotion I at once took up the pursuit of both the philosopher's stone and the elixir of life—although in due time the last quest attracted my undivided attention. Fortune alone was an abysmal ambition; but what fame would accompany the discovery if I could purge the human form of all sickness and disease—and make man impervious to any but a sudden or violent death?

Natural philosophy and chemistry in particular—and the natural genius I possess for it—is the gift which has ruled my fate. I zealously yearned to learn and acquire knowledge, but I always came away from my earlier traditional studies disappointed and dissatisfied. So eventually I entertained the greatest contempt for so-called science which could never penetrate beyond even the threshold of true knowledge— that which pursues power and immortality—so I wondered whether anything of any real depth would or could ever be known. And presently my mind was overrun by one idea, one belief, one design. My very soul cried out loud: so much more, far more, would I do. Pursuing a path already trod I would pioneer a new and un-trodden way, explore mysterious and unseen forces and unveil to all the world the profoundest secrets of Creation.

My intensely scientific study became my sole preoccupation. And my diligence to my research became so devout that the dead of night often gave way to the light of day while I was yet engrossed, heart and soul, in search of secret discovery in my laboratory. Only those who have known it can appreciate this seduction of science: in scientific research alone does there exist constant cause for exploration and discovery! And I constantly pursued the completion of a single goal of research with a single-minded purpose and resolve, becoming absorbed solely in my search: but for what?

One of the things which had particularly intrigued me was the construction of the human form, and for that matter, any creature infused with life. From where, I asked myself many times, did the source of life come? It's an audacious question which has ever been considered a profound secret. But how many countless things are we on the verge of discovering, or learning, if only fear and indifference would not repress our research?

Unless I had been impassioned by an almost superhuman fixation, my diligence to my research would have become unbearably discouraging and disheartening. But to investigate the causes of life we must first resort to death. I became proficient in the science of anatomy but this wasn't enough. I must also examine the natural corruption and decay of the human body. Fortunately my mind was never impressed with any supernatural terror. I never recall shuddering to any superstitious story, or shrinking from any unearthly ghost. Darkness made no impression on my imagination. To me the graveyard was merely the repository of human bodies stripped of life which, from being the vessels of vigor and vitality, were reduced to a great feast for ravenous maggots.

Then I was driven to examine the source and progression of the body's decay, and compelled to spend night and day in crypts and tombs. I devoted my thoughts to all things most destructive to the frailty of human emotions. I watched how the undefiled frame of man was corrupted and consumed. I saw the decay of death replace the fresh bloom of life. I saw how the worm over-swarmed the marvels of the eye and brain. I stopped to examine and analyze all the minutest details of causation—as displayed in the change from life to death, and death to life, until out of the shadows of this darkness a startling light burst in on me—a light so bright and glorious, but so simple, that while I became delirious with the enormity of the prospect which it illuminated I was severely shocked: that among so many men of scientific genius who had concentrated their research on making the very same discovery—that I alone should be singled out to expose so startling a secret.

§

I stepped inside the lecturing hall at the university of Ingolstadt, listlessly at first but then expectantly as I saw my preferred professor of natural philosophy stand at his pulpit and, with head erect, conclude his eloquent tribute to modern chemistry. M. Waldman was a short but decidedly dignified man of about fifty with black hair graying at the temples. His benign face expressed great kindliness as he spoke in surpassingly sweet tones.

"The ancient masters of chemistry promised us the unachievable," he said, "but achieved nothing. Modern masters, on the other hand, promise us precious little: they know full well that metals cannot be transformed by a philosopher's stone and that the elixir of life is a fantasy. But these natural philosophers, whose hands seem capable of only dabbling in dirt, and whose eyes gaze incessantly into the microscope or crucible, have truly accomplished miracles. They penetrate the mysteries of Nature and expose her hidden secrets. They soar among the heavens: they have discovered how the blood circulates and the essence of the air we breathe. They have gained new and almost limitless powers. They can control the thunder in the sky, simulate the earthquake and even taunt the spirit world with its own shadows."

Professor Waldman's words of destiny struck fateful chords throughout my entire being—pronounced to destroy me—as if my spirit suddenly struggled with some tangible enemy. Afterward I went up to him to discuss his thought-provocative lecture.

"I must confess, professor," I told him candidly, "I've long held in contempt the presumed usefulness of contemporary natural philosophy. I've never been satisfied with the finite fruits promised by the modern masters of natural science. It was very different in times past when they pursued infinite power and immortality. Such aspirations were grand even if vain."

"Grandiose and vainglorious!" Professor Waldman exclaimed, smiling decorously.

"Yes," I conceded. "Now I realize that the scientific landscape has changed radically. I've retraced the steps of knowledge over the course of time, and traded the discoveries of contemporary philosophers for the dreams of forgotten visionaries. Now the ambition of the philosopher seems to confine itself to the destruction of those dreams from which my fascination with science comes. I'm compelled to trade visions of infinite imagination for truths of little value."

"Modern philosophers are indeed indebted to the philosophers of old," the professor reassured me, "whose tireless devotion laid most of the groundwork for our present store of knowledge. They left to us a much simpler task of assigning new names and classifications to facts which they, to a great extent, had been the messengers of revelation. The efforts of such men of genius, however misdirected, hardly ever fail to finally work to the definite benefit of mankind."

"Misdirected?"

"By superstition—which is the heresy of any enlightened age. It's simply another feeble excuse for the worst possible kind of darkness."

I looked aghast at the professor with silent expectation.

"Ignorance!" he bluntly blurted out. "But we're here to conduct science—not to pander to superstition."

"Then I put myself at the disposal of science."

"You've shown a serious interest in practicing experimental

surgery, but first you'll have to master anatomy and dissection."

"To what end?"

"To the end that dissection can reveal to us the secrets of life."

"By means of dissecting death?"

"The after-death," he clarified. "Anatomy is the basis for all scientific knowledge of the human body as well as surgical experimentation. It edifies the head, guides the hand and habituates the heart to a kind of necessary inhumanity."

"Inhumanity?"

"To deliberately mutilate the body of another human being demands working beyond the bounds of normal emotions. And to study anatomy by dissection demands that the student effectively suppress those emotions."

"Dissection hardens the heart to a kind of cold-blooded callousness?"

"The materiality of the human corpse is undeniable," the professor explained. "It's a carcass predisposed to corruption, and becomes obnoxious and offensive to the senses, not to mention distressing to the emotions. To treat it as an object of serious scientific study demands a certain suspension of human emotion to counteract any feelings of emotional repulsion."

"So one has to divorce himself from human sensitivity to objectify the human body?"

"Perhaps your heart is too soft to permit you to become proficient at experimental surgery," the professor said dubiously, "but you will realize many practical benefits from careful and meticulous anatomical exploration. You will acquire an intimate knowledge of the structure and function of the human body, sharpen your observational acuity and develop manual dexterity. From this you will cultivate a greater degree of physiological and pathological knowledge, which in turn will greatly improve your ability to experiment and invent innovative surgical procedures."

"I fear the potential danger that this objectification of the human body should be carried over from the dead to the living."

"It's far more practical to objectify a dead body than a living one that's writhing and screaming in agony," he told me coldly.

"Where do I begin to refine this necessary inhumanity?"

"To study those dust-to-dust changes and transformations in the human body which we call decomposition and decay," he said scrupulously, "you must go to a school where only the dead can teach the living."

"School?"

"Yes. If you're disposed to dissect a prime source of dissection material is the grave itself."

"Violate the burial vault?" I asked, disbelieving.

"Quite so," he said in a sly whisper beneath his breath. "You will have to form an unsavory liaison with a resurrection man named Crouch. You will accompany him to the charnel house as an observer until you can accustom yourself to go on your own."

"Resurrection man?"

"Yes," the professor answered me lowly, bristling with bitterness, "one of the lowest scum of the earth, the dregs of degradation, villains of the blackest dye. But we suffer them because disinterment, though loathsome, is often so vital to our research."

"What in God's name is a resurrection man?" I asked, burning with curiosity.

Staggered by my innocent ignorance Professor M. Waldman stared at me stoically.

"A professional grave-robber."

§

A heavy, hulking man Thomas Crouch heaved strenuously

to lift the heavy iron grille of crisscrossed bars from its low-lying base, situated unobtrusively at the secluded corner of the somber churchyard. A pair of outward-opening iron doors was aglow with lambent light thrown aslant by his tilted lantern, which he had set level with the ground. He budged the grinding doors open with difficulty, exposing to view a sunken shaft as dark as a bottomless pit. Taking up his lantern once more he beckoned me to follow him into the gaping hole.

Going slowly down a steep flight of steps leading to a darkened burial vault we came to an arched entry which was barred by an iron gate, grating as we forced our way through. Another step down and our footfalls clattered noisily over a spacious floor of unglazed tiles and bricks. Crouch raised his lantern high in the dank air, shedding its dirty light on the low-ceilinged, panel-vaulted tomb-chamber. A gently curved and barreled brick roof sprang up from sideways plinths of rubble. And all around the chamber's lime-washed, stone-block walls were punched with a neat arrangement of slate shelves and niches set at level intervals. Inside these darkly shelved recesses were stacked so many dismal objects of death: coffins holding the departed dead!

"Welcome to the eternal bedchamber," Thomas Crouch scoffed contemptuously, contorting his coarse features in the shadowy, lurid light. "This is where the pretentious and self-indulgent try in vain to preserve their passing memory from oblivion."

He plunked down his lantern on top of a brick charnel cistern stretching from end to end across the entire length of the vault, and lit up a flambeau suspended from a stone wall already deeply charred with scorch-marks.

"They put the most rotten coffins in there to make room for the fresher ones." He gestured to a deep pit sunk into the floor and lidded with a trapdoor. "They want to make sure the dispossessed dead are entitled to stay within these walls."

I stepped up to a ventilation grille fixed firmly in the wall at one end of the vault, touching the moist surface lightly with my fingertips as I gasped for a breath of the fresh but diffuse air circulating thinly through the heavier, oppressive odor of corruption and decay.

"I feel obliged to tread lightly for fear of waking the dead from their sound slumber." I shuddered from the chamber's deathly cold.

"Don't worry," Crouch scoffed scurrilously. "These idlers have no desire to abandon their comfortable beds."

"Nor to be deliberately disturbed in their beds by the idly curious, no doubt."

"You can't disturb a relic." Crouch gestured complacently to the shelved niches lining the stone walls. "And as sure as death all any of these coffins contain are crumbling and forgotten relics!"

"Human relics," I contradicted him, "momentarily ignored and neglected, perhaps, but not altogether forgotten. Or else we wouldn't be here paying our respects."

"I gather you'll be doing a lot more than merely paying your respects. I've been told you'll be sitting here corpse-watching for a lot longer than the usual vigil."

"Yes, but not to ward off any evil spirits."

Crouch stepped up gingerly to a flat-lidded, shaped-shouldered, velvet-covered coffin laid edgewise across the top of the brick charnel cistern, wrenching loose the recessed lid lined and covered with cambric. He fingered a string of beading affixed to the upper inner side of the lid as he laid it aside.

"Aren't you afraid of evil spirits hovering over this place?" he asked suggestively.

"I'm conscious of the powers of darkness," I told him. "But I also know that the demons of the mind can oftentimes prove more powerful than the demons of superstition."

"For what then?" Crouch took up his lantern again. "To make sure he's dead or to give him a chance to come back to life?"

"To give death sufficient chance to take over the place of life."

Crouch held out his lantern over the padded, elm coffin encased in its lead shell and covered with gilt scarlet velvet.

"Here lies your surrogate of death!" he announced ceremoniously.

Crouch's lantern shone dimly on a young man laid out on a draped mattress, his head resting on a silky pillow. He wore a single-piece, long-sleeved cashmere shroud with rosettes on either side of its turned-down collar; a twisted silken cord tied off his waist. His arms were laid across his breast with his hands pointing toward his opposite shoulders.

"My messenger of mortality," I muttered. "It's hard to believe that this lifeless corpse once sheltered a human soul."

"Death is never a tidy thing," Crouch said scornfully, "though fools try to make it so."

"How do you mean?"

"All that fancy dressing and trimming just to sweeten up a rotting relic!"

"Washing is said to cleanse the sweat of death and the sins of life."

Crouch brought out a hidden jug of wine, making a jaunty display of guzzling from it.

"Every drop of wine that's drunk at someone's burial is a sin which the dearly departed committed in life," he driveled, wiping away the wine dribbling from the corners of his mouth. "So you take away the sins of the dead and take them on yourself. Now that's what I call cleansing."

"Why would you willingly endanger your eternal soul by bearing the sins of another, except for the sake of self-immolation?"

"Maybe because the fate of my soul is open to much doubt."

"The fate of every man's soul is open to doubt. That's why

we speculate about how best to preserve and keep it."

"If you believe in old wives' tales about souls and spirits and such," Crouch jeered. "Rich man or pauper it makes no difference. The fate of this shell we live in is much more certain."

"Nothing in this world is absolutely assured," I told him solemnly, "neither fate nor even death. It's actually possible for a human body to be alive and dead at the same time. The question which remains is: which is more meaningful—life or death?"

"If that's all you came here to decide then it shouldn't take you too long to work out what's meaningful for this dead lad." Crouch shrugged as he gestured dismissively to the nameless young man laid out, cold as pallid marble, before us. "He hasn't been cold long. But one thing's for sure: nothing will warm his blood again anytime soon."

"I've come not to find out what warms the blood but what animates it." I riveted my unflinching eyes on him in deadly earnest. "And whatever animates the blood will animate the dead."

§

So finally I was left alone to watch the young man's corpse decompose over a short span of four weeks. First a greenish blotch of skin tinged his lower stomach, creeping up slowly to his chest while spreading downward to sully his upper legs. A gaseous odor followed the discoloration, bloating the body until it forced the eyes to protrude from their sockets and the tongue from its mouth; after which the greenish skin turned purple and then black, overrunning the whole body until large, smelly blisters cropped up. Sheets of skin peeled off in hefty layers, shredding to pieces. Seeping fluid oozed and ran out of the mouth and nose—the swollen tongue stuck out farther and the entire corpse reeked of a more obnoxious gas.

Hair, nails and teeth loosened until they dropped off. Bowels ruptured and liquefied. What finally remained of the lifeless body was in essence a skeleton masked with putrefied skin.

Bear in mind: I am not recounting the fabrication of a madman. The moon does not glow more surely in the nocturnal sky than that which I now attest is true. Divine Intervention could have created it but the steps to my discovery were decisive and inescapable. After countless days and nights of indescribable toil and exhaustion I succeeded in discovering the source of animation and life. More—I became myself able to infuse lifeless, inanimate matter with animation and life!

FIVE: DAWN OF DEATH

"Life and death appeared to me ideal bounds, which I should first break through, and pour a torrent of light into our dark world."—Victor Frankenstein

JOSEPH COVINO JR

"Incredible!" Captain Robert Walton exclaimed to his convalescent guest. "I cannot believe what my ears have just heard!"

"The utter astonishment I first felt upon making this discovery soon gave way to outright joy and ecstasy," Victor Frankenstein confided from his bomb ship cabin bed. "To finally reach all at once the height of my ambition—after spending so much time in all-consuming toil—was the most satisfying fulfillment of my desires. But this discovery was so remarkable and overpowering that all the steps which had guided me to it were destroyed—and I saw only the first fruits of my labor."

"Which were?"

"What has been the pursuit and aspiration of the wisest men since the earth's creation—and which was now well within my reach. But it didn't reveal itself to me all at once like some mystical event. The secret I had discovered wasn't of a nature that I should reveal the end result already achieved, but rather that I should concentrate my efforts and set my sights on the ultimate purpose of my pursuit."

Captain Walton looked aghast with wide-eyed wonder and opened his mouth to speak, but Frankenstein threw up a cautionary hand to cut him short.

"My friend," Frankenstein said sympathetically, "I see by the anticipation and suspense in your eyes that you expect me to tell you the monstrous secret which only I alone possess. This can never be. Wait patiently until I finish my story and you will readily understand—and appreciate—why I must remain silent on that question."

"I must confess I can scarcely contain my impatience!"

"As rash and reckless as I was I will not guide you to your unfailing ruin and downfall."

"Perhaps you are being somewhat overprotective of my safety."

"Take heed and learn from me," Frankenstein exhorted the

captain, "if not by my warnings then at least by my experience: how perilous acquiring knowledge is—and how much more contented that man is who feels that his native land is all the world than he who strives to become greater than his nature entitles him."

"But I believe that man is worthy of striving beyond mere complacency—to even surpass what his limited nature may appear to allow."

"So too did I believe," Frankenstein conceded. "But when I discovered so awesome a power put into my hands I grappled for a long time with the way in which I should use it."

"No doubt you struggle still with this overwhelming dilemma."

"Can you imagine the multitude of sensations which spurred me on—like some tempest—in my first frenzy of success?" Frankenstein asked excitedly. "Life and death seemed to me to pose only transient barriers, which I should first burst through and shed a flood of light upon our lightless world."

"Tell me everything you thought and felt."

"A new human race would revere me as its creator and source of life. Many benevolent and contented beings would owe their existence to me."

"And their allegiance? Or adoration?"

"Appreciation," Frankenstein sternly corrected him. "And no father could claim his child's appreciation so fully as I should merit theirs."

"Forgive me," Captain Walton apologized. "I often think too rigidly in terms of subordinates obeying their superior commanding officers."

"Following this train of thought," Frankenstein went on un-afflicted, "I speculated that if I could infuse lifeless matter with life then I might over the course of time—even though I then found it hopeless—actually restore life where death had seemingly consumed the body with corruption and decay."

"You did succeed eventually."

"Such aspirations did bolster my resolve and I fell to work with relentless fervor—being so engaged, heart and soul, in this single, solitary pursuit."

"You sound remorseful."

"Because all my senses grew insensitive to even the beauty of Nature herself. And the very same passion which made me overlook the beauty of Creation also made me neglect my most beloved friends and relations, whom I had been absent from for ever so long."

"Explorers and pioneers must always sacrifice so much to reach their greatest goals," the captain said, trying to placate his disheartened guest.

"Indeed," Frankenstein agreed. "Abhorrent in itself I could not turn my thoughts away from my experiment, which had uncontrollably seized my reason. So I wanted to dismiss from my mind anything relating to my feelings of affection until that ultimate pursuit, which consumed every part of my being, should be fulfilled."

"You considered your experiment abhorrent?"

"An exemplary human being," Frankenstein said, "should always keep a calm peace of mind, and never let passion or passing fancy upset his serenity. The pursuit of enlightenment is no exception to this precept."

"How many of us could be considered exemplary?"

"If the pursuit you devote yourself to tends to numb your affections, and to blunt your enjoyment of those simple delights which no profound discovery could possibly create, then that pursuit is most definitely unbefitting the human spirit."

Captain Walton looked spellbound but speechless.

"But I digress unduly," Frankenstein said, "and your expression prompts me to get on with my story."

§

Even though I was possessed of the ability to infuse animation and life, what yet remained a task of unimaginable toil and trouble was to make a framework for receiving it, with all its complexity of muscles, fibers and veins. At first I wondered whether I should try to make a being like myself or rather one of simpler configuration. But my anticipation was much too aroused to let me doubt my capability to infuse with life a creature as complex and marvelous as man. Those materials at my disposal scarcely seemed sufficient for so difficult an experiment. But I never doubted that I should finally succeed.

I made myself ready for a host of setbacks: my efforts might be constantly frustrated and in the end my creation be imperfect. But when I contemplated the advancement which comes about every day in science and mechanics I was heartened to hope my present experiments would at least lay the groundwork for imminent success. Nor would I accept the immensity and intricacy of my undertaking as proof of its impossibility. With these sentiments then I set about to create a human being. Contrary to my original conception I decided to make my being of gigantic size and stature—about eight feet in height and proportionally large—since the smallness of the parts greatly postponed my progress. So after having come to this conclusion, and having spent some time effectively gathering and setting out my materials, I set to work.

§

Lofty towers connected by a battered curtain loomed right ahead, forming a rambling and roughhewn ring punched through with darkened arches which hedged round the castellated keep. Tall, lifeless trees with scraggly, leafless branches stood entrenched in a broken column at irregular intervals along the weather-beaten wall of crumbling brick and stone. Apprehensive as I stepped up to the subjugating gatehouse I fell in with the many men, women and children visitors marching in steady procession in and out of the castle which substituted for the county jail at Ingolstadt.

"State your business," the head turnkey abruptly ordered.

"I'm here to see the prisoner named Davison," I said.

"Davison?" the turnkey snickered. "He's in the condemned hole! That'll cost you plenty."

"By order of the magistrate," I interrupted him, cutting short his expected overture of an extorted fee of admittance by handing over my written injunction, over which the turnkey ran his suspicious eyes, snarling skeptically.

"Right," he finally said in a resigned but indignant voice, "but you'll have to see the superintendent first. Follow me."

Leading the way across a spacious central courtyard, surrounded by darkened cells, the turnkey moved briskly toward a boisterous crowd of spectators clustered about a whipping post situated in the middle, taking me in reluctant tow.

"This prison is the devil's place!" a nameless prisoner screamed in agony. He was shackled in heavy wooden stocks, stripped from his waist upwards, a scaffold rope hung tightly about his neck. "I'll be damned if I ever do another day's work in this accursed pit!"

"So be it!" another man, clothed with authority, answered him back. "Be damned then!"

An emphatic nod of the demanding man's head signaled silently to the hooded hangman to lash out once more—mercilessly—with his flesh-flaying whip. And again the man nodded, only this time with a gesture of mute understanding as he bent an ear to the garrulous turnkey stepping up to speak urgently to him. They talked together and, presently, cast their inquisitive eyes on me.

"Now are you willing to work?" the man in authority asked insistently, throwing up a hand to abruptly stop the flogging.

"No!" the prisoner yelled back at the top of his strained

and anguished voice, sagging weakly in the pillory. "Never! I refuse!"

"Very well," the other man said, resigned but adamant. "You will be asked the same question every twenty lashes until you become willing! Should you persist in your refusal to yield you will be flogged until you drop dead!"

Another emphatic but still silent and stoical signal to the hangman spurred on both the brutal beating and the tortured outcries.

"Herr Frankenstein?" the man in command said, stepping up suddenly to address me. "My name's Ellitson. I'm the director of our lowly little seminary. And I bid you welcome."

"Seminary?"

"Yes," he said proudly, leading me back to the gatehouse, "a seminary of crime. Crime is nothing more or less than a species of sin. And a charitable prison such as ours is bent upon saving the souls of those gone astray. The discipline we administer is a bitter medicine for correcting immoral conduct and an unwholesome way of life. But sinners confined within these walls are presently taught obedience, humility and respect."

"And despair?"

"Atonement and salvation!" Ellitson exclaimed contrarily, raising his voice and looking askance at me. "Prison should be a place of salutary terror for the sinful. I do not count myself among the number of those who, from some misplaced tenderness of heart, would undo the just terror of the law."

"Whose law?"

"The law of the righteous and the just!" he cried. "Prison is a place of penance for sin! And I take no interest in taking away the just terror of punishment by pampering the impenitent and profane."

"The impenitent? Then penance does not always prevail."

"Certain among the ungodly souls," he reluctantly confessed, "are hopelessly lost and beyond all redemption."

"What then is their fate?"

"They are sent to the condemned cells to reflect on their misspent lives," he said solemnly, "before they are put to death."

"Like Davison?"

"Davison is in solitary confinement," Ellitson explained, "which we consider to be a particularly salutary punishment."

"How so?"

"Solitude separates the sinful from the distractions and temptations of the senses so that the innermost voice of conscience can have full sway."

"Then I fear I must invade that solitude," I said regretfully.

"Worse," he objected, "you will disrupt a highly special punishment for, you see, Davison presently lies on the grating."

"Grating?"

"That's of no importance," he hastened to add, gesturing dismissively to his head turnkey who still stayed, awaiting his orders. "Robinson here will convey you to the condemned cell for your interview."

"I thank you."

"You should realize however," Ellitson said, stopping to caution me, "that Davison is destined for dissection as part of his death sentence. His body will be sent to the anatomy hall as soon as he's executed."

"Yes," I said knowingly, "and so I've come: to take special care—to make very sure—that Davison's cadaver arrives safely at the correct hall of anatomy."

Robinson, the head turnkey, led me back across the castle courtyard to the dungeon tower, where we climbed down a flight of spiral steps and stepped up to a solitary cell underground. He budged open its heavy door with a clanking rattle of keys, gesturing for me to keep away from its doorway.

"Stand off to let the stench clear," he warned.

Flinching from the foul odor issuing forth I set my eyes on only part of a cold, stone-flagged floor and a hard board-bed strewn with some straw inside the dark, damp, windowless cell—empty of any prisoner.

"Come on," Robinson said, "let's fetch our hideous guest."

In yet another part of the sunken dungeon the turnkey budged open a different creaking door. By very slow degrees it edged open, grinding as it inched along across the gritty, dirt-covered stone surface, gradually exposing to view a water-filled pit sunk into the ground as deep as a well. Over the watery pit was laid a heavy metal grating. And on top of the grate rested a heavily collapsed and crumpled up human being—a ghastly man of gigantic but monstrous stature!

"Right!" the head turnkey bellowed demandingly. He took up a solid stick left leaning against the outer wall, slapping it hard against his palm. "Come out and get back to your cell!"

Scarcely astir the creature moved listlessly over the grill, laboring to heave himself upright, his weighty fetters clanking with every lumbering movement. Coupled with blocks and chains, shackles clamped down tightly around his bruised and bloodied limbs. His yellow, watery, hate-infested eyes showed through a tattered thatch of long black hair matting his shriveled features. Only with great and strenuous difficulty did he get to his feet. He stood up shakily and shuffled back at a plodding pace to the gaping cavern of the condemned cell, plunking himself down in a lumpish heap on the stone-flagged floor, stoical and silent.

"Must he be put under such severe restraint?" I asked the turnkey, taking pity on the prisoner's wretched plight.

"Don't delude yourself," the turnkey admonished me. "That miserable wretch is put in irons to make doubly sure he stays in custody long enough to justly hang, for he's plenty dangerous."

"What's his crime?"

"He's a bloodthirsty strangler who's murdered men, women and children without compunction. He's threatened to break the neck of many a turnkey like myself. But ironing this incorrigible brute at least assures a certain conduct which I can't effect by simple confinement."

"Utter capitulation," I objected.

"Utter security," he said derisively. "But if it strikes your fancy I should lock him up in a cell along with you without his irons!"

"Only should you be courageous enough to accompany us in unfettered liberty," I answered him back sedately.

"Get in!" he ordered me with a sneering terseness, noisily bolting and locking the door shut behind me once I stepped, quite reluctantly, into the dark, dank cell.

Anxiously I listened as the hollow sound of the turnkey's retreating footsteps and scurrilous laughter echoed lustily throughout the dungeon corridor, falling faintly onto my ears before fading into a startling silence. I felt profoundly afraid and shuddered, struck suddenly with an outright overwhelming, all-consuming, all-pervading fear: for then I knew full well that I was abruptly and altogether alone—together with the monstrous and murderous creature! Slow and irresolute I sat down and settled onto a spare pile of sodden straw, close enough to hear the mammoth creature moan lowly beneath his labored breath as I watched—fearfully with my own bated breath—as he stared, riveting his hate-incensed eyes directly onto me.

"You must be suffering intense pain," I sympathized, running my scrupulous eyes slowly over the length of this pathetic prisoner's bloated and discolored legs, showing piteously through his filthy and tattered rags. "How are you coping?"

"I feel like I'm ready to sink into the earth," he answered

forlornly. "Besides, the pain inflicted on me is supposed to be for my own good."

"Those constricting irons can't be for your own good." I gestured faintly to his hobbled limbs. "They're cutting off your blood flow and causing severe swelling. Should mortification set in you could very well lose your limbs—and even die."

"Mortification?"

"Gangrene."

"I'm already condemned to die!" he scoffed aloud, his voice resounding with a resigned irony. "So there's no help for it. The heavier and tighter the irons the greater the tribute extorted."

"Tribute?"

"That's right. The turnkeys here pluck the prisoners for fees for just about everything they can put a price on."

"They make you pay money?" I asked incredulously. "For what?"

"For the favor of putting the irons on and taking them off," he recited in disparaging detail. "Or for leaving them off entirely. For comforts like better food and warmer clothes. For sleeping on a featherbed instead of straw or boards on the floor. For drinking beer and wine from the prison tap. For receiving visitors—like you. And as you can clearly see I am without means to pay for luxuries such as these, which gives me pause to wonder: what have I done to deserve the charity of this visit?"

Facetiously he paused to ponder my own unexplained presence in his condemned cell.

"I've come to offer to ease the pain of your punishment."

"How would you propose to do that?"

"By royal decree," I explained guardedly, "surgeons are granted the right to take the corpses of certain executed criminals for dissection as part of their punishment. It's an aggravation to their execution."

"It's a sadistic, vindictive act of humiliation!" the creature shrieked contemptuously. "Its only purpose is to deny me a decent burial!"

"Nevertheless," I stressed, "your body will be conveyed from the gallows to the surgeons at the anatomy hall for open dissection and public display."

"It's public butchery!" the creature cried out, violently straining every nerve to shatter his restraints. "Are you one of the butchers?"

"I'm a scientist!" I said with a start. "It's true that dissection is a further terror, for the law expressly decrees that the body of a murderer so condemned shall not be suffered to be buried. But I can spare you such a despicable fate."

"Are you a patron who's come to plead to the judges for my pardon?" the creature asked, suddenly taking heart.

"No," I said, grim-faced. "I'm deeply sorry that I cannot save you from hanging. But I can save your flesh from ever rotting on a gibbet or from being cut up and picked to pieces on some mutilator's dissection table."

"What manner of miracle would you work to effect such a feat?"

"Quite simply," I said, "I've come to buy your body."

"To a wretch like myself," he said spiritlessly, "hanging is nothing but a crooked neck and a wet pair of breeches. And I'd rather be broken on the rack than rot in this prison for much longer. So whatever comes after scarcely matters."

"I was thinking more of what comes before."

"I'm being wasted away by slow starvation," the creature complained bitterly, "unless you think a penny loaf of bread a day is enough to satisfy the cravings of hunger. My limbs are crippled by cold and iron. My body's being devoured by vermin. Of what possible use could I be to you?"

"I could pay to lighten the burden of your confinement."

"You put forth a most tempting proposition," he said distrustfully. "Why?"

"Because of your body's great size and stature."

"Because I'm a monstrosity!" he cried out in protest. "You mean to put me on display in some museum as a freak!"

"I prefer to look on you as a physiological marvel," I calmly contradicted him, "worthy of something more than obliteration at the hands of some anatomist."

"And I should sell my carcass to you?"

"I should make sure you're moved from the common to the master's side of the prison, where you'll enjoy many special amenities and privileges while awaiting punishment."

Looking askance at me the creature chortled cynically.

"What possible purpose is served by possessing a monstrous corpse?"

"What purpose is served by inflicting solitary confinement?"

"They call it confronting your conscience," he said with a simper, "which is supposed to condemn you. Have you too come to condemn me?"

"I've come to offer you a chance to defy death and to confront life after it," I told him in solemn earnest. "Why did you kill?"

"Because I'm a monstrous outcast," he said sullenly. "Because I'm alone, lonely and hated by others. Because I hate myself. Because my existence is unbearable and counts for nothing but wretchedness and misery. And bitterness."

"And so," I condoled, "you took your revenge against all those who stood for everything you could never be, and possessed everything you could never have: beauty, peace, contentment, happiness—and love."

"Yes."

"You've been so overcome by your own pain and misery that you've succumbed to delusion," I said pardonably, "for life can turn ugly and miserable for even the most seemingly prosperous among us. Even they can lose all hope and be defeated by desperation and despair."

"Am I beyond all hope and redemption then?"

"It's not my privilege to judge the fate of your soul," I answered him fatefully, "but it may very well be within my power to determine the fate of your life after your death."

§

On the dreadful day of execution I followed along with a riotous throng of townspeople, crushing against the dirty horse cart which carried its doomed prisoner inexorably to the gallows-field. Davison was sentenced to hang—horribly—in chains. Once we got to the gibbet the rambunctious crowd lustily cheered the condemned man as a noose slipped snugly about his unresisting neck. From among a small circle of constables and magistrates a lone parson exhorted his taunting listeners with his canting sermon:

"Sorry is the state you have brought yourself to," he intoned sanctimoniously. "Judged by the law of your land, and by it deemed unworthy to live any longer, unworthy to walk this earth, or to breathe this air; and that no more good nor use to mankind can be expected from you except the example of your death—as a warning to others against committing the same folly in the future!"

After the punishing deed of death was done the creature's corpse was tarred, harnessed in an iron framework and hung from the gibbet, swaying and creaking in the deathly air like some unearthly scarecrow.

"Unpardonable is this plague of pain and suffering which curses our world!" I wailed aloud, heaving a sorrowful sigh as I sank down to the ground, tears welling out of my eyes, and convulsively cried.

§

During the dead of night the grave-robber called Crouch stealthily helped me to heave Davison's colossal corpse into my house at Ingolstadt and, with strenuous difficulty, haul it upstairs to my garret chamber.

"How did you ever get engaged in such a grisly business?" I finally asked him once we paused to catch our panting breath.

"Like many of my mates in the trade," he explained, "we come naturally to resurrecting the dead. We deal with the dead a great deal purely by occupation: we dig graves, we raise gravestones, we work in the dissection rooms. You could say it's grisliness by association."

"The scientists who employ you seem to hold you in great contempt."

"The hatred's mutual," he said. "We have a grudging dependence on each other—they for the corpses, we for the money—pure and simple."

Thomas Crouch abruptly directed his prying eyes to the corrupting corpse lying at lifeless ease in front of us.

"What use do you mean to make of him?" he asked me at the last.

"He's just a mere mortal about to take on mere immortality," I answered, gravely earnest. "All life is the eternal struggle to resist if not repel the inescapable corruption which finally wreaks havoc on the human form. I mean not only to defy but to defeat that corruption."

§

My face turned deathly pale with exhaustive and searching study; and my body wasted away from isolation. At times on the verge of discovery I failed. But yet I clutched at the bright prospect which the next night or day might hold out in front of me. That lone, solitary secret which I alone controlled was the prospect to which I had totally devoted myself. And the midnight moon shone down upon my nocturnal toil while, with restless and impetuous earnestness, I chased Creation to its most secret retreats. Who can imagine the terrors of my secret struggle as I idled away the time among the unsanctified dankness of the grave to infuse the lifeless flesh and blood with animation and life? Even now the memory makes my flesh creep and my head swoon. But then an irresistible and almost frenzied force spurred me onward.

Except for this lone quest I seemed to have lost all spirit or sensitivity. It was truly just a fleeting faint which made me sense with revitalized penetration that—as soon as that abnormal impulse stopped working—I had gone back to my old ways. I gathered bones from charnel-houses and, with unhallowed hands, desecrated the dead secrets of the human form. In my cloistered chamber, or rather cell, at the top of my house—set apart from all the other flats by a gallery and stairway—I secreted my laboratory of obscene creation. My eyes were straining in their sockets from devoting all my thoughts solely to the particulars of my pursuit. Dens of dissection supplied many of my materials. And many times did my human instinct make me turn away with disgust from my preoccupation, although still spurred on by an earnestness which incessantly intensified, I nearly brought my experiment to an end.

So deeply was I absorbed in my preoccupation I looked more like someone condemned by servitude to sweat in the pit than a craftsman engaged in his preferred pursuit; although my zeal was restrained by my anticipation. Every night I was afflicted with a lingering fever and I grew agitated to an almost agonizing extent. I avoided my fellow human beings as if I had been guilty of committing some atrocious outrage. And at times I looked aghast at the ruined derelict I had become. My strength of will alone sustained me: my toil would soon come to a close and my creation should be finished.

JOSEPH COVINO JR

SIX:
BIRTH OF DOOM

"I considered the being whom I had cast among mankind, and endowed with the will and power to effect purposes of horror, such as the deed which he had now done, nearly in the light of my own vampire, my own spirit let loose from the grave, and forced to destroy all that was dear to me."—Victor Frankenstein

JOSEPH COVINO JR

One gloomy, somber night in November I looked with expectant wonder on the consummation of my ordeal. With an anticipation—and apprehension—which nearly equaled utter torment I gathered my implements of life about me so I might infuse a flame of life into the lifeless being lying at my feet; it was already one in the morning when I bent my knee to kneel down alongside it. And before me was sprawled a monstrous, misshapen creature, beginning to budge with an agitated, half-alive movement and struggling—by the might of some powerful force—to come to life.

Rain pattered drearily on the windowpanes and my candle was almost burnt out when, by the flicker of the half-smothered flame, I watched with bated breath the dull, yellow, watery eye of the creature abruptly fly wide open. It gasped hard and a violent spasm convulsed its whole body. Taut, yellowy skin scarcely masked the musculature and blood vessels underneath. Lustrous, flowing black hair fringed his shriveled face, watery eyes deeply set in ashen sockets and straight black lips which stretched across pearly white teeth.

Spellbound terror and loathing overwhelmed my innermost spirit. Unable to bear the ghastly sight of the creature I had brought into being I hurried out of my laboratory—racing away from my abhorrent handiwork, panic-stricken—and went on for a long time pacing my bedchamber, back and forth, powerless to calm my mind enough to sleep. Finally lethargy followed the restlessness I had suffered earlier; and I flung myself onto my bed still wearing my clothes, struggling to fall for a few moments into welcome oblivion.

But it was to no avail: I sank into senseless oblivion, surely, but I was unsettled by the most frightful nightmare. I dreamed I saw my young wife, Elizabeth, blooming with beauty and vitality, strolling the streets of Ingolstadt, where she had never gone. Jubilant and overjoyed I folded her warmly in my arms, but as I impressed my gentle kiss on her lips they turned pale with the pallor of death: her face transformed and took on the appearance of my dead mother, whose bloodless, shroud-wrapped corpse I embraced, watching with horror while the squirming burial-worms turned and twisted in the creases of her grave-clothes. Now neither brave nor benign this vile and evil mockery of my mother repeated her final, parting words when she tightly clasped and held fast to Elizabeth's hands and mine as she lay, debilitated by scarlet fever, on her death-bed:

"My children," she murmured in a devoutly malevolent tone of voice, "I put my greatest hopes for future joy in the promise of your marriage. These hopes will now give your father comfort. Elizabeth, my dearest, you must take my place for my younger children. I'm sorry I'm being taken away from you, for as happy and loved as I've been, it's so hard for me to leave you all. But these feelings are very unbecoming of me. I will try to surrender myself patiently to death, and will harbor a hope of joining you again in a different world."

I awoke from my frightful sleep with a start: cold sweat burst out on my forehead, my teeth rattled, and my extremities were racked with convulsions. By the lurid, deathly pale light of the moon, as it burst through the window shutters, I set terror-stricken eyes on the wretched creature—the miserable monster I had brought into being! He raised my bed curtain and riveted his unsightly eyes right onto me. His contorted mouth opened and he stood agape, muttering guttural, unintelligible sounds while a ghastly grin creased his shriveled cheeks. Whatever he gave utterance to never caught my ear. He stretched out one misshapen hand, seemingly to hold me back, but I took flight and stole away, racing downstairs. I hid myself in the courtyard of the house where I lived, staying there for the rest of that frightful night, pacing back and forth with the most restless disquiet, listening intently, taking in each noise as if it would give warning of the awful approach of the diabolical creature I had brought so awfully to life.

I spent the night in utter misery. At times my heart beat so hard and fast that I felt the throbbing throughout every blood vessel. At other times I almost broke down and collapsed from sheer exhaustion and fatigue. Wet and gloomy, the light of day finally broke, exposing to view the church of Ingolstadt. I lifted up my eyes fearfully to its lofty white steeple and clock, showing the sixth hour. A porter opened the gates of the court, my sanctuary throughout the night, letting me set out into streets soaked by rain, pouring heavily from a dark and distressing sky.

§

"I took refuge in the church," Victor Frankenstein mused wistfully, "because the very first sight that I saw when I first came to Ingolstadt was the steeple."

"Your creature's ugliness forced you to flee from him?" Captain Robert Walton asked his story-telling guest in a baffled tone of voice.

"No human being could endure the terror of that face!" Frankenstein murmured, heaving a frightful sigh as he cast away the smothering mask of his hands from his downcast face. "No cadaver brought back to life could be so ghastly as that monster. I saw what I had left undone—he was hideous before. But once those muscles and joints were given the power of movement it turned into something which even the Devil himself could not have conjured."

"Perhaps your own wretchedness caused you to exaggerate your dismay."

"How can I express my feelings at this disaster?" Frankenstein hung down his head again, frustrated and disturbed. "Or how describe this monster whom I took such great pains and care to mold and create? His limbs were meant to be well-formed—his face well-favored. Good God!"

"Oftentimes the misfortunes of life are just too capricious."

"But not so much as the reactions of human instinct," Frankenstein lamented grimly. "For nearly two long years I had labored so hard for the sole purpose of infusing life into a lifeless being. For this I had denied myself health and happiness. I had lusted after it with a passion which far surpassed self-restraint. But now that I had succeeded, the allure of the desire had faded."

"What did you do then?"

"I wandered the streets of Ingolstadt aimlessly—as if I connived to evade the monster whom I was afraid would appear at every corner."

"Did you return to your apartment?"

"I didn't dare!" Frankenstein cried with dread. "I felt compelled only to keep on roaming about in a hurry, trying fruitlessly by sheer physical exertion to lighten the load weighing on my mind."

"Where did you finally go?"

"I simply wandered the streets without any definite notion of where I was, much less where I was going, until at last I found myself facing the town inn, where carriages and coaches typically stopped—and where I, too, happened to stop without knowing why."

"What lay in store for you there?"

"As fate would have it," Frankenstein answered, breathing a satisfied sigh of relief at the remembrance, "the Swiss coach from Geneva arrived, delivering to me my dearest and best friend, Henry Clerval, whom I welcomed with the most open arms."

§

Afraid even to look around me I riveted my eyes on the coach moving toward me from the remote end of the street, watching intently as it came near and drew up right where I was standing. Its door flew open and Henry Clerval pounced out at one jump.

"My dear Victor," he cried at setting eyes on me, "how happy I am to see you! And how lucky to find you here the very moment I arrive!"

I pressed his hand and he squeezed mine; and at one stroke I forgot my terror and disaster, feeling for the first time in a very long time a soothing and tranquil peace of mind.

"You may likely think," he said as we started strolling toward my university, "how very hard it was to convince my provincial father that not all essential learning consists solely of the genteel art of accounting. And in fact I think I left him skeptical to the end, for he warned me repeatedly that nothing would ever come of my educational pursuits but failure and futility. But finally his fondness for me overcame his aversion to learning, and he let me embark on this pilgrimage of knowledge to the land of learning, and become your fellow pupil after all."

"I always knew how deeply you felt the disadvantage of being denied a liberal education," I commiserated, "and sensed your reserved but willful determination not to be tied down to the trifling matters of trade."

"We were right not to say farewell when you left us so long ago," he said affectionately.

"I'm so extremely pleased to see you!" I greeted Henry excitedly, "but do tell me: how are my father, brothers and Elizabeth?"

"Happy and in good health," he assured me, "but rather worried that you write to them so rarely. By the way I intend to scold you slightly on their behalf myself."

Henry abruptly cut himself short and stopped to stare straight into my distraught face.

"But my dear Victor," he exclaimed, standing aghast, "I didn't mention before how sick you look—so pale and wasted. You look as though you've been on the alert for many nights."

"You've gathered correctly," I admitted grudgingly. "Lately I've been so preoccupied with one pursuit that I haven't permitted myself enough rest, as you've noticed. But I honestly hope that all these trials are now over, and that I'm finally free."

I shuddered nervously. I could scarcely stand to think much less talk about the horrific events of the night before. Stepping quickly we presently came to my university. Then I reconsidered, for the afterthought made me tremble: the thing which I had left in my apartment could still be there—living and lurking about. I was deathly afraid to find that creature lying in wait for me, or worse that Henry should confront him.

"Wait here for a few moments," I pleaded at the foot of the stairway, throwing up a stifling hand in front of his bewildered face. "I implore you."

I dashed upstairs to my own room. My hand was already grasping the door lock before I recomposed myself. Then I stopped cold as a shivering fear completely overpowered me. I forcefully flung open the door, but nothing betrayed itself inside. I stepped in warily: my apartment was vacant, and my bedroom was equally empty of its ghastly intruder. I could scarcely believe that so miraculous a blessing should fall to my pitiful lot. But once I became reassured that my archenemy— the archfiend—had actually fled, I leaped for joy and rushed downstairs to heartily hail Henry. We climbed the stairs to my room, only I could not restrain myself, for I was possessed not only of jubilation. I felt my flesh creep with acute sensitivity, and my heart pound rapidly. I could not stay still for a moment in any one spot. I vaulted over chairs, slapped my hands and laughed aloud uncontrollably.

"I'm most grateful if I can credit my coming with your curiously high spirits," Henry said cautiously, "but I see a wildness in your eyes which I'm at a loss to account for."

I simply kept on laughing out loud—wantonly and

senselessly.

"My dear Victor!" Henry cried out, taken frightfully aback. "What in God's name is wrong with you? Stop laughing like that! How sick you are! What has caused all this?"

"Don't question me!" I cried, throwing up my protective hands in front of my startled eyes, for I thought I caught sight of the unsightly creature skulking into the room.

"He can answer!" I shrieked at the top of my terror-stricken voice. "Help! Help me! He sees me! He's coming at me! He's clutching at my throat! He's choking me! Help!"

I conjured up a vision of the creature clenching my neck and strangling me; I struggled fiercely and broke down in a fit.

I was listless and did not regain my senses for a very long time. This was the onset of a violent fever which incapacitated me for many months. During the whole time Henry was my sole nurse. But with truth I was very sick, and no doubt nothing but the boundless and persistent care of my friend could have brought me back to life. Very gradually I revived, but with recurring relapses which startled and saddened him.

"The sight of the monster I created is constantly before my eyes!" I raved repeatedly.

"You're overwrought," Henry said, thinking out loud while trying sympathetically to compose my raving. "Your mind is deeply disturbed by some nightmarish hallucination."

But the persistence by which I habitually and unfailingly reverted to the same preoccupation convinced him to reconsider his first conclusion.

"Or else your derangement really owes its cause to some extraordinary and horrible incident," he astutely deduced.

"My dear Henry," I cried, "how very good and kind you are to me! Instead of spending your time in study, as you committed yourself, this whole season has been wasted in my sick room."

"Study would have been a waste if it had distracted me

from restoring you to soundness."

"How will I ever repay you? I feel the deepest regret for the discontent which I have caused. Will you ever forgive me?"

"Forgive what? You will repay me in full if you don't regress and recover as quickly as you can. And since you seem to be in such high spirits, may I talk to you about a matter of particular importance?"

"What matter might that be?" I quaked at the thought of the unthinkable.

"Calm yourself down," Henry said, watching me turn pale. "I won't bring it up if it distresses you. But your father and cousin would be very pleased to receive a letter from you written in your own hand. They scarcely know how sick you've been, and are worried by your long silence."

"My dear Henry," I said, breathing freely a sigh of relief, "is that all? How could you presume that my first concern would not be reserved for my dearest relations whom I love, and who most deserve my attention. I will write them immediately and alleviate any anxiety they might feel."

"My friend," he suggested fatefully, "if this is your immediate mood, perhaps you will be just as pleased to read a letter which has just now come for you: it's from your father, I think."

Clerval watched my face expectantly as I read that letter from my father, shocked to see the depressed spirits overtake the delight I first displayed at taking news from my beloved relations. I tossed the letter onto the table and sank my face into my hands.

"My dear Victor!" Henry cried, watching me burst bitterly into tears. "Are we always to be so miserable? What's happened, my dear friend?"

"My youngest brother, William, is dead!" I blurted out, wailing loudly. "He's been brutally murdered! Strangled to death by some faceless assassin! The mark of the killer's fingers still on his throat!"

I gestured to him to pick up the letter while I paced up and down the room in disordered desperation.

"My friend," he cried, "with tears welling out of his eyes, "can I offer you any comfort? Your tragedy is hopeless."

"First," I insisted irately, pointing straight at my implements of life, "put that apparatus well out of my sight!"

"What are these things?" he asked me, sobbing as he concealed the devices from my view.

"Chemical instruments," I answered hatefully. "They're abominations!"

"What do you mean to do?"

"Go to Geneva right away. Come along with me, Henry, to help me order the coach."

As we hustled together through the streets we abruptly met none other than my professor of natural philosophy at the university, M. Krempe. And all at once I called to mind my very first meeting with this squat, ugly and vulgar little man.

"Have you honestly wasted your time studying such stuff and nonsense?" he asked me contemptuously once hearing me mention the names of certain alchemists and magicians— *Cornelius Agrippa, Saint Albertus Magnus* and *Paracelsus*—as the primary authors I had studied. He lectured me harshly in his gruff tone of voice. "Every moment you have spent reading such books has been totally and utterly wasted. You have contaminated your mind with discredited theories and disreputable thinkers. Good God! What wasteland have you lived in, where no one was charitable enough to tell you that these fantasies, which you've gobbled up so gullibly, are as archaic and corrupt as they are old? I scarcely expected to meet in this enlightened day and age a follower of sorcery. My dear sir, you must undertake your studies completely afresh."

Just then I was duty bound to introduce Clerval to M. Krempe.

"Curse the fellow!" the professor bluntly exclaimed to

Henry. "Why, I promise you, M. Frankenstein has surpassed us all. Yes, gawk if you will, but it's the truth nonetheless. A young man, who just a scant six years ago believed in alchemy as devoutly as Holy Writ, has exalted himself to the utmost summit of the university. And if he isn't presently overthrown we will all fall from grace."

"Yes, yes," the professor callously continued, insensitive to the heartache he saw my face express. "M. Frankenstein is humble, an admirable trait in a young man. And young men, you know, should be unpretentious and unassuming. I certainly was when I was young myself, but that passes in a very short while. Isn't that right, M. Clerval?"

"I wouldn't know, sir," answered Henry, his highly intuitive perceptions ever sensitive to another's feelings. Without a word I gave my friend my heartfelt thanks.

"I must confess," Henry told me after we were alone together once more, "I'm utterly mystified. I sense that you're keeping to yourself some ominous secret, although I'd never try to force it out of you."

"My dear friend," I told him, grasping his shoulders warmly, "I love you with a fondness and respect which has no end. But I could never convince myself to admit that incident which perpetually preoccupies my mind, and which I fear enumerating the particulars to another would only do indelible harm."

"Then I can only express my profoundest sympathy," he said feelingly. "Poor William! Dear beautiful boy—he now rests with his saintly mother! Whoever had seen him so happy and spirited in his youthful glory could only mourn his untimely end. To die so wretchedly. To feel the killer's grip. How much worse a murderer who could eradicate such blameless innocence. Poor little fellow! We have only one comfort: his friends grieve and sorrow, but at least he's at peace. His misery and suffering are over, and forever at an end. Clay covers his fragile frame, and he suffers no pain. He can no longer excite our pity. That we must save for his wretched survivors."

"I bid you farewell, my friend," I told him, scrambling into the coach as soon as the horses strode up.

§

"Noble friend!" Victor Frankenstein cried out, thinking back on their deep-felt words of parting. "How truly did you love me and try to raise my spirits until they were on a plane with your own! A vain pursuit had confined and trapped me, until your loyalty and understanding touched and opened up my heart, and brought out my finer feelings again. I became once more the same happy and smiling person who, just a few years ago, loved and honored by all, had no care or regret."

"I'm in great need of a friend who had compassion enough not to spurn me as a romantic," Captain Robert Walton thought out loud, nodding placidly, "and fondness enough for me to try to order my mind."

"It's always been my tendency to avoid a crowd and to devotedly associate myself with a few," Frankenstein confided with a consoling tone of voice. "So I was mostly indifferent to my schoolmates. But I befriended one among them in the bonds of brotherly friendship, Henry Clerval. Even though his father was a reserved Genevan merchant, Henry was quite an adventurous romantic himself. And I never spurned him."

"And you were blessed with a close and loving family until…"

"Yes, I loved my small family circle so much that I thought myself wholly unsuited for the company of outsiders. My life had been so unusually cloistered and domestic before that I had cultivated a powerful aversion to fresh faces. Study had severed me from the fellowship of my closest and dearest friends and made me even more unsocial."

"Then you were alone?"

"And my own guardian."

"What had kept you in Ingolstadt for so long up to that time?"

"It took nearly two years for my friend to nurse me back to respectable health. After which Henry took up the serious study of Oriental languages at the university. So I put off my return home, reluctant to leave him alone in a foreign place before he could become familiar with any of its townspeople."

"You finally did go back to Geneva?"

"In great haste," Frankenstein answered, nodding ruefully as he renewed his fearsome memory, "no sooner than my father had written me his letter recounting the terrible news that William was gone."

§

My journey was oppressed with unsparing melancholy. As I neared my native land grief and fear overwhelmed me, preying on my mind with countless unknown evils which struck terror into my frightened heart, although I was powerless to account for them. Darkness spread its sunless shadow all over the surrounding black and palatial mountains, putting me in even greater and ghastlier fear.

When I came to the outskirts of Geneva it was dark as pitch, although the sky was placid and unperturbed. Already the town gates were shut for the night. And since I was irrepressibly restless I decided to press on to the precise place where my father wrote and told me in his letter William had been killed: Plainpalais. And since I was barred from passing through the town I was forced to cross the lake in a boat to alight there. Throughout the short crossing I watched lightning blaze across the summit of Mount Blanc in the most dazzling formations. A storm loomed rapidly ahead on the lurid horizon. After I landed I climbed a low hill so I might watch its movement. It gained ground and strength. Above the sky was clouded, and presently I felt the rain falling gently in hefty droplets, but the storm swiftly intensified. I left my spot and passed on, although the darkness and the tempest deepened and thunder pealed overhead with a loud boom. Brilliant flashes of lightning blinded my eyes, lighting up the lake, making it look like a shore-less sheet of smoldering flame. Then for a fleeting moment everything looked pitch dark until the eyesight restored itself after the last flash. While I watched the violent storm, so awe-inspiring and yet so terrifying, I hurried on with a lively step. This exalted clash in the heavens raised my spirits.

"William, precious child!" I cried out, clenching my hands. "This is your last rite! This is your death knell!"

As I muttered these words I saw in the murk a skulking shape which stole away from behind a thicket of trees close to me. I stood fast, staring intently: I could not be wrong. A flash of lightning lit up the thing and sharply exposed its gruesome form to view. Its gigantic size and stature, and the monstrosity of the silhouette, more ghastly and grotesque than can be ascribed to mankind, told me immediately that it was the wretched creature—the infernal devil—whom I had brought to life. What was he doing there? Could he be my brother's murderer? I flinched at the notion, but no sooner did it suggest itself than I became satisfied at its truthfulness.

Its loathsome sight made my teeth chatter, and I was obliged to lean against a tree for comfort. That misshapen shape passed by me swiftly, and I lost sight of it in the murk. No fellow creature in human form could have killed that beautiful boy. He was the killer! I could have no doubts about it. Sheer existence of the thought presented irrefutable proof of its truth. I considered following the foul fiend, but it would have been to no avail; for another flash showed him scaling the rocky heights of the almost sheer slope of the mountain skirting Plainpalais to the south. Rapidly reaching its summit he vanished.

I stayed deathly still. Rain still fell after the thunderclaps stopped, and a murky darkness enshrouded the landscape. I turned over in my mind which up to that time I had tried to think no more of: the complete chain of events leading to the accursed creature's birth; my living handiwork hovering over my bedside; its secret flight. Two years had now almost passed since the fated night on which he first came to life. No one can imagine the agony I suffered during the rest of that night, which I passed restlessly beneath the lowering sky. But I never felt the ruthless discomfort of the elements. My mind was agitated by overwhelming thoughts of disaster and despair.

Captain Robert Walton stood aghast, staring incredulously in fear as Victor Frankenstein addressed him with grim-faced dread.

"Had the monster committed his first atrocity?" Frankenstein grappled gravely with the question. "Had he truly murdered my younger brother? Yes! I had unleashed onto the world a diabolical creature who took perverse pleasure in wretchedness and butchery!"

SEVEN:
INHUMAN SACRIFICES

"Did any one indeed exist, except I, the creator, who would believe, unless his senses convinced him, in the existence of the living monument of presumption and rash ignorance which I had let loose upon the world?"—Victor Frankenstein

"**D**id you ever confront the creature again?" Captain Robert Walton asked, fixing his expectant eyes on his convalescent guest.

"Not immediately," Victor Frankenstein answered, staring at the remembrance with fear and trembling. "My first thought was to reveal what I knew of the killer and instigate an immediate pursuit. But I stopped to reconsider the tale I had to tell."

"For fear you would not be believed?"

"A creature whom I had myself created, and infused with life, had confronted me in the dead of night on the crown of an unapproachable mountain. I recalled as well the crippling fever which had afflicted me from the time I had given birth to the unholy thing, and which would lend an air of lunacy to a story already so utterly unbelievable."

"It would strain the imagination of anyone whose mind was filled with doubt."

"I knew full well that if anyone else had told such a tale to me, I should have looked down on it as the ravings of a lunatic."

"Surely you couldn't permit such a murderous creature to go free and stay at liberty to slaughter others."

"The monstrous nature of the beast would elude all capture, even if I were to be so credible as to convince my relations to attempt it. Besides, what purpose would capture serve? Who could capture a creature able to climb the sheer cliffs of a precipice?"

"What course then did you choose to take?"

"Such considerations prompted me to commit myself to a course of silence."

§

Daybreak came and I bent my steps towards the town.

Finding the gates open I hurried to my father's house. I stepped inside at about five in the morning and went on quietly into the library to await their habitual hour of awaking. I gazed wistfully on the portrait of my mother, Caroline Beaufort, resting on the mantelpiece, from which she exuded—in spite of her pallid cheek and rustic dress—a distinctive air of elegance and nobility. Beneath her portrait was a miniature of William, and my tears burst out when I set downcast eyes on his sprightly blue eyes, dark eyelashes, curly locks and rosy, dimpled cheeks.

"Poor William!" I suddenly heard a warmly familiar voice exclaim. "He was our pride and joy!"

I turned around and saw that my spry and spirited younger brother of sixteen, Ernest, had just then come in.

"My dear Victor!" he greeted me with mournful joy. "If only you had come three months ago, and you would have found us all happy and overjoyed. Now you have come to us to share a sorrow from which nothing can relieve. But I pray your presence will comfort our father, who seems despairing over this tragedy; and your influence will persuade poor Elizabeth to stop her vain and punishing self-recriminations."

Tears welled out of my brother's eyes uncontrollably and I tried to console him.

"Elizabeth most of all needs consoling," Ernest cried, "for she has blamed herself for having caused our brother's death, and that made her profoundly miserable. But since the killer has been exposed..."

"The killer exposed!" I cried incredulously. "Good God! How can that be possible? Who could venture to chase after him? It's not possible! You might as well try to capture a ghost. I saw him as well. Last night he was still at large and scot-free!"

"I don't understand," Ernest said in an unsuspecting tone of voice, "but to us the terrible truth we have found compounds our sorrow. At first no one could believe it, and even now

Elizabeth remains unconvinced, in spite of all the damning evidence to the contrary. After all, who would suspect that Justine Moritz, who was so good-natured and devoted to all the family, could suddenly commit so shocking, so heinous a crime?"

"Justine Moritz!" I exclaimed, raising my voice in disbelief, utterly aghast. "Poor, poor girl! She's the accused? But wrongfully so of course. Everyone must know that. Surely no one believes that?"

"At first no one did," he said in explanation. "But certain facts came to light which have all but imposed the belief upon us. And her own conduct has been so incoherent as to lend weight to the substantial body of evidence that, I'm afraid, leaves no room for doubt. But she'll be put on trial today when all will become known."

"How did poor Justine ever come to be so unjustly accused of this atrocity in the first place?"

"On the morning that William's poor, lifeless body had been found in Plainpalais," Ernest grimly recounted, "the valuable miniature of our mother, which had been believed to be the murderer's enticement, was also found—in the pocket of clothing worn by Justine on the night of the murder."

"You're all wrong," I answered in great earnest. "I know the murderer. Poor, sweet Justine is not guilty."

At that moment my father came in. I saw misery deeply etched in his face, but he tried to greet me joyfully and sorrowfully at the same time.

"Good God, Papa!" Ernest cried out, interrupting us. "Victor says he knows who murdered poor William."

"Regrettably we do too," my father answered mournfully, "for I really would rather have remained eternally oblivious than to have found so much wickedness and ungratefulness in someone I regarded so highly."

"My dear father," I pleaded, "you're wrong. Justine is not guilty."

"If she's not," he said uneasily, "Heaven forbid that she should suffer punishment as guilty. She's to be brought to trial today, and I honestly hope that she'll be exonerated."

"That being so," I breathed a sigh of heartfelt relief, "I'm greatly reassured, for I'm perfectly satisfied that Justine is completely innocent of this crime. I feel confident then that no circumstantial evidence convincing enough to convict her could be given."

"My son," my father said warmly, laying his sympathetic hands on my shoulders, "what a cruel shock it must be when you look forward to a glad and happy reception, only to find instead sadness and misery. Even such a long separation could not have made you insensitive to our joys and sorrows."

"Indeed," I agreed with an emphatic nod, forming in my face a determined but wrathful resolve, "for the efforts to find my brother's murderer will be unrelenting."

"But they will not bring back our beloved William," my father gently admonished me. "Come, Victor—not with seething thoughts of revenge against the killer, but with feelings of compassion and tenderness which will bind rather than lance the wounds of our hearts. Come into this house of mourning, my son, not with bitterness and hatred for your enemies but with love and affection for those who love and care for you."

"I would see justice done out of my care for those who love me," I said solemnly, "and for him who can no longer love me."

"Come, dear Victor," my father heartened me, "only you can comfort Elizabeth. She cries constantly and blames herself unjustly as the cause of William's death. Her rebukes stab my heart. We're all miserable, but shouldn't that be a further inducement for you, my son, to be our comforter? Your dear mother! Victor, I tell you now: Thank God she did not live to see the brutal, wretched death of her youngest dear one!"

Presently Elizabeth came to bear us company, tears falling

out of her eyes.

"My dear niece," my father reassured her, "wipe away your tears. If as you think Justine is not guilty, trust the justness of our laws, and the vigilance with which I will obstruct the slightest hint of prejudice."

Elizabeth greeted me with the deepest affection and we called each other endearingly by our mutually familiar name: cousin.

"My dear cousin," she welcomed me warmly, "your coming gives me hope. Perhaps you will find some way to vindicate my poor innocent Justine. If she can be found guilty of crime who then is safe? I put my trust in her innocence as surely as I do in my own. Our tragedy is doubly difficult for us. We have not only lost that beautiful adorable boy, but this poor girl, whom I honestly love, is to be wrenched away by even a worse destiny. If she's doomed I'll never know true peace of mind again. But she won't be doomed, I'm positive she won't. And then I'll be contented again, even after the tragic death of my little William."

"My Elizabeth," I encouraged her, "Justine is guiltless and that will be proved. Have no fear, but let your spirits be raised by the certainty of her vindication."

"How humane and compassionate you are! Everyone else takes her guilt for granted, and that made me miserable, for I knew full well that it was not possible. And to watch everyone else so prejudiced in so fatal an attitude made me despondent and heartbroken."

She cried.

"How has life passed for you?" I finally asked her with care after Ernest and my father left us alone to talk together.

"Besides the growing of our precious children," she quietly recounted, "little change has happened since you left us. The blue lake and snow-covered mountains—they never change. And I believe our peaceful home and happy hearts are ruled by the same unchangeable laws. My frivolous pastimes take up my time and distract me, and I'm rewarded for any efforts I've made by seeing only happy and cheerful faces around me."

"Time has certainly changed you since I last saw you," I complimented her reverently, "giving you a beauty and grace far surpassing your younger years."

"Dear Victor," she told me with feeling, "one blessed word from you is all that's needed to calm our fears."

"You wrote before, telling me that I would find a happy and cheerful home to come to, and friends who love and care for me deeply."

"How many times have I regretted not taking a journey to Ingolstadt to see you and take care of you, but that was before..."

"When my mother died you held back your own grief and tried to be the comforter to us all. You devoted yourself to those you had come to call your uncle and cousins. Never were you so radiant as at that time when you summoned up the bright light of your smile and shined it upon us."

"You may recall Justine was a pet favorite of yours. And I remember you once said that if ever you were in bad humor, one look from her could dispel it. She always seemed so openhearted and happy. Such is what makes this whole tragedy so utterly unbelievable."

"When my parents adopted you after you were orphaned," I pensively reminisced, "my mother had said she was bringing home a pretty present to give me. And the next day she presented you to me as her promised gift. I literally took her at her word and looked upon you as my own—mine to protect, love and cherish. No word, no power of speech could ever express what you mean to me, and you became my more than sister—the lovely and beloved companion of all my pursuits and pleasures. I was about five years old then, my more than a lifetime ago."

"Oh, God!" Elizabeth lamented, abruptly wringing her hands with a long-suffering sigh. "I'm the one truly to blame for murdering our darling boy! I'm entirely at fault!"

"I refuse to believe that!" I said, startled by her abrupt pronouncement. "How could you make such a grotesque suggestion?"

"On the night he was killed," she recounted heavy-heartedly, "William pestered me to let him wear the miniature of your mother which I possessed. Scarcely an hour before he was missed I hung the picture about his neck. Later it was found in Justine's pocket, and presumed to be the enticement which motivated the murderer to perpetrate the deed."

"Surely the truth of the matter will come out at the trial tomorrow, and Justine will be rightfully vindicated."

§

"Did truth and justice finally prevail at the trial?" asked Captain Robert Walton, shifting restlessly in place.

"During that entire travesty of justice," Victor Frankenstein answered forlornly, "I went through a living hell."

"What did the court decide?"

"When the ballots were thrown all were black. Justine was condemned."

"Condemned? On such obviously paltry evidence?"

"Yes," Frankenstein grimly confirmed, "but not before Justine resigned herself and falsely confessed to the crime. As one imperious officer of the court boasted to me, a confession was scarcely necessary in seemingly so conspicuous a case. But he was actually pleased since the judges supposedly disliked convicting a criminal on circumstantial evidence, however conclusive."

"Surely the court could not have settled the question very decisively based on so flagrant an absence of facts—even with the girl's confession."

"For me," Frankenstein went on solemnly, "the only question to be settled was whether the evil fruit of my petty curiosity and illicit instruments would cause the deaths of my fellow creatures—one an innocent child full of spirit and play; the other far more fearfully murdered—with every mark of infamy which could forever mar her memory."

"You loved her with a tender heart."

"Justine was a girl of excellent virtue and was possessed of traits which promised to make her life extremely happy. But everything was to be eradicated in a degrading grave—and I the reason why! Countless times would I have rather confessed myself as the culprit of the crime blamed on Justine."

"What prevented you from confessing?"

"I was away when the crime was committed," Frankenstein reasoned, "and such a statement would have been dismissed as the ravings of a maniac, and would never have acquitted her who incurred disgrace because of me."

§

Beautiful Justine came into court wearing mourning, looking calm and confident, although solemn and subdued. She glanced around and shortly spotted where we were seated. Tears welled out of her eyes when she saw us, but she quickly composed herself and a look of mournful affection seemed to profess her complete innocence. When she was summoned for her defense her face visibly expressed bewilderment, terror and wretchedness. At times she struggled to fight back tears, but when she finally resolved to testify she collected her faculties and spoke in an articulate but agitated voice.

"God knows," she pleaded, "how completely innocent I am of this crime. But I do not presume that my protests alone should pardon me. I base my plea of innocence upon a pure and simple answer to the charges which have wrongly been brought against me. And I trust that the character which I've always tried to maintain will dispose my judges to a favorable ruling, especially where any evidence seems questionable or suspect."

Nor could Justine account for the damning picture found on her person.

"I realize," the unfortunate victim went on, "how seriously this particular circumstance weighs against me, but I have no means of explaining it. And once I assert my complete innocence I'm left only to speculate about the possibility by which it might have been put into my pocket. But there I'm thwarted again. I have no known enemy in the world, and certainly none would have been so ruthless as to destroy me so viciously. Did the killer put it there? I recall giving him no chance for doing so. Or if I had why should he have stolen the locket only to discard it so quickly?"

"I entrust my fate to the fairness of my judges," she concluded, "but I see no cause for hope. I beg indulgence to examine a few witnesses bearing on my character. And if their testimony will not outweigh my presumed guilt I must be found guilty, even though I would stake my salvation on my innocence."

Overwrought from the prosecution of the trial Elizabeth asked permission to address the court on Justine's behalf.

"I am," she pleaded, "the cousin of the unfortunate boy who was killed, or rather his sister, since I've lived with and was raised by his parents ever since and even long before he was born. It may then be considered improper of me to speak out at this hearing. But when I see a sisterly friend about to die because of the indifference of her faithless friends, I beg indulgence to speak that I may tell what I know of her character. I'm very familiar with the accused. I've lived in the same house with her at one time for five years, and at another for almost two years. During all that time she seemed to me to be the most tender and kindhearted of human beings. She nursed my aunt, Madame Frankenstein, with the most loving care and devotion in her last sickness, and afterwards she took care of her own mother during a debilitating illness in a way which inspired the respect of everyone who knew her; after which she lived once more in my uncle's house, where she was well beloved by the whole family. She was deeply attached to the boy who's now gone and treated him like a most devoted mother. As for me, I say without hesitation—in spite of all the evidence presented against her—I believe and trust totally in her absolute innocence. She had no enticement for such a deed: as for the locket upon which the most incriminating evidence rests, if she had seriously wanted it I should have gladly given it to her, so much do I admire and revere her."

§

"Justine wept even as Elizabeth spoke in her defense," Victor Frankenstein recounted, calling up his heart-stricken memory, "but she never once answered her accusers."

"Her silence must have been construed by the judges as positive proof of her guilt," Captain Robert Walton readily concluded.

"Through the entire trial my own agony and anxiety were extremely acute, but I firmly believed in her innocence. I was certain of it."

"Could you be less certain of it at this moment?"

"I have no doubt of it at all," Frankenstein adamantly affirmed.

"Could you have possibly been led astray?" the captain asked him with reluctance.

"Only by my own absence of mind. I never doubted for a moment that that devil murdered my brother. But could he in his infernal diversion have incriminated the innocent to death and disgrace? But even her torment was unequal to mine. She was heartened by her innocence. Guilt had seized my heart and wouldn't let go."

"You were taken completely unawares by the girl's confession?"

"Curiously…what sense did it make? Had my own senses deceived me? And was I as insane as the whole human race would think me to be if I had exposed the creature of my suspicions?"

§

I hurried to return home where Elizabeth anxiously awaited word of Justine's fate.

"The court has passed judgment," she said despairingly, clearly expecting the worst possible news.

"My cousin," I answered her, pulling a long face, "it was settled as you would have predicted. All judges would rather that ten innocents should die than that one culprit should get away scot-free. Only she has confessed."

"Oh!" she moaned in mournful pain. "How will I ever again trust in human virtue? I loved and revered Justine as my sister. How could she put on those innocent airs only to betray us? Her gentle eyes never seemed capable of any harshness or deceit, and yet she has perpetrated a murder."

"Justine has expressed her wish to see you," I reluctantly revealed. "Your father would rather that you not go, but he leaves you to make up your own mind in keeping with your own conscience and decision."

"Yes," Elizabeth said sullenly. "I will go, even though she's guilty. And you'll go along with me, Victor—I cannot go alone."

To me the thought of that visit was torment but I could not reject it.

§

We stepped inside the somber prison cell and found Justine sitting atop a pile of straw at the far end. She hung her head down on her knees, which she folded in her arms and grasped with her manacled hands. She arose at seeing us come in, but once we were left alone with her she bowed down at Elizabeth's feet, crying convulsively. Elizabeth cried too, blindly stroking Justine's hair.

"Oh, Justine!" Elizabeth sobbed. "You were only twelve years old when we took you away from your abusive mother and brought you to our house. We took you into our family and you were the most grateful little soul in the world. Why did you take away my last comfort? I believed in your innocence, and I'm more miserable now than I ever was."

"And do you also think that I'm so very heartless and cruel?" Justine's voice choked with sobs. "Do you also side with my accusers to destroy me—to condemn me as a killer?"

"Get up, my poor girl," Elizabeth bid Justine, reaching out to hold her up. "Why do you bow your head if you're not guilty? I'm not one of your accusers. In spite of everything I believed in your innocence until I heard that you yourself had asserted your guilt. You say that rumor is untrue. So rest assured, dear Justine, that nothing could shake my faith in you for an instant but your own confession."

"I did confess," Justine admitted defensibly, "but I confessed to a lie. I confessed that I might gain absolution. But now that lie weighs more heavily on my heart than all my other faults. Lord God, forgive me! My confessor has harassed me ever since I was convicted. He threatened and intimidated me until I nearly started to believe that I was the fiend that he said I was. He threatened me with excommunication and everlasting hellfire in my final hour if I persisted with denying my guilt. My dear lady, I had none to stand up for me. Everyone looked down on me as a criminal doomed to disgrace and ruin. What could I do? On an evil day I submitted to a lie. And only now am I truly miserable. My dear lady, I thought with terror that you should think your Justine, whom you held dear and whom your saintly aunt had so highly regarded, was a monster capable of a deed which none but Lucifer himself could have committed. Dear William! Dear blessed boy! I'll soon see you again in heaven, where we'll all be happy. And that comforts me, going as I am to suffer disgrace and death."

"Oh, Justine!" Elizabeth cried, cut short by her own tears. "Pardon me for ever having doubted you for one moment. Why did you confess? But don't fret, sweet girl. Don't be afraid. I'll plead; I'll prove your innocence. I'll soften the hardened hearts of your accusers by my pleas and tears. You will not die! You—my friend, my companion, my sister— die on the gallows! No! I could never endure so terrible a tragedy."

"I'm not afraid to die," Justine said stoically. "That pain is past. God raises my spirits and gives me courage to bear the worst. I leave an unhappy and wicked world. And if you think of me and remember me as one unjustly accused, I've resigned myself to the fate waiting for me. Learn from my tragedy, dear lady, and submit to the will of God!"

I had retreated to the recess of the prison cell where I could hide the ghastly agony which I was possessed of. Justine flinched when she heard me gnashing and grinding my teeth, giving utterance to a mournful moan which came forth from my innermost depths.

"Kind sir," she stepped up to me, "you're very gracious to visit me. I trust you don't think I'm guilty."

"No, Justine," Elizabeth worriedly reassured her, seeing that I was powerless to answer her. "He's more satisfied of your innocence than I was, for even when he heard that you had confessed he didn't believe it."

"I thank him sincerely," Justine said with all her heart. "In these final moments I feel the deepest gratitude towards those who think kindly of me. How comforting is the sympathy of others to such an outcast as I've become! It takes away more than half my misery. And I feel as if I could die in peace now that you, dear lady, and your cousin both believe in my innocence."

"I wish that I could die with you," Elizabeth cried. "I cannot live in this world of wretchedness."

Justine folded Elizabeth warmly in her arms, assuming an attitude of high spirits while suppressing her dispirited tears.

"Farewell, Elizabeth." Her voice only partly smothered her desperate despair. "My dear, sweet lady. My dearly beloved and one and only friend. I'll be forever grateful that being a servant in your house never meant being ignorant or degraded. May God in His grace bless and keep you. May this be the last tragedy that you'll ever endure! Live happily, and help others to."

§

Utter hopelessness! Who dared to speak of that? Even that wretched victim, who was to cross the dreadful border between life and death, could not suffer as I did such profound and painful anguish. So the wretched victim tried to console others and herself. She truly found the surrender she wished for. But I—the real killer—felt the deathless maggot squirm in my breast, giving no hope or comfort. My Elizabeth cried and was also wretched, but hers was the wretchedness of the innocent. Agony and hopelessness had pierced the depths of my soul. I suffered a hell inside me which nothing could quell. So I might pronounce myself a lunatic, but not retract the sentence passed on my witless victim. Justine died on the gallows as a murderess!

"William and Justine," Frankenstein confessed ruefully to Captain Walton, "were the first unfortunate sacrifices to my black arts."

EIGHT: CREATOR CONFRONTS CREATION

"The immense mountains and precipices that overhung me on every side—the sound of the river raging among the rocks, and the dashing of the waterfalls around, spoke of a power mighty as Omnipotence—and I ceased to fear, or to bend before any being less almighty than that which had created and ruled the elements, here displayed in their most terrific guise."—Victor Frankenstein

JOSEPH COVINO JR

"**S**o much grief and guilt preyed on my mind," Victor Frankenstein went on, renewing his fearsome memory, "that sleep forever left my eyes. I roamed about like some aimless ghost, for I had perpetrated acts of such terrible depravity I was satisfied that much, much worse was yet to come."

"But you never intended that the deeds you had done would create evil," Captain Robert Walton consoled him.

"Oh yes!" Frankenstein cried in a self-reproachful tone of voice. "My heart ran over with brotherly love and noble virtue. I had started life with the best intentions and looked forward to the time when I should put them—and myself—to use in humanity's service. Then everything was shattered. Instead of that clear conscience which would let me think back upon the past with self-gratification, and from that to take heart in bright prospects for the future, I was struck by a sense of profound grief and guilt which sentenced me to a place of extreme torment, such as no words can express."

"Was there nothing you could take comfort in?"

"I avoided the society of men. Any semblance of happiness or contentment were sheer torment to me. Isolation was my sole comfort—complete, utter and absolute isolation."

§

I was afflicted with an unsoundness of mind which perhaps had never fully survived the first blow it had suffered. My father watched in pain the drastic change evident in my humor and habits and tried by reasoning—drawn from the sentiments of his clear conscience and faultless life—to inspire me with courage and arouse in me the resolve to disperse the lowering cloud which hovered over me.

"Victor," he asked me solemnly, his eyes falling out with tears, "don't you think that I suffer too? No one could love a boy more than I loved your brother. But isn't it our duty to the survivors that we should avoid aggravating their misery by an excessive display of grief? It's also a duty you owe yourself, for extreme grief hinders recovery or contentment, or even the conduct of everyday employment, without which no man is suitable for society."

Although sound his advice was soundly unsuitable to my situation. I should have been the first to suppress my sorrow and comfort my friends—if remorse had not mixed its heartache, and horror its dread, with my other feelings. Now I could only answer my father with an expression of sadness and try to keep myself out of his sight. I hardly need to explain the emotions of those whose closest bonds are broken by that most incurable curse—the emptiness which overwhelms the soul and the sadness which is shown on the face. I called to mind the feelings I entertained when my dearly beloved mother died.

It took so long before the mind could convince itself that she, whom we saw every day, and whose very life seemed a part of our own, could have left forever—that the light of a beloved eye could have been snuffed out and the sound of a voice so precious and dear to the ear could be silenced—to be heard no more. These are the thoughts of the earliest days. But when the passing of time proves the truth of the curse then the real bitterness of sorrow begins. But from whom has not those fatal jaws of death torn away some precious bond? And why should I express a grief which everyone has felt and must feel? Finally the time comes when grief is rather a self-indulgence than an obligation. And the smile which crosses the lips, although it may be considered an irreverence is not ostracized. My mother had died but we had still duties which we should discharge. We must carry on our course along with the rest and come to believe ourselves fortunate while one survives whom death had not taken.

§

"I was tempted to take my own life many times," Victor Frankenstein went on, surrendering to his wretched recollections, "that oblivion might drown me and my misfortunes in darkness."

"What deterred you?" Captain Robert Walton asked, his heart excited with deep pity for his forlorn friend.

"Thoughts of my brave and broken-hearted Elizabeth, whom I dearly loved, and whose life was so wrapped up in mine—and of my father and surviving brother as well. Should I by my cowardly flight leave them defenseless and vulnerable to the evil of the demon I had unleashed among them?"

"Did nothing promise you hope or peace of mind?"

"Sorrow had snuffed out every ray of hope," Frankenstein said, deeply disheartened. "I had been the creator of irrevocable evil, and I lived in constant dread for fear that the monster I had made should commit some other outrage. I harbored a vague feeling that all was far from over and that he would yet perpetrate some vile atrocity, by which its wickedness should all but obliterate any memory of the past."

"What in particular excited that fear?"

"There was always room for fear so long as anything I loved survived."

"How did you finally face your fear?"

"My hatred of this devil cannot be imagined," Frankenstein said, seething with rage. "When I thought of him I fervently wanted to stamp out that life which I had so mindlessly created. When I thought of his outrages and viciousness my hatred and vengeance had no end of excess. I would have taken the journey to the highest summit on earth could I, once there, have expedited him to its bottom. I wanted to face him once more that I might wreak the greatest measure of havoc on him and avenge the murders of William and Justine."

§

Our house at Belrive—to which we had retreated—was a place of mourning. My father's health was profoundly weakened by the terror of the latest incidents. Elizabeth was sad and despairing. That worst of visitations which is meant to separate us from the world had afflicted her, and its suffocating sway darkened her sweetest smiles.

"I feel so sorry that you no longer take pleasure in your simple pursuits," I condoled.

"All enjoyment seems to me disrespect for the dead," she said despondently. "Perpetual tears and mourning are the rightful tribute I should pay to purity so shattered and spoiled."

"But I lament that you're no longer that spirited creature, who in our tender youth roamed along with me on the banks of the lake, and talked together with joy about our hopes for the future."

"My dear cousin," she told me, "when I think back on the wretched death of Justine Moritz I no longer see the world and its wonders as they looked to me before. Then I considered stories of wickedness and cruelty which I read or heard to be those of times past or whimsical evil. At least they were far removed and more recognizable to reason than to invention. But now wretchedness has come close to home and men look to me like bloodsuckers thirsting after each other's blood. But I'm surely unfair."

"No," I assured her, "you're perfectly right. Wretchedness surely exists and lies all around us."

"Everyone thought that poor girl to be at fault. And if she could have perpetrated the atrocity for which she suffered punishment, surely she would have been the most corrupt of human beings. To have killed the boy of her friend and benefactor, for the sake of a paltry locket, a boy whom she had nursed from his birth, and looked like she adored him as if he had belonged to her!"

"In certain respects he surely was her own."

"I couldn't accept the killing of any human being. But surely I should have believed such a criminal unsuited to stay in human society. But she wasn't guilty. I feel I know full well she wasn't guilty. You think so too and that satisfies me. Victor, when a lie can seem so much like the truth who can guarantee themselves definite contentment? William and Justine were murdered and the killer gets away with it. He goes about the world scot-free and perhaps admired. But even if I were sentenced to suffer on the gallows for the same wrongs I wouldn't trade places with such a villain."

"I would aspire only to destroy him," I said stoically.

I took in this talk with the most intense anguish. I—not in act but in fact—was the real killer.

"My dearest cousin," Elizabeth discerned the agony in my face and warmly took my hand, "you must calm yourself down. These episodes have afflicted me, God knows how poorly. But I'm not so miserable as you are. There's a look of desperation, and at times of vengeance, in your face which makes me shudder."

"My despair surely drives my desire for revenge."

"My dear Victor," she consoled me, "expel these black desires. Remember your nearest friends who pin all their hopes on you. Have we lost the ability of making you happy? So long as we love—so long as we care for each other and hold each other dear, here in this place of peace and contentment, your native land, we may have every good fortune—what can upset our peace?"

§

Could not such words from her whom I dearly loved before every other blessing of good fortune manage to drive off the devil which skulked in my soul? Even as she spoke I moved toward her, as if in horror, for fear that at that very instant the devil had been close to steal her from me. So not the devotion of love, nor the splendor of heaven, nor of earth, could deliver my soul from desolation—the very utterances of love were futile. I was surrounded by a darkness which no heavenly power could penetrate. At times I could contend with the desperate despair which overpowered me. But at times the tortured passions of my soul compelled me to search, by change of place, for some deliverance from my insufferable impressions. It was during an outburst of this sort that I abruptly left my home, and shaping my course toward the surrounding Alpine valleys, undertook in the beauty—the perpetuity of such scenery—to forget myself and my fleeting, because mortal heartache.

It was about the middle of August, almost two months after the death of Justine Moritz—that wretched time from which I marked all my ordeal. I decided to mount the summit of Montanvert by my sure-footed mule. Although steep the rising trail was split into short but continuous windings and turnings, which enabled me to surmount the mountain's rugged steepness. It was a landscape mightily inhospitable. In countless places the remnants of the plummeting avalanche could be seen. Pines lay snapped and scattered on the ground, some totally shattered, others tilted, slanting across the bulging crags of the mountains or other trees. As I climbed higher the trail was crisscrossed by frigid ravines of snow, down which stones constantly tumbled from high up. I surveyed the rugged valley below. Immense mists were rising from the rivers which flowed through it and wafted in dense rings all around the facing mountains, whose peaks were shrouded in thick clouds while rain poured down from the darkened and somber sky.

It was almost noon when I got to the stainless, snowy mountain top. For a long time I sat on the cliff which looked out on the bounding main of ice. A heavy mist hung over it and the surrounding mountains. A gust soon scattered the cloud and I climbed down onto the vast and ever-shifting glacier. Its surface was very irregular, steeply rising and falling like the undulations of a stormy sea, and scattered by deep-seated rifts. Nearly a league in width I spent almost two hours crossing the closely packed ice-field. From the edge where I then stood Montanvert was directly opposite at a league's distance, and overhead soared majestic Mont Blanc in awe-inspiring grandeur. I stayed in a nook of the rock, intently inspecting this wondrous and magnificent vista. That ocean, or rather that stupendous stream of ice meandered among its suspended mountains, whose lofty and glittering peaks overhung its icy ravines. And all over, the shining mountains rumbled with the thunderous noise of cracking and crashing ice.

Commanding this view of the wondrous and sublime valley of Chamounix, through which the rushing Arveiron worked its noisy way, had discernibly lightened the forbidding burden of terror and despair weighing so heavily on my mind. That fearsome sight of the majestic and magnificent in material nature had in reality always the effect of unburdening my mind and making me oblivious to the cursory cares of life. Then once more the benign power stopped working—even as I struggled to forget creation, my fears, and more than everything else, myself: I found myself shackled once more to sorrow and wallowing in all the deep distress of deep reflection.

Surprisingly as I pondered this I saw the form of a human being a long way off, approaching me with inhuman speed. He vaulted over the crevices in the ice, among which I had walked warily. His size and stature as he drew near too seemed to surpass that of a man. I was disturbed: a haze clouded over my eyes, and I felt a dizziness paralyze me, but I was swiftly revived by the frigid air of the mountains. As the figure came closer—gigantic and detested—I saw that it was the monster whom I had made. I shuddered with fury and terror, steeling myself to await his arrival and then grapple with him in a death struggle. He came at me. His face expressed raging agony, mingled with scorn and spite while his diabolical deformity made it almost too terrible for human sight. But I scarcely saw that. Hate and hostility had at first stripped me of speech, and I revived only to overpower him with words suggestive of infuriated hatred and loathing.

"Demon!" I cried out. "Do you dare come near me? Aren't you afraid of the savage revenge I would take on you? Be-gone, foul fiend! Or rather, remain that I might beat you to dirt! Ah! That I could—with the destruction of your wretched life—revive those victims you have so devilishly killed!"

"I expected this welcome," the devil said. "All men despise the wretched. How then must I be despised, who am wretched beyond all living creatures! But you—my creator—hate and scorn me, your creation—to whom you're tied by bonds only broken by the destruction of one of us."

"No bonds exist which tie me to you! None!"

"You intend to kill me. How dare you toy so with life? Do justice to me and I will do justice to you and the rest of mankind. If you consent to my demands I will leave them— and you—unmolested. But if you refuse I will glut the jaws of death until they're gorged with the flesh of your remaining relations."

"Abominable creature! Devil that you are! The torments of hellfire are too tame a revenge for your wrongs. Miserable fiend! You blame me for your creation. Come on, then, that I might stamp out the spark which I so recklessly brought to life."

My fury was boundless. I pounced on him, driven by all the passions which can guard one person against the presence of another.

"Calm yourself down!" He effortlessly averted me. "I implore you to listen to me before you give vent to your hatred of me. Haven't I endured enough that you mean to deepen my pain?"

I lunged at him again to no avail.

"Life," he exhorted me, "although it may merely be an accumulation of agony is precious to me, and I'll protect it. Remember, you've made me much stronger than yourself. But I won't be provoked to contend with you. I'm your creation, and I'll be even gentle and compliant with my natural lord and master if you'll do your part as well—that which you're indebted to me."

"Life means nothing to you. And I owe you nothing."

"Frankenstein," he pleaded, "be not fair to every other and do wrong to me alone—to whom your fairness, and even your mercy and compassion, is most due."

"You're entitled to nothing but my utmost loathing and contempt."

"Remember that I'm your creation, whom you deny happiness for doing no wrong. Everywhere I see happiness, from which I alone am unwillingly left out. I was kind and good. Wretchedness made me a monster. Make me happy and I will again be noble."

"Be-gone! I won't listen to you. There can be no society between you and me. We are archenemies. Be-gone, or let us try our strength in a death struggle in which one must fall."

"How can I reach you?" he beseeched me. "Will no plea move you to look kindly on your creation, who pleads for your pity and compassion? Believe me, Frankenstein: I was good. My spirit overflowed with love and kindness. But aren't I alone, wretchedly alone? You, my creator, detest me. What hope can I put in my fellow humans who owe me nothing? They despise and scorn me."

"And with just cause," I scoffed, "for you're no fellow of humanity."

"Barren deserts or frozen wastes are my only refuge. I've roamed here many days. The caves of ice, which only I am not afraid of, are a sanctuary to me, and the only one which men don't begrudge me. These desolate places I welcome, for they're kinder to me than your fellow humans."

"Since you've so brutally murdered my fellow humans what else should you expect?"

"If the masses of mankind knew of my existence they would follow in your footsteps and devote themselves to my destruction. Should I not then despise them who despise me? I will come to no terms with my archenemies. I'm miserable, and they'll share in my misery. But it's in your power to repay me, and save them from a disaster, which it only remains for you to make so terrible that not only you and your relations, but countless others will be devoured by the fury of its wrath."

"As you will be devoured by the fury of my wrath."

"Let your heart be touched," he exhorted me, "and don't scorn me. Listen to my story: once you've heard it, desert me or take pity on me as you will decide that I deserve. But listen to me. Even the guilty are entitled by human laws—bloodthirsty as they are—to speak out in their own defense before they're condemned. Hear me, Frankenstein. You charge me with murder, and yet you would—with a clear conscience—kill your own creation. Ah, applaud the immortal justice of man! But I don't ask you to spare me. Hear me. And then—if you're able and willing—do away with your handiwork."

"Why do you remind me of things of which I shudder to remember—that I've been the wretched cause and creator? Damned be the day, abominable devil, in which you first saw daylight! Damned be the hands which made you! You've made me miserable beyond description. You've left me no ability to judge whether I'm fair to you or not. Be-gone! Spare me the sight of your loathsome form."

"My creator," he held out his hideous hands in front of my eyes, which I violently threw away from me, "so I spare you. So I cast away from you a sight which you hate. Still you can't listen to me and give me your pity."

"I can feel no pity for you."

"By the virtues I once had I demand this of you. Listen

to my story. It's long and strange, but once you've heard it you can decide. Upon you it depends whether I leave forever the society of man and live a virtuous life, or become the bane of your fellow humans, and the perpetrator of your own swift destruction. The air of this place doesn't suit your sharp senses. The sun's yet high in the sky. Come to my hut on the mountain before it sets to hide itself beyond those snowy cliffs and lighten another world."

As he bid me to go along with him he led the way across the ice and I followed.

§

"Whatever prevailed upon you to follow him?" Captain Robert Walton asked in a bewildered tone of voice.

"My heart was heavy," Victor Frankenstein lamented, "but I never hesitated. And as we went along I considered the arguments which he had made and decided at least to listen to his story."

"His arguments must've proved compelling."

"I was partly prompted by curiosity and pity strengthened my resolve. I had before suspected him of being the murderer of my brother and I anxiously desired an admission or a denial of this belief."

"I gather that something else drove you as well."

"For the first time, yes, I felt what the responsibility of a creator towards his creation was and that I should humor him before I blamed him for his brutality. These considerations moved me to meet his demands."

§

We crossed the ice then and climbed the facing cliff. Cold was the air and the rain once more started to fall. We stepped inside the hut—the demon with an air of bombast and bravado—I with a sinking heart and disgust of life. But I agreed to listen, and seating myself by the fire which my loathsome host had lighted, he so started his story.

"Finally," he concluded, "I wandered toward these mountains and have roamed through their vast recesses, devoured by a burning desire which only you can satisfy. We may not part company until you've pledged to grant my request. I'm alone and wretched. Men won't associate with me. But one as monstrous and grotesque as myself wouldn't deny herself to me. My mate must be one of the same species and possess the same deformities. This creature you must create."

That monster finished recounting his story and riveted his eyes on me in anticipation of an answer. But I was confused, mystified and powerless to collect my thoughts enough to comprehend the full import of his request.

"You must," he insisted, "make a female for me with whom I can live in the mutual sharing of those feelings necessary for my being. This only you can do. And I demand it of you as a right which you cannot refuse to grant."

As he uttered that I could no longer repress the fury fuming inside me.

"I can and do refuse it," I declared, "and no threat will ever force my consent from me. You may make me the most wretched of men but you'll never make me evil in my own eyes. Would I make another like yourself, whose shared evil might devastate the earth? Be-gone! I've given you my answer. You may threaten me but I'll never consent."

"You're mistaken," the demon answered ominously. "And rather than threaten I'm resigned to reason with you. I'm wicked because I'm wretched. Am I not avoided and abhorred by all mankind? You, my creator, would exterminate me and celebrate. Admit that and tell me why I should show man more pity than he shows me."

"Because man hasn't murdered your most beloved relations."

"I have no relations—no family—to be beloved. Besides, you wouldn't call it murder if you could plunge me into one of those ice-crevices and obliterate my form—your own handiwork. Should I revere man when he scorns me? Let him live with me in the bearing of good will, and rather than doing injury, I would do every good turn to him with tears of thankfulness for his approval. But that can never be. Human sight is the impassable obstacle to our unity."

"The only obstacle is your vile and vicious cruelty."

"But mine won't be the surrender to groveling enslavement. I will avenge my injuries. If I can't inspire respect I will inspire fear, and mainly towards you, my archenemy—because my creator—do I swear indestructible hatred. Take care: I will toil at your annihilation, nor stop until I devastate your soul so that you'll curse the moment of your birth."

A fiendlike fury agitated him as he uttered that. His face was contorted into creases too terrible for human sight but shortly he calmed himself down and went on.

"I meant to reason," he said. "This emotion is harmful to me, for you don't think that you're the source of its excess. If any creature felt emotions of tenderness towards me I should return them many times over. For that one creature's sake I would make peace with the entire race! But I now indulge in reveries of rapture which can never be fulfilled."

"You scarcely deserve to revel in rapture."

"What I ask of you is reasonable and sound," he insisted. "I demand a mate of another sex but as monstrous as myself. The satisfaction is slight but it's all that I can take, and it will satisfy me. It's certain we'll be monsters cut off from the rest of the world. But because of that we'll be more attached to each other. Our lives won't be ecstatic but they'll be inoffensive and free of the wretchedness I now feel. Ah, my creator, humor me! Let me be grateful to you for one favor. Let me see that I excite the pity of some living thing. Don't deny me my plea!"

My heart was touched. I shivered when I thought of the

potential results of my acceptance but I felt that there was some merit to his argument. His story, and the emotions he then expressed, showed him to be a being of finer feelings. And did I not as his creator owe him all the share of happiness it was in my power to give? He saw my change of disposition and went on.

"If you accept," he offered, "neither you nor any other human being will ever set eyes on us again. My mate will be of the same nature as myself and we will go to the remotest wilds of the world to live in utter isolation. The proposal which I make is peaceful and humane, and you must think that you could deny it only in the licentiousness of power and neglect. Heartless as you've been towards me I now see pity in your eyes. Let me take advantage of this opportune moment and convince you to pledge what I so fervently yearn for."

"You offer to leave the habitations of man and live in the world's most isolated wilderness. How can you, who yearns for the affection and compassion of man, survive in this seclusion? You will come back and once more seek their sympathy, and you will confront their hostility. Your evil emotions will be revived and you will then have a mate to help you in the work of annihilation. This cannot be. Stop making the argument, for I cannot accept."

"How capricious are your feelings!" he protested. "Only a moment ago you were touched by my expressions, and why do you once more harden your heart to my grievances? I swear to you, by the world in which I live, and by you who created me, that with the mate you make I will leave the domain of man and live, as it may be, in the most desolate of places. My evil emotions will have gone, for I will confront compassion! My life will pass silently away, and in my final moments, I will not curse my creator."

His words made a strange impression on me. I pitied him and at times felt a desire to comfort him. But when I looked upon him, when I watched that ghastly monstrosity which

160

lurked and spoke, my soul languished and my impressions were changed to those of terror and hate. I tried to suppress these feelings. I felt that since I could not empathize with him, I had no cause to keep back from him the small share of happiness which was still in my power to give.

"You swear to be inoffensive," I said, "but haven't you already shown a measure of malevolence which should logically make me mistrust you? May not even this be a pretense which will strengthen your advantage by giving you a broader range for your vengeance?"

"How's this?" he bristled. "I mustn't be toyed with. And I demand an answer. If I have no bonds and no attachments hatred and wickedness must be my share. Another's affection will do away with the source of my sins and I'll become a creature to whose existence everyone will be oblivious. My sins are the spawn of a forced seclusion which I despise. And my virtues will of course come to the fore once I live together with a mate. I will feel the tenderness of a sensitive creature and become tied to the course of existence and events, from which I'm now shut out."

I stopped to ponder everything he had recounted and the different arguments which he had made. Nor were his strength and threats neglected in my considerations. A creature who could survive in the ice-caves of the glaciers, and conceal himself from capture among the ledges of unapproachable cliffs, was possessed of powers it would be futile to contend with. After a long lapse of thought I decided that the justice owed both to him and my fellow humans obliged me to accept his plea.

"I agree to your demand," I turned to him, "on your sacred word of honor to leave Europe forever—and every other place in the community of man—as soon as I will hand over to you a female who will follow you into seclusion."

"I swear," he cried out, "by all the heavenly bodies above, and by the burning desire which devours my heart, that if

JOSEPH COVINO JR

you grant my request, while they endure you will never see me again. Return to your home and begin your work. I will follow your progress with unspeakable anguish. And have no fear but that when you're done I will reappear."

Saying that he abruptly left me, fearing perhaps any change in my feelings. I watched him climb down the mountain at breakneck speed and swiftly lost sight of him among the waves of the bounding main of ice. His story had taken up the entire day and the sun was on the edge of the skyline when he left. I knew I should hurry my climb downward towards the valley since I should soon be enveloped in darkness. But my spirits were depressed and my pace sluggish. Working to meander among the narrow trails of the mountain and bending my steps steadily as I progressed puzzled me, preoccupied as I was by the feelings which the doings of the day had stirred. Dusk had much deepened when I got to the midway resting-place and seated myself alongside the spring. Sparkling stars shone sporadically as the clouds drifted from above them. Darkened pines sprang up ahead of me, and here and there a snapped tree lay broken on the ground. This vista of awesome wonder inspired strange impressions inside me. I cried convulsively.

"Heaven and earth!" I wailed, clenching my hands in anguish. "You both scoff at me. But if you truly pity me blot out all feeling and memory. Let me come to nothing. But if not go away and leave me in blackness."

These were reckless and wretched thoughts which called to mind once more my dearly beloved mother.

NINE:
RETREAT TO THE
REFUGE

"Here then I retreated, and lay down happy to have found a shelter, however miserable, from the inclemency of the season, and still more from the barbarity of man."—Frankenstein's Monster

Deeply devoted as they were to one another my mother and father seemed to tap a limitless wellspring of love to lavish on me as their eldest and, for a time, only child. My mother's gentle affections, and my father's smiles of warmhearted delight while watching me, are my earliest memories. I was their well beloved child—the helpless and innocent creation handed down to them from Heaven, whom to raise for the best and whose imminent fate it was in their hands to guide to happiness or wretchedness. With this deep awareness of what they owed towards the creature to which they had given birth, along with the lively spirits of affection which enlivened both, it may be supposed that while during every interlude in my youth I learned a telling lesson in kindness, compassion and devotion. In light of these thoughts I stirred myself and returned right away to Geneva.

§

"Even in my soul I could give no vent to my emotions," Victor Frankenstein listlessly told his rapt host. "They weighed on my mind with the weight of a millstone and their excess crushed my anguish beneath them."

"What did you tell your family?" Captain Robert Walton asked, listening intently to his convalescent guest.

"I answered none of their questions. I scarcely spoke at all. I felt enjoined—as if I had no right to accept their pity—as if I would never again enjoy their fellowship."

"Surely they loved you to understanding."

"Even as I loved them to devotion," Frankenstein affirmed with a nod. "And to save them I decided to devote myself to my most loathsome chore. The prospect of such a pursuit made every other trial of life pass in front of me like a shadow, and that impression only struck me with the dead certainty of life."

§

A change truly had happened in my life: my health, which had before languished, was now greatly revived. And my spirits, when unfettered by the thoughts of my dismal prospect, were equally raised. My father watched this change with delight and he turned his mind towards the best means of obliterating the remnants of my sadness, which every now and again would come back by fits, and with a devastating darkness overshadowing the sunlight looming ahead. Finally my father took me aside to talk:

"My dear son," he said, "I'm glad to say that you've taken up your past enjoyments and appear to be yourself again. And yet you're still miserable. For a long time I was lost in thought as to the reason for this. But yesterday a thought passed through my mind, and if it's true, I implore you to confess it. Silence in such a matter would not only be futile but bring down untold disaster on us all."

I shuddered uncontrollably at his appeal and my father went on.

"My son, I admit that I've always hoped for your marriage to our dear Elizabeth as the bond of our domestic contentment and the barrier to my waning years."

"We've always been attached to each other."

"From your earliest youth you grew up together and looked—in temperament and judgment—perfectly compatible with one another. But so illusory is the perception of man that what I imagined to be the best partisans of my plan may have completely done away with it. You perhaps consider her your sister, without any desire that she might become your wife. No, you may have found another whom you may love. And believing yourself bound by honor to Elizabeth this conflict may cause the painful torment which you seem to suffer."

"My dear father," I reassured him, "set your heart at

166

rest. I love my cousin dearly and truly. I've never known any woman who inspired as Elizabeth does my deepest respect and devotion. All my hopes and prospects for the future are completely bound up in the anticipation of our marriage."

"My dear Victor," he heaved a satisfied sigh of relief, "the sentiments you've expressed in the matter do my heart more good than I've felt in a long time. If you feel so we'll certainly be pleased, however recent incidents may cast a shadow over us. But it's this shadow which seems to have such a firm hold on your heart that I want to dispel. Tell me then whether you object to an early celebration of the marriage. We've been unhappy and these incidents have distracted us from that daily serenity befitting my age and ailments. You're younger but I don't suspect—blessed as you are with sufficient fortune—that an immediate marriage would at all interfere with any future intention of honor or endeavor which you may have devised. Don't presume though that I mean to impose happiness upon you, or that a postponement on your part would cause me any severe disquiet. Take in my words with frankness and answer me, I implore you, with honesty and conviction."

I listened silently to my father and stayed for a time unable to give any answer. I quickly turned over in my mind a profusion of thoughts and tried to come to some conclusion. To me the thought of an immediate marriage to my Elizabeth was one of terror and dread. I was obliged by a sacred pledge which I had not yet performed and did not dare break. Or if I did what endless tribulations might not hang over me and my beloved family! Could I enter into an engagement with that malignant millstone hanging about my neck and weighing me down? I must fulfill my obligation and let the monster leave with his mate before I let myself rejoice in a marriage from which I looked forward to peace and happiness.

But I could not summon up the courage to resume my task. I was afraid of the dissatisfied demon wreaking vengeance, yet I was powerless to conquer my aversion to the chore which was incumbent on me. I realized that I could not create a female without once more dedicating many months to serious study and diligent discourse. But I held on to every pretext of procrastination and recoiled from setting about an errand whose urgent need started to seem less certain to me. Besides, I had an unconquerable loathing of the thought of devoting myself to my repugnant task in my father's house while going about intimate fellowship with those I cared for. I knew that countless ghastly calamities might happen—the least of which would tell a story to strike terror into everyone related to me. I was conscious too that I should many times lose all self-control—all ability to conceal the wrenching emotions which would seize me over the course of my hellish preoccupation. I must separate myself from everyone I cared for while so preoccupied. Once begun, it would be expeditiously concluded and I might be returned to my family in peace and contentment. My pledge performed the monster would leave forever. Or—so my foolish fancy imagined—some calamity might in the meantime come about to do away with him and bring to an end my enslavement forever.

These sentiments determined my answer to my father. I expressed a desire to visit England, but hiding the real purpose of this proposal I secreted my intent beneath a pretense which raised no question or suspicion while I pleaded my desire with a resolve which readily prompted my father to consent. After so long a time of an obsessive sadness, which looked like lunacy in its frenzy and result, he was pleased to learn that I was able to relish the thought of such a journey, and he took heart that a change of outlook and different diversion would—before my return—have brought me back completely to myself. For England then I was bound and it was accepted that my marriage to Elizabeth should happen right away on my return. My father's age made him intensely hostile to any postponement. For myself there was one consolation I pledged myself—one compensation for my unequaled afflictions: it was the promise of that day when, liberated from my wretched enslavement, I might join Elizabeth and be oblivious to the past in marriage to her.

§

"But one thought haunted me," Victor Frankenstein confided, "which made me tremble."

"What was that?" Captain Robert Walton asked expectantly.

"That while I was away I should leave my friends unaware of the presence of their enemy, and defenseless against his assault, infuriated as he might be at my parting."

"But didn't he pledge to pursue you wherever you might go? And wouldn't he follow you to England?"

"That thought was awful in itself, but comforting, since it presumed the protection of my friends. I was tormented by the thought of the prospect that the opposite of this might take place."

"How so?"

"Throughout the entire time I was the servant of my monster I let myself be directed by the instincts of the moment. And my immediate instinct strongly suggested that the demon would indeed follow me, and spare my family the threat of his evil intent."

§

The term of my absence—several months or at most a year was the time expected—was left to my own discretion. And a well-intentioned protective measure my father had taken was to assure my having an escort. Together with Elizabeth he had, without first consulting me, provided that Clerval should meet me in Strasbourg.

§

"Shouldn't that have intruded upon the privacy you needed for the accomplishment of your task?" Captain Walton asked discerningly.

"At the start of my trip at least," Frankenstein's glance acknowledged his host's insight, "the company of my friend could in no way be an obstacle, and actually I relished that so I should be spared untold hours of lonesome, distressing rumination. Henry might even stand in the way of intrusion by my enemy. Were I alone would he not sometimes impose his repugnant presence upon me—to accost me about my task or to anticipate its completion?"

§

It was in the late part of September then that I once more left my native land. My trip had been my own proposition, and that being so, Elizabeth assented. It had been her concern which afforded me an escort in Clerval: and yet a man is oblivious to the countless precise contingencies which summon a woman's diligent vigilance.

"But I'm filled with fear," Elizabeth confided to me with deep-felt care, "at the thought of your suffering, away from me, the pain of sorrow and despair. I pray you to hasten your return."

Countless, contentious sentiments made her silent as she bid me a grievous, solemn goodbye. I flung myself into the carriage which was to carry me off, scarcely aware of where I was traveling and oblivious to what was drifting about. Haunted by monotonous nightmares my sight was riveted but unperceiving. I could solely appreciate the urgency of my journey and the employment which was to engage me while it went on. After some time spent in leaden idleness, during which I traveled many leagues, I reached Strasbourg where

I awaited Clerval for two days. He arrived. How vast was the disparity between us! He was susceptive to every last prospect.

"This is what it is to be alive!" he cried out. "Here I revel in life! But you, my dear Victor, why are you sad and despairing?"

Truly I was preoccupied by rueful reflection: I, a forlorn sufferer, damned by a curse which frustrated every last expedient of pleasure. We had settled to go down the Rhine in a boat from Strasbourg to Rotterdam, where we might take ship for London. As we drifted down the waterway I lay at the bottom of our boat, desolate in spirit, and my mind continuously disturbed by morose sensations; but Henry felt like he had been conveyed to never-never land and relished a joy scarcely savored by man.

"Oh," he sighed happily, "the ministering spirit who frequents and protects this place possesses a soul in perfect unity with man."

In due course we came to Rotterdam, from which we passed on by sea to England in the last days of October. And London was our immediate place of repose.

I had learned of some discoveries by an English philosopher—the knowledge of which was vital to my attainment. I recalled as well the urgency forced upon me of either traveling to England as I had done, or keeping up a lengthy correspondence with those philosophers of that country, whose knowledge and discoveries were of essential use to me in my immediate venture. Untimely and intolerable was the last means of acquiring the necessary knowledge. If this trip had happened during my term of research and satisfaction it would have given me indescribable delight. But a decay had blighted my life and I merely called upon these people for the purpose of the knowledge which they might impart to me on the question for which my concern was so intense. Society was distressing to me; unfamiliar faces brought back sorrow to my soul. I saw an impassable wall put up between me and my fellow creatures; this wall was finished with the slaughter of William and Justine, and to contemplate the circumstances associated with those human beings overwhelmed my spirit with agony.

I was solemnly employed with the means of acquiring the knowledge essential for the performance of my pledge and promptly resorted to the letters of introduction which I had carried with me—addressed to the most celebrated natural philosopher: Dr. David Seward. I recalled merely—and it was with an indignant agony that I brooded upon it—to direct that my chemical instruments be loaded to go along with me. But when I had prepared to depart from Geneva to travel to Strasbourg to meet Clerval I suddenly realized that I had never in the first place brought back my chemical instruments from Ingolstadt, where I had left them behind, put out of sight in my cloistered laboratory at the top of the house where I had made my monster. I frantically accosted Henry when we greeted each other in Strasbourg.

"In my haste to leave Ingolstadt and go to Geneva upon hearing of William's death," I said, alarmed and shuddering, "I forgot altogether to take them with me."

Then I fixed my eyes on Henry with anxious expectancy.

"Did you pack my instruments to go with you?" I fearfully awaited his answer.

"No, my dear Victor," Henry said hesitantly, uncertain of my reaction, "it was unnecessary to pack them."

"What do you mean unnecessary?" I exclaimed, standing aghast. "Those instruments are of the utmost importance to my present experiment!"

"I mean only that Professor Krempe packed your instruments to go with him," he clarified.

"M. Krempe? Go with him where?"

"To London—where he's to join us."

I pressed him impatiently.

"Join us where?"

"At the asylum of the famed alienist, Dr. David Seward," he told me at the last. "When you wrote to Professor Krempe from Geneva for a letter of introduction he came to me to ask about your condition."

Henry gingerly handed over to me Professor Krempe's letter of introduction which I took tremulously into my fingers.

"Professor Krempe expressed acute interest in your instruments when I recounted how the sight of them had excited such great anxiety in you," he recalled.

"M. Krempe is a professor of natural philosophy just as Dr. Seward, although scarcely on an equal par."

"Professor Krempe proposed to take a sabbatical from the university, pack your instruments with him and meet us at Dr. Seward's asylum in London," Henry recounted warily. "Recalling your vehement aversion to even the term of natural philosophy I determined that it might best benefit your disposition should you travel without those instruments present to distress you."

"I thank you, my dear friend." I squeezed Henry's hand, stoically resigning myself to this troublesome turn of events.

Henry aspired after discourse and fellowship with men of brilliance and learning who thrived in our time; but this was for me a frivolous aspiration. When by myself I could fill my head with the vision of all creation; Clerval's voice comforted me and so I could fool myself into a fleeting calm. And in Clerval I saw the likeness of my past identity; he was curious and eager to acquire knowledge and insight. He was endlessly engaged; and the sole impediment to his delight was my desolate and mournful heart. I strove to secrete this as far as was practical that I might not avert him from the enjoyment essential to someone, who was coming to a new vista of existence, un-afflicted by any concern or hateful memory. I continually declined to keep company with him, claiming another obligation which I might carry on by myself.

§

NEAR PURFLEET ON THE RIVER THAMES

A lone, rotund and castellated tower, rising high up alongside an equally lofty but conical tower on one side of the distinctly Gothic villa, shot up dramatically out of a thick circlet of poplar and willow trees surrounding the country estate's expansive and pendulous grounds. As my clangorous carriage bowled along the road hedging round the embattled stone wall, bound directly for the villa's great north gate, I apprehensively watched those two towers loom ahead until, presently, they hovered ominously overhead. And as I alighted at the gate I first cast my eyes on the faded bronze plaque embedded and embossed in stone: *THE REFUGE*.

A porter met me at the gate and led the way through a small oratory spaced with open niches and iron rails, enclosing an altar and stone basins for holy water. Passing by a small, shadowy cloister we stepped up to the narrow front entry to the house and inside the doorway—overhung with three ancestral shields—which opened up to a small, somber hall hung with gothic paper, paved with hexagon tiles and lighted by two narrow windows of painted glass. We turned off from the hall, going through a small passage and into a great parlor hung with paper in imitation stucco and lighted by windows of fine painted glass. We walked the floor's Turkish carpet and went into a waiting-room where the porter left me alone. I was closely examining a large, ancient altar candlestick of metal, inlaid with gothic inscriptions, when two young men came together into the waiting-room to greet me. Both had strong jaws and good foreheads but were some twenty years apart in age.

"Good afternoon," the older one hailed me, holding out

his hand to press mine. "I am Abraham Van Helsing—head warder here—and we welcome you to the Refuge." He paused to gently lay his hands on the boy's shoulders and hastened to proudly introduce him to me. "This is friend John, Superintendent Seward's son. He serves as an attendant in his father's employ, and already he aspires to read medicine at university in future—and he's all but barely ten years old."

"How do you do?" I said cordially. "I'm very pleased to meet you both."

"I call him friend John," Van Helsing explained with relish, "because once he promptly extracted the poison of gangrene from a knife, which another rather nervous friend of ours had let slip and wounded me with."

"Then friend John has already made a rather resourceful beginning toward realizing his vocation."

"Quite so." Van Helsing sprightly raised his bushy brows. "We're given to understand that you've made something of a serious study of Dr. Seward's vocation."

"Yes," I heartily affirmed, handing over to him my letter of introduction. "I'm most anxious to consult Dr. Seward on a great many subjects of inquiry."

"Likewise," Van Helsing ran his big, dark blue eyes over my letter, "Dr. Seward has awaited your arrival with great anticipation. Will you kindly accompany us so that you might pay your respects?"

"Most certainly."

They escorted me directly to a little parlor, entering a room hung with gothic paper of stone color in mosaic by a door overhung with an ancestral shield of arms and quarterings on painted glass. A tall, stately man stood looking meditatively out a bow window which threw light upon a lustrous table and eight ebony chairs. Atop the table was set an ice-pail of Wedge-wood's ware.

"Dr. Seward," Abraham Van Helsing announced ceremoniously to the mature man so lost in his private thoughts, "might I present Victor Frankenstein?"

"Herr Frankenstein!" the boy's obvious elder exclaimed, arresting his reverie and turning to spiritedly greet those addressing him. "I'm extremely delighted to meet you."

"You honor me, sir," I said. "It's my profound privilege to meet you. And I'm greatly indebted to you for so graciously sparing the time to grant me this interview."

"Not at all," Dr. Seward politely dismissed my deferential overture and gestured to my pair of youthful escorts. "I take it that you've already met my two most excellent attendants."

"Indeed I have."

"I must frequently remind my son, John, in particular to foster his inheritance here," Dr. Seward digressed, "with constant admonishments that power over other people's lives brings along with it certain responsibilities."

"Will there be anything else that you require, sir?" Van Helsing tactfully interjected.

"No thank you, that'll be all for the moment," Dr. Seward said with a curt wave of his hand, "however we will take tea and coffee shortly in the cottage-garden."

"I'll see to it at once." Van Helsing took his cue to take the doctor's son in tow and excuse themselves from the room.

"Abraham comes over to us from Amsterdam and studies in London," Dr. Seward mentioned with almost paternal pride. "He's reading medicine, law, philosophy, metaphysics and literature at university. No doubt he'll eventually surpass us all."

"He must prove to be an indispensable member of your household."

"Admirable," Dr. Seward readily agreed, nodding. "I gather that you yourself are quite an exceptional student of natural philosophy—especially chemistry."

"Of certain necessity I've avidly read all your treatises on the subject with abundant admiration, but I'm yet baffled by certain particulars."

"So you've come over to consult to make a closer inquiry."

"With your indulgence."

"Then we can commence our discourse straightaway."

Dr. Seward showed the way through the tiled hall adjoining the great staircase hung with gothic paper, going through the entrance of a long passage over which hovered an owl in cut paper. We crisscrossed the passage and went out through another entry, emerging inside the columned arcade of a great cloister. Slanting rays of light fell through the shadowy arches and wavered across our faces as we strolled along, talking together.

"As you may know," Dr. Seward said, "I happen to be the resident mad doctor."

"Sir?" I said with a confused frown.

"Forgive me," Dr. Seward apologized, turning with a knowing smile to take notice of my predictably perplexed expression. "In no way do I mean to imply that you must be mad to minister to the mad. But supervision of the insane is often spoken of as the trade in lunacy—or simply the mad-doctoring trade."

"I can appreciate that your trade obliges you to contend with some of the most confounding riddles of the human mind."

"Most assuredly," Dr. Seward said. "Managing men and women of intense sensitivity and contentiousness, such as lunatics commonly are, demands on the part of all attendants a combination of the rarest talents and abilities."

"As well as, I would expect, a degree of devotion prevalent only in those having a true calling."

"Regrettably," Dr. Seward lamented, "my contact with patients is frequently confined to making cursory rounds of the wards, leaving the more meticulous handling of cases to my attendants. I'm inundated with administrative tasks—many of them painfully tedious and trivial. My time is so thoroughly occupied by extraneous matters that I have precious little left to devote to visiting patients. That being the case the more important task of daily, intimate contact with patients devolves on my attendants."

We went out of the great cloister, passing by a blue and white china flower-pot at its end, and bent our steps along a twisting footpath.

"You're doubtless grateful for the service rendered by Abraham Van Helsing," I said. "Evidently he's a most learned and capable fellow."

"Exemplary," Dr. Seward concurred. "Only we've learned by experience that even learning and ability are but imperfect protections against the temptations of insensitivity and neglect."

"How do you mean?"

"To regard these fragile charges as both fellow creatures and mere material creations..." Dr. Seward expounded. "To praise all they do right—and pity without reproving whatever they do wrong—calls for such a habit of reflective thought and charitable consideration as is difficult to attain."

"It must be a blessing at least to hold a position where you have no overseer hovering over you."

"True," Dr. Seward smiled a wry smile. "I do my own work in my own way. And my duties do give me a somewhat prominent position in polite society which I would not have without them, although at times they can prove to be rather burdensome. Even so I consider myself to be a part of an enlightened movement of learning and philanthropy which promises to be enormously beneficial to mankind."

"You refer of course to treatment of insanity at the asylum?"

"Yes," Dr. Seward said. "What was at first conceived purely as a sequestered receptacle and storehouse for the insane has been transformed into an experimental laboratory for developing invaluable new theories about mental alienation."

Piers of artificial stone buttressed the wrought iron gate opening up to the flower-garden. And at the end of our winding walk was a gigantic seat in the curious shape of a seashell, carved out of solid oak, planted at the foot of a great, gnarled tree. Presently we stepped inside the cottage tea-room hung with green paper and prints. Dr. Seward invited me to sit at the tea-table, around which a young maidservant busied herself setting out the tea-service. She had a face of heavenly beauty and expression. Her hair was a shiny, sable-black and oddly braided; her eyes were dark but kindly, although lively; her features were evenly well-formed and her complexion marvelously fair; both cheeks blushed with a pretty pink.

"Sweet Safie here is a voluntary resident who lives and works in the Refuge community," Dr. Seward said with pride, gesturing affectionately to the girl. "She comes over to us from the country near Ingolstadt where you undertook your university studies. We call her our sweet Arabian."

I looked aghast at the lovely young girl, disbelieving my eyes. I had never met nor seen this girl ever before in my life, yet somehow she was compellingly and inexplicably familiar to me. Somewhere—from someone—I had at least heard of her before.

"Safie is a model example," Dr. Seward went on, "of how the Refuge can fulfill its intended purpose: by being a place where the mentally distraught can unburden themselves of their mental torment, and learn anew how to live within the safety of a protected setting."

"Seclusion can frequently serve its own beneficial purpose," I speculated sadly, "as a sanctuary from a scornful world."

TEN:
BEAUTY FLED THE BEAST

"Was I, then, a monster, a blot upon the earth, from which all men fled and whom all men disowned?"—Frankenstein's Monster

S afie poured our tea from a tea-pot of crackled china with blue and brown flowers; filling two handle cups on saucers with dark blue and gold edges and colored flowers, setting out on the tea-table as well a sugar-dish, milk-pot and an octagon green basin and plate with colored flowers. Presently Dr. Seward dismissed her from the cottage after we both tendered our thanks and started to converse between sips of tea.

"I'm simply curious," I confessed. "But why is your asylum situated in such a remote spot? It seems you've been banished from the rest of humanity."

"You make an astute observation," Dr. Seward complimented me. "The decision to establish my asylum in this isolated setting is significant. Humanity demonstrates that it repudiates madness by exiling the insane to out-of-the-way places. Humanity presumes that by putting a discreet distance between the sane and the insane it protects itself from the supposed contagion of the mad."

"Yet you've built your asylum on rather high ground, which still makes it somewhat conspicuous."

"That's quite right. Although we may stay on the cloistered outskirts of polite society we still cast a threatening shadow over it."

"Threatening?"

"For a great many," Dr. Seward clarified, "an asylum serves solely as a repository for violent lunatics."

"This scarcely appears to be a place of violence."

"In our time the asylum has become synonymous with the very notion of unreason. The demented and deranged are not merely disturbed but deeply disturbing: most often themselves in great distress and, at the same time, the source of great distress in the lives of those compelled to cope with them."

"You refer to the disturbance they cause in their own households?"

"For many they pose a great threat—both symbolic and

real—to the very integrity of the social fabric—as well as a great source of anxiety to others trying to go about the business of daily living."

"Certainly not all of the mentally disturbed are overtly disruptive."

"Whether they're ranting or raving, or melancholic and withdrawn, they inflict turmoil and bewilderment at every turn, inciting a gamut of emotions and a host of troubles for relations and society at large: disorder and disarray in the family; shame and humiliation; fear of violence to people and possessions."

"Are those who are dangerous and most difficult to deal with always violently agitated?"

"Mostly," Dr. Seward said. "Families trying to contend with their violently irrational or severely disturbed relations are eager to dispose of the more incorrigible ones at the asylum—in response to conduct which is too intolerable."

"Then the asylum has become an acceptable place for families to relegate relatives whose conduct is too hard to handle in the confined circle of the home."

"Indeed. There is a growing tendency of families to deliver their aged, ailing, invalid or otherwise burdensome relations to the asylum—essentially abandoning their duties of kinship."

"When the asylum relieves a desperate family of an inconvenient relative," I said with marked contempt, "it appears to provide a remarkably simple solution more suitable for the indifferent and irresponsible."

"In the eyes of distressed families," Dr. Seward continued, unperturbed, "most of those who are admitted and remain within the asylum's walls are not so much inconvenient as impossible. And for many families at the end of their rope looking for it the asylum brings relief from impossible hardship."

"Relief as well, I suspect, from caring for an embarrassing relative."

"Surely the asylum spares some families from the disgrace perceived to be related to having a lunatic in the fold, and from the many inconveniences which go along with having to guard themselves against their excesses in the confines of the home, and therefore serves to preserve the family name and honor in the face of madness in a close relative."

"Apparently," I said with some disdain, "the asylum's principal value to the community is as a convenient dumping ground on which to discard the inconveniently impossible."

"From the moment most asylums opened their doors," Dr. Seward conceded, "they functioned as museums for the collection of the unruly and unwanted, selling the promise of silence and secrecy to families anxious to conceal the existence of insanity in their midst."

"How should they conceal their dereliction?"

"High standards of physical care and the alienist's confidence in his own ability could help ease the guilt and helplessness suffered by families who no longer felt able to cope with mentally disturbed relatives, relieving them as well of the responsibility of making decisions for them."

"Choosing to send disturbed relations to an asylum rather than care for them at home obviously means taking a decisive step in itself. And wealthier families, I expect, can well afford to pay to have them put away."

"The wealthy can buy considerably more care and even more reputable physicians," Dr. Seward said ruefully, "but scarcely more cures."

"In effect then an asylum is an expedient for casting out one's undesirables."

"Granted, an asylum is a custodial place and serves mostly a custodial purpose, although at least it has pretensions to therapeutic treatment as well as confinement. Families intend simply to provide accommodation for relations who have lost their sanity. So those who exercise that choice cast out their disturbed relatives into custodial and, they trust, curative care."

"That being the case such confinement could conceivably be considered an act of charity."

"Confinement is scarcely anything but a traumatic experience," Dr. Seward differed, "since families usually resort to an asylum to discipline relations who are of an unruly nature. Tragically most unwanted patients finish in a place which feels like a foretaste of hell, even though there are many gradations to be found there."

"Should not an asylum have the greater purpose of restoring sanity itself, rather than being merely a prison for the insane?"

"A great many families believe that their difficult relations deserve to be taught a lesson, and that a stern reprimand should do them a world of good. From that point of view confinement is eminently effective, for even those who have spent only a few months confined are prepared to go to great lengths to avoid being confined again."

"Then I gather," I said somewhat scurrilously, "that asylums are meant more to be reformatories than refuges."

"Unfortunately," Dr. Seward lamented, "confinement is yet the foremost method affecting those who are thought to be disturbed. Few alienists take any interest in the mental states of their patients. In fact the largest contingent consists of patients who are confined at the behest of their families to discipline their ungovernable relations. And whether it's merely a matter of madness, or objectionable behavior, patients are left mostly to their own devices."

"Is there not at the present time some humanitarian concern for the protection against flagrant abuses of people who must be seen as curable sufferers, whose condition is not at all their fault?"

"Most of those who come into contact with the insane regard them as more of a social than a medical matter, and making any provision for them has been more for the protection of society at large than for the care and cure of mental patients. Where they've appeared dangerously disturbed many patients are people whose derangement is, for whatever cause, deemed to be a threat to public order and safety."

"Then the asylum has yet to legitimize itself as a curative, much less as a compassionate establishment, but serves solely as an instrument of confinement and control—still upholding conventional codes of conduct which risk subversion by the nonconformist lunatic."

"For lunatics whose mental condition compromises public peace and security there can frequently be little prospect of cure, especially since the asylum has so dissipated any pretenses that it could effectively carry out the therapeutic and curative functions attributed to it."

"If such concerns continue to surpass any care for the individual lunatic, or a desire to prepare the patient for reuniting with the greater community, will not the asylum permanently remain a custodial place meant more for confinement than cure?"

"As of now the asylum has become at least a token symbol of official approval that to medicine has been assigned the task of demarcating the limits of so-called normal thought and conduct, even though many a valuable member has been lost to society, either by the disease gaining strength beyond the reach of medicine, or by the patient falling into the unskilled hands of a physician utterly untrained in its treatment."

"I should suspect that many a person of modest means who, laboring under the appalling misfortune of a disordered mind, have no place to retreat but a private asylum, where their expected cure stands a stronger chance of being unduly prolonged for the profit of some mercenary alienist."

"Precisely," Dr. Seward confirmed. "Seeing which way the wind was blowing, I withdrew to set up this relatively small and private asylum in which I treat the insane consistent with the precepts of the current science of mental alienation."

"Then the Refuge is a house of improvement, not correction."

"Correct," Dr. Seward's pride betrayed itself in his eyes. "At the Refuge we attempt to humanize rather than institutionalize the treatment of the insane. This asylum is patterned after the excellent establishments, subject to men of conviction and integrity, who would render certain that most humane care is provided for patients. Here the patients are treated with all the compassion and patience which is compatible with steady and effective guidance."

"If Safie is any sign," I deliberately directed attention back to the young maidservant, "your asylum provides diversion enough to counter the tendency of derangement to degenerate into outright irrationality."

"Our guiding principle here," he explained, "is to inhibit idleness to preserve every power of mind and body constantly engaged, and never to let it languish or to revert on itself."

"And one effectual way of putting that principle into practice is to encourage patients to busy themselves in some worthwhile work?"

"Patients can also enjoy the benefits of fresh, bracing country air," Dr. Seward nodded his affirmation, "as well as the spacious and pleasing surroundings, which contribute to diverting the disturbed mind from its morbid fantasies, replacing their morbid emotions with healthy trains of thought."

"Does Safie suffer morbid fantasies?" Once more I called attention to the delicate maidservant.

"Sweet Safie is an extremely sensitive soul," Dr. Seward said somewhat disconcertedly. "Her presence here spreads happiness and joy throughout the Refuge. She yet laments—with tears in her eyes—the evil lot of the native inhabitants being slaughtered in the newly discovered American hemisphere. Not long ago she went over from Italy to Germany, where she recounted rather obscurely that she saw something quite mysterious—the horror from which, I fear, she may never recover."

"Is Safie not of Arabian ancestry?"

"Safie's father was a Turkish merchant who traded for a long time in Paris when, for some unknown reason, he became loathsome to the French government, which seized and sent him to prison, after which he was tried and sentenced to death. Safie had just come from Constantinople to join him the very day he was arrested."

"For what crime was the Turk finally condemned?"

"All Paris was outraged at the blatant injustice of his sentence, which was passed owing more to his faith and wealth than the crime with which he was charged."

"Was the Turk's punishment finally inflicted?"

"A young descendant of a good family called De Lacey, who was raised in the service of France, had accidentally attended the Turk's trial. He pledged himself to liberate the Turk from prison. His name was Felix. He would also become pledged to wed our sweet Safie."

"Then a day for the Turk's execution must've been appointed."

"But on the night before Felix set him free from his prison, and before morning was gone they were many leagues from Paris, traveling by passports which Felix had procured in the names of his own father, sister and himself. Felix guided the fugitives through France to Lyons and across Mont Cenis to Leghorn, where the Turk had determined to await an opportune time of escaping into some part of the Turkish domain."

"How did Safie's betrothal to Felix finally come about?"

"All throughout the plotting to free him from bondage," Dr. Seward recounted, "the Turk promptly took notice of the feelings Felix cherished for his daughter when she was permitted to visit his dungeon. And he contrived to entrap Felix more completely in his plans by promising him Safie's hand in marriage as soon as he should be delivered to a place of refuge."

"Whatever became of Safie and Felix while they resided at Leghorn?"

"Safie determined to stay with her father until the time of his parting before which the Turk repeated his pledge that she should be wedded to his liberator. Felix stayed with them in anticipation of their marriage. And all the time he enjoyed Safie's companionship and she displayed towards him the purest and most tender of affections."

"Eventually Safie and Felix did marry?"

"The Turk permitted their intimacy to flourish, and falsely raised the hopes of the young lovers, while inwardly he framed a far different scheme," Dr. Seward explained. "He was afraid of the animosity of Felix should he seem indifferent, for he knew that he was yet at the mercy of his liberator should he decide to expose him to the Italian realm where they resided. He hatched a thousand plots by which he should be able to prolong his deception until it might no longer be needed, and secretly take flight with his daughter alone."

"Did the Turk ultimately carry out his plot?"

"His schemes were eased by the news received from Paris. Deeply incensed at the escape of their prey the French state spared no pains to discover and punish his liberator. The plot of Felix was promptly exposed, and his own father and sister were imprisoned. When the news reached Felix he was awakened from his vision of bliss. De Lacey, his blind and elderly father, and Agatha, his gentle little sister, wasted away in a noxious dungeon while he enjoyed the open air and the companionship of her whom he cherished. This notion was torment to him."

"What then was his course of action?"

"Felix promptly made preparations with the Turk that if he should gain an opportune occasion for escape before Felix could come back to Italy, Safie should stay as a boarder at a convent at Leghorn. Leaving then his lovely Safie he made haste to Paris and handed himself over to the mercy of the law, expecting to liberate De Lacey and Agatha by this action."

"Did he succeed?"

"He failed," Dr. Seward looked decidedly downcast. "They stayed imprisoned for five months before being brought to trial—the verdict of which divested them of their modest fortune and sentenced them to eternal exile from their native land."

"To where were they banished?"

"They took up their abode in a wretched cottage in Germany. Felix presently found out that the trustless Turk, for whom he and his family suffered such an unthinkable outrage, upon learning that his liberator was so abased to privation and ruin, betrayed good faith and had left Italy with his daughter, disparagingly sending Felix a pittance of funds to assist him— as he scoffed—in some scheme of prospective support."

"Would Safie and Felix ever reunite with one another?"

"I would rather let Safie relate the rest of her story to you," Dr. Seward took me by surprise by taking notice of my unsuspecting expression. "She is a most intelligent and articulate young woman."

Just then, mildly audible from afar, a girl's singing voice fell upon our ears—a sweet voice which hummed in a sonorous rhythm, rising or fading away like a nightingale of the forest—attracting our rapt attention. Dr. Seward took exceptional notice of me, listening distractedly.

"Safie sings the spiritual songs of her native land in the cottage-garden," he said. "Perhaps you would care to take advantage of this opportunity to introduce yourself and talk with her."

Dr. Seward abruptly stood up to excuse himself.

"I must go to meet another guest at the villa," he said in parting, "a mutual acquaintance of ours. I'll send Abraham presently to fetch you to join us in the round drawing-room."

§

Once Dr. Seward departed the cottage I went out to follow the twisting footpath back to the seashell-shaped seat, where I found Safie sitting and singing her melodious airs.

"You sing elegantly," I complimented her, stepping prudently into view once she paused in her song. She shyly lifted up her eyes to meet mine.

"Please pardon my intrusion," I said. "My name's Victor Frankenstein. I'm a guest of Dr. Seward at the villa. Might I sit with you for just a moment?"

Safie gestured silently and timorously to the spacious part of the oaken seat next to her.

"I gather from Dr. Seward," I reiterated, "that you came over from the country in Germany near Ingolstadt, where I attended university, and that you fled from your domineering father to live with the De Lacey family so that you could marry your betrothed, your beloved Felix."

Safie nodded modestly with downcast eyes.

"Would you mind telling an interested stranger how you came to settle in the German countryside?" I asked her softly.

"My mother was a Christian Arab," Safie recounted enthusiastically, "captured and enslaved by the Turks. She had won the affections of my father, who married her."

"Like you she must have been commended for her beauty."

Safie hung down her head, blushing.

"My mother was born in freedom," she went on, blinking at my compliment. "She scorned the bondage in which she was held."

"What special lessons did your mother teach you?"

"She taught me the beliefs of her faith, and taught me to aspire after a greater strength of mind and an independent spirit forbidden to women followers of Mahomet."

"How did you escape enslavement yourself?"

"I shuddered at the prospect of going back to Asia and being imprisoned within the walls of a harem, permitted only to busy myself with childish diversions unsuited to the nature of my spirit. I had grown accustomed to noble ideas and a pure practice of virtue."

"You also entertained a prospect of marriage."

"That prospect of marrying a Christian and staying in a land where women are entitled to take a station in society entranced me."

"But your father detested the notion that his daughter should be married to a Christian."

"My father dictated that I forget Felix," Safie made a wry face, "and make ready to go back to our native land. I was offended by his demand. I tried to disagree with him but he left me bitterly, repeating his dictatorial edict."

"He left you to go where?"

"He employed a ship to carry him to Constantinople, for which city he should sail alone. He meant to leave me in the care of a confidential servant—to come after at my leisure with the greater part of his property—which had not yet come to Leghorn, where we were exiled."

"Did you make up your mind to carry on a course of action which would become you to follow in that event?"

"A residence in Turkey was repellent to me. My faith and my feelings alike were hostile to it."

"How then did you reunite yourself with Felix?"

"By some papers of my father which came into my hands I heard of the exile of Felix and learned the name of the place where he then lived."

"Did you hesitate to form your resolve?"

"For a time," Safie lowered her tone. "Taking along with me some jewelry which belonged to me and a sum of money I left Italy with an attendant, a native of Leghorn but who understood the native language of Turkey, and set out for Germany."

"You arrived safely?"

"At a town about twenty leagues from the cottage of Monsieur De Lacey, only my attendant took deathly ill. I tended her with the most dedicated care but the afflicted girl died, and I was left alone, ignorant of the language of the country and completely unversed in the customs of the world."

"How did you finally manage?"

"I had good fortune. The girl had mentioned the name of the place for which we were bound, and after she died, the woman of the house where we had lived took care that I should reach the cottage of Felix safely."

"How then did you live in Germany?"

"Rapturously happy and ravished with joy!" Safie cried jubilantly. "At first I grasped very little of the language and spoke only in broken words, but Felix finally taught me how to speak in his native tongue with the most meticulous instruction."

"From Dr. Seward," I gently suggested, "I understand that something happened to cast a gloom on the serenity of your life in the country. Might I ask what was your fate?"

"One winter's day," Safie hesitantly recounted, "when the sun shined on the red leaves scattered about the ground—and spread gaiety even though it withheld warmth—I set out with Felix and his sister, Agatha, on a long country walk, and we left Monsieur De Lacey alone in the cottage by his own choice."

"Do go on," I heartened her.

"At the moment we returned and the cottage door was opened," she recalled falteringly, "we went in. Who can recount the terror and dismay at the sight of...?"

"What?" I asked anxiously. "Tell me. What did you see?"

"Agatha fainted and I hastened out of the cottage, powerless to aid my friend!" she said, fidgeting excitably. "I fled!"

"Fled? From whom?"

"From what!" she shrieked aloud. "A monster! A hideous,

loathsome monster!"

ELEVEN:
INSANITY INCARNATE

"But I am a blasted tree; the bolt has entered my soul; and I felt then that I should survive to exhibit what I shall soon cease to be—a miserable spectacle of wrecked humanity, pitiable to others, and intolerable to myself."—Victor Frankenstein

JOSEPH COVINO JR

Together with Abraham Van Helsing I watched from a paneled doorway while a matron of the asylum put Safie to bed in a cheerful, airy room with a carpeted floor and papered walls. A chest of drawers stood in it, along with a looking-glass, washstand and basin. Most distinctly a large sash window-pane was framed by cast-iron bars divided up into squares, making a double window unfilled with glass.

"How is she?" I asked, concerned. "Is she well?"

"Only mildly agitated," Van Helsing assured me with a confident tone. "She'll be much better for it after a sound sleep."

"Will she need to be sedated?"

"No." He shook his head adamantly. "We prescribe only few medications as such. If on occasion we do have recourse to drugs then it's more for tranquilizing than curative effects. We have a mind to calm the virulence of patients and habituate them to passive compliance, beyond bringing them back to reason."

"You resort to no sedatives at all?"

"Extract of henbane is sometimes recommended for its sedative properties," he said, "although soft opiates have been of late commonly propagated as the so-called sheet anchor of the alienist physician."

Van Helsing gestured for us to depart quietly and gently shut the door to Safie's unadorned bedroom.

"We have found," he affirmed, "that a warm bath, a good supper and a glass of porter are a far more beneficial way of inducing a restful sleep in restless patients."

"Safie's room scarcely looks like a cell in an asylum ward," I observed, pausing just outside the doorway.

"And for good reason," Van Helsing gestured to the door paneling. "Locks and bolts are purposely hidden behind paneling to blend in and downplay the asylum's confining role, as well as to simulate an ordinary domestic setting."

"Much the same as iron bars cast as window frames, I noticed."

"Exactly."

Together we crossed the spacious, grassy tract separating the asylum's patient wing from its main block, where Abraham Van Helsing led me on through the darkened and shadowed arcade of the villa's great cloister. We passed through the sidelong end of the passage flanking the lengthy cloister and onward to the rearward pair of stairs, conversing on our way.

"As you dispense few drugs to your patients," I noted, "I take it that you invariably dispense with resorting to medicine to treat insanity. Don't you believe that it lies within the reach of medical knowledge to discover an effective method of treating insane patients?"

"In most cases of mental derangement," Van Helsing curled his lip, "very little can be done through the medium of medical therapy for the treatment of insanity. And so far, we must shamefully admit, the medical art has acquired very little merit in the cure of insanity. We put very little trust in it then. Nature alone cures all but everything."

"Even if medicine can't cure insanity," I tactfully objected, "certainly it must favorably promote the patient's prevailing health. Medical treatment for physical debility might just as well relieve mental symptoms."

"Although we recognize that an inexplicable sympathy between body and mind exists," Van Helsing conceded with a shrug of his shoulders, "and that medical remedies might lead to relief in the patient's mental condition, madness doesn't appear to be an organic disease which can be relieved mainly by medical means."

"But mental disorder is oftentimes attended by bodily disorder," I argued, "for there's a clear connection between a sound mind and a sound body."

"There's no question of the necessity for some sort of therapeutic treatment," he allowed again, "which until now has been limited to a specious concern for cleanliness and supervision. If anything could add to the calamity of mental derangement it would be the mode which is ordinarily adopted for its cure, for much of what's passed for medical treatment has been cruel quackery."

"How do you mean?"

"Conventional wisdom presumes that insanity is due to afflictions like plethoric inflammation or vascular congestion of the brain, which call for treatment known as depletive therapy."

"Depletive therapy?"

"A polite euphemism which comprises all manner of ineffectual bleeding and cupping," he clarified. "But we resort to none of the primitive practices of blood-letting or venesection here."

"Leeches employed for blood-letting?"

"Controlled topical bleeding at the temples or from behind the ears to relieve cerebral congestion," he affirmed with a nod. "Against mere madness unattended by bodily disorder medicine appears to be as good as powerless."

"Are you convinced then that medicine has no curative effect on mental disorder?"

"Physicians are the most inept and incompetent class of alienist expert," Van Helsing surprisingly said, drawing himself up. "Every man who takes the degree of doctor supposedly becomes—as a consequence of taking such degree—a learned man. And it's slanderous to pronounce him ignorant. A doctor may be deaf, dumb and blind, stupid or mad, but still his diploma shields him from even the implication of ignorance. But as yet medicine possesses deficient means of treating, much less curing, this most grievous of human diseases. So we disapprove of a random application of medical remedies, which should be employed prudently and sparingly."

"What do you conclude when insanity is chronically attended with disease of the brain?"

"Even in dissected brains which show evidence of patholo-
gy or organic lesions, which are typically unrelated to any mental symptoms, we're not likely soon to acquire knowledge of
how far disease attacking any of the afflicted parts of the brain
may enhance, debase or otherwise change its functions."

"Then a systematic method of treating insanity would
seem to call for a strict study of the powers and workings of
the human mind," I proposed.

"Don't be discouraged to discover," Van Helsing admonished me, "that the physician should depend more on the power of mind over matter than of matter over mind."

Abraham Van Helsing led the way up the rear pair of
stairs, which were wide enough for us to step up abreast of
each other. It was a framed-up staircase with no well, constructed in two straight flights of steps, its lower flight coming
up to a half-landing halfway between floors, its upper flight
resuming the ascent. At length he showed me the way to a
round drawing-room hung with crimson Norwich damask, its
floor overlaid with a carpet of the manufacture of Moor-fields.
With a discreet parting gesture he left me alone to meet once
more with Dr. David Seward, who we found standing next to
a green and gold table at the great bow window, absent-mindedly fingering one of two boat-shaped vases of deep blue Seve
china with snake handles. His apparent reverie disrupted he
turned his mind to greeting me. He gestured for us to sit
down across from each other in chairs of Aubusson tapestry in
front of the window, which was growing dim with the fading
light of day.

"It's been said," Dr. Seward asserted solicitously, "that
there's no disease more to be dreaded than madness, for every
willful sin is madness, and madness amounts to the wages paid
for sin."

"And the lunatic is the payment incarnate for that sin?"

"Precisely," his eyes betrayed a suggestive glance. "Would
you then diagnose Safie as being sinful or insane?"

"Being as lucid and benign as Safie appears she should scarcely merit either title."

"Quite right," Dr. Seward nodded his accord. "In spite of the traditional notion that spiritual and mental afflictions are identical insanity is now seen less as a spiritual disease—in which the lunatic, possessed by the devil, is sinful or immoral—and more as an earthbound condition. So insanity is no longer diagnosed in terms of sin or possession by evil spirits. Even certain priests, who sometimes act as witnesses for certification, no longer consider insanity as the work of the devil, much less as a punishment from God."

"How then is insanity ordinarily diagnosed?"

"At present we tend to analyze sudden and substantial disturbances in the lives of prospective patients in trying to explain the reasons why they become deranged."

"Safie's abrupt flight from her country cottage would doubtless fit in consistent with that analysis."

"Like life," Dr. Seward overlooked my allusion to Safie's plight, "sanity hangs on a thin thread, exposed to ten thousand jars and jolts which we can neither see nor avert. I've seen insanity in all its forms and viewed its more subtle shades. And I've come to conclude that insanity is invariably a matter of degree."

"Don't you then draw the line somewhere between the sound and unsound mind?"

"I never saw any human being who was impeccably of sound mind," his tone turned impatient.

"Do you mean that quite literally?"

"Should you believe in God," he answered acidly, "then I dare say that He, and He alone, is of perfect sound mind."

"I've heard it said that the descent into insanity portends the divestment of the rational soul of all its divine and distinguishing endowments," I said, nodding my acknowledgment.

"Reason is seen as the essential trait of our humanity and so as the touchstone of sanity," Dr. Seward said, looking considerably downcast. "Having lost their reason the insane have been perceived purely as animals. This bestial view of the lunatic has been fortified by a much more archaic intellectual notion which regards the world as a great chain of being. Indeed the asylum itself has been regarded as a kind of wild animal farm, and its insane inmates as something akin to captive wild beasts."

"Then the chain of being orders our human existence."

"Man—the middle link in that chain—is situated where the transition takes place from lower sentient beings to higher intellectual ones. But the insane, having lost their reason, have fallen off the lowest rung of humanity and so take on an animal quality."

"Realizing that the essential quality of the insane is irrationality rather than animality must fundamentally affect the treatment of insanity," I suggested.

"Of necessity," Dr. Seward said, "if those deemed insane are believed to partake in some measure of the traits of the rest of humanity then rehabilitation is more likely to be prominent in their treatment. If they are seen as brutes, or as having lost their spiritual element, then discipline and coercion will most likely be the predominant method of treatment."

"To tame the wild beast?"

"That concept of insanity as a condition which demands taming, as somebody might domesticate a dumb animal, renders somewhat more predictable the behavior of the wild beast."

"Don't certain lunatics deport themselves like mad dogs?"

"Some of those who are seized with this disease do appear to act as wild beasts," Dr. Seward declared. "Nor do they differ much from them. They possess a monstrous brute strength and endure as well the severest cold, heat, hunger and thirst without suffering any appreciable harm. Certain lunatics can shatter cords and chains, break down doors or walls and readily overcome many struggling to subdue them. More extraordinarily still they almost never tire. Whatever they suffer or endure they aren't hurt; they bear beatings and punishment without any palpable harm—that's because the spirits, being powerful and persistent, are neither daunted nor take flight."

"What becomes of a lunatic so afflicted?"

"Such a forlorn creature," he heaved a sorrowful sigh, "looks forward to a wretched and humiliating existence: to attack his fellow creatures with ferocity like a wild beast; to be tied down, and even beaten to prevent his doing injury to himself or others; or on the contrary to be sad and desolate; to be continually terrified with vain delusions; to imagine spirits haunting him; and after a life spent in great anxiety to be convinced that his death will be the commencement of everlasting torment."

"Madness," I speculated, "must be as manageable as many other distempers, which are equally fearsome and stubborn, and still are not looked upon as incurable."

"Insanity is a most frightening and mysterious disease," he granted. "Its most extreme manifestations—frenzied ravings, deranged senses, deep depressions—are profoundly disturbing and disruptive events. They prompt a troubling reminder of the transient nature of the rule of reason."

"To what degree might disordered reason be a result rather than a cause of insanity?"

"Our perceptions of insanity are culturally sensitive," Dr. Seward said. "Explanations for what constitutes insanity reflect those beliefs and values prevalent at a particular time in society. Among those are the prevalent notions pertaining to insanity: stressing in patients characterized as insane their uncontrollable passions, an irrational mind and an undisciplined will suggests an implicit contrast with the abstract attributes of the sane. As viewpoints about humanity change so too the bounds between sanity and insanity also change."

"How then is insanity mostly explained at the present

time?"

"Essentially," he said, "insanity is constituted by the unexplained preternatural force with which certain irrational ideas dominate the mind, heedless of the natural corrective practices afforded by experience and conviction. It appears that a lunatic's loss of contact with our consensually defined reality, their spurning of common sense, must somehow reflect how deeply the chains of false impressions and associations are etched on their mentality."

"Notions about our rational nature scarcely evolve in a void," I said. "Certainly they must arise from a sound foundation in social intercourse. Aren't the ways in which mortals look at the world affected by their activity in it?"

"Deluded imagination," Dr. Seward propounded, "which is not only an indisputable but an essential trait of insanity sets itself well apart from all other carnal disorders. Man and man alone is suitably insane, who is utterly and unalterably convinced of the existence or the appearance of any thing, which either does not exist or actually appear to him, and who acts by such erroneous conviction—insanity, or false perception, being consistent then with a preternatural state or disorder of intellect."

"Of late I've heard insanity construed as an incorrect association of ideas."

"A morbid perversion of the passions, sensations and active powers can occur without any delusions or erroneous convictions impressed upon the mind," he clarified. "It sometimes exists with an apparently unimpaired state of mental faculties."

"In that event a particular lunatic could be seen as being responsible for his own affliction to some extent. Irrationality might even be perceived as the end product of individual choice rather than some outside origin."

"In some sense," Dr. Seward acceded, "the insane are in reality architects of their own misfortunes since their control over their emotions is deficient. Outside discipline should then be applied to correct them. Treatment of the insane reflects the extent to which this fluid boundary line between sanity and insanity is perceived as permeable."

"Then perceptions of even the lunatic himself have adapted to certain circumstances in the course of time?"

"At present," he nodded acquiescently, "the lunatic is perceived as a patient: a fellow creature to whom the alienist might minister, rather than an animal to whom he might administer conventional treatment."

"How then did this altered perception of the lunatic take place?"

"Evangelicalism," Dr. Seward explained, raising his eyebrows quizzically, "with its emphasis on the fellowship of man, set about to shatter the intellectual fetters of the great chain of being which before had fortified the belief in the lunatic as an animal. Evangelical influence strives to reunite the insane within humanity precisely because it stresses the essential likeness of all human beings before God."

"Evangelicals indeed!" caustically interjected a repulsively familiar and mocking voice. "Against all knowledge and logic these evangelical fanatics have insisted on inflicting the false hopes and consolations of faith upon those afflicted with insanity. If only these evangelical opiates and ointments could relieve a raving convulsion, or calm the distempers of the mind which are embodied by delusions and morbid animosities. Could they confer a scintilla of intellect on existing imbecility, or incite idiocy into understanding, the cure of this infirmity ought to be exclusively confided to the clergy. If on the other side these spectral therapeutics fail to subdue the disorder of insanity then, presumably, you can make no rational objection to entrust the entire treatment of this infirmity to the alienist practitioner."

And I looked unexpectedly aghast at the squat and squalid figure of M. Krempe, professor of natural philosophy at the university of Ingolstadt, darkening the doorway to the round drawing-room and staring down his surly nose straight at me. At that very same startling moment I worriedly riveted my eyes on a familiar leathern portmanteau which Professor Krempe clutched tightly in his hands. He promptly stepped up and plunked the hefty valise down onto the green and gold tabletop in front of us. I watched anxiously as his wrinkled fingertips tauntingly tapped the rigid rim of the suitcase, arresting my most rapt attention.

"M. Frankenstein," Professor Krempe addressed me jauntily, "I suspect that you've suffered some consternation over the disposition of these rather curious chemical instruments, which I took the liberty of removing to the villa from Ingolstadt on your behalf."

"Yes," my suddenly dry mouth moved feebly.

"Let me set your heart at rest," he hastened to add reassuringly. "I packed and conveyed your property with the most meticulous care."

"I thank you, sir," I said somewhat suspiciously.

"Might you acquaint us then with what function they perform?"

All at once I stood up, laid my grasping hands on my suitcase and cast my anxious eyes nervously back and forth between both professors, struggling desperately to collect my silently frantic thoughts. I sat back down, slowly, laying a firmer hold on my suitcase.

"With your indulgence," I gently suggested, directing my solicitous eyes to Dr. Seward, "I should like to defer my answer to your question until after I've been given leave to consult on a related matter of grave importance."

Dr. Seward nodded his accord.

"Then we shall discuss this apparently critical subject at dinner."

§

A lone footman attired in resplendent livery served our abounding dinner in the late afternoon from a sideboard in the great refectory, hung with paper in imitation stucco and lighted by windows of fine painted glass. We sat in black chairs of a gothic pattern at a table of Sicilian jasper on a black frame. A butler stayed at the sideboard with the wine while the footman waited at our table, treading across the Turkish carpet and setting out our unsparing courses of pike, fried sole, boiled beef, ham, fowls and goose, followed by puddings for dessert. After putting the main meat dish in front of our host to carve the footman attended to our individual desires by taking our plates to the dishes and filling our glasses at the sideboard.

"Permit me to propose a modest toast," I suggested at the last, lifting a customary glass to both Dr. Seward and Professor Krempe, "that we may each profit by a mutually beneficial and enlightening exchange of knowledge."

"What subject of inquiry in particular invites your interest?" Dr. Seward asked.

"Certification," I answered, grim-faced. "How does someone set about securing it for a special patient?"

"Patients are admitted by medical certificate," he explained. "Ordinarily this document originates in the patient's family and calls for signatures of two physicians. Other patients gain mandatory admission by a Lieutenant-Governor's warrant which designates a patient as dangerous either to self or to others. To secure this document petitioners give evidence before a Justice of the Peace who—if satisfied—commits the patient to prison. There the surgeon and one other physician—if in accord—issue a certificate which the county judge is obliged to do likewise. The Provincial Secretary reviews these certificates for completeness and then petitions the Inspector to issue a warrant for transfer of the patient from the prison to an asylum."

"What manner of evidence is given to support that document?"

"A deposition must be sworn. A predisposing or exciting cause for insanity is declared in each instance as gathered from the patient's case history, which accompanies the medical certificate at the patient's admission."

"What occurs once such evidence is given?"

"Petitioners submit the patient for examination by the Justices of the Peace who—if satisfied the patient is insane—commission a physician to conduct a further examination. If all are agreed a certificate of lunacy is duly signed and the patient is conveyed to the asylum."

"Does this procedure hold true for both private and country asylums?"

"Relatives or friends make a formal petition for reception of private patients and provide a formal statement of each case. Those same intermediaries are also constrained to petition a Justice of the Peace and to provide two medical certificates before a patient may be admitted under an ordinary reception order." Dr. Seward gestured suggestively to himself. "Physicians with an interest in a private asylum must certify admissions before two Justices of the Peace to the effect that the patient in question is in fact a lunatic or insane person."

"What other requisite documentation supports assignment of a patient to an asylum?"

"Along with the certificate of lunacy," he related, "must come the order of the Inspector, a copy of the judicial interdiction, letters from the patient's family and friends, as well as the medical certificate, which purports to prove that all attempts at cure have failed and that there is little likelihood of a swift return to reason."

"How reliable is medical diagnosis in such cases of lunacy?"

"Hereabouts," Dr. Seward scoffed contemptuously, "a man's ability to brandish a razor qualifies him to call himself a surgeon."

"Patients at the Refuge are then certified?"

"From its inception," Dr. Seward held up his head haughtily, "the Refuge has demanded a formal deposition from a physician or surgeon certifying that the patient admitted is insane. By law a separate examination and certification by two physicians are called for. So we admit patients either through the courts on a warrant, designating a potentially dangerous patient and demanding immediate confinement, or by a certificate bearing the signatures of two physicians and simply designating a patient of unsound mind."

"Under what circumstances are most patients admitted to the asylum?"

"Many patients are sent indiscriminately to the asylum," he admitted, lowering his tone, "not because they're dangerous or even troublesome, but simply because their relatives want to get rid of them. Most of those who are confined are doubtless at the instigation of relatives or other members of the family, whose depositions are supported by third parties."

"Must relatives invariably certify the insanity of the patient meant to be confined by depositions and witnesses?" I asked cautiously.

"Determined relatives," Dr. Seward cast his curious eyes on me, "can gain mandatory admission by circumventing discretionary certificates and, through testimony as to the violent nature of the patient securing a warrant instead, which of course calls for the intrusion of the courts."

"Before, you mentioned certain predisposing causes of insanity as evidence given for certification."

"Often the cause for admission isn't grossly abnormal or violent behavior but, rather, a determination on the part of the patient's petitioners to free themselves of the care and cost of their demented and comparatively harmless relations."

"I'm wholly determined to be free of him," I said in deathly earnest, abruptly lost in thought, "only he's far from harmless.

He's versed in raising the devil with a vengeance!"

"M. Frankenstein," Dr. Seward addressed me pointedly, "have you a relative whom you desire to dispose of, whose conduct you find so intolerable that you yourself are disposed to resort to certification in spite of the stigma it bears?"

"Perhaps," I said spiritlessly, puzzling in desperate despair over my forbidding predicament, "if only I could substantiate his inordinate insanity."

"In this day and age insanity amounts to unruliness," he said. "Petitions for certification are full of detailed accounts which make it quite evident that the patient to be confined acts in some outlandish fashion, isn't amenable to reason and constitutes a threat both to those closest to him and to society at large."

"His reason is lost," I looked scurrilously grave, "and he constitutes the most sinister threat to all the world."

"Most petitioners phrase things somewhat less harshly," Dr. Seward said, un-afflicted by my withering words, "but the import of their declarations is always the same: their relative is incapable of normal human contact, has no sense of responsibility, is bereft of reason and has turned the lives of the other members of the family into a living hell."

"He's incapable of human contact—normal or otherwise—because he himself is fiendishly inhuman!" I raved, quivering with rage. "He has no sense of humanity, is bereft of all fellow-feeling and intends to turn the lives of my family into a bloodthirsty slaughterhouse!"

"Such petitioners don't fail to declare that their relative is ungovernable, wreaks havoc and threatens to inflict calamity on their closest relations," he added, unperturbed. "Physicians do little more than substantiate their viewpoint."

I seethed, Professor Krempe looked silently thunderstruck and Dr. Seward cast his stoical eyes directly on me.

"Well M. Frankenstein," Dr. Seward repeated sedately, "have you a relative whom you wish to certify and admit to the asylum?"

"Yes!" I snapped. "I have a son! I have a murderous, hell-born, bastard son!"

TWELVE:
A BEING'S BIRTHRIGHT

"I learned from your papers that you were my father, my creator; and to whom could I apply with more fitness than to him who had given me life?"—Frankenstein's Monster

JOSEPH COVINO JR

D r. David Seward slapped down his palms and pressed flat and firm against the jasper tabletop as he abruptly stood up, making a wry face of restless resignation.

"Very well, M. Frankenstein," he said, conspicuously perturbed, "our servants have been promptly dismissed at your request. So now—if you please—will you kindly tell us how you came to the clear conclusion that your own son should be diagnosed as being dangerously and violently insane?"

"Strictly speaking," I hesitantly corrected him, "he isn't my son."

"Then he's illegitimate?"

"In a manner of speaking."

Dr. Seward listlessly threw up his hands and paced back and forth scarcely a few steps before sitting back down at the table, heaving a dissatisfied sigh. I kept cautiously silent.

"Petitioners invariably judge by outward appearances alone," he digressed. "They presume that they can perceive insanity in certain patterns of conduct which they believe are perceptible to almost anyone. They fancy that insanity betrays itself in a great many symptoms: an abnormal manner, a peculiar appearance, a strange way of speaking, eccentric habits. The afflicted patient looks insane, speaks gibberish and acts outlandish. Does this dubious descendant of yours display any such symptoms?"

"Do you doubt my ability to credibly diagnose insanity in my unnatural child?"

"I doubt your ability to diagnose your son—whether illegitimate or otherwise—as being either inhuman or unnatural," Dr. Seward said contrarily. "There's doubtless nothing wrong with a great many so-called lunatic patients. At least they don't demonstrate any mental disturbances or aberrant reactions. Many are confined at the solicitation of their relations purely and simply because they won't conform to prevailing norms of behavior. Many can be blamed for nothing more than that they've misbehaved. Has your own doubtful son misbehaved?"

"He's done the most atrocious mischief and pernicious harm."

"Some families consider confinement as a remedy for other maladies altogether," he shrugged off my disparaging words. "Indeed insanity often serves as an expedient euphemism for disorderly conduct. And certification can protect the family from the patient's aberrant or extreme behavior. Has your own child then been disorderly?"

"In his infernal merriment," I boiled with indignation, "the demon has callously murdered my little brother and false-ly incriminated an innocent girl of purity and virtue to death and disrepute."

"In that event," Dr. Seward finally relented, "certification warrants banishment of a disruptive patient while at the same time promising treatment and a possible cure."

"Suffering the most agonizing pain and punishment think-able is the only treatment which the demon deserves," I said virulently, "for I've unloosed on the world a wicked wretch who wallows in butchery and misery, and for whom there's no tolerable cure but a violent and torturous death!"

"Why do you bedevil us with such invidious words?" Dr. Seward scowled.

"As men who descend from Adam we're nothing but ashes and dust," I sobered down, "with nothing among us but mis-ery and wretchedness, conflict and strife, and this worldly life of ours is full of hatred, hostility and wrath, dissension and sorrow. Why then should we go on searching our bodies for what can't be found in them—and attribute to them faculties which they don't possess? Wouldn't it be better to believe that by patience we can master all things?"

"Including death itself?" Professor M. Krempe blurted out facetiously, finally breaking off his attentive silence. "I suspect rather fearfully that Herr Frankenstein has again reverted to squandering his time, indulging in the frivolous nonsense of alchemists and magicians."

"Only when the mortal body has died and passed away can we begin to search for the immortal body in which we would crave to live," I said, ignoring the professor's reviling words.

"M. Frankenstein," Dr. Seward chimed in, knotting his brows in confusion, "what is it exactly that you're bent on telling us?"

"Simply that nothing is so hidden in the world that man can't learn of it," I said in earnest. "So there's nothing on earth or in the sea, in chaos or in the sky which doesn't manifest itself at the appointed time."

"Then you infer that the appointed time has come for something heretofore hidden to become known?" Dr. Seward suggested.

I grinned a grave, ghastly smile but kept scrupulously silent.

"Will you be good enough then to unburden your mind to us?" he asked, conspicuously impatient.

"I have discovered the source of animation and life," I finally said solemnly. "No, more, I have become myself able to animate and put life into lifeless matter."

At once Dr. Seward and Professor Krempe looked aghast at each other after which they cast their expectant eyes on me.

"I see by the anxiety and awe which your eyes express," I anticipated their imminent inquisitiveness, "that you expect me to make you acquainted with the fatal secret which has come to my knowledge. I'm quite reticent on that subject and propose only to strike a compact with you for a mutual exchange of knowledge."

"What you see expressed in our eyes," Dr. Seward soundly contradicted me, "is considerable doubt and disbelief. How could you conceivably come to such staggering knowledge?"

"To study the source of life," I answered seriously, "I discovered that I had to resort to death."

"What should we be given to understand by that?" he persisted.

"*Paracelsus* was quite right," I recounted, "when he proposed that corruption is the beginning of all birth, and that decay transforms shape and substance—the forces and virtues of Nature. Decay is the instigator of prodigiously great things! It prompts many things to rot so that a noble fruit might be given birth, for it's the reversal—the death and destruction—of the original essence of all natural things. It generates the birth and rebirth of creations a thousand times regenerated."

"Do you imply," Dr. Seward asked skeptically, "that out of physical decomposition comes the creation of living things?"

"Philosophers have struggled to separate the good from the evil—and the pure from the impure—since ancient times," I affirmed. "All living things die but only the soul lives eternal. While the body decays the soul endures forever."

"What sort of living thing comes out of dry rot?" Professor Krempe asked sarcastically.

"What does it mean to rot?" I asked in turn. "Bear in mind that a seed must rot away if it's to bear fruit. To rot means only that the body decays while its essence—the good and the pure: the soul—survives and subsists. And once we appreciate that we possess the pearl of knowledge which contains all the virtues."

"Fewer virtues lie in mystical bombast than do in dry rot," Professor Krempe scoffed, looking down his imperious nose at me with disdain.

"I too was shocked and surprised," I quietly confessed, "that from among so many men of brilliance who had directed their study toward the same science, that I alone should be reserved to discover so astounding—and yet so simple—a secret."

"And precisely what secret is that?" Dr. Seward looked acutely expectant.

Mutely I muttered, straining to let out my reluctant reply.

"How to instill," I said, grudgingly giving grave voice to my averse answer, "a living soul into a lifeless body."

For a long time Dr. Seward and Professor Krempe stared at me incredulously, agape but speechless.

"Apparently," Professor Krempe said at length, sneering, "Herr Frankenstein has elevated himself to the supreme station of deification."

"Of course," Dr. Seward chimed in charily, "you can prove the truth of your rather extravagant assertion."

"My demon son literally embodies the truth of what I maintain," I put on a stoical face. "He's murderously insane and must of necessity be certified, only I can't risk exposing him to any prying Justice of the Peace. His certification must be kept an absolute secret."

"In effect," Dr. Seward said, unconvinced, "you seriously contend that the creature you call your demon son is a lifeless being whom you brought to life by infusing a soul?"

"Yes," I nodded my grudging acknowledgment. "I put life into a condemned killer hanged for strangling his victims to death."

"Perhaps," Professor Krempe mocked, "your questionable son's pec-cant pedigree duly accounts for his murderous tendencies."

"A decision to confine a close relation," Dr. Seward interjected, contriving vainly to discover some secret motive on my part for soliciting certification, "even when it's believed to be in the patient's best interests, can inspire profound feelings of grief and guilt, although treatment somewhat relieves the strong sense of guilt so often felt when confronted with an insane relative. Other afflicted families petition for confinement because they fancy that the conduct of the distraught patient will bring undue disgrace, and as a consequence, compromise their reputation."

"I act with a clear conscience," I said dispassionately, "and

I feel no guilt for conspiring to imprison forever a bloodthirsty monster that deserves to suffer only the most exquisitely painful punishment possible."

"You have no care that you could incur disgrace should your incredible creation reflect dishonor on your good name?"

"Quite the contrary," I differed. "I fear that I should disgrace myself worse should I fail to bury the devil in oblivion."

"Perhaps we shall discreetly resolve your extraordinary predicament after all," Dr. Seward suggested confidently. "Private asylums such as the Refuge can admit voluntary boarders and treat them without precursory certification. We can resort to this practice solely for patients who come voluntarily and comprehend what they're doing."

"You propose then that I should persuade the foul fiend to purposely present himself for reception at the asylum?"

"We should scarcely contain our anxiety while awaiting his most auspicious arrival," Professor Krempe jeered.

"Nor should I contain my own," I ignored his deriding words, "for the demon is in possession of some vitally important papers, which of necessity I must retrieve should you intend to acquire complete knowledge of my creation."

"Papers?" Professor Krempe asked, immediately intrigued.

"He holds my journal of the four months preceding his creation," I clarified, "in which I meticulously relate every step which I took in the course of my work."

A familiar young girl's voice, soft and gentle, unexpectedly interrupted our discourse.

"He must speak the truth," she said sympathetically, "for God lets nothing stand empty but fills everything. What would man be if no soul resided inside him? Man possesses a soul—and by it he and all men live and exist—in fullness and not in emptiness."

Suddenly we directed our eyes to sweet Safie—the sweet Arabian whose well-formed figure darkened the doorway to the refectory, arresting our attention.

"Safie," Dr. Seward addressed her worriedly, "you should be at rest in your room."

"Pray," Professor Krempe rudely interjected, "what has a doubtful God—much less any doubtful deity—to do with some artificial creation?"

"What good would the world be if it did not bear fruit?" Safie answered demurely. "And what good would the fruit be if it were hollow? None at all. Then God created nothing hollow but filled all things."

"I dare say," I hinted, harboring a deliberate design, "sweet Safie herself could very well bear fruit and help answer our purpose."

I caught a glimpse of Professor Krempe turning up his mannered nose at me.

"Don't make light of this treacherous task," I told them grimly, "for I created the thing of superhuman strength and stature. And contending with him could prove to be dangerous and deadly."

§

At the open doorstep to the shadowy anti-chapel I gently dipped my trembling fingertips into a holy-water-pot of earthenware, mildly rippling its placid bowl when I irresolutely crossed myself. In the lurid dark I sat down on an oaken gothic bench facing, directly opposite, a crucifix of bronze which glinted soothingly and protectively in the moonlight.

"Take heart," sweet Safie's voice consoled me from the somber blackness beyond the wrought iron gate, chained and padlocked, barring the entry to the chapel where she lay hidden and unseen. "They're arrogant, proud and imprudent men who imagine that there's no God and that they themselves are the masters of heaven and earth."

"I bear a much heavier burden than laboring in vain to defy the folly of unbelievers," I said solemnly.

"Arabians," she confided, "believe that camels bearing burdens are braced by the singing of their masters."

"Men carrying heavy loads who sing are strengthened as well," I said, "for singing revives and enlivens their strength, pacifies their enemies, calms the raving of madmen and dispels vain inventions."

"So profound is the power of song that it eases the mind, raises the spirit, renews the weary and heartens the desperate," she cheerily chimed in. "Do the canons of *Cornelius Agrippa* also inspire your plea for my song?"

"Only should your song allure the beast," I said, pulling a long face.

Looming ahead in the dead of night the unseen creature spread a towering, pendulous shadow across the woodsy footpath, winding up between facing rows of pedestals bolstering hefty Indian flower-tubs to the lofty chapel nestled snug among tall trees in a cloistered niche of the villa estate. Creeping, the creature moved slowly toward the chapel façade, built solidly of brick with a resplendent front of Portland stone. At length the undulating shadow fell short of throwing itself across the chapel's partly open door, from which flowed sweet Safie's voice in a mellow rhythm, swelling or falling away as she played her guitar and sang sacred airs from her native land.

"Safie's enchantingly sublime song still wrings tears of sadness and joy from my eyes," murmured the familiar but stifled voice of the devil from out of the lurid night.

Stunned, I caught a petrifying glimpse of the demon's gruesome face, reflected grotesquely in the gleaming bronze crucifix suspended dead ahead. Convulsively I flinched, casting my startled eyes on the wide open door, starkly darkened by the demon's huge and hulking form.

"Do you pretend then to possess a sensitive heart?" I asked

scornfully, shrinking and shivering in fear.

"Enlarged knowledge only divulged to me more clearly what a miserable derelict I am," he forlornly lamented. "I harbored hope, truly, but it evaporated when I saw my visage reflected in water, or my figure in the moonlight, even as that fragile image and that misshapen shadow."

"Do you truly suppose that you've acquired some nebulous knowledge?"

"From watching my fellow creatures," he recounted incredibly, "I learned to venerate their virtues and to denounce the vices of mankind."

"You presume too audaciously to fancy yourself to be equal to any mortal," I taunted him.

"From reading books," he rambled, unruffled, "I feel the most devout fervor for virtue swell within me, and aversion to vice, so far as I grasp the import of those terms, comparable as they are—as I employ them—to express pleasure and pain."

"You've become most proficient at inflicting pain!"

"Still I see vice as a remote evil," he harped on inexplicably. "Kindness and charity are ever-present all about me, inspiring inside me an aspiration to become a participant in the active setting where so many exemplary virtues are evoked and practiced."

"You preen yourself well to speak so speciously."

"I'm unformed in mind," he desponded. "I rely on none, I'm related to none, and there's none to mourn my ruination."

"You're as deformed in mind as in body," I said sullenly. "There are plenty to revel in your ruination."

"Like Adam," he deplored, "I'm seemingly joined by no bond to any other living thing. But his predicament was much different from mine in all respects. He was fashioned from the hands of God a perfect creation, happy and thriving, preserved by the special care of his Creator. He was permitted to confer with and learn from creatures of a superior character. But I'm miserable, powerless and alone. Often I see Lucifer as the more suitable symbol of my plight, for many times like him—when I witness the bliss of my fellow creatures—the bitter bile of envy burgeons inside me."

Unexpectedly the demon lumbered bodily through the doorway, stepping up in full view, his ghastly features illuminated by the luminous glow of moonlight. Cringing, I fell back and signaled silently to Safie to keep out of sight in the opaque gloom of the chapel.

"At times I let my thoughts—unrestrained by reason—to roam the gardens of Eden, and ventured to imagine kind and comely creatures condoling with my feelings and gladdening my gloom—their angelic faces breathing smiles of solace," he harped on, hovering menacingly over me. "But it's all a vision. No Eve salves my sadness nor shares my reveries. I'm alone. I recall Adam's plea to his Creator. But where's mine? You've forsaken me, and in the wrath of my heart, I curse you."

"I should curse you for butchering my little brother," I reminded him warily, 'but I pledged my word to create your Eve."

"Redeem your pledge promptly then, for I'm impatient."

"In turn," I insisted, "you must come to my aid whenever I demand it."

"What aid can I lend?"

"You yet carry in the pocket of your dress my journal, which you took from my laboratory."

"No doubt you recall your journal," he answered coyly, reaching deep into his dress pocket with his shriveled, yellowish hands, pulsating with transparent blood vessels as he pulled out into view my coveted record. "Here it is," he boasted, jauntily flaunting it before tucking it back tightly into his pocket, primly patting its protrusion with his gnarled fingertips.

"Everything's recounted in it which alludes to my accursed creation," the demon clamored in anguish. "All the particulars of that succession of odious events which generated it are exposed to view: the most meticulous account of my disgusting and repugnant countenance is rendered—in vernacular which etched your own terrors and made mine indelible. I shuddered at reading it. Detestable day when I came to life!"

"Blessed day when you meet your death!" I retorted unreservedly.

"Accursed creator!" he railed at me. "Why did you fashion a creature so monstrous that even you shrank from me in fear? God—in mercy—created man sublime and alluring after His own image. But my visage is an obscene mockery of yours—more horrific even from the very likeness. Lucifer had his compatriots—fellow demons—to revere and reassure him. But I'm alone and abominated."

"You're held in abomination for as much as you act abominably!"

"On you alone can I rely for comfort," the demon unhappily complained, "although towards you I cherish no feeling but that of hate. Cold-blooded, hardhearted creator! You bestowed on me feelings and emotions and then threw me out at large an object of the contempt and terror of mankind. But upon you and you alone can I lay any claim to sympathy and satisfaction, and from you I resolved to exact that justice which I futilely tried to claim from any other being who was cast in the human mold."

"Apart from dying a violent death," I asked irately, "what justice do you fabricate having a title to?"

"Acquiring knowledge of myself," he pleaded piteously. "My countenance is loathsome and my stature monstrous. What does this mean? Who am I? What am I? Where did I come from? Where am I going? These questions constantly recur but I'm powerless to answer them."

You're a devil from hell where you'll doubtless return, I bethought myself, glowering at him.

"What am I?" he repeated ruefully. "Of my creation and creator I'm completely oblivious. I am, as well, endowed with a countenance loathsomely deformed and hideous. When I look about I see or hear of none like me. From my earliest memory I have been as I now am in size and stature. I've never yet seen a creature who looked like me or who tried to consort with me."

What rational creature should undertake to consort with a vile devil, I bethought myself, still glowering.

"What am I?" he persisted. "The question once more recurs to be answered only with complaint. Am I, then, a monstrosity—a blight upon the world—from which all men abscond and whom all men scorn?"

"Perhaps," I finally relented, "it may be that I should help appease your curiosity and sate this thirst for knowledge in which you wish to wallow."

"I can't relate to you the anguish which these ruminations impose upon me," the devil lamented. "I try to dismiss them but sadness only grows with knowledge."

Surprisingly sweet Safie stepped up out of the somber blackness of the chapel, gently clenching from behind the bars of the wrought iron gate, casting her faultless face into the fluted shadow.

"What's come to your knowledge to sadden you so deeply?" she asked the demon sympathetically.

"Of what a curious character is knowledge!" he bellowed, a grisly grin creasing his yellowish cheeks and straight black lips. "It cleaves to the consciousness—when it has once laid hold of it—like a vine on the trellis. I wanted at times to dismiss from my mind all feeling and emotion, but I discovered that there was but one way to overpower the sensation of pain—and that was death—a condition of which I was afraid but didn't comprehend."

"To every living thing God has allotted a time to grow in lest it ripen before its time," Safie whispered warily. "Much happens before it bears fruit: first come the sprouting buds, then the shoots, then the flowers and then the fruits. But all are exposed to many fortunes, many kinds of danger before they have on their husks and are harvested. It's the same with man: he has his destination in death, for death is the harvester of the human spirit."

"And man cleaves all his days to what he acquired in his youth," I muttered reflectively.

"I draw nearer to my destination than my beginning," the demon moaned, "for I've never tasted my youth. Where after all are my friends and relations? No father watched over my childhood days, no mother favored me with smiles and embraces, or if they had, all my past existence is now a void—a blind spot in which I detect nothing."

"Perhaps," I quietly suggested, "men of learning at the asylum may aid you to understand the total nature of your mystifying existence."

"Indeed," the devil growled gutturally, laying a firm hold of the padlocked chain binding the bars of the wrought iron chapel gate. "Is man at once so powerful, so noble and virtuous, yet so depraved and corrupt?"

With one smooth, swift stroke the devil violently and readily wrenched the padlock and chain free from the bars, and flung them loudly to the floor.

"A feeble precaution," he scoffed defiantly. "Man appears at one time a pure descendant of evil, and at another as all which can be imagined as good and godly. To be a righteous and virtuous man appears the highest honor which can be conferred on a sensitive creature. To be depraved and corrupt, as many recorded have been, appears the worst debasement—a state more wretched than that of the disgusting maggot."

Menacingly the demon hovered high over sweet Safie, who slowly faded back into the chapel blackness, awestruck but undismayed.

"For a long time," he reflected, "I couldn't imagine how one man could go out to kill his fellow. But when I unraveled details of malice and murder my bewilderment ended, and I moved away with abhorrence and aversion."

"For to kill is forbidden under the penalty of forfeiting eternal life," Safie told him in a lenient tone.

"Then the slayer should suffer eternal death," the demon deduced broodingly. "Tell me more of death."

Fronting the chapel gate stood a resplendent shrine of mosaic, three stories in height, beneath which towered a crucifix inlaid with mother-of-pearl. At its foot rested a paneled altarpiece before which Safie bowed down.

"Death is the one who takes our life in many ways," she said solemnly. "Then let us be alert and vigilant, for he guides us to judgment—to render an account of our lives from the beginning to the end. He is the magistrate—the executioner—the summons to the judgment of God. And what does this summons mean? Nothing but this: the journey to God's judgment—at the appointed hour and on the appointed day—on the day of wrath—when heaven and earth will quake and crumble to dust—when the trumpets will awaken him who has been summoned. It's death who brings us the awakening and so returns to us what he's taken from us."

"What thing other than life can death take away from the living?" asked the bewildered devil.

"The very same thing which inspirits the hearer to feel moved by music," she told him tenderly.

"As I felt touched by your stirring song?"

"Truly," Safie said with a delicate nod, "the singer touches the affection of the hearer by her affection, and the hearer's fancy by her fancy, and mind by her mind, and impresses the mind and melts the heart, and pierces even to the innermost recesses of the soul."

"Soul?" the devil questioned, profoundly befuddled. "What pray is a soul? Have I a soul?"

Convulsively I flinched along with Safie when, without warning, a startling lightning bolt flashed across the chapel's painted glass windows, rattled by the booming peal of thunder, threatening the outburst of a rainstorm.

"What is as mighty and so powerful and so marvelous in its strength as lightning?" Safie asked, anxiously glancing all around. "Since Christ foretold that His second coming would be as lightning alighting from Heaven we must of necessity know the nature of lightning, for it strikes hard and heavy, and is so wondrous in Nature that man can scarcely conceive of it. To him who contemplates this let the lightning serve as a warning to commit no sin, or turn aside from the way of God."

What many men have mistakenly misconceived as some mysterious life-giving force, I bethought myself as I woefully watched sweet Safie depart hastily into the sudden downpour, is indeed a foreboding of eternal death!

THIRTEEN:
INSENSATE SENSATIONS

"I was a poor, helpless, miserable wretch; I knew, and could distinguish, nothing; but feeling pain invade me on all sides, I sat down and wept."—Frankenstein's Monster

Past midnight the lumbering devil followed me grudgingly into the great cloister, lagging sluggishly—but guardedly—behind as we slowly passed by eight ancient, turned Welsh chairs and four stands sparsely gracing the shadowed arcade. Going through a tenuous entry and across the impinging passage we reached the rear pair of stairs and climbed down, breathlessly wide-eyed, by fluttering lamplight to the dank and darksome corridor below. I led the devil to a secluded cell with its door already opened outwards. Our feet scuffed across its polished parquet floor as we shuffled together inside, squeezing ourselves into its cramped confines. I enjoined him to sit down on a chair next to a glinting metal bed, a shelf at its head, which was fixed to the floor. Wobblingly he perched himself and indignantly glared at me with his singularly yellow, watery but speculative eyes. I directed his attention to a bedside table set out with some tepid tea and tea cake.

"Refresh yourself and rest here for a time," I invited him.

"Am I to be given benevolent comfort?" he leered ironically at me.

"Your host intends that patients should enter this establishment free from distrust of those to whose care they're about to be entrusted," I said crossly. "He labors under the misguided illusion that even a bloodthirsty lunatic hasn't lost all claim to kindness and consideration."

"Shall I be treated as a patient," the devil asked with a scurrilous sneer, "or put on display as some freak monstrosity purely to appease the idle curiosity of some inquisitive alienist?"

"For the attending alienist at this asylum the lunatic is no longer a beast divested of all vestiges of humanity. To the contrary, he remains in essence a man—a man wanting in self-control and discipline, but a man whose deficient faculties might and must be restored to him."

"Then I should expect to be shown considerable compassion."

"Judicious compassion is reserved for fellow creatures still possessed of their essential humanity," my demeanor turned cold. "As you retain no remnants of humanity you no doubt deserve no such consideration."

"Pray, my dear creator, what remnants of humanity do you yet lay claim to?"

"Precious few to repudiate my despicable pledge to create—for you—a female companion of the same odious species."

"You're sworn," he admonished me menacingly, "to create a being as hideous and horrible as myself, endowed with the same deformities, who won't repudiate me, and with whom I can live as an equal in the mutual exchange of those emotions essential to our existence."

"To redeem my pledge," I reminded him, my attitude adamant, "I must consult together with the most celebrated natural philosopher at this asylum, whose knowledge and discoveries are indispensable to the completion of my most abhorrent task."

"Proceed promptly then with what you alone can do," he insisted, "for I demand it of you as a right which you must not begrudge me to grant."

"Very well," I conceded, heaving a vanquished sigh of surrender and admonishing him as I vacated his cell. "You must wait patiently for me to satisfy your demand while I confer to acquire the knowledge affecting accomplishment of my most detestable task: delivering into your destructive hands a female companion of the same murderous species!"

Sometime later on the weary but curious creature reached out to lay his gnarled hands on the abutting table top, fumbling to grab a crumbly piece of tea cake. He snapped it up and cast his voracious eyes on it. Greedily he gulped it down, swallowing it whole. Next he guzzled the cup of tea. Ruefully he recalled the first time he went in search of a place of shade in the forest close to Ingolstadt. There he lay by the edge of a stream resting from his tiredness until he felt afflicted by hunger and thirst. That stirred him from his almost listless state and he gobbled some berries which he found dangling from trees or scattered on the ground. He sated his thirst at the stream; and then lying down—he called to mind as he clambered laboriously onto the cell bed—he was overpowered by sleep.

Without warning the creature's whole body heaved convulsively. He lurched up in the bed clutching at his throat, retching violently. He recalled that it was dark before when he first awoke; he felt cold and impulsively half afraid, finding himself so miserable. Before he had left Frankenstein's apartment, on a prickling of cold, he had put on some clothes; but those weren't enough to protect him from the night damp. Off the bed and out of the cell he stumbled, vomiting savagely. He was a poor, powerless, forlorn sufferer; he knew and could discriminate nothing; but feeling pain afflict him on every side he slouched down and wailed loudly.

Along the lengthy corridor the devil staggered awkwardly, reeling to and fro, and gagged in wrenching surges. But he stopped dead in his tremulous tracks when he set his bleary eyes on me, darkening the doorway at the corridor's far end. He grinned his grisly smile, creasing his straight black lips as he abruptly came at me—his gangly arms outstretched; his gnarled hands grasping for some unsuspected throat. And as he drew near, lumbering headlong, I suddenly withdrew, disappearing conspicuously behind the darkened doorway. Toward the looming doorway the devil moved slowly and warily, rasping gutturally beneath his strained and strangulated breath. Ponderously he stepped up to the doorway, stumbled and floundered from side to side before stepping inside the lurid void. In another fleeting moment the devil growled and bellowed aloud, letting out a long and harrowed wail which by rapid degrees faded far away. And before long an abrupt and tumultuous splash of water could be heard clamorously filling the nebulous air.

"Wallow in your bath of surprise!" I shouted lustily at the top of my triumphant voice.

Torches ignited in sconces dully lighted up the spacious cellar, wholly wainscotted with coupled panels of Coromandel lacquer screens of China. An attendant of the asylum turned a wooden windlass, strenuously heaving its levers hand-over-hand until a huge iron cage was hoisted—by rolling rope and pulley—high up above the plunge bath sunk deep as a yawning well below the level of the cellar floor. Long arcs of flowing water spilled out from between the bars as the cage was lifted up toward the ceiling. And crumpled up in the bottom of the cage the devil lay still in a lumpish and leaden heap.

"With what did you incapacitate the foul fiend?" I asked Abraham Van Helsing, stepping up beside me.

"We laced the cake and tea with an emetic and sedative mixture," he explained, "combining chloral hydrate and potassium bromide for their sedative properties. Tartrate of antimony was added to induce nausea, which works to quell violence. We strengthened the dosage to compensate for your creature's great size and stature."

"It quenches even the most quiescent wild beast into quietness," boasted Dr. Seward, nodding in proud accord with his novice.

Other attendants scrambled ahead to lay hold of the dangling cage, being lowered heavily by the unwinding windlass, and guide it to the plane surface of the floor. Hurriedly they labored to put the devil under stringent restraint: reaching through the cage bars—without unbolting its shut gate—to bind him with iron handcuffs and leg-locks.

"Under no pretext," Dr. Seward pronounced, "do we tolerate either chains or physical punishment at this establishment. For those patients curiously disposed to mischief however gentle and efficient restraint is sometimes essential."

"Clapping patients in irons scarcely assumes the appearance of gentility," I said complacently, "although I suspect that extraordinary conditions could dictate that certain drastic steps should be taken."

"Originally," he gestured to the capacious chamber encompassing us, "this particular basement served as a wine cellar until uncouth alienists of times past converted it into this place of peculiar treatment."

"Salutary treatment, I trust."

"Salutary effect certainly was attributed to the employment of water euphemistically referred to as hydrotherapy."

"Is salutary restraint thought to be therapeutic too?"

"Absolutely," he asserted. "As a method of restraining the lunatic from acting upon the immediate impulse of his will, unrestrained by reason, external restraint invariably induces internal self-restraint."

"Should the most virulent and violent patients respond to treatment?"

"Restraining their virulence and violence is always essential to avert their hurting themselves or others," he elucidated. "Virulent passions are always rendered more violent by the indulgence of the impetuous notions they invent. And even in lunatics the sensation of restraint will oftentimes avert the efforts which their passion would otherwise excite."

Presently the asylum attendants put the devil under the most stringent restraint: a rigid iron ring was riveted about his neck, from which a short foot-long chain stretched to an iron ring linked to slide up and down on a solid upright bar installed erect into the wall. About his waist a solid iron bar was riveted, which fitted and girt each of his arms, pinning them down tight to his sides. Two bowed bars, hung over his shoulders, were riveted to the rounded body-bar both before and behind. A dual link coupled the iron ring around his neck to the bars on his shoulders, from each of which another short chain stretched to the ring hitched to the upright bar. Presently we stepped up to the devil, lying still and supine on the floor in a hushed, hulking heap.

"No better method could have been invented for restraining a patient of so dangerous a description," Dr. Seward blustered. "This particular contrivance is a convenient vestige of times past, for it kept under restraint one of the most malicious and malevolent madmen ever put on record. This nameless lunatic was reputed to be a most insensible being—little better than a brute—for he had not the least feeling whatever."

"As of now," I said contrarily, "your device restrains a devil unequaled in malice and malevolence."

Abruptly I bent my knee next to the motionless devil while groping his garments.

"I'm looking for my journal," I announced anxiously, "but I can't find it! It isn't here!"

Unexpectedly the devil stirred sluggishly, budged open his yellow, watery eyes, which he riveted venomously on me and grinned the ghastly smile which creased his shriveled face.

"I'm hardly the half-witted fool that you expected," he gloated listlessly. "Am I?"

§

Early in the morning we assembled to discourse atop a pair of stairs in the breakfast-room furnished with blue paper and blue and white linen. In the bow window black and yellow glass was set in plain blue glass. Over the chimney hung a glass framed in ebony, reflecting two blue and white flower-pots of Seve china, and two candlesticks with Chinese figures and china flowers. At the writing-table Dr. Seward jotted down some notes which he laid aside in an inlaid writing-box.

"Your sedative drugs worked wonders at tranquilizing the devil," I commended him.

"We consider these drugs to be conducive to restricting

circular flows of fluid and therefore to reducing congestion in the brain?"

"What of your own insight into the human brain?" I asked him opportunely.

"Knowledge of the brain," he said in a trenchant tone, "is the most difficult and vital aspect of advancing alienist science. Had I the secret of even one such brain—did I hold the key to the mind of even one such madman—I might advance my own branch of brain science to a perfect pitch."

"Your knowledge and discoveries of the brain are what I've come principally to discuss. And now we have captured a subject whose brain we might closely analyze."

"Brain or mind? To which do you allude?"

"Do you distinguish greatly between the two?"

"The faculties of the mind are clearly linked to the brain—or more accurately—are dependent upon that organ."

"Mind and body—being linked—are clearly dependent upon one another," I nodded my accord. "But by what means are mind and matter linked?"

"The mind is merely a function of the brain and wholly dependent upon it," Dr. Seward said assuredly. "Being a function of the brain mental faculties must be equivalent to the physiological processes which are their natural complement."

"Apparently," I said, considerably disconcerted, "you dispute the existence of the duality between mind and body. The mind—which is an immortal, immaterial and imperishable substance—is necessarily forced to function in this world through the medium of a material instrument: namely the brain."

"I'm an unabashed materialist," he admitted immodestly. "I dismiss the notion—or fiction—of some subtle invisible matter, vitalizing the visible textures of living things, as merely a demonstration of that penchant of the human mind, which has motivated men at all times to explain those phenomena—of which the causes are unclear—as the mysterious influence of imaginary supreme beings and their immediate divine intervention."

"Then you deny the divine immortality of the human soul?"

"I simply contend that the subtle distinction between mind and brain is illusory, and that mental events are then mere cerebral phenomena. Mind—so far as any single person's sense and consciousness are concerned—is purely material."

"Don't judge a living thing which will ultimately become visible by its existing and immediate invisibility," I rebutted him. "A child who's being conceived is already a man, although he's not yet visible. Already he resembles the visible man."

"Whether visible or invisible, developed or undeveloped, mature or immature," Dr. Seward shook his head, "man is merely material—not immaterial."

"He's both," I objected. "You must understand that man has two kinds of life—corporeal and sidereal. Therefore man has also a corporeal and a sidereal body—and both are one and are inseparable. The corporeal body—the body of flesh and blood—is in itself always dead. Only through the animation of the sidereal body does the motion of life enter the corporeal body."

"The seat of all natural sensation is in the nerves and the brain alone," unexpectedly interjected Professor M. Krempe, suddenly darkening the breakfast-room door, "and nowhere else."

"Shall we take up this speculative matter with our belatedly created guest?" Dr. Seward suggested—in deadly earnest jest.

§

Presently we stepped up to the sprawled devil, hedged about by a metal partition erected to close in the niche where he was confined. "At long last," Professor M. Krempe mocked flippantly, "I shall be privileged to witness firsthand my illustrious student's prodigiously superhuman creation!"

"However unsightly an apparatus," Dr. David Seward apologized, "it appears to have been, on the whole, rather a lenient and tempered precaution to take than a strict and stern imposition to assure the safety of the other patients and their keepers. At the same time we guard against exposing our distinguished guests and visitors to any potential danger."

As we came up closer to the cage the lolling devil unexpectedly budged, cumbrously hobbled, and struggled laboriously to stand. Professor Krempe recoiled abruptly from the cage, flinching in fear and revulsion.

"Have no care," Dr. Seward reassured him, "for the creature has been put under the most rigorous restraint."

"Good God!" Professor Krempe cried. "That thing deserves to be confined beneath all other beings of an animal nature, for he must have degraded himself in some degree from the human level, only to be reduced to the condition of brute creation, which remains subject to the domain of man!"

"My mind to me a kingdom is!" the devil bellowed.

"What does the accursed creature mean by that?" Professor Krempe scowled.

"As God Himself is infinite," I said, "and cannot be compelled by any, so too the mind of man is free and cannot be forced or bound."

"So you seriously contend that he's no composite, patchwork creature into which you improbably put life?" Dr. Seward asked skeptically.

"Inherent in everything is the virtue of being indivisible and simple—that isn't split apart or torn asunder, but is an undivided whole," I asserted. "What breeches are the best? Whole ones. Those which are mended and patched are the worst."

Looking askance at me, Dr. Seward turned to deliberately

and directly address the devil.

"I grievously regret putting you under such harsh restraint," he apologized, "but we felt we had no other alternative which would guarantee the safety of all patients at the asylum."

"Has my beneficent creator convinced you that I pose some ominous threat to your unprotected patients?" the devil derisively scoffed.

"Only that you bear close watching for safety's sake.

"Listen closely then to my story," the devil implored, "which is long and strange: and judge justly whether it's truly I or my sinister creator—Frankenstein—who poses the most threatening menace to mankind."

§

"It's with great difficulty that I recall the earliest term of my existence," the wretched creature recounted. "All of the incidents of that time seem muddled and vague. A curious profusion of sensations afflicted me and I saw, felt, heard and smelled all at one time; and it was, truly, a long time before I learned to discriminate among the functions of my several senses. Gradually, I recall, a brilliant light oppressed my senses so that I was compelled to close my eyes."

"It was a kind of divine light," I involuntarily volunteered.

"Divine light?" Dr. Seward echoed curiously.

"Knowledge which proceeds from our own reason's earliest impressions brings to light the conclusions at which we arrive," I said.

"Kindly elucidate."

"It's a kind of reality which convinces the understanding to cohere to it above all else," I clarified. "And so it elevates the understanding to something which transcends it, and this is why the mind is left with something of which it has no well-founded knowledge."

"Do you allude to the light by which our bodily sight is empowered to see things?" Dr. Seward persisted. "That light as such gives us no specific knowledge of any particular visible thing since it isn't the visible form of anything in particular."

"The light of rational impressions in the mind is more like the specific forms of visible things," I said, "by which our sight grasps particulars, and so these impressions lead to the specific knowledge of some definite thing."

"Blackness then overshadowed me and disturbed me" the creature complained, "but scarcely had I felt this when, by opening my eyes—as I presently surmise—the light irradiated me once more. I wandered and, I fancy, descended; but I directly discerned a considerable change in my sensations. Before, dark and obscure things encompassed me—immune to my sight or touch; but I immediately discovered that I could roam on at will—with no barriers which I couldn't either circumvent or overcome. The light became more onerous to me; and the warmth fatiguing me as I roamed."

"Nature ordains this order of powers in man," I said, "that by our external senses we might know material things."

"Before long," the creature continued, "a soft light illuminated the sky and struck me with a sensation of delight. I shuddered and saw a luminous and heavenly body arise from among the trees. I stared with a kind of bewilderment. It loomed ahead languidly but it illumined my way. I still felt cold when beneath one of the trees I found a large cape with which I draped myself, and reclined on the ground. No definite notions penetrated my mind. I felt light and darkness, hunger and thirst; infinite noises fell upon my ears; and on every side infinite scents assailed me: the sole thing which I could differentiate was the glowing moon, and I riveted my eyes on that with delight."

"Known to everyone," I told him, "are the five external senses—to which there are apportioned five bodily organs; being so ordered that they which are put in the more preeminent parts of the body possess a greater degree of purity."

"Several spans of night and day passed away," the creature continued, "and the globe of night had considerably waned when I started to differentiate my sensations from each other. I slowly and clearly saw the limpid stream which provided me with drink, and the trees which shaded me with branches and leafage. I was overjoyed when I first found that a sweet sound, which frequently fell upon my ears, emanated from the gullets of the little feathered and winged birds who had frequently obstructed the light from my eyes."

"Purest are those senses which perceive their objects farthest off," I said, "as seeing and hearing. Put in the uppermost place eyes are the purest and have an affinity with the nature of fire and light; then the ears hold the second order of place and purity, and are compared to the air."

"I started too to contemplate—with considerable clarity—the shapes which encompassed me," he related, "and to comprehend the confines of the shining canopy of heaven which overhung me. At times I attempted to mimic the sweet songs of the birds but was incapable. At times I wanted to express my sensations in my own tone, but the gross and garbled sounds which emanated from me startled me into stillness once more."

"Nostrils hold the third order," I said, "and maintain a middle nature between the air and the water: then the organ of tasting, which is grosser and most like to the nature of water: smelling and taste don't perceive but those which are near. Last of all, touching is dispersed through the whole body and is compared to the grossness of Earth. But the touch perceives both ways, for it perceives bodies near; and as sight perceives through the medium of the air, so the touch perceives—through the medium of a stock or pole—bodies hard, soft and moist."

"The moon had vanished from the night," the creature deplored, "and once more—with a diminished shape—manifested itself while I yet stayed in the forest. My sensations had by that time grown sharp, and my mind absorbed every day more impressions. My eyes grew used to the light and to discern things in their precise shapes; I differentiated the worm from the herb and, gradually, one herb from another. I discovered that the sparrow emitted none but coarse tones while those of the blackbird and thrush were lush and enchanting."

"Touch alone is common to all animals," Dr. Seward objected, "for it's most certain that man has this sense—and in this and taste—he excels all other animals, but in the other three he's excelled by some animals—as by the dog who hears, sees and smells more acutely than man; and eagles and the lynx see more keenly than all other animals—and man."

"Just what has any of this mystical drivel to do with that frightful monster there?" Professor Krempe protested, perturbed and pointing at the creature.

"Remember that the four tempers are rooted in the body of man as in garden mold," I said.

"Alchemistic gibberish!" Professor Krempe sniffed.

"The body has four sorts of taste," I disregarded his disdain, "the bitter, the sour, the sweet and the salty. They're to be found in every creature, but only in man can they be scrutinized. Everything bitter is hot and dry—that's to say choleric; everything sour is cold and dry—that's to say melancholic. The sweet gives rise to the phlegmatic, for everything sweet is cold and moist, even though it mustn't be compared to water. The sanguine originates in the salty, which is hot and moist. If the salty predominates in man as compared with the three others he's sanguine; if the bitter is predominant in him he's choleric. The sour makes him melancholic, and the sweet—if it predominates—phlegmatic."

"Pray," Professor Krempe interrupted impatiently, "what temperament predominates in that ghastly monstrosity?"

"Everything that's within can be known by what's without," I answered assuredly. "We men discover everything which lies hidden by external signs and manifestations. There's nothing that man is unable to discover; everything's revealed to him by corresponding signs."

"What kinds of signs?" Professor Krempe sniggered.

"There's nothing in man which isn't marked in his exterior," I said, "so that by the exterior we can discover what's in the being who bears the sign."

"How then shall we interpret the signs which mark the exterior of this unsightly creature?" he scoffed.

"I'd marveled at the flawless forms of human beings," the caged creature surprisingly responded, "their delicacy, comeliness and graceful aspect: but how I was horrified when I saw myself in a limpid pool! At first I sprang back, unable to accept that it was truly I who was mirrored in the reflection; and when I became completely persuaded that I was indeed the monster that I am, I was infested with the bitterest sensations of dejection and degradation. Alas! I still didn't fully know the lethal aftermath of this wretched disfigurement."

"Any signs which mark the exterior of this monstrous beast," I said with scurrilous contempt, "are strictly choleric."

FOURTEEN:
EMOTIVE EMOTIONS

"If such lovely creatures were miserable, it was less strange that I, an imperfect and solitary being, should be wretched."—
Frankenstein's Monster

"Once when I was afflicted with cold," the creature recounted, "I found a fire which had been abandoned by some roaming paupers, and was overwhelmed with joy at the warmth I felt from it. In my euphoria I plunged my hand into the smoldering cinders but quickly pulled it out again with an outcry of searing pain. How curious, I thought, that the same source should enkindle such reverse results! I inspected the embers of the fire, and to my delight found it to be made of wood. I hurriedly gathered some branches; but they were moist and wouldn't burn. I was disappointed at that; and sat silent watching the working of the flame. The moist wood which I had put next to the heat dried and itself ignited. I contemplated that; and by handling several branches I ascertained the source, and occupied myself with gathering an abundant amount of wood that I might dry it and have an ample store of fire. When night fell and induced sleep I was deeply afraid for fear that my fire should be snuffed out. I covered it with dried wood and leaves and put moist branches on it; and then, spreading my cape, I lay down on the ground and slipped into sleep."

"All things must go through fire to attain to a new birth," I said, "in which they're useful to man."

"It was daybreak when I awoke," the creature continued, "and my first concern was to examine the fire. I uncovered it and a mild breath of air swiftly blew up a flame. I noticed that too and fashioned a fan of branches, which enkindled the cinders when they were almost smothered. When night fell once more I discovered—with delight—that the fire emitted light as well as heat; and that the detection of this element was of use to me in my food, for I found some of the remnants which the ramblers had left behind had been roasted, and tasted much more flavorful than the berries I picked from the trees. I attempted then to cook my food in the same way, putting it on the smoldering cinders. I discovered that the berries were ruined by this action, and the nuts and roots much enhanced."

"Nature is the artisan," I attested. "She endows everything with the form which is also the essence, and so the form reveals the essence. There's nothing which Nature hasn't signed in such a way that man may discover its essence."

"Food, though, grew scant," the creature lamented. "And I frequently spent the entire day looking futilely for a few acorns to ease my pangs of hunger. When I discovered that, I decided to leave the spot which I'd before haunted to search for one where the few cravings I felt would be more readily gratified. In this migration I supremely deplored the loss of the fire which I'd acquired by chance, and knew not how to reconstruct it. I spent several hours giving earnest thought to this predicament; but I was compelled to give up all attempts to resolve it; and, bundling myself up in my cape, I set out across the woodlands towards the sinking sun. I spent three days in this roving and finally found the free spaces. A heavy flurry of snow had fallen the night before, and the fields were one un-separated sheet of white; the sight was desolate and I felt my feet chilled by the pinching dampness outside which overspread the ground."

"The same is true of man," I said, returning to my uncompleted sentiment.

"What's true?" Professor M. Krempe snickered.

"Man is endowed with a form corresponding to his inner nature, for the human shape is a sign which reveals what a given man is. Let the devil tell how the countryman he encountered interpreted the outward signs which betrayed his innermost nature."

"It was almost seven in the morning," the creature continued, "and I yearned to find food and sanctuary; finally I sighted a little hut on sloping ground, which had no doubt been raised for the use of some shepherd. This was a fresh sight to me; and I inspected the structure, burning with curiosity. Finding the door ajar I stepped in. An old man sat inside fast by a fire, over which he was cooking his breakfast. He turned upon hearing a sound; and seeing me bellowed aloud, and leaving the hut scurried across the fields at a pace of which his feeble frame scarcely seemed capable. His face—more distinctive than I'd ever before seen—and his flight rather startled me. But I was entranced by the aspect of the hut: here the rain and snow couldn't infiltrate; the ground was dry; and it accorded me an excellent and exemplary refuge. I gluttonously devoured the vestiges of the shepherd's breakfast, which was made up of bread, cheese, milk and wine; the last though I disliked. Then, overwhelmed by exhaustion, I lay down among some straw and went to sleep.

"It was noon when I awoke; and enticed by the warmth of the sun, which blazed brilliantly on the white ground, I resolved to resume my migration; and, putting away the remnants of the peasant's breakfast in a pouch I found, I rambled across the fields for several hours until at sundown, I came to a village. How marvelous did this look! The huts, the tidier cottages and majestic houses struck me with awe by turns. The vegetables in the gardens, the cheese and milk which I saw put in the windows of some of the cottages tempted my appetite. One of the best of these I went in; but I had scarcely set my foot on the doorsill before the children squealed and one of the women fainted. The entire village was incited; some ran away, some assailed me—until badly battered by stones and many other sorts of projectiles—I absconded to the free spaces and frightfully took sanctuary in a low hovel, quite empty, and assuming a miserable appearance after the mansions I'd seen in the village. This hovel though abutted a cottage of a tidy and dainty aspect; but after my last costly experience, I dared not venture into it. My place of asylum was made of wood, but so low that I could scarcely sit erect in it. Now wood though was put on the ground which made up the floor, but it was dry; and although the wind infiltrated it by countless crevices, I found it a pleasant sanctuary from the rain and snow."

"When a carpenter builds a house," I said, "it first lives in him as an idea; and the house is built by this idea. From the framework of the house you can make inferences about the carpenter's ideas and images."

"As soon as day broke," the creature continued, "I crawled from my hovel that I might inspect the adjoining cottage and learn if I could stay in the hovel I'd found. It was set up against the rear of the cottage and encircled around the edges which were exposed to a pigsty and a limpid pool of water. One section was open and by that I'd crawled in; but now I covered every crack by which I might be seen with stones and wood, but in such a way that I might remove them occasionally to go out: all the light I relished passed through the sty and that was enough for me. Having so put in order my hovel and overspread it with fresh straw I slept; I had first though supplied my subsistence for that day by a loaf of grainy bread, which I pilfered, and a cup with which I could drain, more readily than from my hand, from the clear water which streamed by my refuge. The floor was slightly elevated so that it was kept impeccably dry, and by its proximity to the chimney of the cottage it was bearably warm."

"What Nature has in view," I said, "no one can know until it has assumed form and shape. Now note well that virtue fashions the shape of man just as the carpenter's ideas manifest themselves in his house; and a man's body takes shape by the nature of his soul. Nature acts no differently. She endows man with an outward appearance which is consistent with his inner constitution. And each man's soul can be recognized just as the carpenter can be known by his house."

"Being so provisioned," the creature concluded, "I decided to dwell in this hovel until something should happen which might change my decision. It was truly an Eden contrasted with the desolate forest, my past habitation, the rain-dripping branches and damp earth."

"Tell us more then of what transpired while you dwelled in this hovel," urged Dr. Seward, visibly intrigued.

"Upon inspecting my hovel," the creature continued, "I discovered that one of the windows of the cottage had before adjoined a section of it, but the panes had been shut up with wood. In one plank was a threadlike and nearly indiscernible crack through which my eye could barely see. Through this crack a small room was exposed to view, neat and whitewashed, yet mostly empty of furnishings. My style of life in my hovel was monotonous. During the morning I observed the activity of the inhabiting cottagers; and when they were engaged in their many employments I slept; the rest of the day was spent in watching these neighbors. When they had gone to sleep—if there was any moonlight or starlight—I ventured into the woodlands and gathered my own food. I spent my whole winter in this way."

"Can you render an account of these cottagers?" Dr. Seward asked.

"There were three," he enumerated. "The youngest was a tender girl of gentle disposition who tempted my affection. She was shabbily clothed, a coarse blue petticoat and a linen jacket being her only dress. Her fine hair was braided but not arrayed; she looked subdued but sad. She occupied herself carrying pails of milk squeezed out from one cow in their milk-house, preparing food, putting their cottage in order and tending their yard and garden."

"And the others?"

"There was a young man," the creature said, "whose face expressed a profounder sadness and who pronounced sounds with an air of despair. He busied himself toiling in the fields with his tools, drawing water from their well, and carrying loads of firewood gathered for the family fire on his shoulders. In one niche of the cottage, fast by a small fire, often sat an old man resting his head on his hands in a dejected and reflective posture. The silvery hair and kindly face of the venerable cottager inspired my respect. The young man was continually occupied outside and the girl in several arduous tasks inside. Together they would go into the garden and engage themselves, digging and grubbing up plants and roots, soaking them in water and then cooking them on the fire. The old man, whom I directly discerned to be blind, filled his idle hours on his musical instrument or in deep reflection. Nothing could surpass the affection and esteem which the younger cottagers demonstrated towards their venerated elder. They discharged towards him every small duty of devotion and regard with tenderness; and he repaid them by his kindly smiles."

"What qualities possessed by this family in particular intrigued you most?"

"The mild deportment and delicacy of the cottagers deeply enamored me of them," the creature declared. "When they were sad I felt downcast; when they exulted I empathized with their jubilation. The old man, I could discern, frequently tried to hearten his children—as at times I discovered that he called them—to dispel their despair. He would speak in a cheery tone of voice with a look of kindliness which afforded pleasure even on me. The young girl listened with due respect, her eyes at times welling out with tears, which she attempted to wipe away unseen; but I mostly discovered that her face and feeling were more contented after having heard the counsel of her elder. It wasn't so with the young man. He was always the unhappiest of the three, and even to my unskilled senses, he seemed to have endured more profoundly than his companions. But if his face was more mournful his voice was more joyful than that of the girl, especially when he spoke to the old man."

"What other activity in particular attracted your attention?"

"Every day at noon," the creature recalled, "the old man, leaning on the arm of the young man, strolled in front of the cottage in the sun for a time when it didn't rain—as I discovered it was called when the heavens spilled their water. Nothing could surpass in splendor the disparity between these two exemplary creatures. One was old with silvery hair and a face glowing with kindness and affection: the younger was slender and willowy in his shape and his face was cast in the finest form; but his eyes and his demeanor expressed the utmost depression and despair.

"Night would quickly fall; but to my utter astonishment I discovered that the cottagers had a method of protracting light by the employment of tapers, and was pleased to discover that the sunset didn't bring to an end the enjoyment I experienced in scrutinizing my fellow creatures. In the evening the old man once more picked up the musical instrument which emitted the heavenly sounds which had fascinated me in the morning. As soon as he had finished the young man started, not to play but to give utterance to sounds which were monotonous and sounded like neither the tones of the old man's instrument nor the songs of the birds: I since discovered that he read aloud to his companions, but at the time I was ignorant of the art of words or letters."

"How did you acquire knowledge of words and letters?"

"Gradually I made a discovery of great import," the creature explained. "I discovered that these people commanded a medium of expressing their emotions and experiences to each other by eloquent sounds. I discerned that the words they uttered at times evoked pleasure or pain, sadness or joy in the minds and faces of the listeners. This was truly a heavenly art and I fervently aspired to acquaint myself with it. But I was frustrated in each effort I made for this object. Their articulation was fast; and the words they gave utterance to—not having any seeming correlation to seeable things—I was unable to find any solution by which I could decipher the secret of their association. By great diligence, though, and after having stayed during a span of several rotations of the moon in my hovel, I found the names which were assigned to some of the most recognizable subjects of conversation."

"Names such as?"

"I mastered and used the words bread, milk, fire and wood," the creature roistered. "I mastered too the names of the cottagers themselves. The old man answered to only one, which was father. The young girl was called Agatha or sister, and the young man, Felix, brother or son. I can't express the gratification I felt when I mastered the concepts assigned to each of these sounds and was able to enunciate them. I differentiated several other words without being able just then to comprehend or employ them, such as dearest, good, unhappy."

"How did you differentiate between reading and speaking?"

"Felix reading to the old man and Agatha had confounded me deeply at first," the creature complained. "But gradually I found that he pronounced many of the same sounds when he read as when he spoke. I supposed then that he perceived on the paper signs for speech which he comprehended, and I fervently yearned to conceive these as well; but how was that thinkable when I didn't even comprehend the sounds for which they signified as signs? I developed though perceptively in this art, but not enough to carry on any conversation, although I employed my whole mind to the effort: for I readily discerned that although I earnestly yearned to reveal myself to the cottagers, I shouldn't make the effort until I had first become adept at their language; which mastery might empower me to compel them to ignore the ugliness of my form. These notions elated me and inspired me to persevere with fresh fervor to master the art of language. My voice was really rough but pliable; and although it was very different from the sweet tones of their speech, I still verbalized such words as I knew with passable skill."

"What motivated your desire to divulge yourself to the cottagers?"

"What mostly affected me," the creature said, "was the gentle deportment of these people; and I yearned to join them but dared not. I recalled too well the treatment I had endured before from the barbaric villagers, and determined—whatever line of conduct I might eventually consider it proper to prosecute—that for the time being I would stay still in my hovel, observing and striving to find the intentions which motivated their conduct."

"What course of action did you finally decide to adopt?"

"My thoughts presently grew more astute," the creature construed, "and I yearned to ascertain the aims and emotions of these delicate creatures; I was curious to learn why Felix looked so forlorn and Agatha so mournful. I fancied—witless outcast!—that it might be in my power to restore contentment to these exemplary people. When I slumbered or slipped away the faces of the revered blind father, the gentle Agatha and the noble Felix darted in front of me. I imagined them supreme beings, who would be the judges of my imminent fate. I conjured up a thousand visions of introducing myself to them and their reception of me. I presumed that they would be repelled until, by my mild manner and reassuring words, I should first earn their esteem and afterwards their affection."

"Did you perceive that something depressed the family's spirits?"

"They were not wholly happy," the creature condoled. "Felix and Agatha frequently went alone and seemed to cry. I saw no source of their sorrow but I was profoundly moved by it. But why were these kindly creatures sad? They had enjoyed a cozy cottage—for such it was in my mind—and every comfort; they had a fire to warm them when cold and delectable food when hungry; they were clothed in admirable garb; and—yet more—they rejoiced in each other's companionship and conversation, exchanging every day expressions of endearment and tenderness. What did their weeping mean? Did it truly express distress? I was at first incapable of answering these questions; but persistent scrutiny and time clarified to me many sights which were at first mystifying."

"Did you finally find the cause of their distress?"

"A substantial lapse of time passed before I found one of the sources of the anxiety of this kindly family," the creature deplored. "It was privation and they endured that evil to a very deplorable degree."

"How did you determine that?"

"They frequently—I think—endured the pangs of hunger very painfully, especially the two younger cottagers; for many times they put food in front of the old man when they saved none for themselves."

"That act of kindness affected you?"

"This quality of kindness touched me deeply," the creature confided. "I had been used—during the night—to pilfer a portion of their hoard for my own ingestion; but when I discovered that in doing that I inflicted suffering on the cottagers I abstained, and appeased myself with berries, nuts and roots which I collected from a bordering woodland."

"Did you do anything else to unburden their plight?"

"I found as well another medium through which I was empowered to lighten their labor. I discovered that Felix spent a great deal of every day gathering wood for the family fire; and during the night I frequently took his tools—the use of which I readily mastered—and carried firewood enough to furnish their home with fuel for several days."

"How did the family respond to your act of kindness?"

"I recall the first time that I did that, Agatha, when she opened up the door in the morning, looked deeply dumbfounded upon beholding a huge heap of firewood on the outside. She blurted out some words in a clamorous voice and Felix joined her, who also expressed bewilderment. Then he carried firewood from the out-house where—to his neverending amazement—he discovered his store always restocked by some unseen hand. When I returned from gathering firewood from the cottage—as frequently as it was needful—I cleared their footpath from the snow and discharged those duties which I had observed done by Felix. I afterwards discovered that these exertions—done by some unseen hand—deeply astounded them; and sometimes I overheard them on occasions give utterance to the words ministering spirit and miraculous; but I did not then comprehend the significance of these words."

"What lessons about humanity did your humble experience teach you?"

"Each conversation of the cottagers then opened my eyes to new marvels," the creature rejoiced. "The curious arrangement of human society was described to me. I heard of the distribution of property and wealth; of aristocratic rank, titled descent and noble lineage. The terms motivated me to turn my mind inwardly towards myself. I learned that the possessions most prized by your fellow creatures are highborn and uncorrupted descent coupled with riches. A man might be esteemed with only one of these conditions; but without either he was considered—except in highly uncommon cases—as a pauper or a serf destined to waste his talents and abilities for the advantage and gain of the select few!"

Dr. Seward turned to me with a simpering smile showing on his face.

"Do you still contend that this creature is wanting in sanguine, phlegmatic or even melancholic tempers?" he smirked.

"If we want to make a serious statement about a man's nature on the basis of his physiognomy," I granted grudgingly, "we must take everything into account: it's in his distress that a man is tested, for then his true nature is revealed; for in their most extreme things reveal their nature and show themselves in their truest light. Then we can judge: he's an honest man, a forthright man, a steadfast man—he betrays his innermost being. One man reveals more traits of loyalty and less of disloyalty; one man is to a great extent this, another that. Therefore we should examine closely the outward characteristics which Nature endows a man by casting him in a certain mold."

"Then this wretched creature is wholly human," Dr. Seward scrupulously concluded, "but whether you actually infused life into him is another matter altogether."

"The nature of each man's soul accords with the design of his arteries and lineaments," I insisted. "The same is true of the face, which is fashioned and shaped by the composition of his mind and soul, and the same is again true of the proportions of the human body; for the sculptress of Nature is so artful that she does not mold the soul to fit the form, but the form to fit the soul."

"In other words..."

"The form of a man is shaped by the conduct of his heart."

"One man is large in his limbs," a familiar, gentle voice interjected, "another to the contrary is slender and slight. Which of the two should be commended and which condemned? Neither: for both have hearts, stomachs and intestines, red flesh, red blood, bones, marrow and hair. Their brains are developed, although they may be wanting in intelligence. Therefore you shouldn't judge men by their size and stature, but honor them all equally. What is in you is in all. Each has what you also have within you. And the poor grow the same plants in their gardens as the prosperous."

Safie, the sweet Arabian, suddenly darkened the cellar door and stepped up softly to the creature's cage, surprising us.

"The just way resides in work and action," she said, "in doing and producing. The perverse man does nothing but talks a lot. We mustn't judge a man by his words but by his heart. His heart speaks through words only when they are demonstrated by deeds."

"What else except murderous deeds have demonstrated the devious words which flow from that devil's wicked heart?" I seethed.

"Once," the creature lifted his stifled voice, startling us, "Agatha took something out of a drawer which occupied her hands and sat down alongside her father, who picking up his musical instrument started to play and to give out sounds more lush than the song of the thrush or the nightingale. It was a beautiful sight, even to me—wretched outcast!—who had never seen anything of beauty before. He played a sweet sorrowful song, which I noticed wrung tears from the eyes of his tender daughter—of which her father gave no attention until she cried audibly; he then uttered some sounds and the delicate creature, stopping her task, knelt at his feet. He lifted her and smiled with such tenderness and affection that I felt emotions of a curious and overwhelming nature: they were a combination of pain and pleasure such as I'd never before felt—either from hunger or thirst, cold or warmth—and I moved away from the window unable to endure these emotions."

"All of us should know," Safie gently exhorted us, "that art, science and skill exist only to be conducive to peace, joy, unity, purity, dignity—to gratify our needs and help us to serve our fellow man. This is also true of music. It's the remedy for all who suffer melancholy and delusion—disorders which ultimately make them desperate and solitary. But music has power to keep them in human company and preserve their minds."

"Now I remember everything," the creature murmured, looking upon Safie with a knowing and melting expression. "You remind me of events which impressed me with emotions which, from what I had been, have made me what I am."

"I humbly beg your pardon," Safie craved the creature contritely, "for when I first beheld you I fled from you in terror and dismay. I am sorry for it and I ask for your forgiveness."

Startlingly Safie held out her fragile hand, reached easily through the partition bars and caressed, softly and soothingly the creature's shriveled face, pulsating with its transparent arteries and musculature. She cast her gentle eyes, penitent and imploring, directly onto the creature's eyes—yellow, watery, no longer speculative but stirred, softened and welling out with untrammeled tears.

FIFTEEN:
A MONSTER'S ENMITY

"There was none among the myriads of men that existed who would pity or assist me; and should I feel kindness towards my enemies? No: from that moment I declared ever-lasting war against the species, and, more than all, against him who had formed me, and sent me forth to this insupportable misery."—
Frankenstein's Monster

JOSEPH COVINO JR

Thunderstruck Dr. David Seward stood aghast.

"When did you first set eyes on our sweet Safie?" he asked the creature incredulously.

"It was on a refreshing spring day," the creature reminisced, "when my cottagers customarily rested from toil—the old man played on his guitar and his children listened to him—that I noticed the face of Felix was sad beyond expression. He sighed often, and once his father ceased in his music I surmised from his manner that he asked the source of his son's sadness. Felix answered in a blithe tone, and the old man was resuming his music when somebody rapped at the door."

"Someone paid your cottagers a visit?"

"It was a lady on horseback," the creature attested, "attended by a countryman as a guide. The lady was attired in a dark suit and wrapped with a thick black veil. Agatha asked a question—to which the visitor only answered by enunciating, in a sweet accent, the name of Felix. Her voice was lyrical but unlike that of either of my neighbors. Upon overhearing his name Felix stepped up impatiently to the lady, who when she recognized him, cast off her veil. It was sweet Safie."

"They must've been overjoyed to greet each other again."

"Felix looked enraptured with joy when he saw her, every suggestion of sadness faded from his face, and it immediately expressed a rapturous delight of which I could scarcely have thought it capable. His eyes flashed as his cheek blushed with bliss; and at that instant I believed him as sublime as the visitor. She looked afflicted by disparate emotions; wiping some tears from her beautiful eyes she held out her hand to Felix, who kissed it sumptuously and called her—as well as I could tell—his sweet Arabian. She didn't seem to understand him but smiled. He helped her to dismount, discharged her guide and led her into the cottage. Some conversation was being carried on between him and his father; and the young visitor knelt at the old man's feet and would have kissed his hand but he lifted her, and enfolded her lovingly."

"How did your French family manage to communicate with their sweet Arabian?"

"I soon discerned," the creature explained, "that although the visitor enunciated eloquent sounds, and seemed to speak a language of her own, she was neither understood by, nor herself understood the cottagers. They made many signs which I didn't understand; but I perceived that her presence spread delight throughout the cottage, dispelling their sadness. Felix appeared exceptionally pleased, and with smiles of joy embraced his Arabian. Agatha, always gentle, kissed the hands of the beautiful visitor; and gesturing to her brother, made signs which seemed to me to mean that he had been sad until she came. So some time passed while they, by their faces, expressed rapture—the source of which I didn't understand. Soon I discovered, by the constant recurrence of some sound which the visitor repeated after them, that she was struggling to learn their language; and the notion immediately suggested itself to me that I should take advantage of the same guidance to the same goal. The visitor learned about twenty words at the first lesson, most of them—truly—were those which I had before mastered, but I benefited from the others. I fervently desired to understand them and strained every nerve toward that end, but at first found it totally unthinkable."

"How did you progress in learning your linguistic lessons?"

"Springtime passed peacefully as before," the creature recalled, "with the only change that happiness had replaced sadness in the faces of my neighbors. Safie was ever cheerful and joyous; she and I advanced quickly in the knowledge of language, so that in two months I started to understand most of the words pronounced by my neighbors. My time was spent in rapt attention that I might more quickly learn the language; and I might gloat that I advanced more quickly than the Arabian, who grasped very little and spoke in broken accents while

I understood and could mimic almost every word which was said. While I developed in speech I also mastered the art of letters as it was taught to the visitor; and this opened up before my eyes a vast horizon of wonderment and delight."

"Did you come to read something actually printed?" Dr. Seward cast curious eyes on the creature.

"One night," the creature recounted proudly, "during my usual excursion to the bordering woodland, where I gathered my own food and carried home fuel for my neighbors, I found on the ground a leathern portmanteau holding some books. I anxiously grabbed the prize and went back with it to my hovel. Fortunately the books were written in the language—the rudiments of which I'd mastered at the cottage. The possession of this prize afforded me profound pleasure; I then constantly studied and applied my mind while my neighbors were engaged in their customary employments."

"Did this discovery significantly affect you?"

"I can scarcely relate to you the weight of these books. They excited in me an immensity of fresh images and emotions which at times roused me to rapture, but more often plunged me into the deepest despair. As I read, though, I applied much in particular to my own emotions and predicament. I found myself alike but at the same time curiously unlike the creatures about whom I read—and to whose conversations I was a listener. I empathized with and partly comprehended them, but many things I read exceeded my knowledge and experience. My emotions became every day more turbulent."

Dr. Seward stopped to collect his thoughts.

"Although experience be our only guide in reasoning about matters of fact," he pondered aloud, "it must be acknowledged that this guide is not wholly infallible, but occasionally is liable to lead us into error."

"Precisely to which matter of fact do you refer?" Professor M. Krempe asked, perturbed.

"Whether we're bearing witness to a miraculous feat of

science, of sorcery or simply a frightful freak of nature."

"A scientist adjusts his judgment to the authenticated facts," Professor Krempe preached. "In such conclusions as are drawn from an infallible experience, he anticipates the result with a conclusive degree of certainty, and considers his past experience as a perfect proof of the future reality of that result."

"The precept by which we commonly conduct ourselves in our reasoning," Dr. Seward agreed, "is that the things of which we have no experience resemble those of which we have—that what we've found to be most usual is invariably most probable."

"Nevertheless," I pointed out emphatically, "things do exist which are in reality far beyond our limited earthbound experience!"

"The corruption, decay and dissolution of Nature which you hold so dear," Professor Krempe interjected cynically, "is a result rendered probable by so many resemblances—that everything which seems to have a tendency towards that catastrophe comes within the reach of human experience if that experience be very extensive and consistent."

"Only there's no immaterial corruption in immaterial things," I objected. "After all, there are found in immaterial things immaterial emotions and afflictions such as anger, envy, hatred and heartache—all of which aren't only emotions and afflictions but even the worst of torments. What more perfect proof of this monster's soulful experience could probably exist?"

"It is experience only which gives credence to human testimony," he persisted, "and it's the very same experience which assures us of the laws of Nature."

"Known laws of nature," I stressed contrarily, "which must be both experienced and understood."

"When experience then contradicts the known laws of Nature," Dr. Seward calmly acquiesced, "we have nothing to do but to take away the one from the other and embrace a belief—either on one side or the other—with the assurance which comes out of whatever is left over, preferably founded on the most past experience."

"Very well," Professor Krempe sneered resignedly, throwing up his hands in disdain, "let the revolting beast testify more about his immaterial emotions, presumably to prove by his experience the existence of his immaterial soul."

Discerning that we directed our eyes and devoted our thoughts to him once more, the creature returned to his stirring story.

"I venerated virtue and fellow-feeling and adored the mild manners and kindly qualities of my cottagers," he lamented, "but I was shut out of fellowship with them, except by virtue of stealth when I was unknown and unseen, and which rather heightened than gratified the longing I had to become one among my fellow creatures. The gentle expressions of Agatha and the heartening smiles of the enchanting Arabian weren't for me. The tempered admonitions of the old man and the cheerful conversation of the beloved Felix weren't for me. Forlorn, wretched outcast! These were the musings of my time of my sadness and seclusion."

"Could you devise no way to surmount the difficulty of your prominent deformity?"

"When I considered the virtues of the cottagers, their kindly and tender dispositions, I convinced myself that when they should become aware of my veneration of their virtues, they'd pity me and ignore my peculiar deformity. Could they bar from their door one, however monstrous, who implored their compassion and fellowship? I determined at least not to despond, but in every way to prepare myself for a meeting with them, which would decide my destiny. I delayed this design for some months more; for the stress laid on its success excited me with awe for fear that I should fail. Besides, I discovered that my comprehension developed so much with each day's experience that I was reluctant to undertake this venture until a few more months should have enhanced my capacity. I strove to quash these cares and to strengthen myself for the ordeal, which in a few months I decided to endure."

"How did you expect to benefit by such a meeting with the cottagers?"

"After summer and fall had passed I turned my mind more towards the cottagers. The more I watched them the deeper became my desire to crave their compassion and kindness; my heart longed to be known and beloved by these tender creatures—to see their kindly expressions directed towards me with fondness was the highest limit of my aspiration. I dared not believe that they would turn them from me with scorn and terror. I craved—it was true—for greater gifts than food or drink; I needed kindness and compassion; but I didn't think myself undeserving of it."

"How then did you plan to proceed?"

"The winter progressed and a complete turning of the seasons had passed since I awoke to life. My mind at this time was only turned towards my design of introducing myself into the cottage of my neighbors. I turned over in my mind many schemes; but that upon which I finally settled was to enter the cottage when the blind old man should be alone. I had acumen enough to know that the monstrous grotesqueness of my form was the foremost object of terror with those who had before seen me. My voice, although rough, had nothing terrifying in it; I believed then that if in the absence of his children—I could win the sympathy and intervention of the old man—I might by his virtue be indulged by my younger neighbors."

"How did your meeting finally come about?"

"One day," the creature recounted, "Safie, Agatha and Felix set off on a long country walk and the old man was left by himself in the cottage. Once his children had gone he picked up his guitar and played several sorrowful but sweet songs, more sweet and sorrowful than I had ever heard him play before. At first his face was brightened by delight, but as he played on reflection and gloom followed; finally, setting aside his musical instrument, he sat preoccupied with contemplation. My heart beat fast; this was the time and moment of truth, which would determine my aspiration or reap my dread. All was quiet in and about the cottage: it was an auspicious chance; but when I proceeded to perpetrate my plan my limbs wobbled and I crumpled to the ground. Once more I arose; and exerting all the strength of which I was master I displaced the planks which I had put in front of my hovel to hide my haven. The bracing air refreshed me and—with restored resolve—I stepped up to the door of their cottage."

§

"Who's there?" the old man asked once I finally knocked. "Come in."

"Forgive my intrusion," I apologized, going in. "I'm a traveler in need of some rest. You would help me much if you would permit me to stay a few moments in front of your fire."

"Come in," the old man bid me, "and I'll try in whatever way I can to satisfy your needs. But regretfully my children are away from home—and as I can't see—I fear I shall find it troublesome to provide food for you."

"Don't distress yourself, kind sir. I have food. It's rest and warmth only that I want."

I sat down and kept silent. I knew that each moment was dear to me, but I remained uncertain of what way to begin the conversation when the old man addressed me.

"By your language, sir," he said, "I gather you're my compatriot. Are you French?"

"No," I admitted, "but I was taught by a French family and know that language only. I'm now going to crave the safety of some friends whom I truly hold dear, and on whose help I pin my hopes."

"Are they Germans?"

"No, they're French. But let us talk about something else. I'm a hapless and abandoned being. I look all around and I have no friend or relation in all the world. These kindly people to whom I go have never met me and know nothing of me. I'm afraid, for if I'm unsuccessful there I'm a pariah in the world forever."

"Don't lose heart. To be friendless is truly to be unblessed. But the souls of men—when unprejudiced by any selfish conceit—are full of good will and generosity. Depend then upon your hopes. And if these friends are good and kindly don't give up hope."

"They're good and kind. They're the most exemplary people on earth. But regretfully they're prejudiced against me. I have excellent inclinations. My life has been before inoffensive and in some measure helpful. But a deadly prejudice obscures their eyes—and where they should see a gentle and sensitive friend—they see only a loathsome monster."

"That's truly tragic. But if you are truly guileless can't you disabuse them?"

"I'm about to attempt that task. And it's for that reason that I feel so many overpowering horrors. I dearly love these friends. I have—unsuspected by them—been for a long time given to everyday kindness towards them. But they think that I want to harm them, and it's that prejudice which I want to surmount."

"Where do these friends live?"

"Close to this place."

"If you'll forthrightly tell me the details of your story," the old man went on after a pause, "I perhaps may be of service in disabusing them. I can't see and can't read your face, but there's something in your voice which convinces me that you're sincere. I'm destitute and displaced, but it'll give me real joy to be in any way of service to a fellow creature."

"Noble man! I thank you and accept your gracious offer. You raise my spirits from the depths by your generosity. And I trust that—by your help—I shall not be expelled from the fellowship and favor of my fellow creatures."

"God forbid! Even if you were truly treacherous, for that can only drive you to despair and not inspirit you to virtue. I too am unblessed. I and my family have been found guilty although guiltless. Decide then if I'm not sorry for your troubles."

"How can I thank you, my truest and only protector? From your mouth first I've heard the words of tenderness directed towards me. I shall be eternally thankful. And your present charity reassures me of acceptance by those friends whom I'm on the verge of greeting."

"Will you tell me the names and home of your friends?"

I froze. This, I thought, was the moment of truth, which was to deprive me of or grant gladness to me forever. I strove to no avail for resolve enough to answer him, but the strain demolished all my remaining stamina. I collapsed on the chair and cried aloud. At that instant I heard the steps of my younger neighbors. I hadn't a moment to lose, so clutching the old man's hand I cried out loud.

"This is the time! Preserve and protect me! You and your family are the friends whom I crave. Don't forsake me in the hour of my ordeal!"

"Good God!" the old man cried. "Who are you?"

At that moment the cottage door was opened and Safie, Agatha and Felix came in. Who can recount their terror and dismay at seeing me? Agatha fainted and Safie, unable to assist her friend, hastened out of the cottage. Felix rushed ahead, and with superhuman strength wrenched me from his father—to whose feet I cleaved: in a fit of rage he knocked me to the ground and struck me savagely with a stick. I could've ripped him to pieces. But my heart collapsed inside me—as with crippling debility—and I restrained myself. I saw him on the brink of repeating his stroke—when overpowered by pain and agony—I left the cottage and—in the prevailing turmoil—absconded unseen to my hovel.

§

"Accursed, accursed creator!" the creature growled gutturally as he lurched forward, straining violently against his irons and wrenching his collar-chain until it turned taut with tension. "Why did I live? Why in that moment didn't I snuff out the flame of life which you had so capriciously conferred? I don't know; hopelessness hadn't yet overpowered me; my emotions were those of wrath and vengeance. I could with relish have demolished the cottage with its dwellers and have gorged myself with their screams and anguish."

Un-appalled Professor Krempe stepped up to the partition enveloping the creature and glowered at him regard-fully.

"If Frankenstein put life into you," he asked audaciously, "then when were you born?"

"I'm oblivious to my birth," the creature answered, looking deeply perplexed.

"What is imperishable must also be un-producible," Professor Krempe challenged him pugnaciously. "You're supposed soul then—if incorruptible—existed before your birth. Your obliviousness—before the birth of your body—seems to sensible reason a proof of a comparable condition after death."

"Sense differs greatly from intellect in that respect," I objected. "The more some things are sensible the more they harm the impressible sense; but the more the objects of the intellect are powerfully intelligible the more they entrance and stimulate the intellect—even should they incense the intellect as the rest of his story shall attest."

"When night fell," the creature continued with a stoical nod of acknowledgment, "I left my shelter and roamed through the woodlands; and then—no longer deterred by the dread of detection—I vented my agony in fearsome wailings. I was like a savage beast who had snapped the snare, smashing the things which hindered me and roving fast and furious through the woodlands. What a wretched night I spent! I—like the foul fiend—carried a hellfire inside me, and finding myself un-pitied, wanted to uproot the trees, wreak havoc and ruin all around me, and then to have sat down and delighted in the destruction. But this was an extravagance of emotion which I couldn't bear; I grew weary from overindulgent physical effort and collapsed on the moist grass in the disabling paralysis of despair.

"When I contemplated what had transpired at the cottage I couldn't help thinking that I'd been too impetuous in my judgments. I'd surely behaved rashly. It was evident that my conversation had concerned the father in my interest—and I was a halfwit in having displayed myself to the terror of his children. I should've acquainted the old man with me and gradually to have revealed myself to the rest of his family—when they should've been readied for our meeting. But I didn't think my mistakes to be irremediable, and following much deliberation I decided to go back to the cottage, seek out the old man and by my expressions win him to my side."

"Did you honestly expect another meeting to prove less startling for the family?"

"The boiling of my blood didn't permit me to be afflicted by heartening visions. The terrible recollection of the day before was perpetually floating before my eyes; the women were fleeing and the enflamed Felix wrenching me from his father's feet. I bent my steps towards the familiar footpath which led to the cottage. Everything there was quiet. I crawled into my hovel and stayed in mute anticipation of the customary time when the family awoke. That time passed, the sun rose, but the cottagers didn't materialize. I shuddered restlessly, sensing some forbidding disaster. The inside of the cottage was pitch dark and I heard no movement; I can't relate the anguish of this apprehension."

"Did the family finally appear?"

"Presently two countrymen passed by; but stopping close to the cottage they carried on a conversation, making vehement gestures; but I didn't comprehend what they said as they spoke the language of the land, which differed from that of my neighbors. Shortly after though Felix came up with another man; I was confused as I knew that he hadn't left the cottage that morning, and anxiously awaited to learn from his conversation the import of these curious manifestations."

"What in particular did you hear them discuss?"

§

"Do you think that you'll be compelled to pay three months' rent and to lose the yield of your garden?" his acquaintance asked him. "I don't want to take any unjust advantage and I pray then that you'll take some time to reconsider your decision."

"It's totally futile," Felix answered. "We can never again stay in your cottage. The life of my father is in the gravest peril due to the awful event that I've recounted. My wife and my sister will never recover from their terror. I implore you not to argue with me anymore. Reclaim your cottage and let me escape from this place."

Felix shuddered wildly as he said that. He and his acquaintance went into the cottage—in which they stayed for a few moments—and then left. I never saw any of the family ever again.

§

"How then did you react to the family's flight?" Dr. Seward asked him.

"I went on for the rest of the day in my hovel in a state of stark and senseless dismay. My neighbors had absconded and had broken the only bond which bound me to the world. For the first time the emotions of vengeance and hate filled my heart and I didn't try to restrain them; but letting myself be swept away by the tide I turned my mind towards hurt and death. When I recalled my neighbors—the kindly voice of the old man; the soft eyes of Agatha; the graceful delicacy of the Arabian—these impressions disappeared and a torrent of tears rather comforted me. But once more when I reconsidered that they had repudiated and abandoned me wrath returned—a ferocity of wrath—and unable to harm anything human I directed my wrath towards lifeless things."

"What did you trample under foot?"

"As night fell I put an assortment of inflammables all about the cottage," the creature recounted resentfully if rather regretfully. "And after having ravaged every remnant of cultivation in the garden, I remained with imposed impatience until the moon had set to start my activities. As the night fell, a stormy gust blew up from the woodlands and swiftly scattered the clouds which had lingered in the sky—the storm ripped along like a powerful landslide and provoked a kind of frenzy in my heart which burst all limits of reason and rationality. I lighted the dry branch of a tree and romped with rage all about the dedicated cottage, my eyes yet riveted on the western skyline—the brim of which the moon almost skimmed. A part of its sphere was finally concealed and I twirled my torch; it set, and with a powerful outcry, I ignited the straw, heath and shrubs which I'd gathered. The breeze blew up the flames and the cottage was swiftly engulfed by the fire, which stuck to it and darted across it with its thorny and deathly tongues. As soon as I was persuaded that no aid could salvage any part of the cottage I left the spot and searched for sanctuary in the woodlands."

"Pray," Professor Krempe asked cynically, "what do we gather from the enmity expressed by a wretch who vents his hostility against the objects of his unrequited affections?"

"That the disposition of enmity is nothing else but a certain inclination of one thing to another," I promptly answered, "desiring such—and if such a thing be absent and to move toward it—unless it be impeded—and to submit to it when it's obtained—avoiding the contrary and dreading the approach of it—and not resting in or being contented with it."

"This creature wanted acceptance but found it wanting," Dr. Seward deduced. "He approached it and was indeed impeded, and couldn't plausibly submit to what he lost. And so he avoids rejection and dreads its incursion, and scarcely takes heart or comfort in it."

"In particular," I elucidated, "the inclinations of enmity are the disgust, anger, indignation and a certain sort of obstinate contrariness of temperament so that anything avoids its contrary, and drives it away out of its presence."

"As the De Lacey family drove this creature from their presence?"

"As I would drive the devil from my presence and into oblivion were I empowered to do it."

"Ignoring his evident deformity," Dr. Seward persisted, "why should you hold your own creation in such profound abomination?"

"All things have enmity among themselves," I said with indignant irritation, "and everything has something which it dreads and fears—that's deadly and destructive to it—and an enemy: and that devil is my archenemy—the archfiend whom I'm bound to blot out of earthly existence!"

SIXTEEN:
A MONSTER'S SOUL

"I felt as if I had committed some great crime, the consciousness of which haunted me. I was guiltless, but I had indeed drawn down a horrible curse upon my head, as mortal as that of crime."—Victor Frankenstein

JOSEPH COVINO JR

L ustily the creature strained every twitching nerve to break free of his bonds, riveting his resentful eyes upon me.

"And then," he rasped spitefully, "with all the world in front of me, where should I direct my course? I decided to abscond far from the place of my calamities; but to me, abhorred and scorned, every land must be equally terrible. Finally the remembrance of you passed through my mind. And among the lessons which Felix had taught Safie geography hadn't been ignored: I'd ascertained from these the comparative locations of the different lands of the world. You had designated Geneva as the name of your native town; and towards that place I decided to proceed."

"How then did you wend your way?" Dr. Seward asked him.

"It was late in autumn when I left the region where I'd so long lived. I journeyed only at night for fear of meeting the face of a human being. Oh, world! How many times did I curse the source of my life! The gentleness of my nature had absconded, and everything inside me was turned into hostility and hate. The closer I came near to your home place the more acutely did I feel the fervency of vengeance inflamed in my heart. The anguish of my emotions permitted me no repose: no event happened from which my wrath and wretchedness couldn't draw its sustenance; but an incident which took place when I came to the frontiers of Switzerland established in a special way the animosity and terror of my emotions."

"You could enlist no one to lend their aid?"

"My nocturnal treks among the moonlit woodlands were a great enjoyment to me, although they were substantially short-ened by the late setting and the early rising of the sun, for I never rambled abroad during daylight, for fear of encountering the same treatment I had before suffered in the first village which I came to. I usually rested during the day and jour-neyed only when I was hidden by night from the sight of man.

One morning, though, discovering that my footpath thread through a particularly thick woodland I dared to resume my migration after the day had broke."

"What was it about that morning which struck you as being so remarkable?"

"That day after I had destroyed the cottage, which was one of the first days of spring, enlivened even me by the brilliance of its sunlight and the mildness of the air. I felt sensations of softness and serenity, which had long seemed extinct, recover inside me. Half baffled by the freshness of these feelings, I permitted myself to be carried away by them and, overlooking my seclusion and disfigurement, I ventured to be content. Tender tears once more moistened my face, and I even lifted up my wet eyes with gratitude towards the sacred sun, which conferred such happiness upon me."

"Did such sentiments temper at all your bitter disposition towards mankind?"

"I resumed treading among the footpaths of the woodland until I got to its border, which was bound by a deep and speedy river over which many of the trees bowed their branches— then blossoming with the crisp spring. There I stopped—not precisely knowing what footpath to follow—when I overheard the noise of voices which prompted me to hide myself beneath the shadow of a cypress. I was hardly hid when a young girl came hurrying towards the place where I was hidden, giggling as if she fled from somebody in fun. She resumed her path along the steep edges of the river when, unexpectedly, her foot tripped and she tumbled into the swift stream. I hurried from my hiding-place and—with desperate effort from the strength of the current—rescued her and yanked her to the bank. She was insensible; and I attempted—by every power in my possession—to reanimate life when I was abruptly disrupted by the approach of a peasant, who was presumably the one from whom she had frolicsomely absconded. On beholding me he bolted towards me, and ripping the girl from my grasp, hurried towards the remoter parts of the woodland. I pursued swiftly, I scarcely knew why; but when the countryman watched me come near he pointed a gun, which he bore at my frame, and shot. I dropped to the ground and my aggressor—with an undiminished speed—absconded into the woodland."

"What construction then do we put on that particular story?" Dr. Seward asked inquisitively.

"That a being who suffers pain in this way isn't injured in his essence," I readily answered. "So as the injury of the thing doesn't affect the essence of its possessor, so the injury of this sort isn't essential. So it doesn't bring about essential failure or injury."

"By a being's essence then you allude to its supposedly immortal soul?"

"Let me illuminate its immortality in another way," I nodded my accord. "A sense isn't applied to things which are sensed without its being likened to them. So sight isn't applied to what's bright or dim without becoming dazzled or blurred, and touch to what's hot or cold without becoming burned or cooled, just as smell or taste aren't applied to what's pungent without becoming so. Even hearing isn't applied to what's loud or soft without becoming stunned or tempered. Whenever we sense something we necessarily become whatever is sensed, for there's no fuller or more powerful application of sensations to the senses than the sensing of them."

"To what do you point by employing doubtful metaphors?" Professor Krempe protested, perturbed.

"That the immortal intellect acts in quite the opposite manner in that respect, for whenever we understand something we don't in any way become what's understood. There's no alteration except by the agent's application to—or unity with—what's altered, and there's no more fitting unity, no more powerful application of the intellect to intelligible or sensible things than the very understanding of them."

"So," Dr. Seward concluded sedately, "it's evident by your

inventive interpretation of immortality that the intellect cannot essentially be altered or at least cannot be injured by sensible things."

"Exactly!" I gestured assertively to the unearthly monster. "That creature felt—and sensed—the pain inflicted by the shot which penetrated him. But his essential understanding of his wound—being impenetrable and impervious to injury—cannot be shot, penetrated or hurt in any way."

"This was then the reward of my kindness!" the creature clamored vociferously. "I had rescued a fellow creature from extinction, and as a reward I then squirmed under the wretched anguish of a wound which smashed the flesh and bone. The emotions of mildness and tenderness, which I had harbored only a few moments before, gave way to infernal fury and grinding of teeth. Angered by agony I swore everlasting hate and revenge to all mankind. My wretchedness was aggravated as well by the severe sense of unjustness and ungratefulness of its infliction. My everyday pledges grew for vengeance—a profound and lethal vengeance such as would atone for the injuries and agony I had suffered. All happiness was only a sham which outraged my wretched condition, and forced me to feel more hurtfully that I wasn't created for the pleasure of bliss."

"Where were you wounded?" Dr. Seward asked curiously, stepping up closer to the partition to examine the creature intently.

"The ball had penetrated my shoulder," the creature lamented in pain, straining his eyes to point out the part shot, "and I didn't know whether it stayed there or went through; in any event I had no way of extracting it."

"Take no pity on that crafty devil," I exhorted them. "Rather, let him tell you how he slaughtered my beautiful little brother so wretchedly. Nothing but a fiend in deformed human shape could have destroyed that delicate child."

"Following some weeks," the creature continued stoically,

"my wound mended and I resumed my migration. But my pains came near an end, and in two months from that time, I arrived at the vicinity of Geneva. It was sundown when I got to the town, and I retreated to a hiding-place among the plots which encompass it to contemplate in what way I should petition you. At that time a scant sleep soothed me from the distress of contemplation, which was disrupted by the approach of a lovely boy, who came racing into the niche I had picked with all the vivacity of youth. Unexpectedly—as I looked upon him—a notion struck me that this delicate creature was unprejudiced, and had lived too brief a time to have absorbed a terror of disfigurement. If then I could capture him and cultivate him as my companion and fellow, I should not be so lonely in this populated world. Encouraged by this urge I snatched the boy as he passed by and tugged him towards me. As soon as he perceived my shape, he put his hands in front of his eyes and let out a sharp squeal."

§

"Boy!" I yelled, wrenching his hand forcefully from his face. "What's the purpose of this? I don't mean to harm you! Hear me!"

"Let go of me!" he screamed, squirming frantically. "Monster! Horrible devil! You want to devour me and rip me to pieces! You're a ghoul! Let go of me or I'll tell my papa."

"Boy, you'll never be with your father again. You must stay with me."

"Disgusting monster! Let go of me. My papa's a magistrate—he's M. Frankenstein—he'll arrest you. You don't dare hold me."

"Frankenstein! You belong then to my foe—to him towards whom I've vowed eternal vengeance. You shall be my first sacrifice."

Still the boy squirmed and called me names which broke

my heart. I clutched his throat to stifle him and in an instant he dropped dead at my feet. I looked upon my prey and my soul surged with joy and infernal victory.

"I too can deal destruction!" I cried, slapping my hands. "My foe isn't invincible. This killing will depress his spirits—and countless other afflictions shall torture and devastate him."

"As I riveted my eyes on the boy I spotted something glinting on his bosom. I snatched it; it was a picture of a very sublime woman. Despite my enmity it melted and enticed me. For some moments I looked with relish upon her black eyes, fringed by dark lashes, and her lush lips; but presently my fury came back: I recalled that I was eternally denied the enjoyments which such enchanting beings could confer; and that she whose likeness I appreciated would—in observing me—have turned that air of heavenly benevolence to one exuding revulsion and fear. Can you imagine that such reflections lashed me into a fury? I only marvel that at the instant, rather than expelling my emotions in outcries and anguish, I didn't plunge among mankind and die in my endeavor to devastate them.

"While I was overpowered by these emotions I departed to the place where I had murdered the child and, searching for a more remote hiding-place, I went into a stable which had looked to me to be bare. A girl was asleep on some straw; she was youthful: not really so refined as her whose picture I took; but of a pleasing look and blossoming in the beauty of youth and vitality. There, I thought, is one of those whose pleasure-giving smiles are conferred on everyone but me. And then I stooped over and gasped. The sleeper moved; a tremor of horror penetrated me. Should she actually awaken and see me, and swear at me and condemn the killer? So would she surely behave if her dark eyes opened and she saw me. The notion was insanity; it provoked the demon inside me—not I, but she shall grieve; the killing I've perpetrated because I'm eternally deprived of everything which she could grant me she shall regret. The offense had its origin in her: be hers the penalty! Thanks to the instructions of Felix and the heartening laws of men I'd learned how to do harm. I stooped over her and put the picture snugly in one of the flaps of her frock. She budged once more and I absconded."

§

Enraged I lunged wildly at the foul fiend, thrust my out-stretched arms through the partition bars and tightly clenched with both hands the foot-long chain linked to the iron ring riveted about his neck. I heaved hard, forcefully wrenching the chain with all my might, yanking him violently awry. He toppled over, legs buckling, and battered the partition before collapsing heavily to the rough floor. I flung my foot through the bars, kicking him savagely in his face.

"Oh," he groaned gutturally, "that I had eternally stayed in my native woodland, nor experienced nor endured anything beyond the sensations of hunger, thirst, cold and heat!"

"You learned how to do harm!" I roared furiously. "Let me teach you a lesson in how to do harm to a vile devil!"

He tilted headlong against the partition, grunting in crip-pling pain. Underfoot I stamped on his neck-chain—stretched taut to the other iron ring which slid noisily down the solid bar bolted upright to the wall. His head sagged with a walloping thump to the unyielding floor.

"Pray!" I raved, quivering with rage. "Tell us what other lessons you learned!"

"Other lessons were impressed on my mind even more deeply," he moaned achingly. "The patriarchal lives of my neighbors made these impressions wholly occupy my mind. I heard of all the relationships which join one human being to another in common bonds of union. But where were my dot-ing father and protective mother?"

"Where's my sweet, innocent little brother?" I bellowed, convulsed with rage, lashing out at the defenseless devil once more.

"Where were the growth of my mind and the gathering of knowledge in my nonexistent youth?" he retorted resentfully.

Dr. Seward grasped my shoulders firmly, keeping me back. I sank down, collapsing slowly to the floor.

"We're born to be awake—not to be asleep!" I raved, unburdening myself.

"Make sense, man!" he reprimanded me. "What are you ranting about?"

"In man," I maundered, "the capacity to practice all arts and crafts is innate, but not all these abilities have been brought to the light of day. Those which are to become manifest in him must first be awakened. What can be learned isn't precisely learning, because everything is prefigured even in the child; it must only be awakened and summoned forth in him. The child is still an unformed being, and he takes his form in accordance with the potentialities which you awaken in him. If you awaken the stonemason in him he'll be a stonemason; and if you awaken the scholar in him he'll be a scholar. And this is so because all potentialities are innate in him. What you awaken in him comes forth from him; the rest remains un-awakened—absorbed in sleep."

"The ability to develop and mature must be awakened as well," Dr. Seward scolded me, gesturing to the forlorn devil languishing behind the partition. "Only he enjoyed no childhood, much less was he awakened to humanity. You failed to civilize and humanize him. All you awakened in that wretched creature was the potentiality to kill and wreak havoc. You have summoned forth a destroyer."

§

I awoke, astir and agitated, lying restless in the villa's red bedchamber hung with crimson paper. By the bed were arranged a red and white flower-pot, a cup, saucer and sugar dish of Seve porcelain, and a ewer and basin of Chantilli porcelain. Sluggishly I struggled to raise myself up to reach for the ewer, grasping it to pour into the basin water which I splashed on my face to refresh myself, sprawling back on the bed in a shadowy haze of lurid light. Around me in crimson Norwich damask chairs sat Dr. David Seward and Professor M. Krempe, their faces displaying worried expressions. Sweet Safie, smiling benignly, arose from an arm-chair of patch-work to hold out a draught of laudanum for me to take, but which I pushed aside, looking askance at her.

"It's only a mild sedative," Dr. Seward assured me, "a small tincture of opium is all."

Once I shook my head contrarily Dr. Seward nodded beckoningly to two stalwart attendants abruptly emerging from the room's murky gloom. Nimbly they laid hold of my arms and pinned me down to the bed while Abraham Van Helsing, who unexpectedly materialized, forcibly wedged a piece of curved metal piping through the gap between my tightly clenched teeth—into which he injected from a syringe a potent dosage of drug.

"That should quench the pitiful sufferer into quietness," I heard Dr. Seward whisper among them as I blacked out, lapsing into deep sleep.

Abraham Van Helsing reached through the nebulous murk to tightly clutch my outstretched hand, trembling with grief and guilt.

"Your master blames me for making a monster," I bellowed aloud.

"You made your monster a madman," he said dispassionately, "for misery makes madness."

"He deserves his misery," I said, furiously sullen, "for he made himself a murderer."

"You neglected to consider the longings of the human

soul," he sympathized, "insofar as it's human."

"He's nothing if not fiendishly inhuman."

"Any human soul has a noble being in which it surpasses the carnal soul."

"His soul should never surpass the bestial level."

"Every human soul has a natural desire for true happiness and an aversion to true misery—indeed a dread and hatred of it. Happiness befits the noble part of the human soul but misery doesn't."

"Misery befits his ignoble outrages all too well."

"But some human movements are purely physical while others are purely spiritual. Fear is spiritual flight and hope is spiritual pursuit."

"What have flight and pursuit to do with that vile devil?"

"Just as fear is by itself the way of attaining evasion," he elucidated, "and desire is by itself the way of attaining what's coveted, flight is by itself the way of attaining evasion and pursuit is the way of attaining possession. And since spiritual things are acquired just as physical ones are it's likewise essential that there be—for those who acquire them—ways of attaining them in a befitting manner. These ways cease when they've been attained just as in the attainment of physical things."

"That devil has no fear and nothing to fly from. He has no desire except to wreak havoc, which is his sole pursuit."

"Our most natural faculty is a natural desire for the happiness which is most befitting to it and a natural flight from—indeed a natural dread and hatred of—its own wretchedness and misery."

"Then death and slaughter most befit that devil."

"There's nothing in vain—nothing without a purpose among those things which come about naturally—but these movements are in vain and without a purpose if this evasion from misery is naturally impossible and if the attainment of such happiness is impossible. It's essential then that evasion from its misery and the attainment of its happiness is possible for this noble soul."

"For a monster whose only possible happiness is carnage his misery is inevitable."

"His misery was made inevitable by his deformity and his constant ostracism by mankind."

"I'm guilty of creating his deformity," I contritely admitted. "But am I responsible for the prejudices of mankind? Or for the demon's violent and murderous rampages?"

"That by which this faculty is naturally cultivated, enlightened and perfected to this extent cannot be violent," Van Helsing said disinterestedly, "for everything violent obstructs and is hurtful to the nature for which it's violent."

§

Professor M. Krempe emerged abruptly from the room's murk.

"If you possess this supposed almighty and all-powerful secret of life and death," he defied me, hissing through his scurrilous smile, "then why didn't you bring your unfortunate little brother back to life?"

"No man has the power to reanimate that which has died a natural death and which Nature—or some unnatural thing in Nature—has killed at the predestined time," I lamented ruefully. "Only by God can it be done—or by another at God's command. Nor can man reanimate what Nature has consumed. Only what he himself has broken can he repair and then again break it. More man cannot do by his own power. If he were to presume further he would trespass on the power of God, and still his endeavors would be in vain. What dies naturally has reached its appointed time. Therein lies God's will and command. Even if death happens through accident or infirmity no reanimating is possible. There is then no protection against fate and against the predestined end."

"I dispute the existence of any doubtful deity," Professor Krempe sneered, waving his hand dismissively, "or preordained destiny."

"To the contrary," I challenged him, "the true knowledge of man's essence can be attained only on the basis of his eternity. It cannot be understood by any other sign, for the great truth is such that all the forces of Nature are silent and surrender in the face of a mighty God-given power on earth. With one single, solitary word it can resurrect the dead."

Professor Krempe raised his facetious voice angrily.

"It's inconceivable that manipulated matter should receive life, be brought to life, come to life or assume any other fanciful noble form!"

"Why is it more than probable that all men must die and less than probable that all men must live forever?"

§

Suddenly Dr. David Seward came at me out of the room's lurid shade.

"Pray," he importuned me, "enter then into the details of your creature's creation. Recount for us your concept of soul and how you infused life into lifeless matter."

"The soul of man is both a certain divine light," I explained drearily, "as well as a certain divine substance—indivisible—and wholly present in every part of the body. Being such it's joined only by masterly means to man's grosser body."

"Specify what you mean by masterly means."

"The soul of man is first infused into the midmost point of the heart—which is the center of man's body—and from there it's diffused throughout all the parts and members of his body."

"So the seat and home of the soul is in the heart in the center of man?"

"The soul dwells within man in the place where life is and

against which death contends."

"And over which death triumphs."

"For which death changes," I corrected him. "When by a disease or some mischief the body fails then the soul musters itself, and flows back into the heart which was its first receptacle: but the spirit of the heart failing, and the natural heat being extinct, the soul leaves him and man dies."

"This philosophical drivel means nothing," Dr. Seward objected, shaking his head. "Man is scarcely capable of understanding his corporeal body much less some incorporeal soul—should it truly exist. We ourselves understand almost nothing at all and can simply judge perishable things."

"And so," I refuted him, "philosophy is nothing other than the knowledge and discovery of that which has its reflection in the mirror. And just as the image in the mirror gives no one any notion about his nature, and cannot be the object of knowledge, but is merely a dead image—so is man considered in himself: nothing can be discovered from him alone, for knowledge comes only from that outside being whose mirrored image he is."

"You allude to that god after whose image man was supposed to be made?"

"After whose image man's soul was made," I elaborated, "for as God cannot be touched, nor heard by the ears, nor seen with the eyes, so the soul of man can neither be seen, heard nor touched."

"Man's senses can indeed perceive when man perishes and dies."

"Death is an empty concept," I told him solemnly, "and even as nothingness is nowhere so also is death; then when a man dies—when his body and soul are separated—nothing of them perishes or is turned into nothing."

§

Surprisingly sweet Safie issued from the room's darksome gloom.

"When then the best proportioned soul is joined to the best proportioned body," she said, "it's manifest that such a man also has received a most fortunate lot in the bestowal of gifts."

"When the eternal Creator of the world was to put the soul into the body," I nodded, surprised at her perception, "as into its abode—first made a suitable dwelling worthy to receive it—and endows the most exemplary soul with a most splendid body, which then the soul knowing its own divinity frames and adorns for its own dwelling."

§

Most unexpectedly the demon himself—the foul fiend in human shape—loomed large in the room's lowering gloom.

"Seeing that man is the most magnificent and beautiful work of God," he angrily snarled his grisly grin, "and his image of the most perfect composition—and in him the supreme workmanship—in whose hideous and monstrous image was I made?"

"By your savage outrages you made your own image hideous and monstrous!" I snapped. "I only rendered it ugly."

"The gallantry of the mind does indeed depend upon the goodness of the body," Safie gently interjected, abruptly reappearing.

"There's no defect," Dr. Seward agreed, reappearing alongside her, "and no deformity in the body which the vice and intemperance of the mind doesn't emulate, because it's assured that they do develop, thrive and evolve by the aid—one of the other."

"None of that exonerates the monster from the atrocities he committed!" I protested vehemently.

"But the will as the master of all these powers at pleasure—being joined with the superior intellect—is always tend-ing to good," Van Helsing chimed in, rematerializing, "which intellect indeed does always expose a pathway to the will as a candle to the eye; but it moves not itself but is the mistress of her own power, from which it's known as free will; and although it always tends to good as an object suitable to itself: yet sometimes being blinded by error—the carnal power forc-ing it—it chooses evil, wrongly believing it to be good."

At the last the squat, uncouth and repellent countenance of Professor M. Krempe rematerialized.

"M. Frankenstein has indeed surpassed us all!" he spouted contemptuously.

Over me the mammoth monster hovered high once more—his ghastly grin creasing his leathery lips and cheeks, stretching out his gnarled, palpitating hands to clutch at my throat. I shrank and flinched with petrifying fright. And I abruptly awoke from my nightmare with a twitching start, deathly startled, wet and steaming with shivery sweat!

JOSEPH COVINO JR

SEVENTEEN:
A MAKER'S MISERY

"For a moment my soul was elevated from its debasing and miserable fears.....For an instant I dared to shake off my chains, and look around me with a free and lofty spirit; but the iron had eaten into my flesh, and I sank again, trembling and hopeless, into my miserable self."—Victor Frankenstein

JOSEPH COVINO JR

Sometime later on I awoke in the red bedchamber, lying listless on one side and casting my leaden eyes on a crucifix of ivory by my bed, blurred by a beamy but murky haze. Sweet Safie materialized once more and gently held up to my lips a glass of barley water, from which I sipped feebly. Once I grasped the glass she resumed mixing a certain concoction for me in a pewter bowl—into which she beat up the yolk of an egg after stirring up a teacupful of milk, some sugar and brandy.

"Drink this," she urged, holding out the bowl for me to take, "as you're rather reduced."

After I dutifully drained the somewhat bitter draught Safie warmly squeezed my hand.

"Here your researches must cease," she implored me inexplicably, "for you must declare that wonderful are the works of the Lord and His ways are beyond discovery."

Promptly she left—immediately after which Dr. David Seward, Abraham Van Helsing and Professor M. Krempe together shuffled in and, seating themselves in the bedchamber's crimson Norwich damask chairs, surrounded my bedside.

Attentive to my debilitated condition they talked together quietly among themselves at first.

"Physiologically speaking," Dr. Seward said lowly, "the mind—the grand prerogative of the brain—is simply a function of that organ. So symptoms of insanity possess the same relation to the brain as cough and asthma to the lungs; heartburn, indigestion and vomiting to the stomach; or any other disordered functions to their corresponding organs. Disease in the organ of the brain—and not in the mind—is the source of all nervous disorders and derangement."

"In all cases where derangement of the mind is detectable," Professor Krempe stressed, nodding his accord, "from the slightest peculiarity to the farthest departure from reason—it must and can only be attributed directly or indirectly to the brain."

"Then there can be no such thing as mind disease," Van Helsing interjected. "All the afflictions generally referred to as mental derangement are only evidences of cerebral afflictions—disordered symptoms of that organ whose sound action produces the phenomena termed mental—that's to say symptoms of the diseased brain."

Feebly I raised a dissenting hand.

"The intellect doesn't have an organ in the body," I objected. "The intellect doesn't have a determinate part that is its organ. The intellect—in its being and in its kind—is form in itself."

"From a strictly somatic standpoint," Dr. Seward disputed, "derangement is no longer deemed a disease of the understanding—but of the center of the nervous system—upon the unimpaired condition of which the function of the understanding depends. At fault is the brain and not the mind."

"From an impairment to the central compartment of the brain," I insisted just as contrarily, "the function of understanding may appear to be impeded or completely destroyed, but the intellective power doesn't have in the body an organ for its function."

"As a material organ," Dr. Seward argued, shaking his head in disagreement, "the brain is subject to irritation and inflammation, and it's these which induce insanity. But let this affliction of the brain be relieved—this irritation removed—and the mind revives in its native strength: clear and calm, unimpaired, immutable and—so to say—immortal."

"It's impossible for thought to consist of a material substance, for the soul is immaterial."

"Our concept of substance, much less the soul, is completely confused and imperfect."

"Our experience of substance however is more meaningful and complete."

"Experience—being the sole source of our judgments of this nature—we cannot know from any other principle whether matter, by its structure or construction, may not be the source of thought."

"But our power of judgment depends entirely upon the essence of the mind," I persisted, "which isn't at all dependent upon the body."

"Abstract speculations cannot settle any question of fact or existence," Dr. Seward finally relented, reconciled to my resolute rebuttal. "Let's withdraw to the drawing room to continue our discourse once you've regained your strength."

And they promptly left the bedchamber, looking perplexed as they retired from sight.

§

Abraham Van Helsing led me once more to the round drawing room hung with crimson Norwich damask. A carpet of the manufacture of Moor-fields softened our footfalls as we strode straight over to the great bow window—in which Professor M. Krempe already sat in one of the chairs of Aubusson tapestry at a table framed in green and gold. Dr. David Seward walked the floor close to the chimney-piece inlaid with white marble, fronted by a screen chased in chenille and flanked by two silver sconces. Presently he attended us and invited us to sit together at the table beneath the dusty fretwork of light shed by the round, frieze-grated window in the ceiling above.

"By supposing some spiritual substance to be scattered throughout creation and to be the sole essential substance of thought," Dr. Seward suggested solicitously, "we have cause to conclude from analogy that Nature uses it after the style she does the other substance: matter. She manipulates it as a sort of paste or clay; molds it into a variety of shapes and forms; dissolves after a time each alteration, and from its substance fabricates a fresh form. As the same material substance may successively make up the bodies of all animals, the same spiritual substance may make up their minds: their consciousness—or that seat of thought which they formed during life—may be continuously dissolved by death. Even the most assertive testifiers of the mortality of the soul never doubted the immortality of its substance. And that an immaterial substance—as well as a material—may lose its consciousness appears inescapable from experience if the soul be immaterial."

"If the activity of a substance doesn't depend upon the body," I contradicted him, "its essence doesn't depend upon the body, for the essence of any substance must be freer from the body than the activity. Since then the activity of the human soul—the activity of that which is most subtle and noble in the human soul—doesn't depend upon the body—as is the case with the activity of the intellect—its essence doesn't depend upon it either. So it's naturally separable from the body and has life apart from the body."

"From the analogy of Nature," Dr. Seward declared, "the physical logic for the mortality of the soul is powerful. Where any two things such as mind and body are so closely connected that all alterations—which we've ever seen in the one—are accompanied by proportionate alterations in the other: by all rules of analogy when there are still greater alterations produced in the body—and it's totally dissolved—there follows a total dissolution of the mind."

"If the activity of a power isn't impeded by the body," I argued, "its existence of essence doesn't depend upon the body. It's evident that the intellective power is of this sort—because the more it becomes involved with and immersed in the body—the more its intellectual consciousness will be obscure, dull, slow and filled with errors. But the more it separates and disconnects itself from the body the more it will be sharp, clear, quick and free from errors. By that I allude to spiritual not bodily separation. The essence then of the intellect doesn't depend upon the body—since its proper activity is impeded by it and through it."

"Quite the contrary," Professor Krempe objected, "the essential activity must depend upon the body to exist and last. Everything is common between mind and body. The organs of the one are all of them the organs of the other. The existence and lastingness of the one must be dependent upon the other."

"In infancy," Dr. Seward chimed in with him, "the weakness of the body and that of the mind are exactly proportionate; their vigor in manhood, their sympathetic disorder in sickness, their common gradual decay in old age. The step further appears inescapable: their common dissolution in death."

"Far from it," I persisted. "If the essence of the intellect depends upon the body the strengthening of the intellect should follow the strengthening of the body and the weakening of the intellect should follow the weakening of the body. But in fact the entire matter is exactly the opposite, for the weakening of the body occurs in old age and the vigor of the intellective power is then greatest—and the intellect in every way is strongest. From this it's clearly evident that the intellective power is rejuvenated in old age."

"The last symptoms which the mind manifests," Abraham Van Helsing said deliberatively, "are disorder, debility, insensibility and stupidity—the harbingers of its annihilation. Further progression of the same causes—generating the same effects—entirely extinguishes it."

"True," I granted, "everything mortal is gradually weakened by its duration and fails until it comes to its final failure which is death. But the intellective power makes progress through its duration and grows stronger so that—the longer it lasts and the older it gets—the stronger it is in every respect. The intellective power then is immortal and it's evident—that it not only cannot age or approach failure by reason of its duration—but that from its duration it rejuvenates and is further removed from failure and death."

"Sleep," Professor Krempe proposed, "a very slight effect on the body is attended with a temporary extinction—or at least considerable confusion in the soul. This intellective power is doubtless impeded and weakened when the body is impeded and weakened—as in those who are ill, delirious, deranged, melancholic or mentally alienated in some other manner."

"To impede or impair isn't the same as to preoccupy," I repudiated him, "for our external sight or hearing don't impair or impede the intellect, but they truly preoccupy the human mind so that it isn't free at that time for intellective activity because it's distracted—and drawn—through sight or through hearing to particular external things."

"Emotions in those under their influence must distract the intellect as well," Van Helsing astutely affirmed.

"Emotions," I explained, "are like recurring dreams which persist on account of impressions which cannot be readily removed. As dreams then grip the mind—or the soul preoccupied with and bound by phantasms—so do these alienated mental states. They don't impair the essence of the intellective power, but impede its activity by preoccupying it. When the mind has been liberated and cleansed completely from these impressions, the intellective power returns to its proper activities as though it had sustained no impairment in its essence."

"No form," Dr. Seward insisted, "can continue when transformed to a condition of life drastically different from the original one into which it was put. What reason then to imagine that a vast alteration—such as is done upon the soul by the dissolution of its body—and all its organs of thought and sensation—can be produced without the dissolution of the whole?"

"In the complete separation from the body—which is death—the intellective power is in full vigor," I answered sedately.

"Nothing in this world is perpetual!" Professor Krempe, irritable and irate, blurted out. "Everything, however seemingly firm, is in continual flux and change: the world itself shows symptoms of frailty and dissolution. How contrary to reality then to imagine that one single form—seemingly the frailest of all, and from the objects and causes subject to the greatest disorders—is immortal and indissoluble? What a daring theory is that! How lightly—to say nothing of how rashly entertained!"

"Every substance whose form isn't corruptible is incorruptible," I said stoically. "And every intelligent substance is of this sort, because only substances in which there are material forms are corruptible. But no intelligent substance has any of the material forms as its own—that is, as natural and essential. Since then only a material form is corruptible and an intelligent substance cannot have that sort of form as natural or essential, it's manifest that an intelligent substance is incorruptible since its essential form is incorruptible."

"By what analysis or analogy," Professor Krempe asked, conspicuously disconcerted, "can we prove any state of existence which no one ever saw—and which no way resembles any that ever was seen? Who will put such trust in any spurious philosophy as to accept on its testimony the truth of so extravagant a presumption? Some new species of logic is imperative for that purpose—and some new faculties of the mind that they may empower us to grasp that logic."

"Even the so-called dumb animals don't possess the powers of mind to perceive and understand the very same realities of the world which we know to be real and true," I challenged him, "but their unawareness—their inability to know—makes the actual existence of those realities no less real or true. So why should man presume so imperiously that he indeed knows and understands all the realities of our existence?"

"Then some realities of our tenuous existence are beyond our limited capacity to comprehend," Van Helsing astutely suggested.

"Nothing may be perpetual in the world which we know," I allowed, "but we necessarily have no conception of another world in existence—in which everything isn't only perpetual but imperishable. In that other world the eternal essence of the human mind endures forever and never dies, for it is deathless and immortal. Bodily disorders such as disease or madness may displace or disrupt it—just as sleep may distract or divert it—but no bodily state may ever destroy it."

"Except death!"

"Death may simply transfer—or transport—the eternal essence of the mind to that other eternal but unknown world."

My definitive rebuttal reduced the three learned men to insensible silence. After a time Dr. Seward finally heaved a heavy sigh of surrender.

"I must admit," he stated stoically, "we're all at a loss about whose mind to diagnose as the most unsound—that of your captive creature or your own—for misery may have made him mad, but obsession has made you similarly or more so."

"I'm guilty of the most derelict neglect," I contritely confessed, "for no passion or emotion can of itself enkindle an essential failure of the human soul since its essence doesn't depend upon the essence of its body. What I negligently ignored was the sober reality that misery or madness—in the extreme—can of itself indeed induce the soul to abscond from the body."

Unexpectedly Dr. Seward produced a document with which he presented me to inspect.

"As I explained," he reminded me, "a private patient must have a friend or relation petition for reception at the asylum and supply a formal statement of the case. The Refuge has initiated its own formal certificate in which that intimate is asked to answer questions about the patient's history and a physician is to complete the statement as indicated."

I took the document and examined it intently, reading aloud:

"I do hereby certify, after personal examination of the patient identified herein, that I believe him to be insane and a fit object for confinement in a house for the reception of lunatics."

He slowly arose from the table and gazed gravely upon me.

"We'll leave you alone now to consider whether you'll certify and commit your exceptional son to our asylum for reception and therapy," he abruptly announced.

Professor Krempe arose after, demurely looking down his disdainful nose at me.

"Perhaps you should consider as well whether you'll voluntarily admit yourself to the asylum for treatment," he sneered, "for you've clearly overtaxed your capacity to contrive fantastic metaphysical theories."

Van Helsing arose last but simply stared down at me in spellbound silence, speechless, appearing perplexed, stupefied and strangely sympathetic. After the others left he stayed behind to accost me.

"We received a letter for you from someone in Scotland," he told me, handing it over.

"Thank you," I said, briefly reading the envelope. "It's from an acquaintance in Perth who's before been our visitor at Geneva."

"In all manner of evasive explanations," he intimated, deftly shifting the subject, "you've rendered various accounts of what you've purportedly created and why, although you've most carefully and consistently refrained from entering into any of the precise particulars of your extraordinary experiment—that's to say how you animated your creation."

"My friend," I asked him tellingly, "where will your fatuous curiosity take you? Would you make for yourself and the world a demonic nemesis? Heed my madness and misery— and don't endeavor to instigate your own."

"I understand," he nodded knowingly, holding out his hand to warmly press mine for the last time; and then he left me alone.

§

Lost in thought I strayed sometime after into the adjoining tribune, which was square with a semicircular recess in the middle of each side, painted stone-color with gilt ornaments together with niches and windows surrounded by the most splendid mosaics of the simplest taste. A star of yellow glass terminated the roof, throwing a golden gloom all over the room, lending it the solemn air of a rich chapel. Through the grated door I passed and crossed the carpet, taken from the mosaic of the windows, and stood in the middle which mirrored the reflection of the star in the ceiling. Glancing around I directed my eyes to an altar of black and gold—with a marble slab of the same colors—standing on the right side flanked by two silver sconces. In front of the altar on a bench silently sat two young women wearing gray-woolen gowns, shawls, stockings and wooden clogs. Closest to me sat sweet Safie, whom I delightedly recognized, caressing a miniature cross of cedar inlaid with mother-of-pearl.

"Pardon this intrusion into your devotions," I apologized, stepping up to them softly, "but I must bid you a most regretful goodbye. I've determined to quit this place at the first opportunity, for I've failed to acquire the knowledge which I'd hoped to discover here."

"This search for elusive knowledge has deeply troubled you," she perceptively observed with a sympathetic tone.

"This has been to me like the torment of solitary drops of water repeatedly dripping on my head," I lamented. "Every thought devoted to it has been a grievous agony, and every word that I've uttered with relation to it has made my mouth quiver and my heart flutter."

"We pray at this altar," she related with a reverent gesture, "for it symbolizes the ultimate presence of God among these outcasts forsaken by the rest of humanity—by all sane human beings."

"No one's secure from going mad," I said, heaving a flustered sigh as I sat down expectantly beside her. "Whatever occasioned your coming to this asylum?" I asked her at the last.

"I came of necessity to help care for my dearest friend, Agatha, whom monsieur De Lacey committed here for treatment before he himself died of despair!" she softly exclaimed, confounded by my question.

Rigidly I sat upright, looking greatly aghast—first at Safie and next at her quietly downcast companion. Slowly the girl, sitting so listless alongside Safie, lifted up her fair face and gentle eyes to directly confront the outright fright betrayed by mine.

"Felix's sister?" I asked, my startled heart standing still as I tensely turned back to face Safie's confused countenance.

"Agatha's quite well," Safie assured me with her furrowed brow, "for little addles her mind. Although her heart has sunk exceedingly low she has kept her spiritual strength."

"Whatever became of her brother, Felix?" I asked with bated breath.

"Something was amiss with his senses," she staidly confided, "but he hadn't the same binding round his mind which we had."

"What do you mean?" I asked, growing increasingly anxious.

"Ever since he confronted your creature at the cottage of the De Lacey family," she told me, "Felix has hated and hunted him, for he blames him for the death of his father and the seemingly incurable despair of his sister, Agatha. Even now he chases after the creature, for should he ever overtake him he intends to take his revenge and kill him."

"Where's Felix now?" I asked, almost frantic.

"He migrated to the frontier of Switzerland where the creature was shot by the rustic, and even to the environs of Geneva itself, but he lost the creature's trail. He's written to say that he's making his way back to us—he could return at any moment."

"Safie," I implored her solemnly, my eyes pleading, "I must leave this place immediately, along with the creature. And you must help me."

§

Through the metal partition bars I reached my reluctant, outstretched arms, slowly, watchfully. My irresolute hands trembled uncontrollably as I tried so deliberately to handle the clanking keys taken from one of the asylum attendants lying sprawled, quiescent and unconscious alongside his toppled teacup on the stone cold cellar floor. By slow, tremulous turns I only grudgingly unlocked and unshackled the rigid irons restraining the listless creature, sitting upright but torpid against the wall, staring rancorously at me. After the last fetters clanged to the floor he gave out a long, low, infernal growl.

"We must leave this place at once," I told the devil slyly. "I've collected the materials necessary to construct my other creation, and I've resolved to complete my labors in some remote retreat in the northern highlands of Scotland."

Safie, wrapped up in her homespun gown and headscarf, stepped up softly in slippers as the partition creaked open and the creature emerged, looming monstrously ahead. Tightly I clutched the leathern portmanteau containing my chemical instruments.

"We must make haste," she exhorted us urgently, "for the sedative should daze the guards for only a short time."

Safie shuffled on before us—out of the cellar, along the somber corridor, up the pair of stairs, across the adjoining passage and cloister and out into the lurid dead of night. Together we hurriedly crossed the wooded grounds to the villa stable.

Guardedly we edged through the creaking gate, budging it open by slow degrees, stepped inside the looming stable and strained our eyes, peering through the shadowy darkness at seven sodden stalls, reeking of mustiness and manure. Behind us lumbered the hulking devil.

"Hold this, will you, while I harness one of the horses?" I asked Safie, gingerly holding out to her my leathern portmanteau of chemical instruments.

"Yes," she readily consented, grasping the portmanteau with care, "but you must work quietly, for the coachman's room lies directly above the coach house."

Unknown to us someone else quietly lurked, unheard and unseen in the nebulous half-light of the clustered hayloft above. In the darksome moonshine glinted the sharp prongs of an upraised pitchfork. At one desperate jump the spry and strapping shape of a young man leapt from the hayloft, pouncing on the devil from high up and plunging the pointed pitchfork forcefully into his monstrous back—blood spurting instantly from the deep impalement. Convulsed with rage the inflamed devil let out a clamorous cry of agony as he bodily hurled his assailant on his head and let him fly.

"Felix!" Safie shrieked, throwing up her hands in horror as she watched the youth tumble down heavily against some stacked bales of hay.

Felix heaved himself feebly to his feet, swiftly snapping up a sickle from the stable floor and wildly lunging at the devil once more. With the stiff pitchfork loosely lodged and dangling from his bloodied back the devil deftly dodged every blow struck as Felix lashed out again in a relentless frenzy. With one of his huge, gnarled hands the devil caught Felix by his sickle-wielding wrist, clenching it in a bone-crushing grip, wrenching the sickle free from his crippled fingers. His other hand quickly clutched Felix by his brittle throat, choking his neck with a slow, strangulating squeeze.

"I could tear you limb from limb!" the devil growled angrily as he lifted Felix off the ground with effortless ease, his legs dangling in the air, violently throttling him at the end of his outstretched arm.

"Stop!" I shouted at the devil. "If you put the print of your murderous hands on his neck I shall never deliver into them the female devil who'll follow you into your exile."

Downstairs from his room aloft clumsily stumbled the night-clothed coach man, frightfully drawn towards the bedlam.

"What goes on here?" he cried.

"The monster from the asylum is loose!" Safie frantically warned him, inciting him to bolt from the stable. "Flee for your life!"

From the devil's loosened hold Felix tumbled down heavily to the ground and collapsed into a crumpled heap, desperately clutching at his own tortured, retching throat. Safie rushed to bend and fold him in her arms.

"How could you bear me such malice?" the devil implored Felix—his voice incredulous. "I watched you fetch with delight for your sister, Agatha, the first tiny white flower of spring which peeked out from underneath the frigid ground."

"I consent to your ultimatum," I reminded the devil, yanking the pitchfork from his brawny back and holding it up before his desiccated face, "on your solemn vow to leave Europe forever and every other place in the community of man."

"Retreat to your remote niche in the northern highlands of Scotland," the devil bid me with a nod of accord as he ran his speculative eyes over the bloodied prongs—oblivious to any injury, "and finish your work: I shall observe your progress with unspeakable anticipation; and don't worry but that when you're prepared I shall appear."

Saying that he abruptly left us; we watched him set out into the gloomy dead of night with scrambling speed and rapidly disappear among the shadowed woods. Immediately I bent down to bid the two tearful youths a sad goodbye.

"It's for the better," I consoled them, "that I should endure my inroads of misery and madness far away from you."

"Love is merely a madness," Safie said devoutly, "and deserves as well a safe house and an open heart as madmen do; and the reason why they're not so rescued and cured is that the madness is so ordinary that the doctors are in love too."

Together with my chemical instruments I cast myself into the coach that was to carry me off, scarcely knowing where I was going, and heedless of what was passing by. I could only brood upon the burden of my expedition and the work which was to preoccupy me while it proceeded.

EIGHTEEN:
A MONSTER'S MATE
LOST

"How mutable are our feelings, and how strange is that clinging love we have of life even in the excess of misery."—Victor Frankenstein

JOSEPH COVINO JR

After spending some months in London an acquaintance in Scotland, who had before been our guest at Geneva, sent us a letter. He alluded to the loveliness of his native land, and asked us whether that was not enough enticement to prompt us to extend our excursion as far north as Perth, where he lived. Henry anxiously wished to take that invitation; and I, although I loathed society, yearned to see once more mountains and streams, and all the miraculous marvels with which Nature graces her choice habitations.

We had reached England at the start of October, and it was then February. So we decided to embark upon our expedition towards the north at the end of another month, determined to reach the finish of that trip around the end of July. We left London on the 27ᵗʰ of March.

I relished this prospect; and yet my relish was poisoned both by my remembrance of the past, and my apprehension of the future. I was fashioned for tranquil contentment. Throughout my youth bitterness never afflicted my spirit; and if I was ever overpowered by monotony, the spectacle of what is sublime in nature, or the search for what is admirable and superb in the inventions of man, would always stir my heart, and impart vitality to my soul.

The relish of Henry was proportionately deeper than mine.

"I could spend my life here," he told me, "and amidst these heights I should scarcely miss Switzerland and the Rhine."

The time of our meeting with our Scotch acquaintance drew near, and we journeyed ahead. For my own part I had no regret. I had then postponed my pledge for some time, and I feared the consequences of the devil's vexation. He might stay in Switzerland, and take his revenge on my relations. This notion haunted me, and tortured me at every instant from which I might have taken rest and tranquility. I awaited my letters with frenzied anxiety: if they were detained, I was wretched, and overpowered by countless qualms; and when they came and I saw the inscription of Elizabeth or my father, I scarcely ventured to read and learn my lot. At times I felt that the demon followed me, and might hasten my neglect by killing my friend. When these impressions preoccupied me, I would not leave Clerval for an instant, but shadowed him as his ghost, to protect him from the suspected wrath of his slayer. But I was restless to reach the end of our excursion.

We arrived at Perth, where our acquaintance anticipated us. Only I was in no humor to revel and converse with strangers, or entertain their caprices and preparations with the high spirits expected from a visitor; and so, I told Henry that I desired to make the trip of Scotland alone.

"Do you," I said, "enjoy yourself, and let this be our rendezvous. I might be gone for a month or two; but do not intrude on my movements, I implore you: leave me to my own devices in peace and privacy for a brief period; and once I come back, I trust it will be with better humor, more agreeable with your own good nature."

Clerval wanted to discourage me; but sensing me intent upon this purpose, he desisted to dissuade. He implored me to write frequently.

"I had rather remain with you," he told me, "in your lone travels, than with these Scotch people, whom I do not know: hurry, then, my good friend, to come back, that I might once more feel myself rather at ease, which I cannot do with you gone."

Having taken leave of my friend, I resolved to sojourn in some secluded place in Scotland, and complete my task in isolation. I had no doubt but that the fiend followed me, and would betray himself to me once I should have finished, that he might accept his mate. So I packed up my chemical instruments and the materials I had gathered, deciding to complete my work in some remote corner in the northern highlands of Scotland.

FRANKENSTEIN RESURRECTED

With this resolve, I traveled the northern highlands, and settled on one of the most isolated of the Orkneys as the site of my task. It was a setting suited for such toil, being scarcely more than a stone, whose lofty surfaces were constantly battered by the waves. The earth was sterile, barely providing pasture for a few wretched cows, and oatmeal for its dwellers, which comprised five people, whose gangly and ragged limbs betokened their wretched sustenance. Bread and vegetables, when they luxuriated in such indulgence, and even fresh water, was to be acquired from the mainland, which was roughly five miles off.

On the entire island there were just three wretched huts, and one of these was tenantless when I alighted. This I rented. It consisted of just two rooms, and these displayed all the squalor of the most wretched poverty. The thatch had caved in, the walls were un-tarred, and the door hung off its hinges. I directed it to be patched, procured some furnishings, and took up my abode; an event which would, no doubt, have evoked some bewilderment had not all the faculties of the cottagers been blunted by dire distress and privation. As it was, I subsisted un-gawked at and undisturbed, scarcely requited for the paucity of rations and garments which I donated; so much does misery deaden even the crudest senses of mortals.

In this refuge I dedicated the morning to work; but in the night, when the climate allowed, I wandered on the rockbound coast of the ocean to hear the rollers as they rumbled and smashed underfoot. It was a tedious yet ever-shifting sight.

In this way I allotted my activities once I first alighted; but as I progressed in my task, it grew each day more terrible and troublesome to me. At times I could not persuade myself to step inside my laboratory for many days; and at other times I labored night and day to finish my task. It was, in reality, an obscene occupation in which I was employed. During my first attempt, a sort of frenzied enthusiasm had blinded me to the

321

terror of my endeavor; my thoughts were resolutely bent on the completion of my task, and my eyesight closed to the terror of my procedure. But then I went to it coldheartedly, and my spirit frequently revolted by my handiwork.

So installed, engaged in the most odious employment, submerged in a seclusion where nothing could for a moment divert my attention from the true situation in which I was involved, my soul grew agitated; I turned restive and unsettled. Every instant I was in fear of encountering my oppressor. At times I sat with my eyes riveted on the floor, afraid to lift them up, for fear that they should meet the thing which I so strongly shuddered to see. I dreaded to stray from the vicinity of my neighbors, for fear that once by myself, he should appear to take possession of his mate.

In the meanwhile I labored on, and my work had by then notably progressed. I anticipated its accomplishment with a nervous and anxious apprehension, which I did not risk trusting myself to dispute, but which was intermingled with murky premonitions of calamity, that made my spirit shrink in my breast.

I sat one night in my laboratory; dusk had fallen, and the moon was just hovering over the ocean; I had not enough light for my occupation, and I stayed unoccupied, in a lull of contemplation of whether I should quit my task for the night, or expedite its completion by a relentless preoccupation with it. As I sat, a current of thought struck me, which compelled me to contemplate the consequences of what I was then doing. Three years earlier I was employed in the same way, and had made a monster whose unequaled brutality had devastated my spirit, and filled it eternally with the most virulent regret. I was then about to create another creature, of whose temperament I was likewise unwitting; she might turn countless times more malevolent than her companion, and revel, for its own sake, in carnage and misery. He had vowed to leave the community of man, and secrete himself in wastelands; but she had not;

and she, who in all likelihood was to turn into a rational and thoughtful creature, might reject consent to a pact stipulated before her creation. They might even abominate each other; the beast who already breathed despised his own monstrosity, and might he not construct a stronger animosity for it once it floated before his eyes in the womanly form? She too might shrink with loathing from him to the surpassing splendor of man; she might abandon him, and he be once more by himself, infuriated by the new indignity of being forsaken by one of his own kind.

Even if they were to quit Europe, and haunt the wilds of the new world, yet one of the first fruits of those emotions for which the devil hungered would be children, and a race of demons would be procreated throughout the world, who might make the very presence of the family of man a predicament perilous and fraught with horror. Had I a prerogative, for my own advantage, to impose this scourge upon untold descendants? I had before been touched by the sophistry of the monster I had made; I had been struck dumb by his diabolic threats: but then, for the first time, the outrage of my pledge exploded upon me; I trembled to speculate that succeeding generations might condemn me as their curse, whose arrogance had not scrupled to purchase its own complacency at the cost, perhaps, of the existence of the entire human species.

I shuddered, and my heart fluttered inside me, when, lifting up my eyes, I saw, by the moonlight, the devil at the casement. A grisly grin creased his lips as he glared at me, where I sat discharging the duty which he had appointed to me. Indeed, he had shadowed me in my excursions; he had lingered in woodlands, secreted himself in caves, or taken shelter in vast and barren heaths; and he then came to inspect my advancement, and take the consummation of my oath.

As I watched him, his expression exuded the utmost degree of depravity and malevolence. I contemplated with an inkling of insanity my oath of making another akin to him, and shuddering with rage, pulled to pieces the thing in which I was engrossed. The monster watched me eradicate the creation on whose imminent presence he relied for contentment, and, with an outcry of demonic desperation and vengeance, departed.

I quit the room, and, latching the door, pledged my sacred word in my own breast never to continue my task; and then, I bent my shaky steps toward my own apartment. I was by myself; none were close to me to dispel the despair, and comfort me against the disgusting persecution of the most horrible visions.

Many hours went by, and I stayed close to my window staring at the ocean; it was nearly still, for the currents were calm, and all creation slumbered beneath the glimmer of the tranquil moon. Several solitary fishing boats spotted the sea, and once in a while the mild wind carried the utterance of voices as the fishermen called out to each other. I sensed the stillness, although I was scarcely aware of its utmost intensity, until my attention was abruptly attracted to the plying of oars close to the shore, and somebody alighted near my hut.

Several minutes later, the creaking of my door caught my ear, as if somebody tried to budge it open quietly. I shuddered from top to toe; I sensed a foreboding of who it was, and wanted to waken one of the peasants who stayed in a cottage at no great distance from mine; but I was overwhelmed by the impression of paralysis, so frequently sensed in frightening nightmares, when you to no avail try to flee from an imminent threat, and was pinned to the place.

Shortly the sound of footsteps reached my ear; the door budged open, and the monster whom I abominated materialized. Closing the door, he drew near and said in a stifled voice—

"You have destroyed the creation which you started. What is it that you mean to do? Do you dare to break your word? I have suffered so much pain and despair."

"What do you know of either?"

"I left Switzerland with you. I followed you along the shores of the Rhine, crossed its islands, and climbed its peaks. I have roamed for many months the heaths of England and the deserts of Scotland. I have endured unending hunger, cold, and fatigue. Do you dare destroy my dreams?"

"Away with you! I do break my word. Never will I make another like yourself—identical in ugliness and depravity."

"Peasant! I before pleaded with you, but you have proved yourself undeserving of my indulgence. Remember that I possess power. You think yourself wretched, but I can make you so miserable that the breath of life will be abhorrent to you. You are my maker, but I am your master. Obey!"

"The time of my indecision is no more, and the time of your power is now. Your threats cannot force me to commit an act of abomination. But they strengthen in me a resolve not to make you a mate in brutality. Shall I, coldheartedly, loose upon the world a devil, whose pleasure is in death and misery? Away with you! I am resolved, and your talk will only aggravate my wrath."

The demon saw my resolve in my expression, and ground his teeth in the paralysis of rage.

"Shall each man," he exclaimed, "take a wife to his breast, and each beast have a mate, and I be by myself?"

"What makes you think you are either man or beast?"

"I felt emotions of tenderness, and they were repaid with loathing and contempt. Betrayer! You may abominate, but take care! Your time will pass in fear and despair, and soon the death blow will come which must ravage your happiness forever. Shall you be happy while I wallow in the depths of my misery?"

"I should be happy to deliver to you your death blow."

"You can destroy my other emotions, but vengeance remains—vengeance, from this time more precious than life itself. I may die, but not before you, my oppressor and torturer, shall curse the light of day."

"To this day I curse you!"

"Take care; for I am unafraid, and therefore invincible. I will watch and wait with the cunning of a serpent, that I might bite you with its fangs. Betrayer, you shall regret the wrong that you do."

"Demon, desist; and do not corrupt the air with the sound of your spite. I have asserted my resolve to you, and I am no craven to flinch from talk. Away from me; I am unwavering."

"Very well. I will leave; but do not forget, *I shall visit you on your wedding-night.*"

I lurched ahead, and cried, "Scoundrel! Before you pass my sentence, be certain that you are yourself protected."

I would have grasped him; but he escaped me, and left the hut with haste. At a stroke I watched him embark in his boat, which scudded across the sea with an expeditious speed, and was promptly lost amidst the billows.

Everything was once more quiet; but his pronouncement resounded in my ears. I quivered with rage to chase the slayer of my tranquility, and expedite him into the sea. I paced back and forth in my apartment impatiently and agitated, while my mind's eye conjured up countless visions to torture and distress me. Why had I not chased after him, and grappled with him in a death struggle? But I had permitted him to escape, and he had steered his course toward the mainland. I trembled to speculate who might be the next prey slaughtered for his voracious vengeance. And then I pondered once more his pronouncement—"*I will visit you on your wedding-night.*" That then was the time set for the accomplishment of my fate. At that time I should perish, and at the same instant gratify and quench his spite. That outlook did not inspire fear; yet when I considered my beloved Elizabeth—her weeping and unending sadness, once she should discover her beloved so savagely seized from her—tears, the first I had burst out with in many a month, flowed from my eyes, and determined not to falter before my foe without a death struggle.

The night went by, and the sun arose from the sea; my emotions became composed, if it might be termed composure, once the outbreak of fury plummets into the bottomless pit of futility. I quit the hut, the horrific site of the past night's confrontation, and trudged on the strand of the sea, which I nearly considered to be an insurmountable obstacle between me and my fellow mortals; rather, a desire that such should prove true crept over me. I wished that I might waste my existence on that stark stone, arduously, it is sure, but undisrupted by any abrupt stroke of wretchedness. If I went back, it was to be slaughtered, or to watch those whom I most cherished, perish beneath the clutches of a devil whom I had myself made.

I roamed around the island like a restless ghost, severed from everything it adored, and wretched in the severance. When it came to be midday, and the sun climbed higher, I sprawled on the grass, and was overwhelmed by a heavy sleep. I had been awake all of the night before, my wits were disturbed, and my eyesight irritated by strain and wretchedness. The sleep into which I then lapsed revived me; and when I awoke, I once more felt like I was related to a family of mortals like myself, and I began to contemplate what had happened with considerable calmness; but still the utterances of the monster resounded in my head like a funeral dirge; they materialized like a nightmare, but explicit and withering as actuality.

The sun had distantly set, and I still sat on the strand, gratifying my hunger, which had become voracious, with an oaten cake, when I sighted a fishing-boat landing near me, and one of the men carried a package to me; it contained letters from Geneva, and one from Henry beseeching me to meet him. He wrote that he was spending his time futilely where he remained. He could no longer postpone his departure for London; so he beseeched me to apportion as much of my company to him as I could share. He implored me, then, to quit my isolated isle, and to join him at Perth, that we might continue southward together. His letter to some extent brought me back to life, and I resolved to leave my island at the end of two days.

But, before I left, there was a chore to complete, which I trembled to contemplate: I must pack up my chemical apparatus and for that object I must return to the chamber which had been the place of my loathsome task, and I must manipulate those implements, the sight of which was revolting to me. The next morning, at the break of day, I plucked up enough courage, and unbolted the door of my laboratory. The remnants of the half-completed being, whom I had pulled to pieces, lay strewn on the floor, and I nearly felt like I had mutilated the living tissue of a fellow creature. I stopped to compose myself, and then stepped inside the room. With shaking hands I carried the instruments out of the apartment; but I considered that I ought not to abandon the vestiges of my task to inspire the terror and consternation of the peasants; and so I placed them in a basket, with quite a number of rocks, and, piling them up, resolved to cast them into the ocean that very evening; and in the meanwhile I sat upon the strand, engaged in washing and putting in order my chemical apparatus.

Nothing could be more thorough than the change that had occurred in my emotions since the night of the arrival of the devil. I had before considered my pledge with a forlorn futility, as something that, with whatever results, must be redeemed; but then I felt like a veneer had been stripped from my sight, and that I, for once, saw plainly. The notion of resuming my task did not for one moment suggest itself; the threat I had taken oppressed my mind, but I did not accept that a discretionary deed on my part could thwart it. I had formed a resolve in my own heart, that to make another like the monster I had first created would be a deed of the vilest and most flagrant conceit; and I banned from my brain every consideration that could come to a contrary conclusion.

Between two and three in the morning the moon loomed; and I then, placing my basket on board a small skiff, I sailed out almost four miles from the strand. The setting was utterly isolated: several boats were steering towards shore, but I sailed away from them. I felt like I was conspiring to commit an awful crime, and shunned with shuddering dread any contact with my fellow mortals. All at once the moon, which had before been unclouded, was abruptly overshadowed by a dense cloud, and I exploited that instant of blackness and cast my basket into the ocean; I heard the gurgling noise as it submerged, and then sailed away from the spot. The sky was clouded over; but the air was fresh, although crisp from the north-east gust that was then gathering. But it revived me, and pervaded me with such pleasant impressions, that I decided to extend my stay at sea; and, setting the rudder in a fixed position, sprawled myself at the bottom of the boat. Clouds covered the moon, all was murky, and I heard merely the creaking of the boat, as its keel sliced through the billows; the sound soothed me, and soon I slept deeply.

I do not know how long I stayed in that condition, but when I woke up I discovered that the sun had already climbed conspicuously. The current was squally, and the billows incessantly menaced the stability of my small skiff. I discovered that the current was north-east, and must have driven me a long way off from the strand from which I had sailed. I struggled to alter my course, but promptly discovered, that if I once more launched forth, the boat would be immediately flooded with water.

So stranded, my sole recourse was to steer before the storm. I admit that I experienced some emotions of horror. I possessed no compass, and was so narrowly familiar with the geography of that part of the earth, that the sun was of scant advantage to me. I might be driven to the vast Atlantic, and suffer all the torments of starvation, or be engulfed by the boundless, bounding main that rumbled and battered all around me. I had already been afloat for untold hours, and suffered the torture of a searing thirst, an overture to my other ordeals. I contemplated the skies, which were overspread by clouds that scudded before the storm, merely to be supplanted by others: I contemplated the ocean, it was to be my tomb. "Monster," I cried, "your work is already done!" I brooded upon Elizabeth, Henry, and my father—all abandoned, on whom the fiend might gratify his murderous gluttony. That notion submerged me into a nightmare, so daunting and dreadful, that even then, when the vista is on the verge of sinking into oblivion in front of me forever, I tremble to contemplate it.

NINETEEN:
A FAMILY REUNITED

"Death snatches away many blooming children, the only hopes of their doting parents: how many brides and youthful lovers have been one day in the bloom of health and hope, and the next a prey for worms and the decay of the tomb!"—Victor Frankenstein

FRANKENSTEIN RESURRECTED

SWONA, IN THE ORKNEY ISLANDS

Between Caithness on the northern Scottish mainland and the Orkney Islands beyond flows the perilous Pentland Firth—a relatively narrow channel, widening from six to eight miles with swirling tidal currents surging up to twelve knots. Swona, the bleak speck of rock upon which I then subsisted, lies far out amidst scattered, low-lying rock skerries in the thick of the fiercely turbulent Firth. Roughly only one and one-half miles long and a half-mile at its widest the scrubby island was effortless to traverse on foot. From the coastal heath atop the red sandstone cliffs at its eastward side to its lush grassy pasturage, battered at its jagged edges by constantly crashing waves, the island is wholly enveloped by an eerie atmosphere of intensely intermingled but drab color, fog, light and shade, buffeted by blustering winds and utterly destitute of trees.

After my distasteful encounter with the monster, I left my crofter's hut in haste and rambled at random all around the inconsiderable island, trudging lustily, and treading a haphazard path across its sandy clay loam until finally, completely spent, I crumpled to the sodden ground from utter exhaustion and lapsed into a deep sleep. At length I awoke, sprawled awkwardly atop the loftiest eastward cliff which plummeted one hundred thirty-four feet to the tumultuous waters below. Slowly aroused by the rhythmic sound of the sea sloshing convulsively through the towering gloup, which cut a roughhewn passage through the rock, I arose and tread a westward path until I caught sight of a fiery, flickering light in the offing.

Instinctively I tramped toward it—a dim, distant glow which turned into a blazing flame the closer I came. As I ploddingly approached I made out a cluster of several standing but slanted stones, poking obliquely out of the tufted grass at the lower edge of the stone-cluttered seacoast. In the midst of those tall, tilted stones lay discarded upon the ground a smoldering heather torch—the burning beacon which lured me with its strangely seductive, silent but irresistible invitation: to enter the island's sole prehistoric round-covered chambered *cairn*.

Upon the burial chamber's central sinuous axis was laid its ingoing access passage through which I would insinuate myself and guardedly thread my way. So overpowering was the impulse to penetrate its dark, gaping depths that I unhesitatingly snapped up the torch and directly proceeded to step inside.

Two pairs of opposing slabs were upraised crosswise to the central passageway, partitioning the *cairn* into three stalled compartments. The first pair of slabs separated an antechamber from the principal chamber. The second pair of slabs formed a portal to an inner sanctum of the principal chamber. Dry flagstone and sandstone masonry made up the rough-hewn passage and chamber walls. False-corbelled vaults were erected above the principal part of the chamber.

My heather torch, held out before me at arm's length, threw its blazing light upon the facing upright slabs and side-long walls linked by tiers of massive stone lintels overhead. Underneath shorter, protruding pairs of facing slabs with sill-stones between them partitioned the lengthy inner compartment. Level shelves in the flanking walls subdivided the innermost section.

Between a pair of low-set portal stones I cautiously entered the innermost cell composed of rough-cast walls and overhung by a capstone. Bound between the crosswise slabs along the side walls were slab benches of solid stone buttressed by stones set on end upon the clay floor. Underfoot a profusion of unseen brittle objects crunched noisily. I lowered the torch, shedding an outspread spangle of light about my feet, and looked aghast at all manner of human bones accumulated and scattered all over the floor. Gradually lighting up the rest of the confined cell I cast my startled eyes on heaps of human skulls piled against the back-slab of the rearward wall. By slow degrees I illuminated the sidelong walls, exposing to sudden view their crowded horde of inhumed human skeletons, crouched intact upon the cell's slab-benches. One after the other the blazing light of my torch passed over the wall-to-wall rows of crouched skeletons until I abruptly started at catching sight of some slight movement in their tomblike midst. Straining my eyes I cringed in mortal fear at making out the unmistakable shape of the misshapen monster whose startling and grotesque visage made my heart stand still! Paralyzed with fear I stopped cold and stared agape, shuddering uncontrollably as I directed my panic-stricken eyes to the lifeless object which the monster unexpectedly tossed into a shallow, stone-lined pit scooped out of the clay—a fragile human skull which wobbled to a deathly standstill atop a heap of equally breakable skulls piled into the circular cist at my feet. His hideous features were at once brightly irradiated and darkly shaded by the firelight.

"The dead sleep in their beds," he muttered in his smothered voice, creasing his straight black lips and shriveled yellow cheeks with his grisly, malign grin.

"It is quite seemly, then, that you skulk here since you should soon join them!" I blurted out, holding before my drastically bated breath.

"As well you should yourself," he rejoined, his yellow, watery eyes squinting malignantly. "Remember, *I shall visit you on your wedding-night!*"

§

Several hours elapsed so; but gradually, as the sun set upon the skyline, the wind subsided into a soft sea breeze, and the ocean grew rid of rollers. Only those gave way to a strong surge; I felt queasy, and barely capable of gripping the rudder, when unexpectedly I sighted southward a sea line of lofty land.

Nearly worn out, as I was, by exhaustion, and the awful anxiety I suffered for some time, this sureness of survival surged like a torrent of exquisite euphoria, and tears burst out of my eyes.

I fabricated another sail with a portion of my garb, and anxiously steered toward land. It possessed a rugged and wild landscape, but, as I hugged the shore closer, I readily discerned the vestiges of tillage. I sighted boats close to the coast, and found myself abruptly carried back to the community of civilized humanity. I meticulously followed the meanderings of the land, and signaled a steeple which I eventually sighted rising from behind a prominent headland. Since I was in a condition of intense infirmity, I decided to steer straight towards the town, as a refuge where I could most readily obtain sustenance. Luckily I had funds with me. As I rounded the headland, I sighted a tidy little town and a safe harbor, which I infiltrated, my spirit leaping with joy at my surprising deliverance.

While I was engaged in repairing the boat and organizing the sails, some people thronged toward the site. They looked greatly aghast at my outward appearance, but rather than volunteering any aid, murmured in concert with motions which at any other moment might have evoked in me a scant impression of apprehension.

"My dear friends," I hailed them. "You speak English. Would you be so good as to tell me where I am and acquaint me with the name of your town?"

"You will find that out in due time," a man answered in a raspy voice. "Perhaps you have landed someplace that will not prove much to your liking. But you will not be conferred with as to your lodgings, I assure you."

I was extremely stupefied at hearing so curt a retort from a stranger; and I was also distressed at discerning the scowling and irate faces of his compatriots.

"Why do you accost me so harshly?" I asked them. "Certainly it is not the habit of Englishmen to greet strangers so ungraciously."

"We haven't the remotest idea what the habit of the English might be," the man snapped. "But it is the habit of the Irish to detest scoundrels."

While this curious conversation carried on, I discerned that the crowd quickly swelled. Their faces displayed a combination of curiosity and animosity, which disturbed, and to some degree startled me.

"Can anyone tell me the way to the inn?" I asked them; but no one answered.

I then pressed forward, and a muttering noise emanated from the crowd as they swarmed and encircled me; when a sickly looking man stepping up, rapped me on my shoulder.

"Come, sir," he commanded. "You must accompany me to Mr. Kirwin's, to give an explanation of yourself."

"Who is Mr. Kirwin? Why must I give any explanation of myself? Is this not a free country?"

"Aye, sir, free enough for honorable people. Mr. Kirwin is a magistrate; and you are to give an explanation for the death of a young man who was discovered murdered here last night."

His reply shocked me; but I directly regained myself. I was guiltless; that could readily be demonstrated: so I accompanied my escort quietly and was conducted to one of the better houses in the town. I was on the point of collapsing from exhaustion and hunger; but, being encircled by a crowed, I felt it prudent to muster all my strength, that no bodily infirmity might be interpreted as anxiety or cognizant guilt. Little did I then anticipate the catastrophe that was in a few minutes to crush me, and eradicate in terror and futility all dread of disrepute or death.

I must stop here; for it demands all my strength to call to mind the frightening incidents which I am about to recount, in fastidious detail, to my remembrance.

§

I was promptly ushered into the chambers of the magistrate, an elderly and kindly man, with a gentle and temperate comportment. He inspected me, however, with some measure of strictness; and then, facing my escorts, he asked who attended as witnesses at this proceeding. Some six men presented themselves; and, one being designated by the magistrate, he testified.

"I had been out fishing the night before with my son and brother-in-law, Daniel Nugent," he recounted. "At about ten o'clock we noticed a strong northerly gust blowing up, so we put in for port. It was pitch dark since the moon had not yet risen. We did not land at the harbor, but as was our wont, at a stream about two miles south. I went ahead first, carrying some of our fishing gear, and the others followed behind at some distance. As I walked along the strand, I hit my foot against something, and fell headlong to the ground. My mates came to my aid, and by the light of their lantern, we discovered that I had stumbled upon the body of a man, who by all appearances looked dead. We first suspected that it was the corpse of somebody who had drowned, and was washed up on shore by the waves, but on closer inspection, we discovered that the clothes were not wet, and even that the body was still warm. We immediately carried it to the cottage of an old woman close to the place, and tried to revive it, but to no avail. He looked like a handsome young man, about five and twenty years old. He had evidently been strangled, for there were no signs of violence, save the black mark of fingers upon his neck."

The first part of his testimony did not in the least concern me; but once he alluded to the black mark of the fingers, I recalled the murder of my brother and I became intensely disturbed; my limbs quivered, and a haze clouded my eyes, which forced me to lean on a chair to stand. The magistrate regarded me with an eagle eye, and naturally came to an inauspicious conclusion from my demeanor. The fisherman's son corroborated his father's testimony; but then Daniel Nugent was summoned.

"Right before my friend fell," he deposed definitely, "I saw a boat, with a man in it, at a short distance from the beach. And, so far as I could tell by the light of some stars, it was the very same boat in which the Englishman has just landed."

"I live close to the shore," a woman testified, "and was standing at the door of my cottage, waiting for the fishermen to return, when I saw a boat with a man in it, push off from that part of the beach where the body was later found."

"The fishermen brought the body to my house while it was still warm," another woman testified. "They laid it on a bed and rubbed it. Daniel went to town for an apothecary, but life was quite extinct."

"With the strong north wind that blew up in the night," several other men questioned about my landing testified, "it was most likely that he had floundered about for many hours, and was forced to go back to roughly the same place from which he embarked. Besides, it looked like he brought the body from another place, and it was likely, since he did not know the coast, that he had put into the harbor unaware of the distance of the town from the spot where he had abandoned the body."

Mr. Kirwin, on listening to this testimony, ordered that I should be conducted to the room where the corpse lay for burial, that it might be examined what effect the sight of it would provoke in me. That notion was likely prompted by the intense disturbance I had displayed once the method of the murder had been recounted. I was then led, by the magistrate and several others, to the inn. I could not help being impressed by the curious coincidences that had occurred during that unforgettable night; but, realizing that I had been talking together with several people on the island I had occupied about the time that the corpse had been discovered, I was completely calm as to the outcome of the incident.

I stepped inside the room where the body lay, and was taken up to the coffin. How can I recount my emotions at setting eyes on it? I feel still withered with terror, nor can I contemplate that horrible moment without trembling and anguish. The interrogation, the attendance of the magistrate and witnesses, drifted like a dream from my mind, once I viewed the dead body of Henry Clerval laid out in front of me.

I gulped for breath; and flinging myself on the corpse I cried, "Have my deadly devices deprived you, my dear Clerval, of life as well? Two I have already killed; other sacrifices await their fate: but you, Henry, my friend, my confidant..."

The human body could no longer bear the anguish that I suffered, and I was conveyed from the room in convulsive seizures.

A delirium followed this. I lay for two months at death's door: my ranting, as I was later told, was frightening. I named myself the slayer of William, of Justine, and of Henry. At times I implored my keepers to help me in the extermination of the monster by whom I was tortured; and at others, I felt the hands of the fiend clutching my neck, and shrieked aloud with anguish and horror. Luckily, as I spoke my mother tongue, Mr. Kirwin by himself understood me; but my agonizing outcries were enough to frighten the other witnesses.

Why did I not perish? More wretched than man ever was before, why did I not fall into oblivion and sleep? Of what stuff was I formed, that I could so withstand so many tribulations, which, like the turning of the screw, constantly repeated the torment?

But I was condemned to live; and in two months, found myself as starting from a nightmare, in a jail, laid out on a miserable bed, hemmed in by jailers, turnkeys, locks, and all the wretched contrivances of a prison. It was morning, I recall, once I so awoke to consciousness: I had forgotten the details of what had occurred, and just felt like some mighty calamity had abruptly overpowered me; but when I glanced around, and beheld the barred windows, and the squalor of the cell in which I was, everything ran in my head, and I moaned mournfully.

This noise disturbed an elderly lady who slumbered in a chair alongside me. She was an appointed nurse, the wife of one of the turnkeys, and her face displayed all those ill attributes that frequently represent the breed. The features of her face were harsh and rough, like that of those used to seeing without empathizing with the sights of wretchedness. Her speech voiced her complete unconcern; she accosted me in English, and the voice impressed me as one that I had heard throughout my affliction:--

"Do you feel better, sir?" she asked.

I answered in English, with a faltering voice, "I think I do; but if everything be real, if truly I did not hallucinate, I feel sorry that I live to feel this wretchedness and terror."

"Indeed," remarked the old lady, "if you refer to the gentleman you killed, I think that it were better for you had you died, for I suspect it will go rough on you! But then, that's none of my concern; I am sent to tend you and make you better; I do my duty with a clear conscience; it were well if everyone did likewise."

I turned with disgust from the old lady who could give utterance to so insensitive a diatribe to a patient barely spared, at the very point of death; but I felt listless and powerless to ponder all that had happened. The entire sequence of my existence materialized before me as a nightmare; at times I wondered whether indeed it were all real, for it never suggested itself to my consciousness with the power of truth.

As the pictures that drifted in front of me grew more distinct, I became feverish; a blackness enveloped me: no one was close to me who consoled me with the soothing tone of tenderness; no helping hand braced me. The doctor came and prescribed medications, and the old nurse prepared them for me; but extreme neglect was manifest in the first, and the expression of indignation was prominently displayed on the face of the second. Who would be concerned with the destiny of a killer, but the executioner who would earn his payment?

These were my first ruminations; but I presently I discovered that Mr. Kirwin had demonstrated to me ample compassion. He had arranged the best cell in the jail to be prepared for me(miserable in fact was the best); and it was he who had engaged a doctor and a nurse. It is certain, he rarely came to visit me, for although he fervently yearned to ease the misery of every fellow creature, he did not want to witness the anguish and wretched ranting of a killer. He came, then, at times to make certain that I was not neglected; but his visits were brief, and with lengthy intermittence.

One day, while I was slowly recuperating, I was slumped in a chair, my eyes half shut, and my cheeks pallid like those in death. I was overwhelmed by despondency and wretchedness, and frequently contemplated I had better court death than seek to stay in a world which to me was full of misery. Once I pondered whether I should not confess myself culpable, and endure the punishment of the law, more guilty than poor Justine had ever been. Such were my ruminations, when the door of my cell was opened, and Mr. Kirwin stepped inside. His face displayed pity and compassion; he drew a chair near mine and greeted me in French—

"I am afraid that this place is most distressing to you; can I do anything to make you more at ease?"

"I thank you, but everything that you suggest matters little to me; in the whole world there is nothing in which I am able to take comfort."

"I realize that the pity of a stranger can be but of little comfort to someone weighed down as you are by so curious a misadventure. But you will, I trust, presently leave this unhappy place; for, no doubt, evidence can readily be given to acquit you of the criminal complaint."

"That is my least worry: I am, by a strange turn of events, become the most wretched of creatures. Oppressed and tormented as I am and have been, can death be any harm to me?"

"Nothing indeed could be more grievous and distressing than the curious accidents that have recently happened. You were cast, by some unexpected chance, on our shore, celebrated for its hospitality; arrested immediately, and accused of murder. The first sight put before your eyes was the body of your friend, killed in so incomprehensible a fashion, and put, in a sense, by some monster in your way."

As Mr. Kirwin uttered this, despite the trepidation I suffered on this remembrance of my tribulations, I also felt extreme bewilderment at the familiarity he appeared to have regarding me. I suspect some surprise was displayed in my face; for Mr. Kirwin hastened to add—

"Immediately upon your falling ill, all the papers that were in your pockets were delivered me, and I studied them that I might learn some clue by which I could render to your relatives an account of your misadventure and infirmity. I discovered several letters, and, among others, one which I learned from its opening to be from your father. I immediately wrote to Geneva; almost two months have passed since the sending of my letter:--But you are unwell, even now you shiver: you are unsuited for trepidation of any sort."

"This apprehension is countless times worse than the most terrible incident: tell me what latest act of death has been committed, and whose I am then to deplore?"

"Your family is perfectly safe," Mr. Kirwin said, with consideration: "and someone, an acquaintance, has come to call on you."

I know not by what train of thought, the notion suggested itself, but it immediately came into my head that the killer had come to scoff at my affliction, and mock me with the death of

Henry, as a fresh provocation for me to submit to his infernal demands. I placed my hand in front of my face, and wailed in anguish—

"Oh! Send him away! I cannot face him; for God's sake, do not let him come in!"

Mr. Kirwin observed me with a disturbed expression. He could not help considering my outcry as a presumption of my culpability.

"I should have thought, young sir, that the arrival of your father would have been agreeable rather than provoking such vehement aversion."

"My father!" I cried out, while every lineament and every sinew was relieved from agony to gladness: "Is my father really arrived? How generous, how very generous! But where is he, why does he not hurry to me?"

My change in demeanor shocked and satisfied the magistrate; possibly he thought my prior outcry was a momentary relapse of raving, and then he immediately returned to his previous kindliness. He stood up, and left the cell with my nurse, and in an instant my father stepped inside.

Nothing, at that instant, could have done my heart more good than the coming of my father. I held out my hand to him and wept—

"Are you, then, well—and Elizabeth—and Ernest?"

My father pacified me with reassurances of their well-being, and attempted, by harping upon those topics so arresting to my heart, to lift my depressed spirits; but he presently felt that a jail cannot be the place of happiness.

"What a hole is this in which you waste away, my son!" he said, looking sorrowfully at the barred windows, and miserable appearance of the cell. "You journeyed searching for peace of mind, but a calamity seems to stalk you. And poor Henry..."

The name of my hapless and strangled friend was a trepidation too extreme to suffer in my decrepit condition; I burst into tears.

"Alas! Yes, my father," I answered; "Some fate of the most terrible sort hovers over me, and I must survive to fulfill it, or certainly I should have died on the coffin of Clerval."

We were then permitted to talk together for any lapse of time, for the critical condition of my health made every precaution imperative to ensure placidity. Mr. Kirwin stepped in, and asserted that my strength should not be depleted by excessive exertion. But the presence of my father was to me like that of my ministering spirit, and I slowly reclaimed my health.

As my illness left me, I was preoccupied by a desolate and dark despondency, which nothing could dispel. The face of Henry was perpetually in front of me, deathly and killed. More than once the trepidation into which these ruminations plunged me made my companions fear a perilous recurrence. Alas! Why did they spare so wretched and despised a life? It was certainly that I might fulfill my fate, which was then coming to a close. Before long will death quell these fits, and ease from me the weighty burden of agony that presses me to the dirt; and, in conducting the reward of righteousness, I shall also lie down to rest.

I had already spent three months in jail; and although I was still infirm and in constant risk of a recurrence, I was compelled to journey almost a hundred miles to the county-town, where the court was conducted. Mr. Kirwin took upon himself every responsibility for gathering witnesses, and organizing my defense. I was saved the humiliation of being put on trial publicly as a culprit, since the case was not brought before the court that judged life or death. The grand jury dismissed the case, on its being established that I was on the Orkney Islands at the time the corpse of my friend was discovered; and a fortnight following my delivery I was released from jail.

My father was overjoyed on finding me delivered from the bitterness of a criminal complaint, that I was once more permitted to breathe the fresh air, and allowed to go back to my native land. I did not partake in these emotions; for me the walls of a prison or a palace were equally abhorrent. The breath of life was stifled forever; and although the sun beat down upon me, as upon the joyful and jubilant of spirit, I saw about me nothing but a thick and forbidding blackness, pierced by no light except the glow of two eyes that stared down upon me. At times they were the expressive eyes of Clerval, succumbing to death, his dark eyes almost closed by the lids, and his long dark lashes fringing them; at times it was the watery, murky eyes of the monster, as I first sighted them in my apartment at Ingolstadt.

TWENTY:
A FAMILY RAVAGED

"Then the appearance of death was distant, although the wish was ever present to my thoughts; and I often sat for hours motionless and speechless, wishing for some mighty revolution that might bury me and my destroyer in its ruins."—Victor Frankenstein

My father attempted to arouse in me the emotions of devotion. He spoke of Geneva, to which I should presently sojourn—of Elizabeth and Ernest; but his expressions merely elicited loud moans from me. At times, in fact, I felt a yearning for serenity; and dreamed, with mournful euphoria of my beloved cousin; or yearned, with a ravaging nostalgia, to behold again the blue lake and rapid Rhone, that had been so precious to me in early boyhood: but my prevailing condition of sensation was a languor, in which a jail was as luxurious a retreat as the heavenliest setting in creation; and these seizures were scarcely disrupted but by convulsions of agony and despondency. At these times I frequently attempted to make an end of the life I abhorred; and it demanded ceaseless scrutiny and watchfulness to deter me from perpetrating some awful act of fury.

But one responsibility remained to me, the remembrance of which finally prevailed over my mundane despondency. It was imperative that I should return without procrastination to Geneva, there to protect the lives of those I so devotedly cared for; and to lie in ambush for the killer, that if any accident brought me to the place of his hiding, or if he ventured once more to devastate me by his existence, I might, with unfaltering aim, make an end of the life of the monstrous countenance which I had endowed with the sham of a soul yet more monstrous. My father still wanted to defer our leaving, afraid that I could not endure the exhaustion of a trip: for I was a smashed ruin—the ghost of a mortal creature. My might was lost. I was a bare skeleton; and delirium day and night ravaged my decrepit form.

Yet, as I pressed our departure from Ireland with such restlessness and impetuosity, my father judged it beneficial to acquiesce. We took ship aboard a vessel bound for Havre-de-Grace, and sailed with a gentle breeze from the Irish coast. It was the witching hour. I lolled on the deck, lifting up my eyes to the stars, and listening to the crashing of the waves. I welcomed the blackness that blocked Ireland from my sight; and my pulse throbbed with a frenzied euphoria once I pondered that I should presently sight Geneva. The past materialized in the gloom of a forbidding nightmare; but the vessel in which I lay, the wind that blew me from the forsaken coast of Ireland, and the ocean which encompassed me, affirmed too forcefully that I was beguiled by no illusion, and that Henry, my friend and dearest confidant, had fallen prey to me and the monster of my making. I retraced, in my mind, my entire existence—my tranquil serenity while living with my family in Geneva, the loss of my mother, and my relocation to Ingolstadt. I recalled, trembling, the frantic fervor that hastened me on to the making of my monstrous foe, and I recollected the night in which he first breathed. I was incapable of following the current of thought; countless emotions oppressed me, and I wept violently.

Ever since my recuperation from the delirium, I had been in the habit of taking each night a minute amount of laudanum; for it was with the aid of this drug solely that I was enabled to attain the rest essential for the support of life. Burdened by the remembrance of my varied calamities, I then consumed twice my customary portion, and shortly slept deeply. Only sleep did not offer me reprieve from reflection and wretchedness; my nightmares conjured up countless visions that frightened me. Towards dawn I was seized by a sort of hallucination; I felt the archfiend's clutches at my neck; and could not liberate myself from them; moans and outcries pierced my ears. My father, who was looking after me, discerning my disturbance, woke me; the crashing waves were all around: the overcast sky overhead; the archfiend was not there: a perception of protection, an impression that a peace was appointed between the present time and the inevitable, calamitous future, endowed me with a sort of tranquil oblivion, to which the human mind is by its formation particularly vulnerable.

Our voyage came to a close. We disembarked, and pressed

on to Paris. I presently discovered that I had overexerted my strength, and that I must rest before I could resume my journey. My father's care and concern were tireless; but he did not realize the source of my misery, and attempted faulty means to restore the hopelessly indisposed. He wanted me to pursue diversion in society. I loathed the countenance of man. Oh, not loathed! They were my fellow creatures, and I felt drawn even to the most repellent amongst them, as to beings of celestial essence and angelic quality. But I felt that I had no claim to partake in their fellowship. I had unloosed a nemesis amongst them, whose pleasure it was to slay them, and to wallow in their moans. How they would, each and everyone, abominate me, and hound me from the world, did they realize my profane deeds and outrages which had their origin in me!

My father acquiesced finally to my determination to desert society, and endeavored by varied rationalizations to dispel my despondency. At times he surmised that I felt profoundly the debasement of being compelled to respond to an accusation of murder, and he strove to demonstrate to me the futility of conceit.

"Alas! My father," I said, "hardly do you know me. Human beings, their emotions and sensitivities, would really be debased if such an outcast as I felt conceit. Justine, poor hapless Justine, was as blameless as I, and she endured the same accusation; she perished for it; and I am the source of this—I killed her. William, Justine, and Henry—they all perished at my hands."

My father had frequently, throughout my confinement, listened to me make the same recrimination; when I so reproached myself, he at times appeared to want an account, and at others he seemed to interpret it as the product of raving, and that, throughout my sickness, some notion of this sort had suggested itself to my invention, the recollection of which I retained in my recovery. I evaded explanation, and retained a constant reticence regarding the monster I had made. I had a conviction that I should be presumed insane; and that in itself would permanently have stifled my voice. But, besides, I could not make myself reveal a secret which would fill my listener with dismay, and make dread and monstrous terror the captives of his chest. I repressed, then, my restless craving for pity, and was quiet when I would have given everything to have divulged that deathly secret. But even so particulars like those I have recounted would erupt untrammeled from me. I could render no account of them; but their reality partly lightened the weight of my secret enemy.

Upon this opportunity my father said, with a tone of boundless bewilderment, "My dearest Victor, what obsession is this? My dear son, I implore you never to make such a profession again."

"I am not insane," I exclaimed trenchantly, "the moon and the stars who have witnessed my actions, can testify to my veracity. I am the murderer of those most blameless prey; they perished by my plotting. Countless times would I have murdered myself, by slow degrees, to have spared their lives; but I could not, my father, I could not exterminate all of humanity."

The end of this tirade persuaded my father that my notions were demented, and he immediately altered the topic of our discourse, and tried to change the direction of my reflections. He wanted as fully as possible to eradicate the remembrance of the incidents that had happened in Ireland, and never spoke of them, or permitted me to mention my calamities.

As time elapsed I became more composed; wretchedness had her abode in my soul, but I no longer spoke in the same irrational method of my own offenses; enough for me was the awareness of them. By the utmost self-stringency I controlled the dominant expression of misery, which at times aspired to proclaim itself to all creation; and my demeanor was composed and more collected than it had ever been since my expedition to the ocean of ice.

These musings called to mind what I had before misremembered, the menace of the demon—"*I will visit you on your wedding-night!*" Such was my punishment, and on that night would the devil resort to every device to crush me, and wrenched me from the sight of contentment which proposed in part to soothe my affliction. On that night he resolved to achieve his outrage by my demise. Well, so be it; a death struggle would then surely occur, in which if he were triumphant I should be at rest, and his control over me ended. If he were defeated, I should be liberated. Alas! What liberation? Such as the countryman experiences when his family have been slaughtered before his eyes, his hovel burnt, his lands laid in ashes, and he is driven astray, dispossessed, distressed, and abandoned, but liberated. Such would be my deliverance, except that in my Elizabeth I was possessed of a treasure; alas! Offset by those terrors of grief and guilt, which would haunt me until death.

Precious and dearly beloved Elizabeth! Some tender emotions crept into my spirit, and ventured to murmur heavenly visions of affection and happiness; but my hopes were already withered. Yet I would perish to bring her happiness. If the wretch carried out his threat, demise was inescapable; but, once more, I contemplated whether my wedding would expedite my destiny. My downfall might indeed come a few months earlier; but if my tormentor should surmise that I delayed it, swayed by his threats, he would assuredly discover other and possibly more awful means of vengeance. He had sworn to visit me on my wedding-night, but he did not deem that threat as obliging him to humanity in the meanwhile, for as if to demonstrate that he was not yet glutted with blood, he had killed Henry instantly following the utterance of his threats. I determined, then, that if my impending wedding with my cousin would contribute either to hers or my father's contentment, my enemy's schemes against my existence should not impede it a solitary moment.

In about a week we departed from Paris and returned to

Geneva. The precious girl embraced me with tender affection; but tears welled out of her eyes; as she discerned my wasted form and fervid face. I perceived a change in her as well. She was thinner, and had lost a lot of that pleasant exuberance that had before enchanted me; but her softness, and gentle expressions of tenderness made her a more apt companion for one shattered and wretched as I was.

"My dear cousin, how much you must have suffered!" Elizabeth exclaimed caringly. "You look even more poorly than when you left Geneva. This winter has been passed more wretchedly, tormented as I have been by restless anxiety; yet I had hoped to see peace in your face, and to find that your heart is not completely empty of comfort and serenity. Yet I am afraid that the same feelings even now persist that made you so wretched a year ago, even perhaps aggravated by time."

"I am afraid, my beloved one," I affirmed with a solemn nod, "that little joy remains for us in this world; yet everything that I might one day relish is centered on you."

"I would not trouble you at this time," she faltered, "when so many difficulties burden you; but I have often craved to express something to you, but have never had the strength to start."

"You well know, Victor," she explained, "that our marriage had been the fondest desire of your parents ever since our childhood. We were told this when young, and brought up to expect it as an occasion that would definitely happen. We were loving playmates during childhood, and, I think, precious and prized friends to one another as we grew up. But as brother and sister often cherish a warm regard for each other, without craving a more affectionate attachment, may not such be our condition as well? Tell me, dearest Victor, answer me, I beseech you, by our shared happiness, with plain truth—do you not love another?"

"Dispel your futile fears," I reassured her, "to you only do I devote my life, and my attempts at happiness."

"You have rambled: you have spent several years of your life at Ingolstadt; and I admit to you, my cousin, that when I saw you last fall so miserable, fleeing to seclusion, from the society of every being, I could not help suspecting that you might lament our attachment, and think yourself obliged in good faith to honor the wishes of your parents, although they contradicted themselves your inclinations. But this is faulty logic. I admit to you, my cousin, that I love you, and that in my wishful dreams of fate you have been my fast friend and confidant."

"In you I confide only the most devoted love."

"But it is your happiness I wish for as well as my own, when I proclaim to you that our wedding would make me infinitely unhappy, unless it were the bidding of your own free will. Even now I lament to think that, burdened as you are by the severest hardships, you might suppress, by some point of honor, all hope of love and happiness which would by itself restore you to yourself. I, who have so dispassionate an attachment to you, might aggravate your tribulations a thousand-fold by being a hindrance to your desires. Ah! Victor, be assured that your cousin and confidant has too devoted a love for you not to be made wretched by this suspicion."

"My devotion to you, dearest, admits of no doubt or suspicion."

"Be happy, my cousin; and if you comply with this one plea, stay content that nothing in this world will have the power to disturb my serenity. Do not let me distress you; do not answer if it will cause you pain; and if I see but one smile on your face, occasioned by this or any other effort of mine, I shall need no other comfort."

"I harbor one secret, Elizabeth," I reluctantly conceded, "an awful one; when discovered to you, it will strike terror into your heart, and then, far from being shocked at my wretchedness, you will only marvel that I survive what I suffered. I will divulge this story of terror and torment to you the day after our wedding shall take place, for, my precious cousin, there must be absolute secrecy between us. But until then, I implore you, do not mention or speak of it. This I most seriously beseech, and I know you will respect."

The serenity which I then relished did not last. Remembrance brought derangement with it; and when I contemplated what had happened, I was possessed of a true madness; at times I was infuriated and convulsed with rage; at times dispirited and downcast. I neither spoke, nor faced anyone, but sat listless, perplexed by the profusion of tribulations that overpowered me.

Elizabeth alone had the strength to wrench me from these throes; her soft voice would comfort me when overcome by convulsions, and inspirit me with human sensations when plunged into stupor. She cried with me, and for me. Once rationality returned, she would reproach, and attempt to inspirit me with capitulation. Ah! It is well for the hapless to capitulate, but for the culpable there is no comfort. The miseries of remorse corrupt the intemperance there is otherwise at times found in wallowing in the indulgence of despair.

Shortly after my coming, my father spoke of my impending wedding with Elizabeth. I stayed quiet.

"Have you, then, another attachment?"

"None in the world. I idolize Elizabeth and await our marriage with relish. Let the date then be set; and on it I will dedicate myself, in life or death, to the happiness of my cousin."

"My dear Victor, do not speak so. Grievous adversities have beset us, but let us only hold tighter to what is left, and render our devotion to those whom we have lost to those who still live. Our society will be small, but united by the bonds of devotion and shared adversity. And when time shall have tempered your despair, fresh and precious objects of care will come into being to replace those of whom we have been so brutally bereft."

Such were the admonitions of my father. But to me the recollection of the threat returned: nor could I doubt that, formidable as the foul fiend had still been in his feats of gore, I should nearly deem him indomitable; and that once he had uttered the words, *"I shall visit you on your wedding-night,"* I should deem the threatened destiny as inevitable. But death was no atrocity to me, if the loss of Elizabeth were offset with it; and I then, with a satisfied and even glad expression, concurred with my father, that if my cousin would acquiesce, the wedding should occur in ten days, and so sealed, as I supposed, my doom.

Good God! If for one moment I had suspected what might be the infernal intent of my demonic enemy, I would rather have exiled myself forever from my native land, and rambled a dispossessed derelict around the world, than have accepted this wretched wedding. But, as if master of mystical powers, the monster had secreted his true intent; and when I suspected that I had designed my own demise, I expedited that of a much more precious sacrifice.

As the time set for our wedding neared, whether from timidity or a portentous presentiment, I felt my spirit sink inside me. But I hid my emotions by a demeanor of mirth, that brought smiles and delight to the face of my father, but scarcely fooled the ever-vigilant and observant eye of Elizabeth. She anticipated our wedding with quiet serenity, not detached from some anxiety, which past calamities had instilled, that what now looked assured and palpable happiness, might presently disperse into a flighty nightmare, and leave no vestige except profound and perpetual grief.

Arrangements were made for the affair, complimentary visits were entertained, and all displayed a mirthful demeanor. I closed up, as much as I could, in my own spirit the apprehension that haunted there, and took part with apparent determination in the arrangements of my father, although they might only act as the ornaments of my own catastrophe. Through my father's efforts, a portion of the inheritance of Elizabeth had been returned to her by the Austrian government. A modest estate on the shores of Lake Como belonged to her. It was agreed that, right after our wedding, we should travel to Villa Lavenza, and pass our early days of happiness beside the resplendent lake close to which it stood.

In the meanwhile I took every precaution to protect my person, in the event the foul fiend should overtly assault me. I carried pistols and a dagger continuously about me, and was ever watchful to avert artifice; and by these means acquired a deeper sense of serenity. Truly, as the time drew near, the threat seemed more like an illusion, not to be deemed as deserving to trouble my tranquility, while the joy I wished for in my wedding displayed a fuller semblance of assurance, as the time set for its celebration neared, and I overheard it constantly alluded to as an event which no mishap could conceivably obstruct.

Elizabeth appeared happy; my calm deportment helped considerably to ease her mind. But on the day that was to perfect my aspiration and fate, she was dispirited, and a premonition of calamity permeated her; and possibly too she contemplated the awful secret which I had pledged to discover to her on the day after. My father was in the meanwhile ecstatic, and in the fluster of arrangement only perceived in the sadness of his niece the modesty of a bride.

After the ceremony was conducted, a considerable party gathered at my father's; but it was agreed that Elizabeth and I should embark on our voyage by water, sleeping overnight at Evian and resuming our journey the next day. The day was fine, the wind fair, everyone reveled in our marital departure.

Those were the final moments of my existence during which I relished the impression of happiness. We passed speedily on: the sun was blood-hot, but we were shrouded from its beams by a type of canopy, while we relished the loveliness of the vista, at times on one side of the lake, where we contemplated the pleasing mounts, slopes, and in the distance, culminating all, the breathtaking Mont Blanc, and the assortment of snow-covered mountains that to no avail strive to rival her; at times drifting along the facing shores, we sighted the indomitable Jura averting its somber side to the aspiration that would depart from its native land, and a nearly invincible obstacle to the aggressor who should crave to subjugate it.

I held the hand of Elizabeth. "You are sad, my love. Ah! If you knew what I have endured, and what I might yet suffer, you would try to let me appreciate the peace and release from misery that this one day at least allows me to relish."

"Be happy, my dearest Victor," Elizabeth answered; "there is, I hope, nothing to disturb you; and be assured that if a joyful smile is not engraved on my face, my heart is satisfied. Something mutters to me not to rely a lot on the prospect that is held out in front of us, but I will not heed such an ominous voice. What a heavenly day! How joyful and tranquil all creation seems!"

So Elizabeth tried to distract her ruminations and mine from all contemplation of sorrowful subjects. But her disposition was vacillating; mirth for a few moments gleamed in her eyes, but it incessantly gave way to detachment and daydreaming.

The sun set lower in the skies; we passed the river Drance, and discerned its course through the ravines of the higher, and the valleys of the lower hills. The Alps here drew nearer to the lake, and we neared the arena of mountains which fashions its eastern edge. The peak of Evian gleamed beneath the woodlands that encompassed it, and the pinnacle upon pinnacle by which it was surmounted.

The wind, which had before conducted us along with astounding speed, plummeted at twilight to a gentle breeze; the calm current scarcely rippled the water, and stirred a soothing rustle amongst the trees as we neared the coast, from which it wafted the most fragrant scent of flowers and hay. The sun set below the skyline as we disembarked; and as I set foot on the shore, I sensed those anxieties and worries return, which presently were to clutch me, and cleave to me forever.

It was eight o'clock when we disembarked; we strolled for a brief time along the shore, relishing the fleeting light, and then withdrew to the inn, and appreciated the picturesque vista of waters, woods, and mountains, blurred in blackness, but yet exposing their dark silhouettes. Situated on the fronting strand of the lake at the foot of a narrow and winding hedged lane was the square, stone-built, two-story chalet, sequestered itself by a grove of forest trees and separated from the water's edge only by a small vineyard overgrown with thickets, to which we at last retired. Situated at the extremity of the chalet terrace was a safe harbor and secure little port where the boat was moored.

The wind, which had waned in the south, then arose with intense turbulence in the west. The moon had attained her crest in the skies and was starting to set; the clouds scudded across it faster than the griffon and clouded her beams, while the lake mirrored the vista of the lively skies, made yet livelier by the choppy billows starting to swell. Abruptly a violent torrent of rain fell.

I had been composed throughout the day; but so soon as night darkened the outlines of things, countless cares preyed on my mind. I was restless and vigilant, while my right hand gripped a pistol which was secreted in my breast; every noise horrified me; but I determined that I would trade my existence devotedly, and not cringe from the struggle until my own life, or that of my foe, was eradicated.

Elizabeth watched my trepidation at some length in anxious and nervous quiet, but there was something in my gaze which conveyed horror to her, and shuddering, she asked, "What is it that disturbs you, my dearest Victor? What is it you are afraid of?"

"Oh! Hush, hush, my love," I answered; "this night, and

everything will be well: but this night is awful, decidedly awful."

I spent an hour in this condition of mind, when unexpectedly I considered how frightening the conflict which I immediately anticipated would be to my bride, and I urgently urged her to withdraw, deciding not to join her until I had acquired some knowledge as to the condition of my adversary.

She quit me, and I resumed some time pacing back and forth the halls of the house, and investigating every niche that might provide a refuge to my archenemy. But I found no sign of him, and was starting to suspect that some auspicious accident had interceded to avert the perpetration of his threats; when unexpectedly I heard a piercing and awful shriek. It came from the room into which Elizabeth had withdrawn. As I heard it, the total reality hastened into my head, my arms collapsed, the movement of every fiber of muscle was paralyzed; I could feel the blood running cold in my veins, twinges in the tips of my limbs. This condition persisted but for a moment; the shriek was echoed, and I hurried into the darksome room.

Good God! Why did I not then die! Why am I here to recount the brightest hope, and the purest being in creation. She was there, dead and gone, flung across the bed, her head dangling down, and her pallid and contorted features partly draped by her hair. Everywhere I go I see the same form—her ashen arms and motionless figure slung by the killer on its marital pall. Could I look on this, and exist? Alas! Existence is tenacious, and cleaves strongest where it is most detested. For an instant only did I lose memory: I sunk unconscious to the parquet floor.

When I revived, I found myself encircled by the patrons of the inn; their faces displayed speechless horror: but the terror of others seemed only as a parody, a ghost of the emotions that afflicted me. I absconded from them to the room where lay the corpse of Elizabeth, my beloved, my wife, so recently alive, so virtuous. She had been moved from the position in which

I had first seen her; and then, as she lay, her head against her arm, and a handkerchief tossed across her face and neck, I may have surmised her asleep. I hurried towards her, and enfolded her with fervor; but the deathly listlessness and frigidity of the limbs told me, that what I then folded in my arms had ceased to be the Elizabeth whom I had adored and idolized. The mortal mark of the demon's grip was on her neck, and the breath had ceased to emit from her lips.

While I yet hovered over her in the anguish of grief, I happened to lift up my eyes. The windows of the room had before been blackened, and I felt a kind of dread on discerning the dull yellow light of the moon lighten the room. The shutters, before closed, had been slung back; and, with an impression of terror not to be related, I perceived at the open window a shape the most monstrous and abominated. A smirk was on the countenance of the monster; he appeared to sneer, as with his infernal finger he pointed towards the body of my bride. I hurried towards the window, and drawing a pistol from my breast, fired: but he escaped me, jumped from his position, and, rushing headlong, leaped into the lake.

The shot of the pistol attracted a party into the room. I pointed to the place where he had vanished, and we followed the wake with boats; nets were cast, but to no avail. After spending several hours, we returned despairing, most of my escorts thinking it to have been a vision conjured up by my invention. After having disembarked, they pressed on to search the countryside, parties dispersing in different directions amongst the thickets and woodlands.

I tried to go along with them, and advanced a short span from the house; but my head spun, my steps were like those of someone in a fog, I dropped at length in a condition of arrant fatigue; a haze masked my eyes, and my skin was scorched with the delirium of fever. In this condition I was carried back, and laid on a bed, scarcely aware of what had occurred; my eyes flitted about the room, as if to search for something that I had missed.

After a time I rose, and, as if by intuition, crept into the room where the body of my beloved lay. There were women wailing about—I hovered over it, and mingled my mournful tears with theirs—all that time no definite notion suggested itself to my mind; but my ruminations roamed to numerous things, brooding perplexedly upon my calamities and their source. I was confused, in a haze of bewilderment and terror. The killing of William, the execution of Justine, the killing of Henry, and finally, Elizabeth; even at that instant I knew not that my only remaining relations were protected from the enmity of the demon; my father even then might be squirming in his clutches, and Ernest might lay lifeless at his feet. That notion made me tremble, and summoned me to action. I sprang up, and determined to return to Geneva with all possible haste.

There were no horses to be hired, and I had to return by the lake; but the wind was inclement and the rain poured in spates. Still, it was barely daybreak, and I might plausibly expect to alight by nightfall. I engaged men to row and laid hold of an oar myself; for I had always taken comfort from mental torture in physical exertion. But the overwhelming wretchedness I then endured, and the glut of trepidation I felt, made me powerless to exert myself. I cast away the oar, and laying my head against my hands, I succumbed to every despondent notion that ensued. If I lifted up my eyes, I sighted vistas which were familiar to me in happier times, and which I had pondered but the day before in the companionship of her who was then but a specter and a remembrance. Tears flowed from my eyes. The rain had stopped for a time. Nothing is so distressing to the human mind as an extreme and abrupt change. The sun might beat down, or the clouds might loom ahead: but nothing could look to me as it had done the day before. A demon had plucked from me every prospect of impending joy: no being had ever been so wretched as I was;

so frightening an incident is unique in the chronicle of man.

But why should I harp upon the events that succeeded this final overpowering incident? Mine has been a story of terrors; I have attained their apex, and what I must then recount can but be tiresome to you. Know that, in their turn, my relations were taken away; I was left forlorn. My own strength is spent; and I must relate, in not many words, what is left of my frightful account.

I reached Geneva. My father and Ernest were still alive; but my father collapsed beneath the word I brought. I perceive him now, benevolent and virtuous old man! His eyes flitted in emptiness, for they had missed their grace and gladness—his Elizabeth, his more than child, whom he loved with all that feeling which a man cherishes, who in the ebb of life, having few attachments, cleaves more resolutely to those that survive. Woe, woe to the devil that brought wretchedness on his gray head, and condemned him to waste away in misery! He could not survive beneath the terrors that were amassed about him; the reflexes of life abruptly succumbed: he was incapable of arising from his bed, and in several days he died in my arms.

EPILOGUE:
THE CREATOR
RESTORED

"But it is even so; the fallen angel becomes a malignant devil. Yet even that enemy of God and man had friends and associates in his desolation; I am alone."—Frankenstein's Monster

JOSEPH COVINO JR

In Continuation, Aboard H.M.S IMMORTAL, 26 August 1797

"What then became of me? I know not," Victor Frankenstein lamented ruefully, gripping the arm of Captain Robert Walton at his bedside in deathly earnest. "Oh! When will my ministering spirit, in guiding me to the devil, permit me the rest I so much want; or must I perish, and he yet survive? If I die, swear to me, Walton, that he will not escape; that you will pursue him, and appease my vengeance in his destruction."

Captain Walton stared aghast and agape, attempting to no purpose to part his lips to speak, paralyzed with speechlessness.

"And do I dare to beg of you to embark on my mission, to suffer the difficulties that I have endured?" Frankenstein clenched Captain Walton's arm even more firmly. "No; I am not so mercenary. But, after I am dead, if he should show himself; if the messengers of revenge should guide him to you, swear that he will not survive—swear that he will not prevail over my amassed afflictions and live to enlarge the catalog of his savage outrages. He is articulate and convincing; and once his words had even a hold upon my heart: but believe him not. His heart is as infernal as his form, full of duplicity and diabolical malice. Listen not to him; summon the spirits of William, Justine, Henry, Elizabeth, my father, and of the miserable Victor, and plunge your blade into his black heart. I will hover close, and drive the steel straight."

"Will you not enter into the details of your being's creation?" Captain Walton asked him bluntly.

"Are you mad, my friend, or where does your foolish curiosity guide you? Would you also make for yourself and the world a devilish foe? Hush, hush! Heed my wretchedness, and do not endeavor to aggravate your own."

"Let me see the notes you have made relating to my story," Frankenstein asked the captain, who readily handed them over. "Since you have preserved my account, I shall correct and perhaps expound upon it. I would not that a distorted version should pass on to posterity, particularly pertaining to those dialogues with my archenemy."

"When younger," Frankenstein pondered aloud introspectively, "I thought myself fated for some noteworthy undertaking. My emotions are deep; but I was possessed of a serenity of intellect that suited me for remarkable accomplishments. This conviction about the value of my character bolstered me, when others would have been overburdened; for I considered it unconscionable to squander in worthless distress those abilities that might prove beneficial to my fellow beings. When I contemplated the work I had accomplished, nothing less than the creation of a reasoning and emotional creature, I could not classify myself with the flock of conventional experimenters. But this belief, which had bolstered me in the beginning of my calling, now works only to bury me deeper into the dirt. All my propositions and prospects are as nonexistent; and, like the angel ambitious for all power, I am shackled in an everlasting inferno. My invention was vivid, yet my gifts for experiment and research were acute; by the unity of these traits I conjured up the vision, and achieved the creation of a man. Even now I cannot recall, without exhilaration, my visions while the creation was unfinished. I strode Eden in my visions, then reveling in my powers, then seething with the concept of their consequences. From my youth I was infused with bright prospects and an exalted aspiration; but how am I fallen! Oh! My friend, if you had known me as I once was, you would not recognize me in this condition of degeneration. Despair scarcely afflicted my spirit; a great fate seemed to sustain me, until I sank, never, never again to stand."

"Can I not reconcile you to life?" Captain Walton warmly covered the weakening hand clenching his arm with his own. "I have yearned for a friend; I have searched for one who would empathize with and revere me. Mark, on this barren ocean I have found such a one; but, I am afraid, I have found him only to appreciate his worth, and lose him."

"I thank you, Walton, for your charitable designs towards so wretched an outcast," Frankenstein said, looking repulsed. "But when you speak of new bonds, and fresh attachments, think you that any can replace those who are missing. Can any man be to me as Henry was; or any woman another Elizabeth? Even when the attachments are not powerfully swayed by any surpassing virtue, the friends of our youth are always possessed of a certain power over our hearts, which scarcely any later friend can acquire. They know our youthful inclinations, which, however they may be later altered, are never eliminated; and they can deduce our conduct with more definite decisions as to the honesty of our intentions. A brother or sister can never, unless indeed such signs have been exhibited early, suspect the other of deception or falsehood, when another friend, however devotedly he may be attached, might, in spite of himself, be preoccupied with suspicion. But I relished friends, dear not only through custom and connection, but from their own virtues; and wherever I am, the consoling voice of my Elizabeth, and the conversation of Henry, will be always reach my ear. They are dead and gone; and but one emotion in such an isolation can convince me to sustain my life. If I were occupied in any lofty enterprise or venture, filled with vast benefit to my fellow beings, then could I survive to complete it. But such is not my fate; I must hunt and decimate the creature to whom I bestowed life; then my destiny in the world will be fulfilled, and I might die."

§

5 September 1797

Frankenstein's withering health was every day on the wane:

369

a fervid flame still gleamed in his eyes; but he was spent, and when abruptly aroused to any effort, he rapidly lapsed once more into apparent death. That morning, as Captain Walton sat scrutinizing the waxen face of his friend—his eyes partly shut, and his limbs dangling sluggishly—he was aroused by six seamen, who demanded admittance to his cabin.

"Me and my comrades have been appointed by our ship-mates to come to you in deputation," their leader addressed the captain upon entering, "to make of you a request, which, in all fairness, you cannot refuse."

"Indeed?"

"We are beset by ice, and should likely never escape; but we are afraid that if, as is possible, the ice should disperse and an unobstructed passage be opened up, you should be reckless enough to resume our voyage, and lead us into new perils, after we might gladly have overcome that. We demand, then, that you should pledge your solemn word, that if the ship should be liberated you will immediately steer our course southwards."

"This talk disturbs me," the captain grudgingly considered aloud. "I have not given up; nor have I yet entertained the no-tion of returning, if liberated. Yet can I, in all fairness or even in all likelihood, refuse this demand?"

Frankenstein, who had at first stayed quiet, and, indeed, looked scarcely to possess strength enough to listen, then aroused himself; his eyes twinkled, and his face blushed with fleeting vitality.

"What do you mean?" Frankenstein asked, turning to-wards the seamen. "What do you demand of your captain? Are you then so easily dissuaded from your purpose? Did you not call this a glorious adventure? Not because the passage was calm and smooth as a southern sea, but because it was full of perils and horror; because, at every new episode, your cour-age was to be summoned, and your bravery displayed; because peril and death besieged it, and these you were to defy and de-feat. For this was it a glorious, for this was it an honorable endeavor. You were henceforth to be hailed as the heroes of your race; your names revered, as belonging to valiant men who met death for honor, and the good of mankind. And now, look, with the first sighting of peril, or, if you will, the first potent and formidable test of your valor, you cower away, and are satisfied to go down as men who had not stamina enough to stand cold and danger; and so, sad souls, they were cold and went back to their warm hearths. Why, that demands not this provision; you need not have sailed this far, and hauled your captain to the disgrace of failure, simply to show yourselves craven cowards. Oh! Be men, or be above men. Be steadfast to your designs, and hard as iron. This ice is not made of such stuff as your spirits might be; it is malleable, and cannot resist you, if you resolve that it shall not. Do not return to your relations with the brand of dishonor stamped upon your heads. Return as champions, who have fought and triumphed, and who know not what it is to retreat from their enemy."

The seamen looked at each other, and were powerless to respond.

"Withdraw," Captain Walton told them, "and ponder what has been said. I will not lead you farther north if you vigorously insist upon the contrary; but I trust that, with deliberation, your fortitude will return."

They withdrew, and the captain turned towards his friend, but he was slumped in lethargy, and nearly depleted of life.

§

11 September 1797

On all sides the ice started to shift, and rumblings like thunderclaps were heard a long way off, as the floes split and splintered in all directions. In the most impending danger was the mighty bomb-ship, which could merely remain as crippled as her captain's un-blest guest, whose sickness intensified to

371

such an extent that he was wholly bound to his bed. Astern the ice cracked, and was forcefully driven northward; from the west a boisterous breeze blew up, and the southward passage opened up freely. When the seamen saw that, and that their return to their native soil was evidently settled, an outcry of riotous jubilation broke out, uproarious and continuous.

"What is the cause of the commotion?" asked Frankenstein, who was dozing but awoke.

"They cheer," answered Captain Walton, whose vital attention was absorbed by his convalescent guest, "since they will presently return to England."

"Do you then truly return?"

"Alas! Yes; I cannot resist their demands. I cannot guide them grudgingly to danger, and I must return."

"Do as you see fit; but I cannot. You may abandon your ambition, but mine is divinely appointed, and I dare not. I am infirm; but certainly the spirits who sustain my revenge shall accord me enough strength."

Uttering that, he strove to bound from the bed, but the effort was too strenuous for him; he dropped back and passed out.

It was a long time before he was revived; and the captain frequently believed that life was utterly nonexistent. Finally his eyes opened; his breath was labored, and he was incapable of speaking. Before long the young ship surgeon administered to him a comforting draught.

"Leave him undisturbed," Doctor Abraham Van Helsing ordered the captain gravely. "Your comrade surely has few hours to live."

Frankenstein's death sentence was passed; and Captain Walton could merely mourn, and remain resigned. He sat beside his bed, regarding him; his eyes were shut, and the captain believed he dozed; but presently he cried out in a faltering voice, craving the captain to come close.

"Alas!" Frankenstein deplored his predicament, "the

strength I depended on is lost; I sense that I shall soon perish, and he, my nemesis and oppressor, might yet be in existence. Think not, Walton, that in the final moments of my life I harbor that violent hatred, and insatiable lust for vengeance, I expressed before; but I believe myself warranted in wishing the demise of my nemesis. During these final days I have been preoccupied with pondering my past behavior; nor do I deem it reprehensible."

"Nor do I sit in judgment of either it or you, my dear friend."

"In a frenzy of irrepressible insanity I made a reasoning being, and was beholden to him, to ensure, as much as was in my power, his happiness and contentment. This was my responsibility; but there was another yet superior to that. My obligations to the creatures of my own race had greater rights to my consideration, since they comprised a greater portion of happiness or wretchedness. Motivated by this conviction, I refused, and I did proper in refusing, to make a mate for the original being. He displayed unsurpassed enmity and meanness, in wickedness; he exterminated my friends; he dedicated to death creatures possessed of acute sensitivity, serenity and understanding; nor do I know where his craving for revenge might end. Wretched himself, that he may make no other miserable, he should perish. The duty of his demise was mine, but I have failed. When moved by mercenary and wicked motives, I entreated you to take up my unfinished task; and I repeat this plea now, when I am merely motivated by reason and rightness."

"And I am sympathetic to your plight..."

"But I cannot ask you to abandon your fatherland and countrymen, to discharge this duty; and now that you are going back to England, you will have little opportunity of encountering him. But the contemplation of these points, and the proper balancing of what you might regard as your responsibilities, I leave to you; my judgment and notions are already troubled by the near coming of death. I dare not ask you to do what I believe right, for I might still be misguided by emotion."

"You are rightly guided to see justice done."

"That he should survive to be a perpetrator of atrocity troubles me; in other respects, this moment, when I presently anticipate my demise, is the only pleasant one I have relished for several years. The figures of the dear departed pass in front of me, and I hurry to their embrace. Godspeed, Walton! Pursue happiness in serenity, and shun ambition, even if it be just the ostensible innocuous one of distinguishing yourself in exploration and discovery. But why do I tell you this? I have myself been dashed in these hopes, but another might prevail. In the end, man bears responsibility and guilt for his own fate, whether it has brought him fortune or misfortune."

His voice turned soft as he spoke; and finally, spent by his exertion, he lapsed into peace. About half an hour later he strove once more to speak, but was powerless; he squeezed my hand weakly, and his eyes shut eternally, while the radiance of a kindly smile faded from his lips.

§

After an absence Captain Robert Walton stepped inside the cabin where lay the body of his un-blest but commendable friend. Over him hovered an indescribable figure: monstrous in size, but hulking and misshapen in his dimensions. As he hovered over the coffin, his countenance was covered by long locks of frayed hair; but one huge hand was outstretched, in complexion and evident texture like that of a cadaver. When he heard the noise of the captain's coming, he stopped articulating utterances of distress and terror, and vaulted towards the window. Captain Walton closed his eyes, instinctively, at the frightful sight of the monster's grotesque countenance, which was of such abhorrent, yet disgusting ugliness.

"Stay!" Captain Walton called out, recalling what his responsibilities were with relation to this exterminator.

Halting, the monster cast his yellow, watery eyes on the captain, lost in wonder; and, once more, turning towards the inert figure of his maker, he appeared to overlook the captain's appearance, and each feature and gesture looked incited by the fiercest wrath of some unrestrained fury.

"That too is my sacrifice!" he ejaculated: "in his killing my crimes are culminated; the wretched cycle of my existence has run its course! Oh, Frankenstein! Charitable and self-dedicated creature! What does it serve that I now beg you to forgive me? I, who unalterably exterminated you by exterminating all you held dear. Alas! He is cold, he cannot rejoin me."

His voice sounded smothered. Captain Walton moved toward this gigantic creature; he dared not once more lift up his eyes to his countenance, there was something so alarming and uncanny in his hideousness. The captain tried to talk, but the words faded from his lips. The monster went on blurting out violent and irrational self-recriminations. Finally the captain mustered the resolve to accost him in a pause of the storm of his fury: "Your remorse," he said, "is now useless. If you had heard the voice of conscience, and heeded the pangs of repentance, before you had instigated your fiendish revenge to this extreme, Frankenstein would yet have survived."

"And do you imagine," said the devil; "do you believe that I was then numb to anguish and regret?—He," he went on, pointing to the body, "he suffered not in the culmination of the act—oh! Not the infinite share of the agony that was mine throughout the prolonged particulars of its performance. A frightening conceit hastened me on, while my spirit was corrupted with regret. Believe you that the moans of Clerval were music to my ears? My spirit was formed to be vulnerable to affection and pity; and once wrested by wretchedness to wickedness and enmity, it did not survive the severity of the alteration. Following the killing of Clerval, I returned to Switzerland, brokenhearted and crushed. I felt for Frankenstein; my sympathy amounted to terror: I abominated myself. But once I learned that he, the instigator at once of my being and of its inconceivable tortures, dared to expect happiness; that while he amassed misery and futility upon me, he pursued his own pleasure in emotions and sensations from the gratification of which I was eternally banned, then ineffectual jealousy and spiteful enmity infested me with a voracious craving for revenge. I recalled my warning, and decided that it should be achieved. I realized that I was contriving for myself a lethal torment; but I was the servant, not the lord, of a compulsion, which I despised, but could not resist. But once she perished!—nay, then I was not wretched. I had shed all emotion, vanquished all agony, to rampage in the excess of my distress. Incited thus far, I had no alternative but to adapt my character to a component which I had freely chosen. The culmination of my devilish scheme became a ravenous greed. And now it is over; there is my final sacrifice!"

Captain Robert Walton at first looked moved by the monster's professions of his wretchedness.

"Frankenstein warned me of your powers of speech and persuasion," he recalled aloud, directing his eyes to the inert figure of his friend, reigniting the wrath within him. "Monster! It is well that you come here to weep over the havoc you have wreaked. Hypocritical devil! If he whom you grieve yet survived, still would he be the prey, once more would he become the quarry, of your damnable revenge. It is not sorrow that you feel; you mourn merely because the sacrifice to your enmity is wrested from your control."

"Oh, it is not so—not so," interjected the creature; "but such must be the impression imparted to you by what seems to be the import of my conduct. But I look not for sympathy in my wretchedness. No pity may I ever find. When I first looked for it, it was the regard for goodness, the emotions of joy and tenderness with which my entire existence was overwhelmed, that I wanted to be shared. But now, that goodness has become to me a ghost, and that joy and tenderness are turned into spiteful and detestable futility, in what should I look for pity? I am satisfied to suffer alone, while my afflictions shall last; when I perish, I am well convinced that hatred and humiliation shall permeate my memory. Once, my imagination was consoled with visions of nobleness, of glory, and of gladness. Once, I deceptively expected to encounter creatures who, forgiving my outward aspect, would revere me for the admirable attributes which I was able to display. I was nurtured with lofty notions of dignity and dedication. But now outrage has debased me beneath the basest brute. No atrocity, no outrage, no enmity, no wretchedness, can be deemed comparable to mine. When I turn over in my mind the frightening chronicle of my crimes, I cannot believe that I am the same being whose mind was once filled with exalted and noble thoughts of the glory and grandeur of goodness."

"My sole impression is that you unduly flatter yourself as being possessed of an extremely exaggerated sense of sensitivity!"

"You, who call Frankenstein your friend, appear to possess an impression of my transgressions and his tribulations. But, in the particulars which he rendered you of them, he could not recount the hours and months of wretchedness which I suffered, spent in crippled emotions. For, while I demolished his dreams, I did not gratify my own aspirations. They were eternally fervent and ravening; even so I craved affection and companionship, and I was still scorned. Was there no inequity in this? Am I to be considered to be the sole culprit, when all mankind transgressed against me? Why do you not despise Felix, who drove his benefactor from his door with contempt? Why do you not detest the rustic who tried to exterminate the rescuer of his child? Nay, these are the exemplary and impeccable creatures! I, the wretched and the deserted, am a monstrosity, to be scorned, struck and stamped on. Even now

I burst with anger at the remembrance of this inequity."

"And what of the atrocious and bloodthirsty injustices you yourself have done?"

"Yes, it is true that I am a monster. I have killed the comely and the defenseless; I have choked the blameless as they slept, and throttled to death his throat who never harmed me or any other living being. I have dedicated my maker, the choice model of everything that is deserving of affection and veneration among men, to wretchedness; I have hunted him even to that irrecoverable destruction. There he lies, pale and cold in death. You abhor me; but your loathing cannot match that which I deem myself. I examine the hands which did the deed; I contemplate the heart in which the vision of it was conjured up, and yearn for the instant when these hands will encounter my eyes, when that vision will obsess my mind no more."

"If only you should haunt this world no more."

"Be not afraid that I shall be the perpetrator of impending injury. My task is almost finished. Neither yours nor any man's demise is demanded to culminate the cycle of my existence, and achieve that which has to be done; but it demands my own. Do not believe that I shall be remiss in making this sacrifice. I shall depart your ship, and shall make for the northernmost limit of the earth; I shall gather my funeral pile, and cremate to cinders this wretched form, that its remains may provide no light to any inquisitive and unsanctified outcast, who would make such another as I have been. I shall perish. I shall no longer suffer the afflictions which now devour me, or be the victim of emotions ungratified, yet unsatisfied. He is gone who brought me to life; and when I shall be no more, the very recollection of us both will quickly disappear. I shall no more contemplate the sun or stars, or feel the breezes blow upon my face. Light, impression, and sensation shall melt away; and in this state I must discover my joy. Some time ago, when the sights which this world offers stood forth before me, when I felt the soothing warmth of summer and heard the swish of leaves and the singing of the birds, and these were everything to me, I should have deplored to die; now it is my only solace. Corrupted by crimes, and ripped by the angriest regret, where can I find respite but in death?"

"Where indeed?"

"Farewell! I take my leave of you, and in you the last of mankind whom these eyes shall ever see. Farewell, Frankenstein! If you were still living and still harbored a craving of vengeance against me, it would be better sated in my preservation than in my devastation. Yet it was not so; you did pursue my destruction, that I might not instigate mightier misery; and if yet, by some means unfamiliar to me, you had not ceased to sense and feel, you would not crave against me a revenge stronger that that which I feel. Tortured as you were, my anguish still surpassed yours; for the biting sting of regret shall not cease to fester in my wounds until death shall seal them forever."

"Not a moment too soon!"

"Yes, soon!" he bellowed, with somber and sullen assurance, "I shall perish, and what I now suffer be no longer endured. Soon these searing afflictions shall be destroyed. I shall climb my funeral pile victoriously, and rejoice in the anguish of the tormenting flames. The glow of that blaze will die out; my embers will be blown into the ocean by the sea breezes. My soul shall rest in peace; or if it senses, it will not certainly sense so. Farewell."

He vaulted from the cabin window, as he uttered that, upon an ice-raft which floated near the ship. He was swimmingly carried away by the billows, and lost to sight in murk, remoteness and gloom.

Just as abruptly the young ship surgeon, Doctor Abraham Van Helsing, burst into the captain's cabin, gesturing excitedly to the still and supine frame of Victor Frankenstein.

"We haven't a moment's time to lose!" he urgently ex-

claimed in a commanding voice. "We must remove Frankenstein to the sick bay at once!"

At first Captain Robert Walton froze, struck dumb with
wonder, and stood speechless, looking aghast.

"At once!" Van Helsing again demanded.

§

Presently Captain Walton and Doctor Van Helsing stood
with bated breath in the ship's sick bay hovering over the supine frame of Victor Frankenstein, connected to metal an-
klets, bracelets, clamps and collars attached by metallic wires
to some strange electrical apparatus, astir with rhythmically
heaving bellows-like air pumps and pulsating with a greenish glow, throwing its eerie light upon their expectant expressions. Half-covering Frankenstein's face was a rubbery, tube-
tied mask which swelled and shrank in rhythmic unison with
his perceivably heaving chest. He looked quite breathtakingly
alive!

"What is it?" Captain Walton asked of the contrivance
with wonder.

"A regenerator," Van Helsing explained complacently,
"which operates by means of galvanism or galvanic action—
that is to say, electricity produced by chemical action."

"What does it do?"

"It simply keeps the heart beating, the blood circulating
and the lungs breathing so that the body's cells and vital organs continue to rejuvenate and receive oxygen through the
blood. After this fashion the body's vital organs are revived
and revitalized, and life itself is thus preserved."

"I was so certain that he had breathed his last."

"The draught that I dispensed induced him to assume
merely the semblance of death."

"Whatever drove my friend Frankenstein to undertake
so destructive and ruinous an experiment?" Captain Walton

asked reflectively.

"Human thoughts and aspirations are free and subject to no rule," Van Helsing pondered aloud. "Upon them rests the freedom of man. And they tower above even the light of Nature herself; for thoughts give birth to a creative force that is neither of the earth nor the stars. Thoughts create a new firmament, a new source of energy and power from which new arts flow. When a man undertakes to create something, he establishes a new heaven, as it were, and from it the work that he aspires to create flows into him; for such is the immensity of man that he is mightier than heaven and earth."

"That sounds utterly blasphemous not to speak of presumptuous."

"Presumption can indeed degenerate into blasphemy. Such is no doubt the reason why that afflictions and suffering are granted by God; nothing—not even those—derive from man. There are those afflictions which arise in a natural way, and those which set upon us as scourges from God; for He has sent us some afflictions as punishments, as warning signs by which we realize that all our affairs are nothing, that all our presumed knowledge rests upon no firm foundation, and that the ultimate truth is unknown to us; but that we are inadequate and incomplete in all ways, and that no capacity or knowledge is our own alone."

"Has this device the capacity to restore my friend Frankenstein fully to life?" Captain Walton gestured irresolutely to the quietly kinetic apparatus.

"For an indefinite time it has the capacity to keep his body and soul together," Van Helsing said gravely. "He is as good as dead already, I'm afraid, for his body is broken beyond repair. His only possible prospect of survival demands that Frankenstein be given not a new heaven but a new body."

"What, sir, do you seriously suggest?" the captain asked, thunderstruck with staggered belief.

"Quite simply," Van Helsing answered with the utmost solemnity, "that you must of necessity and with all due dispatch respect Frankenstein's last request and go immediately in pursuit of his creature—but capture him—*alive!*"

Postscript: Look for the sequel—*FRANKENSTEIN EXHUMED.*

FOOTNOTE: FRANKENSTEIN— A PROFOUNDLY CHRISTIAN PARABLE

"Evil thenceforth became my good. Urged thus far, I had no choice but to adapt my nature to an element which I had willingly chosen. The completion of my demoniacal design became an insatiable passion."—Frankenstein's Monster

JOSEPH COVINO JR

J oyce Carol Oates, in her interpretive essay titled *Frankenstein's Fallen Angel,* rendered her rudely revisionist version of Shelley's remarkably brilliant novel for a supposedly cerebral University of California Press(1984)edition, questioning witlessly at the outset whether it's even a "novel at all." Well, nothing's more irritating if not infuriating—to say nothing of outright insulting to Shelley's incomparable epic accomplishment—than pompously and pretentiously pseudo-intellectual analyses and commentaries artificially contrived to propagate misguided academic agendas or wistful pet theses; except perhaps self-indulgent major motion picture film atrocities like Kenneth Branagh's, "Mary Shelley's Frankenstein"(1994). My own novel, I trust, pays proper tribute to Shelley's impeccable genius by putting a lot to rights.

"Central to Frankenstein....is a stroke of lightning that appears to issue in a dazzling 'steam of fire' from a beautiful old oak tree....: the literal stimulus for Frankenstein's subsequent discovery of the cause of generation and life," Oates illiterately conjectures in the incessantly insipid tradition of all the rest who redundantly but fallaciously attribute Frankenstein's life-giving secret to "electricity and galvanism," which Shelley alludes to only once throughout her entire novel with reference to Frankenstein's youthful intellectual pursuits before attending the university of Ingolstadt, where he studies "natural philosophy"(physical science or physics)or, more specifically, chemistry.

More often than not, Frankenstein refers repeatedly instead to the three mentor intellects who most influenced and made the utmost impression upon his own learning: *Cornelius Agrippa*(magician and occultist), *Albertus Magnus*(a Dominican theologian)and *Paracelsus*(the reputed "father of chemistry")—not only alchemists and mystics but devout Christians all!

"From this day(after meeting his primary professor M. Waldman)," Frankenstein recounts flatly to Captain Robert

Walton, "natural philosophy, and particularly chemistry, in the most comprehensive sense of the term, became nearly my sole occupation." Frankenstein was, finally and once and for all, not an electrician but a chemist—pure and simple—fruitlessly seeking the ever elusive "elixir of life!" Likewise his infamous life-giving device was not galvanic but rather chemical, referred to just as repeatedly as his "chemical apparatus" or "chemical instruments" of life, which are compact enough to get just as repeatedly "packed up" in a suitcase to accompany him whenever and wherever he travels!

"But no one in Frankenstein is evil—the universe is emptied of God and of the theistic assumptions of 'good' and 'evil,'" Oates posits even more witlessly. "Hence its modernity."

EMPTY of God, good and evil? *REALLY?* Equally exasperating are revisionist rationalists who demonstrate all too blatantly by their incomprehension—if not by their outright illiteracy—their arrant incapacity to read much less fully appreciate, comprehend, grasp and understand Shelley's masterpiece. Just look and *LISTEN* to Frankenstein pensively ponder his past to Captain Walton:

"Thus strangely are our souls constructed, and by such slight ligaments are we bound to prosperity or ruin. When I look back, it seems to me as if this almost miraculous change of inclination and will was the immediate suggestion of the guardian angel of my life—the last effort made by the spirit of preservation to avert the storm that was even then hanging in the stars, and ready to envelope me. Her victory was announced by an unusual tranquility and gladness of soul, which followed the relinquishing of my ancient and latterly tormenting studies. It was thus that I was to be taught to associate evil with their prosecution, happiness with their disregard.

It was a strong effort of the spirit of good; but it was ineffectual. Destiny was too potent, and her immutable laws had decreed my utter and terrible destruction."—Victor Frankenstein

In just one solitary eloquent breath Frankenstein contemplates not only good and evil but guardian angels, miracles, souls and spirits as well! He uttered a host of similar sentiments like:

"Chance—or rather the evil influence, the Angel of Destruction, which asserted omnipotent sway over me from the moment I turned my reluctant steps from my father's door— led me first to M. Krempe, professor of natural philosophy."

"Come, Victor," Frankenstein's father, Alphonse, preaches Christian forgiveness following the monster's murder of his youngest son, William, "not brooding thoughts of vengeance against the assassin, but with feelings of peace and gentleness, that will heal, instead of festering, the wounds of our minds. Enter the house of mourning, my friend, but with kindness and affection for those who love you, and not with hatred for your enemies."

"….; my imagination was busy in scenes of evil and despair," Frankenstein laments William's death. "I considered the being whom I had cast among mankind, and endowed with the will and power to effect purposes of horror, such as the deed which he had now done, nearly in the light of my own vampire, my own spirit let loose from the grave, and forced to destroy all that was dear to me."

"The God of heaven forgive me!" the imprisoned family servant falsely accused of killing William, Justine, exclaims to Elizabeth. "….I do not fear to die; that pang is past. God raises my weakness and gives me courage to endure the worst. I leave a sad and bitter world; and if you remember me and think of me as of one unjustly condemned, I am resigned to the fate awaiting me. Learn from me, dear lady, to submit in patience to the will of heaven!"

"I had been the author of unalterable evils," Frankenstein repents following Justine's execution for William's murder, "and I lived in daily fear lest the monster whom I had created should perpetrate some new wickedness."

"The immense mountains and precipices that overhung me on every side—the sound of the river raging among the rocks, and the dashing of the waterfalls around," Frankenstein muses while wandering in mourning amidst the Swiss Alps, "spoke of a power mighty as Omnipotence—and I ceased to fear, or to bend before any being less almighty than that which had created and ruled the elements, here displayed in their most terrific guise."

Conveniently and obstinately overlooked by revisionist rationalists like Oates, in their futile attempts to force Shelley to conform to some feigned form of fanatical feminism, is Safie, the "sweet Arabian" and beloved betrothed of Felix, son of the hovel family observed by Frankenstein's monster. Look and *LISTEN* to Shelley's quite overt testimonial to Christianity couched in her description of Safie's character:

"Safie related that her mother was a Christian Arab, seized and made a slave by the Turks; recommended by her beauty, she had won the heart of the father of Safie, who married her. The young girl spoke in high and enthusiastic terms of her mother, who, born in freedom, spurned the bondage to which she was now reduced. She instructed her daughter in the tenets of her religion and taught her to aspire to higher powers of intellect and an independence of spirit forbidden to the female followers of Mahomet. This lady died; but her lessons were indelibly impressed on the mind of Safie, who sickened at the prospect of again returning to Asia and being immured within the walls of a harem, allowed only to occupy herself with infantile amusements, ill-suited to the temper of her soul, now accustomed to grand ideas and a noble emulation of virtue. The prospect of marrying a Christian and remaining in a country where women were allowed to take a rank in society was enchanting to her."

Far from being a simple fable, giving stale and tiresome "rejoinder" to Milton's *Paradise Lost* as Oates and countless others so tediously suggest, Frankenstein is a profoundly sophisticated Christian parable of obsessive revenge and its ruinous consequences(both physical and spiritual)dramatized with remarkable depth by two mortal archenemies locked in a relentless and ruthless death struggle for revenge—the monster wreaks vengeance for his consuming misery and wretchedness; his maker wreaks vengeance for the monster's wholesale annihilation of Frankenstein's family and friends.

My own novel adaptation of the *Frankenstein* saga, without artificially manipulating or tampering with one solitary iota of Shelley's original creative concept, strives at once humbly and proudly to bring to perfection its ultimate culmination: a close and direct encounter with the human soul!

"It was necessary that I should return without delay to Geneva, there to watch over the lives of those I so fondly loved;" Victor Frankenstein recounts to Captain Walton, hinting unintentionally but conclusively at the irreducible essence of his horrific secret, "and to lie in wait for the murderer, that if any chance led me to the place of his concealment, or if he dared again to blast me by his presence, I might, with unfailing aim, put an end to the existence of the monstrous Image which *I had endued with the mockery of a soul* still more monstrous."

That's why, at the last, this terrible tale raises its impassioned voice and makes a forceful stand against so-called "embryonic stem cell research":

"The soul is born in this way: when the child is conceived in the womb— that is to say, born into its seed—a word from God enters into this carnal conception, which gives the flesh its soul. Thus the soul—take good note of this—becomes the centre of man, in whom now both good and evil impulses dwell. The body is the house of the soul, but the soul is the house of the good and evil spirits which dwell in man."—Paracelsus, Frankenstein's mentor intellect